LONG
LANKIN

LONG LANKIN

LINDSEY BARRACLOUGH

CANDLEWICK PRESS

First U.S. paperback edition 2014

First published in 2011 by The Bodley Head, an imprint of Random House Children's Books

Library of Congress Catalog Card Number 2011047030
ISBN 978-0-7636-5808-3 (hardcover)
ISBN 978-0-7636-6937-9 (paperback)

16 17 18 19 BVG 10 9 8 7 6 5 4 3 2

Printed in Berryville, VA, U.S.A.

This book was typeset in Palatino.

Candlewick Press
99 Dover Street
Somerville, Massachusetts 02144

visit us at www.candlewick.com

For Richard, Eleanor, Imogen,
Christian, Rowena, and Benjamin,
and the other Richard

Said my lord to my lady as he mounted his horse:
"Beware of Long Lankin that lives in the moss."

Said my lord to my lady as he rode away:
"Beware of Long Lankin that lives in the hay.

"Let the doors be all bolted and the windows all pinned,
And leave not a hole for a mouse to creep in."

The doors were all bolted and the windows all pinned,
Except one little window where Long Lankin crept in.

"Where's the lord of this house?" said Long Lankin.
"He's away in fair London," said the false nurse to him.

"Where's the heir of this house?" said Long Lankin.
"He's asleep in his cradle," said the false nurse to him.

"We'll prick him, we'll prick him all over with a pin,
And that'll make my lady to come down to him."

So he pricked him, he pricked him all over with a pin,
And the nurse held the basin for the blood to flow in.

"The nurse how she slumbers, the nurse how she sleeps.
My little son John how he cries and he weeps.

"How durst I go down in the dead of the night
Where there's no fire a-kindled and no candle alight?"

"You have three silver mantles as bright as the sun.
Come down, my fair lady, all by light of one."

My lady came down then, all fearful of harm.
Long Lankin stood ready, she fell in his arm.

Here's blood in the kitchen. Here's blood in the hall.
Here's blood on the stairs where my lady did fall.

"O master, O master, don't lay blame on me.
'Twas the false nurse and Lankin that killed your lady."

Long Lankin was hung on a gibbet so high
And the false nurse was burned in a fire close by.

✣ CORA ✤

There's too much sky, and the farther out of London we go, the more of it there is.

I twist round in my seat and rub the back window with a wet finger until the skin goes brown. I lick it again, and it tastes bitter. Through the smear on the glass, I see the edge of the city moving away. In the grey rain, the crowded buildings that filled my sky at home stick up like rotten teeth.

Mr. Bates didn't want to bring Mimi and me all the way out here. He was only doing it to pay Dad back a favour.

Somewhere past Barking, we stop to get petrol. Mr. Bates starts arguing with the garage man, saying he hasn't filled the tank right up and he's fiddling him. The man wants his money. Mr. Bates gets out of the car but only comes up to the man's nose. A gust of wet wind catches Mr. Bates's hair and blows it sideways off his bald patch. The garage man says Mr. Bates's petrol pointer can't be working properly because he can't get any more ruddy stuff in and he can ruddy well try himself if he doesn't believe him.

The garage man looks over at us and raises his eyebrows. He thinks Mr. Bates is our dad. Mimi smiles. I slide down the back seat and stare out at the road. Our dad would have had a laugh with the garage man—if we'd had a car, that is; if we had, it wouldn't be a dirty old Austin like Mr. Bates's; it would be a nice two-tone job like the one parked outside Farrows and Atkins every morning. Anyway, our dad looks like Tyrone Power in *Zorro*, not like Mr. Bates, with a safety pin through his braces holding up his trousers, and hairs on his stomach that I can see because two of the buttons have burst off his shirt.

The garage man says he's going to call a copper. Mr. Bates makes a hissing noise through his teeth, then slaps the money in the man's hand, gets back into the car, and slams the door so hard that the window handle falls off.

Fewer and fewer houses slip by until there are hardly any at all. The fields stretch away on both sides of the road, flat and a dull grey-green. I try playing I Spy with Mimi, thinking it will help her learn her letters, but give up after a while because there's only *G* for *grass* and *R* for *rain*, and she's not bothered anyway.

I notice the big hand on Mr. Bates's watch has gone right round twice since we started out.

A small run-down old pub called the Thin Man comes up on the left, set back a bit off the road with a bench

2

outside. Mr. Bates parks in front, then goes inside with his scrappy bit of paper. He takes half an hour to ask for directions while Mimi and I stay in the back of the car.

The engine clicks as it cools. We breathe in the stale smell of Mr. Bates's armpits. The windows steam up.

We're hungry. Dad gave us the same sandwiches he'd made on Saturday when we were supposed to come, but even then the cheese was the cracked bit off the end, and today the bread was all curled up, hard enough to do your teeth in. We ate them ages ago, going through East Ham. I've still got a lump in my throat from a crust that didn't go down.

Through the misty glass, I see Mr. Bates coming out again, buckling up his belt. He burps so loudly we can hear it ten feet away with the windows up. He hasn't brought us any peanuts, or a cream soda with two straws, like Dad would have done.

When he opens the door, I smell wet grass and soil. The rain has stopped. Mr. Bates squeezes his big stomach in behind the wheel and wipes his mouth with the back of his hand.

"Ain't we there yet?" I ask.

"Mind your own bloody business," he says, and beery spit flies out of his mouth and lands on the windscreen.

He reaches into his pocket for his tin of Golden Virginia and rolls himself a cigarette, thin, bent, and wrinkly, with bits of tobacco sticking out the end. While he's driving, he can make them with one hand, balancing the tin on his knee. Most of them last only a couple of puffs. When he starts sucking like mad, you know they've gone out. He takes his time with this one, slowly blowing out the smoke until it fills up the car and makes our eyes water.

"Bloody cavemen out 'ere," he says, pushing open the quarter-light to clear the windows.

We turn down a road almost opposite the pub. The name is painted on a piece of wood nailed to a stick— **OLD GLEBE LANE**. The road is narrow and rough, with scruffy hedges on either side.

A high wall and some huge wrought-iron gates loom up on the right. I catch a glimpse of a wide, freshly mown lawn and long, curving flower beds. Mr. Bates lowers his head to look as we drive by.

"And that ain't Guerdon Hall," he says, "just in case you was wonderin'."

After a short while, the car slows and I peer over Mr. Bates's shoulder to see out. We are at the top of a steep hill.

Below us, a small church steeple rises up out of a cluster of trees standing at the edge of a sweeping wasteland of marshes. Thick fingers of sunlight pierce the clouds and stretch down to the earth in long pale rods that dip in and out of the scattered pools and

4

snake around the reed beds along the silvery ribbons of water, until in the far distance the glittering liquid threads merge into a faintly shimmering line that hovers between the land and the sky.

"What's right over there, then?" I ask.

"What's bloody what?"

"Right over there." I point past his ear to the horizon.

"What do you ruddy well think it is?" he says. "It's the ruddy river, innit! And over there's the flippin' sea!"

"So where does the river stop being the river and the sea start being the sea?"

"How the flamin' hell should I know!" he says. "Shut up and stop asking bloody stupid questions! I'm givin' you a lift in me blimmin' car. It don't mean I've ruddy well got to 'ave a conversation."

We bump slowly all the way down the hill, with Mr. Bates swerving to avoid the big holes, muttering *flippin'* this and *bloody* that. At the bottom, the lane carries on towards the church and the trees, and another, far muddier track goes off to the right. Mr. Bates stops the car and switches off the engine. He looks at his grubby piece of paper again.

"The house is up the end," he says, pointing down the muddy track with his yellow finger. "But if you think I'm blinkin' well driving down there, you've got another think comin', and it ain't Christmas!"

Mr. Bates gets himself out and pulls the front seat

forward so Mimi and I can wriggle out with our duffel bags. "That flamin' hill's shot me suspension up. You'll 'ave to walk the rest of the way yerselves."

"Ain't you comin' with us? What if it ain't the right house?" I shout as he gets back into the car and bangs the door shut. "Ain't it against the law to leave kids all by theirselves in a strange place?"

He doesn't take a blind bit of notice, but quickly turns the engine back on.

"Oi! You could get done for this!" I yell over the noise.

Mr. Bates scrapes the gear into reverse. The car turns, squealing and throwing up lumps of wet earth. We jump out of the way. It roars back up the hill, the rattle of the exhaust pipe growing fainter and fainter, until I'm not sure whether I can hear it or not.

The wind stirs the long grass. Some far-off bird calls, but nothing answers it.

Mimi starts sniffing.

"Put a sock in it," I say.

She wipes her nose on Sid, her knitted thing, then rubs her finger on the little worn patch on his head, like she does before she goes to sleep. Once, Sid was a fat blue soldier, but now he's just a woolly grey sausage that smells of sick. Mimi found him in Mum's drawer at home, and Mum said his name was Sid and Mimi couldn't have him because he was old and dirty, but Mimi kept getting him out. In the end Mum gave in, but you could see she couldn't stand Sid lying around. Once I saw her kick him round the back of the chair. I don't know why she kept him in the first place.

I give Mimi the old hankie out of my pocket. It's got a half-eaten sherbet lemon stuck to it. She pulls the sweet off and puts it in her mouth.

"Sherbet's all gone," she says, sucking.

Thin trees line the side of the track, their spindly trunks bent almost double, whipped over years by the wind blowing across the empty spaces from the river.

A narrow ditch, half-hidden in the grass, runs along the front of the trees, giving itself away only by the sound of the trickling water.

I hang the two bags over my shoulders by the strings. The track is all mud and puddles. The soles of Mimi's shoes have come away from the uppers around the toes. I try to keep her on the tufts of grass so her feet stay dry. My scuffed brown sandals aren't much better. The water comes through the little holes that make the pattern on the top. I hate them because they go *flup flup flup* on the pavement and I've always wanted shoes that go *click click click* like Lana Turner's at the pictures, but I have to have Monica Horgan's old shoes because she's older than me. The last ones were black lace-ups like a boy's. They're in the cupboard for Mimi.

As we work our way down the track, I hear the constant muffled sound of running water, as if secret streams are flowing down the hill and under the road, feeding and swelling the ditch below the trees. At its widest point, the ditch curves towards the road and disappears beneath it.

My neck aches with looking down to avoid the mud. I stretch up for a moment and see that some old red chimneys have appeared over the tops of the trees.

We come round a bend, and there is Guerdon Hall, half sinking into the ground.

The chimney bricks are set in patterns of squares, diamonds, and even twisted spirals like the cough candy Mrs. Prewitt has in big jars in her shop, threepence for two ounces. The crooked roof, dotted with pincushions of green moss, overhangs the dark little windows. The reflected light from the high white sky is distorted, rippling unevenly in the old glass.

A deep, open channel of water, at least ten feet across, encircles the house and its garden like a moat, spanned by a wide, flat bridge covered in a layer of earth tufted with grass and dandelions. Down the middle of the bridge, the soil has worn thin over the bare wooden planks.

The garden is a wilderness of bent, half-dead trees, strangled by bindweed, that lean over tangled masses of brambles, wild rosebushes, stinging nettles, and dry yellow grass.

I can't think how Auntie Ida can live in such a place.

Mimi whispers, "Someone's looking."

"Don't be daft," I say. "There ain't nobody here."

"Look."

She points, and I see a boy sitting on a broken wooden fence on the other side of the track, staring. I feel I ought to say something, but I'm not sure they even speak English out here.

Then he says, "Hello. What are you doing?"

I say, "Ain't nobody told you it's rude to gawp?"

"What are you doing, then?"

"We're stopping here. Is this Mrs. Eastfield's house?"

"Yes, it is," he says. "What are you staying for?"

"She's our Auntie Ida. Is she nice?"

"Don't you know your own auntie?" he says, sliding down off the fence. There's a ripping sound. He winces, but only for a second.

"We ain't seen her before."

"Isn't she too old to be your auntie?"

"She ain't that sort of auntie," I say. "She's our grandma Agnes's sister—our mum's aunt—except Grandma's dead. Dad says Auntie Ida's about sixty or something."

"That's your great-aunt, then," he says, rubbing the seat of his trousers. "I've got one as well—Auntie Ethel. She lives over at the seaside at Wrayness. Her garden's just about on the beach."

Keeping his eyes on us all the time, the boy walks backwards into some muddy water—a good thing he's got rubber boots on.

"That Mrs. Eastfield . . ." he adds, still moving away. "I'd watch myself if I were you. She's a witch."

The boy turns quickly and runs off, splashing in and out of the puddles.

As I watch him, I notice for the first time high wooden poles, with wires stretched between them, spaced out in a line along the length of the track. The last pole stands by the bridge. The wire goes down to the house and disappears under the roof.

"It mightn't be as bad as it looks," I say to Mimi. "I think Auntie's on the electric."

✎ ROGER ✐

Mum's going to kill me when she sees I've torn my trousers. There must have been a blinking nail sticking out of the fence and it's gone right through and cut my backside, but I can't see round. I'll need to look at it in her bedroom mirror to weigh up the damage.

I had to decide which was worse, me looking like a dope walking backwards or those two girls catching sight of my bottom. If that nail was rusty, I'm most probably going to die from lockjaw, so I'll have to keep checking to see if I'm smiling when I don't want to, because that's what happens when you get lockjaw—you can't stop yourself smiling. It's the most dreadful way you can die that there is, even though you look happy when you're doing it. I don't know whether a dab of Germolene will stop you getting lockjaw—maybe I should rub the whole tin in, just to make sure.

Trouble is, I can't tell Mum because she'll start asking questions and I'm not supposed to go down to Mrs. Eastfield's.

But I like it down there. It's nice and quiet.

Our house is specially noisy on Mondays because Mum does the washing. The whole place smells of Baby Pamela's nappies boiling in the big pan on the gas stove. Even if I manage to hide these trousers in the dirty basket before Mum sees them, there won't be any others I can put on secretly because they'll all be in the washer, so I'll have nothing to wear to make my escape in. The other annoying thing about going home is that Pete and I have had a row because I trod on one of his soldiers and broke its leg off, and he'll be hopping mad because I've sneaked off and left him to do the wringer on his own.

I was down near Mrs. Eastfield's checking over a spot I thought would be good for a camp—three trees leaning towards each other, almost touching at the top like a wigwam. Me and Pete could live there if we wanted.

We could catch fish to eat, though I don't really like fish unless it's fish paste.

We've got camps all over the place, Pete and me. We've even got one in the woods near where that woman keeps wild pigs. At least, we haven't seen the pigs ourselves, but Tooboy swears blind she's got some and he says they've got big tusks with blood on the ends.

Trouble is, if we did make the wigwam, it would be a bit close to Mrs. Eastfield's. Pete and me are pretty sure she's a witch, like old Gussie Jetherell, just down from us—though *she* definitely is. She's got lots of cats, and that's a sign. I've never seen any cats at Mrs. Eastfield's, but there's a great big dog that comes out over the bridge, barking its head off. Sometimes I dare Pete to see how close he can get before it starts, but he's really scared, and if the dog sees him, Pete legs it and doesn't stop running till he gets to the end of the Chase. The Chase is Mrs. Eastfield's road.

I'd love to go into Guerdon Hall. If we asked those girls, they might get us into the house to have a good look around. One's about my age, and the little skinny one's more like Terry. Their shoes were all holes, and their clothes were too small for them and, if I'm honest, a bit dirty. They certainly don't come from anywhere around here. I could tell because the older one left the *h* off of *house*, and nobody here talks like that. Grandma would say they were common.

Poor things, having to stay with Mrs. Eastfield.

Pete and me can hear chickens clucking round the back. Pete reckons they're probably children Mrs. Eastfield's caught and put a spell on. I'd try creeping round to see, but Pete won't, even for a dare, even if we left the dog some meat with sleeping powder on. He says he doesn't want to be turned into a chicken and eat rubbish seeds and have to push eggs out of his backside all day long.

∽ CORA ∽

We stood by the bridge, Mimi clinging to my hand. On the other side of the channel, two rusted iron gates lay half-hidden among the weeds, left where they'd fallen from the gateposts long ago.

The water level was dropping, making a quiet gurgling sound as it went, leaving behind white frothy bubbles on the thick dark mud, just as it did when the tide was going out on the river at Limehouse. Perhaps the channel was not a moat at all, but a loop at the end of a salty tidal creek.

I looked back to the broken fence the boy had been sitting on. It ran along the front of two small ruined cottages. One of the roofs had sunken in, and the other was nothing more than a jumble of wooden sticks. Dirty splinters of glass from smashed windows stuck out of the long grass behind the fence.

Farther away, standing across the end of the track, was an old barn with a wide-open doorway and a long low roof full of holes. Tangled heaps of rusty machinery were piled up in the yard.

Suddenly the deep, hollow sound of barking and the thumping of heavy paws echoed off the walls of the house. An enormous dog came bounding round the corner. Two long strings of dribble flew out of its slobbering mouth and streamed down its shoulders as it ran.

Mimi let go of my hand and fled back down the track. I should have gone after her, but I didn't want to turn my back on the dog. I glanced behind and saw her slip on the mud into a pool of water.

"Shut up, you!" I shouted at the dog. "Look what you've flippin' well made my sister do!"

It leaped up, but I wasn't scared. There were dogs like this at home. I stuck my hand out, palm upwards. The dog slowed down a bit, stopped, and sniffed my hand. Then it lolled out its long drippy tongue, moving from one front paw to the other, and gave another few barks, but not so loud this time. I patted its big head, then wiped the dribble off my hand on my skirt. Mimi, grizzling, got up on her own. There were muddy streaks down her coat. Her hands and knees dripped brown water.

"You flippin' clot," I said, brushing her down. "What's

Auntie Ida going to say? Oh, it's all right, Mimi, for Pete's sake. He's just a noisy beggar. Stick your hand out like this. Let him sniff you. Blimey, you smell flippin' awful now. Look, even the dog's backing off."

Mimi wouldn't go over the bridge. "Ain't goin'," she said with a sniff. "Don't like it."

"You have to. Come on."

"Won't."

I stooped down, picked a dandelion clock, and blew towards the house.

One o'clock, two o'clock, three o'clock—the little parachutes streamed across the water.

Mimi stepped closer—*six o'clock, seven o'clock*—

"I ain't never known one do the right time yet," I said.

Mimi bent down and tore one up for herself. She blew—*one o'clock, two o'clock*—and followed the swirl of seeds as they floated over the bridge in a cloud of tiny white stars.

✿ ROGER ✿

I called in at the post office on the way back to see if Mrs. Wickerby had any more soldiers.

Pete and I hate Mrs. Wickerby, because when we did "Penny for the Guy" on Bonfire Night, she wouldn't let us do it outside her shop because she said it was begging, so we had to drag our guy over the road to outside Mrs. Aylott's instead. We told Mrs. Aylott we were getting money for the poor, but all we got was threepence from Mr. Rust, which we thought wasn't going to be much use to the poor, so instead we went into Mrs. Wickerby's and bought some bubble gum.

There were loads of soldiers in a cardboard box on her counter. I thought it would be easy to take one without Mrs. Wickerby seeing because the three old Death sisters were in the shop having a chinwag with her. They're called Beattie, Jessie, and Elsie, and they all wear the same white hats that look like meringues.

My hand was near the box with the soldiers in, luckily hidden behind Jessie Death's elbow. I was reaching over the edge when, just at that moment, Mrs. Wickerby stuck her pointy little weasel's face round the Death sisters and said, "Can I get you anything, Roger, or are you just looking as usual?"

"Just looking," I said quietly, and left the shop quick.

When I got home, Baby Pamela wouldn't stop crying. It drives me potty sometimes when she goes on and on and you can't do anything with her. Mum gave her to me while she went out to hang up the sheets. I jiggled her around for a minute, but she started to stink and she puts snot on you, so I gave her to Terry and told him he had to look after her or old Gussie would get him.

I went in the garden with Pete and Dennis to look for lizards, but it wasn't really dry enough. They like to sit on rocks in the sun or on the concrete fence post that's come down by the big conker tree. We don't tell Terry we're looking for lizards because he's cruel and swings them around by their tails until they fly off into the garden. Sometimes the end of the tail comes off in his hand. I know they grow back, but then they always have a kink in. Once he tried it with a newt from the pond, but it dropped before he could whirl it round. They're a bit more rubbery and slip out of your fingers, and their tails never ever come off.

We had sausages and mash for dinner. Mum sticks the sausages in the spuds like they do in *The Beano*. I started to tell her about the two girls at Mrs. Eastfield's, but she had her hands full with Pamela and told me to tell her later. It's a good job she wasn't really listening or she'd have known I'd been down near the church. I nearly put my foot in it there.

I'll go back tomorrow with Pete and see if the girls are still around. If they are, we'll tell them about Mrs. Eastfield capturing a German airman during the war when his plane crashed on her farm, because they most probably won't know about that. Mrs. Eastfield gave the chap a cup of tea, then stood over him with her shotgun until the police arrived to take him away. I once said to Mum I thought Mrs. Eastfield was brave to do that, but

Mum said people didn't like her. They talked about her behind her back.

CORA

Thick dirty grey roots of ivy were clinging to the crumbling front wall, the leaves brown and crispy, coated with dust. Only a few small green shoots up near the roof showed the plant was still living.

Not quite in the middle of the house, a huge porch, with a room above, jutted out onto the path. The dog followed us in, its paws clattering on the uneven stone floor. Dead leaves had blown into piles in the corners. It smelled mouldy.

The massive front door was studded with big iron nails. Threads of spiders' webs, spotted with the dried-up bodies of little flies, fluttered lightly in the cracks. Long deep lines ran down the door, as if the dog had got into the habit of standing up on its hind legs, scratching to come in.

I lifted the great iron knocker—the head of a lion with a ring hanging out of its mouth. It was so stiff it would only go down slowly. When it made its dull thud against the door, some dust fell down on us from the rafters.

"She obviously doesn't have a lot of visitors," I said to Mimi.

I shouted, "Auntie Ida! Auntie Ida! It's us!" but it just made the dog bark and start dribbling again.

"Let's go round the back," I said, leaving the porch and turning to the left along the weedy path. I expected Mimi to follow, but I'd got all the way to the corner of the house before the dog whined and I looked back.

Mimi was standing on the path, staring up at the arch over the porch. I'm not sure I would have noticed it myself—an old piece of wood nailed lopsidedly across the angle of the arch, a couple of feet long, bent, cracked, blackened round the edges as if it had been burned. There was some carving on it, worn almost smooth in places—probably from hanging outside in the wind and rain for years on end.

As I got nearer and saw it more closely, I caught hold of Mimi's coat sleeve and tried to pull her away, but she wouldn't come.

"Who is it?" she said.

"How the hell do I know?" I said. "It's like—well, I think it's supposed to be a baby. Hard to see it really."

"Why's it crying?" she asked.

"Perhaps it's hungry," I said. "Come to think of it, I'm a bit peckish meself. Come on."

She wouldn't move.

"What's the writing?"

19

There were two words under the face, carved out roughly in thick capital letters, but they weren't like words I'd ever read anywhere.

"I don't know. Must be foreign. Come on, Mimi. You can see it later." She wouldn't move. "Look, I'll fetch you one if you don't hurry up."

"Will Auntie Ida eat us with mash?" she asked as we walked round the corner of the house.

I looked over to the deep ditch as it curved around the overgrown garden. There was hardly any water left in the bottom. At the edges, the drying mud had begun to crack.

"Don't be daft," I said, pushing Mimi in front of me. "We're family, ain't we?"

⋖ IDA EASTFIELD ⋗

Finn is scrabbling at the gate. One of the hinges is half off—he'll push the whole fence down one of these days if I don't see to it.

What's he barking at? If it's Harry's girls—God, I hope it isn't Harry's girls—the man will just have to take them straight back.

The letter said Saturday, definitely Saturday, not Monday. I was so relieved when they didn't turn up.

20

I bend to get through the henhouse doorway. Only four eggs today. Is it really worth hanging on to these wretched chickens? Pushing Finn away, I shut the gate in the fence behind me, then pull a piece of straw out of my hair and tuck my fringe under my scarf. Then I catch a movement.

Oh, God, there they are, the two of them standing on the path beneath the washing line, under the row of laddered stockings.

For a sickening moment, I see Susan and Anne.

I shut my eyes and rub my forehead, then look again.

It isn't Susan and Anne, but Susan's daughters. They are scruffy, unwashed.

"Hello, Auntie Ida," says the older one, almost bobbing to a curtsey. "I'm Cora."

My mouth has gone dry. I can't remember the last time I spoke to a child.

"I—I thought you weren't coming. I was expecting you on Saturday."

"Yeah, well, that's when Mr. Burridge was supposed to bring us," Cora says, "but we waited and waited and he didn't turn up. Then Dad asked Mr. Bates because Mr. Bates owed him one, and Mr. Bates is a bookie, so he's busy doing bets of a Saturday, then yesterday his car wouldn't start for love nor money, but Mr. Harrow couldn't fix it because he had to get hold of this special bit and it was Sunday, so he had to do it first thing this

21

morning. You ain't got no telephone or Dad would've rung you from the pub."

Finn barks. The little girl jumps.

"All right. Quiet, Finn, quiet!" I say. My head aches. I am shaking a little, along my arms and in my chest.

"This here's Mimi," Cora says, pushing the little girl towards me.

"What sort of silly exotic name is that!" I snap at her. "Isn't she Elizabeth?"

"Yeah, well, she's Mimi because she used to run after me when I went playing," Cora says in a rush, "and she used to call 'Me! Me!' because she wanted to come, too, and my pals used to say, 'Oh, Gawd, it's that "Me Me" again,' and after a while it stuck, and now she really thinks that's her name."

"It's utterly ridiculous," I say. "Not that it matters, because you're not staying here—not for a moment. Nobody asked me if I minded you turning up, and the fact is, I *do* mind, so you're going straight back to London, where you came from. Where's this Mr. Burridge?"

"It weren't Mr. Burridge. I told you," says Cora. "It were Mr. Bates."

"Where's this Mr. Bates, then?"

"He dumped us at the end of that muddy road there—"

"The Chase—"

"Yeah. He's gone."

"What? You mean he just left you on your own?"

"Yeah, I suppose. He didn't want to get his wheels stuck. Mimi fell in a puddle when your dog came out."

"He's called Finn—"

"Yeah, Finn then," says Cora. "If you want us to go home, you'll have to leave a message for Dad with Alf at the Half Moon. We ain't got no telephone neither. Then maybe Mr. Bates or somebody'll come back and get us. Or you'll have to write a letter. D'you know where we live? We're at number nine."

"We have white eggs," Elizabeth says.

I notice she is rubbing her cheek with an old, filthy, stuffed woollen toy. I look more closely and am overcome by a hot wave of anxiety. I've seen it before. My heart begins to thud. My head feels as if it's being pressed in a vice.

They can't stay here.

They mustn't stay here.

❧ CORA ❧

Don't do this—don't do that—don't go here, there, upstairs, except to your bedroom or the bathroom—don't go round that side of the garden, because there's an old well there and you or Elizabeth ("It's Mimi, Auntie Ida; she don't know she's

23

Elizabeth") *might fall in—you absolutely must not go down to the marshes—it's extremely dangerous there—don't even think about going down to the old church—absolutely forbidden—don't open the windows—ever!* (That's why the house is so stuffy you almost can't breathe, and it smells horrible.) *Don't even try to get into the locked rooms. Lock the back door when you come in and hang the key up on the big iron hook* (there are scratches on the back door as well, and next to it on the inside a great huge axe on the wall with such a long handle it takes three hooks to hold it up). *Always check who's at the door before you let anybody in—not that anyone ever comes. I'm writing the letter to your father this evening, so don't get any ideas about getting too comfortable* (no chance of that in this dump). *If you hear any strange noises, it'll be the parrot* (really old and half-bald—hasn't even got a name, not even Polly) *in the sitting room through there. Don't—never—mustn't— can't—don't—never—mustn't—can't—* (Like a flippin' prison.)

Auntie points out her bedroom door. I lean over the heavy rail and look down the huge staircase, at the monstrous carved post that marks the place where the stairs bend at a right angle and go down past the window towards the hall. The edges of the treads have worn pale and smooth and slippery. Next to the bottom step is a tall clock. Even from here, I can see that it doesn't stand straight. The wooden floors slope so steeply in places that you start to walk faster without being able to help yourself. The clock is silent. All the clocks in Guerdon Hall are unwound.

Above me, cobwebs hang down from the ceiling in loops and bunches like dirty lace, swaying in the draughts that come under the doors or up through the narrow gaps between the floorboards. Dust lies in strips along the skirtings and outlines with grey the curves of the carvings on the spindles. I blow on the dust, but it is so thick that it doesn't move.

Our bed is huge, with a faded pink quilted eiderdown. Auntie turns down the top sheet and plumps up the pillows and tells us the bathroom's down the landing to the left.

When we're sure she's gone all the way back down the stairs, Mimi and I bounce and bounce on the eiderdown. Dust floats down on us from the rafters overhead. Auntie comes thundering back up and shouts that we'll break the bed and we're not to fib about it because she heard the springs going.

We have two eggs each for our tea, with bread-and-butter soldiers for dipping. Auntie only boils the eggs for a couple of minutes so there is jelly around the yolks. I peep under my first strip of bread and see it is flecked with green. I worry Mimi might make a fuss, but she doesn't notice the mould under the butter and is so hungry she spoons up all the runny egg and scrapes out both her shells afterwards.

Auntie says it's time for bed, and I daren't argue even though it's so early, especially for me. We go back upstairs. I get our pyjamas out of our duffel bags and take Mimi to the bathroom.

I push open the door. It isn't a bathroom at all but a shadowy room full of old paintings. The Guerdons look down on us from the walls as we stand in the doorway. I see no likeness to myself at all, dark haired and dark eyed as I am, but in almost every face I see Mimi's pale eyes, Mimi's mouth, and her fluffy fair hair.

The walls are covered with red material, most of it torn and faded. Up near the ceiling on the outside wall are dark patches of damp, and some of the fabric has come away and hangs loose and frayed over the window.

In a dark corner nearby is a portrait of a lady with the same straight nose as Auntie Ida, but she is young and pretty, in a pink dress and lovely shiny pearls. I can't resist running my finger along the top of the frame to see how much dust there is. It comes down in a long thick string and I sneeze two huge sneezes, which makes Mimi laugh.

Beside the fireplace, there is a short dark passage. At the end of it, I can just make out the shape of another door. "Must be the bathroom down there," I say to Mimi, and push her in front of me.

Suddenly, without warning, she opens her mouth and screams—so loudly that the sound bounces from one side of the passage to the other.

Something crashes in the kitchen downstairs.

"What on earth's the matter? Be quiet, Mimi—*shh*."

I clamp one trembling hand over Mimi's mouth and fumble for a light switch with the other but find nothing.

I look up. On the wall over the bathroom door is the face of an old man, glaring down at us out of the darkness. His eyes are two piercing white dots. A few thin grey wisps of hair hang down on each side of his skull. His outstretched hand is raised, the curved fingers spread out towards us like a claw.

I hear Auntie Ida rushing up the staircase. She is out of breath, her face white. She follows our gaze. I expect her to be angry, but when she sees the painting, she just shuts her eyes for a moment, panting slightly.

"Oh," she says quietly, putting her hand on Mimi's shuddering shoulder, "that's—that's only—we called him Old Peter. He's been up there for years and years. You get used to him. It's all right—really. There's no lamp here, but leave the doors open when you come out, and the light from the bathroom window will brighten up the passage a bit. I'll—I'll wait for you here while you get washed, and take you back to your bedroom. Be careful: there are three steps down behind that door."

What a daft place to put steps. If she hadn't said anything, we most probably would have fallen smash down headfirst on the hard wooden floor and broken our necks.

Behind the door is a little room with two more doors. The one to the right is the toilet, and the other is the bathroom.

At home the privy is outside in the yard. I think it's cleaner than having one in the house like this. Ours has been leaking for a couple of weeks, so we've had to share with the Woolletts next door. Mrs. Woollett's mother, Mrs. Bracegirdle, is always in the privy because she's got a disease. Sometimes we have to stand outside, hoping we won't burst before she comes out. Mimi hates going to the Woolletts'. She hangs on in our house till she's desperate.

She's never going to go here with that man hanging on the wall.

I open the bathroom door and blink. The light is green and cold. The ivy outside has grown almost completely over the small arched windows. Some of its stems have crept through gaps and are inside, feeling their way upwards towards the ceiling.

Long ago, it must have been a different kind of room altogether, not a bathroom at all. When I stand in the corner behind the door, in that dusky half-light I can see shapes on the walls — shapes of people, trees, and flowers that were once there but have since been painted over. Now they are nothing more than ghosts, their pale colours faded almost to nothing. The shadowy people look at me, look out at me from the past. Their eyes are barely visible. They watch me in secret. Only when I stand in that special place, and turn my head in a certain way, can I peer into their hidden world and watch them back.

A huge bath, stained with long streaks of brown and green, sits on iron legs right in the middle of the room. The right tap drips now and then.

Dad didn't put any washing stuff in our duffel bags. I brush our teeth with a nasty old toothbrush that lies on a shelf under the mirror and use some vile pink powder in a tin next to the brush. At least, I hope it's toothpaste and not something for cleaning out the sink. I wipe Mimi over with a hard old flannel full of holes that was wrapped around one of the taps. There's only cold water coming through.

Auntie Ida is waiting outside. I see her eyes going to the worn patches around my knees, and I cover up the holes in the elbows with my hands. She says our pyjamas are too small. My teeth begin to chatter. The house must be perishing in the winter, the sort of place to give you the rheumatics.

When we come back down the passage, I don't look behind me at the old man on the wall, but I can almost feel two needles of light coming out of his eyes and boring into my shoulder blades.

I lie in the big bed next to Mimi and try to get to sleep. She goes off straight away, rubbing Sid's little worn patch, but her gentle snoring doesn't soothe me at all.

The night closes in, and the house wraps us up in itself, making its own noises in the dark—muffled clicks, soft thuds from unknown rooms, the rustling of mice in their secret scratchy places underneath the floors. I can hear beetles creeping along the cracks in the old hairy plaster, and above my head, in the angles of the beams, big black spiders are spinning, softly spinning in the shadows.

I hope Auntie Ida is writing her letter so Dad will come and fetch us home.

Late, but I don't know how late, I hear slow creaking on the stairs. A gleam of soft candlelight flares under our door for a moment as Auntie passes on her way to bed.

IDA EASTFIELD

My worn-out tweed skirt lies over the back of the chair. The hem's been hanging down for weeks. Will's old shirt is in a heap on the floor, and I'll just pick it up and put it on again tomorrow, along with the brown cardigan I knitted before the war, the one I wore today, and yesterday, and the day before that.

I know what I have become. I find in some small hidden room of myself a little corner of shame, but I quickly shut the door on it.

I used to smile at my reflection in the mirror there and carefully arrange that jewelled butterfly comb in my hair—the comb that lies in the dust on top of the chest of drawers, with three of its teeth missing. How smooth my skin was then. Now the lines on my face are like the cracks in the dried-up mud at the bottom of the creek when the tide goes out.

I was so slender in the blue silk dress that even now hangs beside the door. The colour has faded on the outside of the pleats, where the light strikes them, but when I press them apart with my fingers, the gleaming turquoise shines out with the brilliance of years ago.

His letter is still in its envelope, tucked into the pocket.

Louvaincourt, January 1917
. . . Last night was a night as bitter as any I've ever known. I couldn't sleep for the cold, even with my boots and great-coat on. I gave up and went out of the dugout and walked along the service trench for a while and had a smoke to stop my teeth chattering. They made such a noise I thought they

might draw fire. I leaned my back against the sandbags and kept my head down so the Huns wouldn't see the light from my cigarette.

There was no moon and the frost was beginning to crust the top of the parapet. I looked up and saw the sky was ablaze with stars. I made your face out of the constellations, and tied up your hair with the long pale ribbon of the Milky Way. . . .

Why am I thinking of that now? Why didn't they leave me alone . . . ?

Why am I lying awake? What am I listening for?

They should have left me alone. . . .

They can't stay here.

✑ CORA ✑

I'm lying in the ditch, the muddy water soaking my back and legs. The more I try to drag myself out, the farther in I sink. My arms reach up to grab the long grass on the bank.

The bed was warm and wet.

"Flippin' heck! Mimi! Wake up! Look what you've flippin' done! Blinkin' hell!"

"Sorry . . ."

"Flippin' hell . . ."

"I had to go . . ."

"Flippin' hell . . ."

The bed was getting cold and beginning to smell.

"For God's sake, get up! Have you finished or is there any more coming?"

"'S all gone."

I rolled back the eiderdown and blankets. Luckily they were dry, but the sheet and underblanket were sopping. I pulled them off, rolled them up, and threw them on the floor. The mattress was wet, too, but I couldn't do anything about that now. I took off our sodden pyjamas, wrapped us both up in the prickly woollen blankets, then covered us with the eiderdown.

Mimi went back to sleep, but I lay awake, itchy in the blanket, worrying about how I was going to ask Auntie Ida to move the painting of the old, bald man with the hand like a claw.

⊙ ROGER ⊙

I love sunny mornings in the summer holidays. I lean over Pete from the top bunk and drop something on him, like a piece of Plasticine or a slipper.

"Oi! Leave off, will you!"

Then he gets up and tries to hit my legs. I push the ladder down so he can't get up, and then he goes off to the bathroom, sulking. It's usually something like that.

We have a bit of toast, if there's bread left, or make ourselves some shredded wheat if the milkman's been, then we leave the house quickly in case Mum nabs us. If you hang around the house for too long, she'll find you jobs to do. You've only got to walk past the door and she'll ask you to make her a cup of tea. Once I thought I'd give myself a bad accident with the boiling water—that would teach her to ask a child to run round after her—but I couldn't do it in the end, in case it went wrong and I ended up in hospital for six months with no skin.

Depending on how we feel, we might go down to the woods and see if Tooboy's around. He's got a scary older brother, Figsy, who has a greasy quiff and wears tight black trousers so his legs look like two sticks of liquorice. Now and then he rides a moped around the path in the woods. We call it his pop-pop and keep out of the way if we hear it coming. Tooboy lets us play on the big rope-swing Figsy made with his gang. You have to climb a tree to get to it, it's so high, but if we hear the pop-pop, we scarper real quick, even Tooboy, and hide in the trees till Figsy's gone.

Sometimes we go over to the Patches and check on our camps, though if there's anyone about, they look at us a bit sideways as people from Bryers Guerdon tend not to go there. The Patches are a long way down Ottery Lane, almost to North Fairing. Dad said East Enders from London came out to the country between the two world wars and built houses for themselves on plots of land sold off or rented out by one of the North Fairing farmers. We've always called them the Patches — patches of land, I suppose.

Best of all, though, we like going down to the marshes. There's a great hill on the way to the church — that's All Hallows, stuck all by itself away from the village. It's smashing whizzing down the hill on your bike with your feet off the pedals, but Pete's got a puncture. Mum won't let me take any more spoons outside, and if I haven't got spoons, I can't get the inner tube out. She says I left them in the garden last time, and she didn't have enough for the prunes. I told her Terry had taken them out to eat mud with, but she didn't believe me.

I told Pete about the two girls I'd seen. He didn't seem too keen, but I told him they might be good for a snoop around Mrs. Eastfield's house. He wanted to go down to the church, but I told him he had to come and sit on the fence with me and wait for them. He nearly went into a mood, but when I told him about the plans for the new camp, he came up the Chase with me to have a look.

✤ CORA ✤

Auntie Ida said she wasn't moving the horrible man. She said he'd been there forever and she wasn't getting a ladder out, and anyway she couldn't do it on her own as it would be much too heavy, and we'd have to put up with it and she didn't have anywhere to put him anyway, and she was really cross about the sheet and the blanket and would have to spend hours scrubbing the mattress with Dettol, and where was she going to find a rubber sheet for the bed, and Mimi should have grown out of that by now, and I was a really cheeky girl, only just arrived and telling her what to do about the painting, and what was Dad doing sending us with no change of clothes, only our pyjamas (that she'd had to stick in the kitchen sink for soaking, and however were they to get properly dried and aired by tonight with the weather so changeable she had no idea), and a couple of pairs of knickers and some socks with holes in, and if Mimi was so silly that she wouldn't go to the toilet upstairs, there was another one by the back door she would have to use.

Then Auntie said she had to go on an errand and she'd be about an hour and a half but we weren't allowed to stay in the house on our own. We were to go up to the village, Bryers Guerdon, to Mrs. Wickerby's to post the letter she'd written to Dad last night. Auntie gave us threepence for the stamp, but nothing extra for sweets or anything.

She opened the back door and squinted, looking across and down the garden. Finn pushed past her and ran up the path, round the henhouse and back.

She said we weren't ever to go out in the garden when the tide was out in the creeks because Mimi might get sucked down in the mud, which wasn't fair if we had to stay in with all the windows shut and boil up like we were in a jungle or something. When I asked why the windows stayed closed all the time, she told me to hold my tongue. I thought it'd be even more dangerous if the tide was in because Mimi might fall in the water and get herself drowned, and that would be much worse than getting stuck in the mud, because at least then I could always pull her out before her head went under, but I didn't dare say anything.

Auntie gave me very clear directions how to get to Bryers Guerdon and said we weren't to dawdle and were absolutely not to go down to the old church — absolutely not, under any circumstances, she said; it was completely forbidden. I had to check the time by the big clock in Mrs. Wickerby's, and after an hour and a half Auntie would have got back. Whatever happened, we were absolutely not to go down to the church, absolutely not. If she hadn't returned, we were to wait for her in the Chase, and not come back over the creek into the garden, and she said most particularly we had to wait just by the old farm cottages, and not near the bridge. She made me promise, so I crossed my heart and licked my finger and spat, but she looked a bit shirty, as if she didn't like me doing it.

Mimi and me went round to the front of the house, out through the gateway and over the bridge. Sitting on the fence, in exactly the same place as yesterday, was the boy, but this time he had another boy with him, a bit smaller.

"Spent a night in the haunted house, then?" the big boy said.

The smaller boy lifted up his arms, wobbled his fingers, and went "Wooooo!" like a ghost and nearly fell off the fence.

Their voices sounded the same, and I guessed they were brothers.

"I'm Roger, and this is Pete," said the older one.

"I'm Cora, and she's Mimi." I jerked my thumb behind me at her.

"Mimi! Ooh-la-la!" said Pete, jumping down and wiggling his hips from side to side. I suppose he thought that's what French people did all day—wiggled their hips and said "Ooh-la-la."

"It's not Mimi like that," I said. "It's a nickname. She's Elizabeth really."

As we walked along, Roger said he'd got three brothers—Dennis, Terry, Pete of course—and a sister, Baby Pamela.

"Baby Pamela's all right for a name," said Roger, "but I reckon if you've waited that long for a girl, you should call her something a bit more interesting, like Aspidistria or something."

We were at the end of the Chase.

"Fancy coming down the church?" Roger asked. "Pete and me are always playing around there."

"Auntie Ida said we wasn't supposed to go," I said. "Went on and on, she did. Made me promise, and I did the special sign."

"Mum's always saying we're not to either, but we just don't say," said Roger. "There's loads to do down there. Won't take long to show you."

"We're supposed to go and post this letter," I said.

"You can post it after," said Roger.

"Better not. I promised," I said.

"Doesn't matter, then," said Roger.

"There's graves so old they're half sticking up out of the ground," said Pete. "We dig around them sometimes."

"I've got to post this," I said. "It's for Dad to come and take us home."

"But you've only just got here," said Roger.

"I know."

"Where's your mum, then? Can't she come and get you?"

"She—" I began, not sure how I was going to finish. "She ain't at home at the moment."

"When's she coming back, then?"

"Um . . . sometime—not quite sure right now."

"See you, then," said Roger. "Pete and me are going down."

"Ta ta, then."

Mimi and me stood and watched while they went towards the church. I looked at the envelope in my hand: *H. R. Drumm, Esq.* I imagined Dad would get the letter the next morning, which was Wednesday, and might come in the afternoon, or Thursday at the latest, so if we were going home nearly straight away, maybe it wouldn't matter if we just popped down and had a little look at the church; then we could go up to the post office afterwards.

"Hang on!" I shouted, shoving the letter in my pocket. "Wait! We'll come an' all!"

Roger and Pete looked back, then stopped to wait for us.

"Don't want to," Mimi said.

"You'll do what I blimmin' well say!"

"Auntie said not to."

"Don't flippin' well tell her, then."

"Don't like it."

"Stay here on your own, then!"

Mimi's lower lip wobbled. She rubbed Sid's worn patch, then put her small soft hand in mine.

We walked down the lane until we came to a large gate standing all by itself on the left-hand side of the road. It had a tiled roof, held up by a wooden arch supported by stone pillars. Like the roof of Guerdon Hall, it was sunken in and soft with green moss. The wooden gates in the middle looked half-rotten. They'd been lashed together with bunches of old ropes and rusty chains. The pillars were messy with brambles and wild rosebushes, and the stinging nettles were nearly as high as our shoulders.

"This is a funny old gate," I said, standing in front. "Why's it all tied up, then?"

"I don't know," said Roger. "It's always been like that. You ever made itching powder out of the middle of rose hips?"

"Nah, does it work?"

"Yeah, brilliant. Have you tried blackberries?"

41

"Won't you get poisoned, just eating stuff by the road?" I said.

"No, but you've got to eat the black ones."

I put one in my mouth. It was really sour.

"We haven't had enough sun," Roger said, screwing up his face. "Maybe in another week or so."

As I spat out the blackberry, I saw something small and pale moving on an enormous, ugly old tree far away on the wild edge of the churchyard, beyond the gravestones. Leafy branches grew out of the massive trunk, but no farther up than halfway. The tree had no crown. Instead, a huge, bare white branch towered high above the cluster of branches lower down, ending in a gigantic hook split into two.

Roger followed my gaze. "We don't like that tree, Pete and me," he said. "Most of it's dead. It's most probably a gypsy tree."

"What's a gypsy tree, then?"

"Well, if you give a gypsy some money or buy some pegs or something, then they'll hang a rag from a tree near your house so the next gypsy who comes along knows you'll give them something as well."

"But there ain't no houses here. Why do you think it's a gypsy tree?"

"Because there's things on it," said Pete, "and when there's things on a tree, it's a gypsy tree."

"It's like it's got a dead heart," I said.

A little way down the road was a wide iron gate, opening onto the dirt path that led to the small church, its warm stone walls flickering in the swaying shadows of the fat overhanging trees.

We cut across in front of the tower, weaving our way around the weathered, ivy-choked crosses and tomb-stones and trying not to trip over the tops of the ancient graves hidden in the long grass. As we drew nearer to the far boundary of the churchyard, I felt my shoes and socks becoming sodden. The ground was growing spongier, and the small rounded hummocks of moss began to give way under our feet so that we were trailing through shallow water. We came close to the tree at last. I saw that the great thick roots facing us were rising up out of a boggy pool, ringed with reeds and bulrushes. There was higher ground at the back where the ground seemed to be dry, and on that side the tree appeared to be well rooted in the shaded earth.

Odd things hung from the branches—dirty rags, shredded by the wind, all faded to the same shade of greyish white, fastened on with rusty wire so long ago that the bark of the tree had grown around it; the remains of children's shoes; an old leather sole; a small buckle. Nailed to the trunk was a little, rough square of wood, covered with faint scratches that might once have been writing; other rusty nails stuck out with nothing on them at all, as if the things had long blown away and

43

rotted in the soil or had fallen off to be lost in the green stagnant water.

I looked up. A face with one eye stared down at me. It was the broken head of an old doll tied onto a branch by its long dirty hair.

✧ ROGER ✧

A pile of brown, rotting flowers was stacked up against the wall on the dark side of the church.

"They're from people's funerals," I told Cora as she picked up some soggy little cards in cellophane covers. "Old Mr. Hibbert comes down and tidies up the newer graves and chucks the old wreaths on this heap. He's done it for years. Once, Pete and I had to hide for two hours while he was pottering about. If he'd seen us, he would have sneaked on us to Mum."

"You know, some of these flowers are still all right," Cora said. "They've got little wires coming out of them." She held up the rusting frame of a square wreath. "Look, we could make new wreaths with flowers that ain't mouldy yet and put them on them poor old graves from hundreds of years ago where nobody visits."

My first thought was that Gary Webb in my class would probably beat me up or something if he found out I'd been playing with flowers. I'd had a lot of trouble one way and another with Gary Webb. I saw his mum at the Confirmations and she'd got the same sort of sticking-out teeth.

The worst thing happened when we had a new teacher in our school, Miss Doyle, who was a real person and not a nun. She asked us if we had anything interesting to tell the class about where we lived, and I put my hand up and said we had some beavers living in the pond by our woods, and they'd made a big house out of sticks.

"A lodge," she'd said.

"Yes, that's right, a lodge," I said, and by the end of my story, I almost believed it myself, I could see the beavers so clearly in my mind.

Then, later, when we were in the lines waiting for the school buses, Gary Webb waited until Sister Laserian, who was on duty, turned her back. Suddenly his two best friends, Leonard Ricketts and Vincent Grossit, took hold of my arms. Then Gary Webb punched me really hard in the stomach with his fist and said I was a liar about the beavers. He said I was really stupid and that everybody knew you only got beavers in Africa.

I thought I'd die from pain and no breath. Then Sister Laserian came back. I didn't want to cry, but these big tears just spurted out on their own. I could never have told her what had happened. She shook me really hard and told me not to be such a big baby, in front of all the bus lines. The worst thing was, Pete was in the line a bit back from us, and I saw him turn away and go red and embarrassed because I was his brother.

Then I remembered that Gary Webb lived over on the other side of Daneflete, nearly to Lokswood, so how was he ever going to know about it? I could do whatever I wanted down here.

We found enough good flowers to make three really nice wreaths and wound them onto the frames with the little bits of rusted wire. Mimi brought some buttercups she'd pulled up, and we stuck those on as well, then filled out the gaps with bunches of hawthorn berries from the bushes.

Cora chose one of the old gravestones. Only about six inches of it stuck up out of the ground. We pulled the grass away and tried scraping off some of the moss with the sides of our shoes, but it was much too old to clean. We let Mimi pop the wreath over the stone, then stood back to admire our work.

"I bet the man in heaven who's buried there is saying thank you," said Pete. "We should say a prayer."

The only prayer Cora knew was the grace from her school dinners, so we joined our hands and said, "For what we are about to receive, may the Lord make us truly thankful. Amen."

"Let Mimi choose the next grave," I said.

"Pick a grave, Mimi," said Cora, prodding her in the back. "Then we can put some more flowers on it."

"How about this one, Mimi?" called Pete.

He was standing a few feet away from the side of the church, just along from the porch, next to a long stone box shaped like a coffin, its sides rising a couple of feet out of the grass. The narrow end of the grave had sunken much deeper into the ground than the wide end, and the stone lid, knotted with ivy, had slipped slightly sideways and backwards, leaving a dark opening.

"Don't like it," Mimi said.

"You're not supposed to like it," said Cora crossly. "We're only going to stick flowers on it. Choose another one if you want, but hurry up."

"Don't want to," she said, her mouth turned down.

"Shove it on, Pete," I called, throwing him the second wreath. "Can you see in the hole—where the lid's tipped off?"

"I'm not looking in there," said Pete, tossing the wreath on the grave from at least three feet away. "There might be a skeleton in it."

He came back over to us, holding his nose. "That grave really stinks," he said. "I bet it's the dead person inside making a smell."

All at once, the birds shot out of the trees and whirled high in the sky, crying as they flew.

"Who's that?" Cora said suddenly.

My heart dropped into my boots. I knew it had to be Gary Webb; I just knew it. I couldn't look up for shame.

Cora pulled at my jumper. "Over there, by the old gate. Look."

She turned her head back. "Oh," she said, "he's gone."

"Hell," I said. "Was he big and ugly, with buckteeth?"

"He was . . . I don't know. . . . Where could he have got to?"

We were all looking now. The tall nettles nodded, and the frayed ends of the old ropes on the gates lifted in the breeze, but there was nobody there.

"It was your himagination," said Pete.

"No, honestly, I swear," said Cora, frowning. "Cross my heart and hope to die, stick a needle in my eye. It was this man, with long black clothes on. He was looking at us. I—I've seen his face somewhere before, but I can't remember where. . . . He looked like he'd been in an accident or something. His skin was all twisted and horrible. . . ."

"Don't be daft," I said. "If there was a man there, we'd have seen him."

"I tell you, I ain't fibbin'!"

"It were Peter," said Mimi, rubbing the worn patch on Sid's head.

"What? Rubbish!" said Pete. "I'm right here, aren't I?"

"No," she said, staring back at the old gate, "the other Peter—over at Auntie Ida's—Old Peter. . . ."

✌ CORA ❧

We don't play the game anymore. Roger puts the last wreath over a headless angel standing on a grave beside the path. Without saying a word, we go back through the iron gate and into the lane.

I search for footprints or flattened grass around the gate with the roof, but everything is just the same as before. The only footprints in the wet earth are ours. Roger kicks the dirt about, and Pete won't look at me. They obviously think we were lying. Mimi stands quietly, rubbing Sid's patch with the side of her finger.

I'm cross. I pick up a stone and throw it high at the gate. It bounces off and nearly hits me in the face. As I dodge, I think I glimpse something written on the cross-piece of the wooden arch that holds up the roof. I stretch up, but my fingers won't quite reach. Moving backwards a little, I shade my eyes with my hand, but the arch is in shadow.

"Hey, you lot, I think there's words up here," I call. Roger and Pete come over and screw up their eyes.

"Can't see it. . . ." Pete squints.

"We need to climb up on something," says Roger, "though it probably just says *DM loves SS*—that's Derek Meacock, who lives next to Mrs. Aylott's, and Sylvia

Sparks. He writes it up all over the place. It's on the lamppost outside Mrs. Wickerby's, and on the bus shelter on the main road, but Sylvia never goes out with him. I asked Mum why once, but Dad butted in and said he couldn't understand it because Sylvia's a tart and would go with anybody for a free ticket to the pictures. Then Mum told him off and said he wasn't to say things like *tart* in front of us, but I didn't know what he meant, anyway. I thought a tart was just something you ate with custard."

"No," I tell him. "A tart's a lady what puts on bright red lipstick and dyes her hair yellow and puts it up in a bouffong with loads of lacquer to keep it stiff. We've got one in our street called Viv."

We look around for something to stand on. There's a big stone by the side of the road, but it's too heavy to move. Roger tries jumping but goes up so high the second time that when he comes down again, he falls over in the mud.

"Let's see if there's a chair in the church to stand on," says Pete. "It's always open. *Nyaaaah!*" He goes whizzing off up the path with his arms out like an aeroplane.

"Good idea," Roger calls after him as he brushes down his knees.

The musty smell in the church porch is like the smell of Guerdon Hall. There are dingy old notices nailed to the wall. Roger lifts the iron latch and pushes open the big wooden door.

"Don't like it," says Mimi. "It ain't nice—ain't goin' in."

"You blinkin' well are," I say, pulling her sleeve.

I've never been inside a church ever before. The quiet is almost like something you can put out your hand and touch. I can hear my ears singing. Our footsteps echo off the polished tiles up into the rafters.

The church is very small, with only eight pairs of pews, each one closed in with a little hinged door.

The walls are plain, but up towards the timber beams, some of the white paint is peeling away and pale pictures are showing through the flakes, like the faded figures on the walls of Auntie Ida's bathroom. Jagged scratches mark the plaster lower down, but somebody has painted over those as well. A dirty mossy stain about a foot high rises up the walls from where they meet the stone floor, continuing in a green band all around the inside of the building.

"Is that mould down there?" I whisper.

"Well, I think it might be, because there was this enormous huge flood when Dennis was a baby," says Roger in a lowered voice. "The water came right up onto our veranda, and we were marooned. When it went back, there were dead fish in the garden from our pond. It was really exciting, and we were lucky because the flood didn't actually get in the house—missed the doors by an inch—but down here I'd have thought it would

51

have been quite bad. Maybe the walls have never dried out properly. Smells, doesn't it?"

Brasso and polish, damp earth, wax and old wood, and underneath, a stink like — like dead rats. I know the smell, metallic and sweet at the same time, because once we found a dead rat in the cupboard under the kitchen sink at home. It stank the place out for at least a week till we had a good search and I noticed its tail curling round a packet of Flash. Dad wrapped it up in the *News of the World* and chucked it in the dustbin.

On our left, a huge arch opens out into the bottom of the tower. A thick embroidered curtain is hanging against the wall to one side, and on the other is a wooden door. In the middle of the floor is a carved stone basin covered with a wooden lid, pointed at the top like a steeple.

"What's that for?" I whisper. "That pointy thing?"

"It's a font, for baptizing babies," says Roger. "This is a Protestant church, so they call it christening. You pour water over the baby and it gets its name. The nuns say we're not allowed to come into a Protestant church, but Pete and me do anyway."

Three thick ropes are looped up to hooks in the wall.

"They pull the bells with those," Roger goes on. "The fluffy bits in the middle stop you getting blisters. If there's a funeral, Mr. Hibbert rings one bell on its own. It's that one over there, that plain old rope hanging down by itself. You can hear it even from our house, all that way. Sometimes, when I'm in bed at night and there's a real wind blowing, I can hear it ringing, even if there's nobody here. Honest, I really can."

I look up to see where the ropes disappear through holes in the ceiling. To my surprise, I suddenly feel uneasy, light-headed. I sway a little, unsteady on my feet.

"Blimey! You all right?" says Roger. "You've gone all white."

"Yeah, yeah," I say, rubbing my head. "What's up there?"

"Dunno. Just the bells, I suppose, and the steeple."

"I don't like it in here."

"Come and look at the big window, then." Roger pulls me by the arm. "It's really nice."

At the other end of the church is a huge stained-glass window. People dressed in scarlet, purple, brilliant yellow, and emerald green are dancing upwards towards a golden point radiating lines of light across a deep blue sky.

"Who are all them people?" I ask.

"It's the holy souls," says Roger, "going up to heaven."

As we stand there gazing, the sun suddenly bursts out from behind a cloud beyond the window and we see everything—the walls, the pews, the stone floor, the glass lamps, even our faces—blazing with moving bands and patches of coloured light, as if the church has been scattered with rainbows.

Roger whispers, "It's like that poem we do in Elocution with Mrs. Lipkiss—"

"Oh, yeah," says Pete, suddenly flinging himself down on the floor, kicking his legs, and grabbing his stomach. "'When they shot him down on the highway'—aargh—'Down like a dog on the highway'—aargh—"

"Shut up! Not that one, you dope," Roger whispers loudly. "You'll go to hell making all that noise in a church. Get up! I mean that poem about the stately Spanish galleon coming through the isthmus."

"Eh?" says Pete, standing up again.

"You know . . . 'with a cargo of diamonds, emeralds, amethysts, Topazes, and cinnamon, and gold moidores.'"

"What's gold moidores?"

"Don't know. I'll have to look it up."

"What's cinnamon, then?"

"Oh, leave off—I don't know, something sparkly. Now, shut up. Look, Cora, this is the altar."

Under the window is a long table covered with a clean white cloth edged with lace and lined with sharp creases like Nan Drumm's starched Sunday tablecloth. In the middle towards the back is a brass cross with three tall creamy candles in fancy silver candlesticks on either side of it. A long heavy curtain like the one in the tower, with a fringe and tassels, hangs behind the altar.

A huge wooden eagle with its face turned sideways and a narrow ledge on its back for a book stands on the floor in front of the pews. I run my fingers over the feathers carved on its outstretched wings. The wood feels warm and smooth.

"Get out of that pulpit, you ninny!" Roger turns and hisses to Pete, who, with furrowed brow and arms raised, is about to deliver a sermon. Muttering to himself, Pete comes down the steps and goes back down the aisle to where Mimi is waiting. She hasn't moved an inch from her spot near the door since we came in.

"Here, this'll do," Pete calls, lifting up a chair from a line of three standing along the back wall. There's a box on the back of it with a couple of books inside.

When we get the chair down to the old gate, Roger stands on it while I keep it steady.

"There's definitely writing here," he says, "but it's in the shadow. Hang on, I've got an idea." He jumps down. "In my encyclopaedia it tells you about doing rubbings."

"What are you going on about now?" I say.

"Look, you get a bit of paper and you put it over the thing you want to copy, like some old tree bark or something, then you rub it with a crayon and the thing comes out on the paper."

"So where are we going to get a crayon and some paper out here?"

"I've got a pencil. It's still got some lead in," says Pete. He turns out his pocket and holds out his palm. Pulling away some grubby fluff with his finger, he uncovers a few bits of dead bird, a couple of Quality Streets with bite marks, a dried-up spider with half its legs missing, and the chewed stub of a pencil.

"For heaven's sake, put that stuff away," says Roger. "It's worse than one of Baby Pamela's nappies."

"I ain't touching that pencil," I say. "You could get typhoid fever from that."

"I'll do it, then. Give it here," says Roger, grabbing it. He spits on it and rolls it dry on his trousers. "Now, where are we going to get paper?"

"Look, here's some," I say, taking out one of the books from the back of the chair. *"Hymns Ancient and Modern."*

I open it in the middle and rip a page out. It's hymn numbers 109 to 112.

"Flippin' heck!" yelps Roger. "That's a huge sin, most probably mortal!"

"Well, it's too late now," I say, giving him the paper. "You should've warned me."

"You might be all right," says Pete. "It's a Protestant book. I don't think Protestants do mortal sins."

Roger climbs back onto the chair and places the paper

on the beam of the arch. The chair legs wobble danger-
ously as he scribbles with the stub of pencil.

"This paper isn't big enough," he calls down. "I can
only get a bit of the writing on."

As I've already torn one page out, I don't suppose the
sin will get worse if I pull out hymn number 113 as well.
Roger hands me the rubbing he's finished and starts on
the next.

Jagged white capital letters stand out against the
rough grey scribble: CAVE.

"What's *cave*, then?" I say.

"We all know what a blinking cave is," says Roger,
"but there aren't any round here. Can you pass up
another bit of paper? I've run out again."

"Can't make head nor tail of it," I say, looking at the
second sheet he's given me. "It says *best*."

Pete looks over. "Doesn't make sense," he calls up to
Roger. "*Cave best*. Are you sure you did it right?"

"'Course I did." Roger comes down off the chair with
the last page. "Anyway, it definitely doesn't say anything about Derek Meacock and Sylvia Sparks. This is
it. There's no more. It says *iam*."

"*Cave best iam*," I say. "It's a load of rubbish if you
ask me."

"I expect he's got bad breath," says Pete thoughtfully.

"What are you going on about now?" says Roger.
"Who's got bad breath?"

"Derek Meacock. That's why Sylvia Sparks won't go to the pictures with him."

"Oh, leave off, will you?"

We stare at the paper.

"Hmm, *Cave best iam*," says Roger, scratching his head. "*Cave best iam*. No idea."

"It must be foreign," I say. "Oh, that's funny. I said that before. Yesterday. At Auntie Ida's."

❧ ROGER ☙

We were really nervous, Pete and me, going over the bridge to Guerdon Hall. I got a nasty dry taste in my mouth, and I could see Pete looking around with eyes as big as Ping-Pong balls.

"Where's the dog?" he whispered.

"Auntie Ida said she was going out," said Cora. "She's most probably taken him with her. Look, Mimi, promise me you won't tell Auntie we've been down the church."

"Why?"

"Because she said we wasn't to go, remember? If you tell, I'll—I'll chuck Sid down the toilet."

"All right."

"It's here, the writing," Cora said to us, pointing up as we got close to the house.

A cracked piece of wood was nailed up over the porch at a wonky angle. It had a rough carving of a baby's face on it. Underneath, all worn and chipped, were the same words as on the gate down at the church: CAVE BESTIAM.

"That's not a very nice thing to have on the front of your house, a blinking crying baby, so you have to look at it every time you go in," said Pete.

"We don't go in here," said Cora. "We go round the back. Come and see."

We were a bit worried about this, to be honest. Round the back was where the chickens were. Pete and I sort of dragged our feet a bit.

"What's the matter?" said Cora. "Ain't you coming?"

"Well," I said quietly, "it's the chickens."

"Don't tell me you're scared of a load of flippin' chickens!" said Cora.

"Well, for a start, are you sure they're chickens?" said Pete.

"What do you mean, *sure they're chickens*? What else would they blinkin' well be—blimmin' vultures?"

"Nah, well," said Pete, "we think they're children Mrs. Eastfield's put a spell on."

"Pete does," I said quickly.

"What a load of stupid rubbish," Cora said, annoyed. "We had their eggs for tea yesterday."

"Doesn't mean they weren't children first, before they

59

laid eggs," said Pete. "If you're turned into a chicken, you couldn't be a real one if you didn't lay eggs."

"It's still rubbish," said Cora, and we might have stood there talking about this a lot longer, but there came the sound of barking, and the big dog bounded over the bridge and down the path. Pete jumped behind me.

Then Mrs. Eastfield appeared, carrying a huge, scruffy leather suitcase with its straps straining. She had to lean to one side to balance herself.

"Crikey! We're trapped!" Pete whispered to me.

Mrs. Eastfield saw us and put the suitcase down. The lines on her forehead set themselves into a nasty frown.

"Cora!" she said. "I thought I told you to stay in the Chase if I wasn't back—near the cottages, I said!"

"Blimey, I forgot—"

"I will not be disobeyed! While you're here, you'll do what I say! I won't have this, Cora! I won't!"

"Sorry, Auntie."

Mrs. Eastfield wiped her forehead with the back of her hand. Then she took off her scarf and, fanning herself with it, looked Pete and me over. I felt hollow around my knees. Pete's eyes had grown into tennis balls.

"And who are you?" she said.

"Roger and Peter Jotman," I blurted out. Crikey! I'd actually talked to Mrs. Eastfield.

"Jotman? Two of the Jotman boys? Does your mother know you're here?"

"Um, pardon?"

"You heard me. Does she know you are here?"

"Er—"

"Obviously not! You know full well she would be furious if she knew you had come down to Guerdon Hall."

I heard Pete gulp at the same time as me.

"Better go. Bye, Mrs. Eastfield. Thank you, Mrs. Eastfield," I said.

Pete and me shot off like lightning bolts. Halfway down the Chase, we stopped to get our breath.

"Cor, narrow escape, there," panted Pete, leaning forward with his hands on his knees.

"Yeah, but what was in that great big suitcase?"

"Most probably stuff for spells," said Pete. "New supplies."

❦ CORA ❧

Auntie Ida wouldn't open the suitcase until she'd had a cup of tea. Mimi and me stood quietly on the sunken floorboards by the kitchen door while she made it. I knew the case had to be something to do with us or Auntie wouldn't have kept us waiting there. When she finished her tea, she put the cup and saucer in the big stone sink. Then, with a grunt, she lifted the suitcase up onto the kitchen table, undid the strap buckles, and threw the lid back. As the case burst open, I caught a wave of light-coloured material and a lovely fresh smell on the air, but Mimi and I stayed where we were, not daring to move until Auntie called us over.

The case was full of lovely clean clothes—perfect, no holes or patches or darning: gingham dresses for me, one blue and one mauve with a white collar; skirts; green trousers with yellow stitching on the pockets; a white cardigan with pink roses in two lines next to the buttons; flowery pyjamas; and (I couldn't believe it) a pair of red slip-on shoes without any straps or buckles. Amazingly, they fit pretty well. There were dresses for Mimi, too—one pink with coloured smocking, another in white—pairs of knickers with rows of lacy frills, socks, little black shiny shoes, and pyjamas with yellow ducks on. At the bottom of the case, wrapped in brown paper, were some wellingtons.

Everything was much nicer by a million miles than anything we had in London. Clothes went round in Limehouse, all used before, the elbows worn out by some other child, the patches sewn on by someone else's mum. The only things I ever had new were the jumpers Nan knitted, striped in odd colours from old scraps of leftover wool. When I grew out of them, Nan unravelled them, washed the yarn to get the kinks out, then knitted bigger ones, the stripes always in different places to where they'd been before.

It was wonderful of Auntie Ida to go to all this trouble for us, to buy all those lovely things, but I didn't say anything other than a quiet "Thank you, Auntie Ida," because it wasn't good manners to draw attention to the fact that money had been spent. Dad always said there was quite a lot of it—money, that is—on that side of the family, Mum's side. He even said that they were actually toffs, but that my Grandma Agnes, Mum's mother and Auntie Ida's sister, had been a black sheep. I know that that sort of black sheep has got nothing to do with the nursery rhyme. It means somebody in your family who has done a bad thing and can't ever be forgiven for it.

❧ ROGER ❧

Pete and I walked back up the hill.

"What do you reckon *Cave bestiam* means, Pete?"

"I dunno," he said, shrugging. "'Best cave' or something. I dunno. Is it French? You've done French in your class."

"Yeah, but only counting to ten and days of the week, and I can't remember anything after Thursday," I said.

"It's not German, because it doesn't sound like a war film, like when they're escaping from a prisoner-of-war camp."

We spent a bit of time discussing how we would have got out of Stalag Luft 5.

"Do you know what *Cave bestiam* sounds a bit like to me?" I said after a while. "I think it sounds a bit like Latin."

"Like in church?"

"Yeah, the priests are always saying *quoniam*s and *gloriam*s. *Bestiam*'s the same."

"I dunno. Maybe. *Cave* is English, though. How could we find out?"

"We'll have to have a think. We can't ask Mum. You know what she's like, and Dad'll just go along with her. She won't stop asking questions, like where did we get it from. We'll have to ask someone clever."

"Crikey. Where are we going to find someone clever?"

"I dunno. I wonder what we're having for dinner. Hope it's rice pudding for afters. If it is, I bags the skin."

"That's not flippin' fair. Let's dip for it."

❧ CORA ☙

Auntie Ida put plaits in so tight I could hardly get my fingernails through my hair to scratch my scalp.

She looked out of the window at the dark grey sky and said the tide was in, so Mimi and I could put on our boots and go and see if the chickens had laid any eggs, but we'd best be quick before the heavens opened.

We unlocked the back door, walked across the cobbles of the small paved yard between the two wings of the house, and took the narrow path that led down the garden.

It was damp and chilly. Rain had fallen in the night. The wet grass was sprinkled with drops like shiny glass beads, each one separate from the others. The branches of the overgrown shrubs arched over the path with the weight of dripping water, their drooping leaves showering us as we brushed by.

Mimi held the basket, and I pushed open the old gate in the wire fence round the henhouse. Our boots soon became clogged with mud and feathers, straw and chicken muck. When we went through the door, the chickens bobbed and jerked and looked us up and down with their little beady eyes, clucking like a lot of old women gossiping.

A huge cockerel with a big fancy-coloured tail and spikes on the back of its feet came over and started pecking around Mimi's legs. She took hold of my arm, grizzling to go out. I told her she was to give the old bird a kick if it pecked too hard.

Auntie Ida said we had to be firm with the chickens and stand no nonsense. I took a deep breath, stuck my hand under the backside of a big brown hen sitting in its box full of straw, and pushed it off. It rose up, squawking in a flurry of flying feathers and scratchy claws, starting all the other chickens off. They went scattering into the air and scrabbling for the door, making a silly racket. In the empty boxes, I found five warm eggs altogether and let Mimi help me get them safely into the basket.

It started to spit as we pulled the wire gate shut. I rested one hand gently on the eggs while we ran back along the path towards the house. By the time we'd reached the back door, dashed inside, taken off our boots, and put them in the crate like Auntie told us, the rain was falling in heavy drops. We rushed down the stone passage to the kitchen in our socks and showed her the eggs. She was really pleased with us and said we'd done well for townies. For a moment, I thought a smile was coming, but it never did.

The rain went on all day. We listened to the wireless,

and Mimi cut pictures out of old magazines and newspapers and stuck them onto bits of cardboard with glue that Auntie made out of flour and water. I thumbed through the stack of papers. Most of them were old and yellow, some even from before the war.

I didn't realize I'd started drumming on the kitchen table until Auntie told me to stop it. With a big sigh, she went into the pantry and brought out a cardboard box full of plums from the garden. Many of them were over-ripe and speckled with dots of white mould, but Auntie said if I helped her pick them over and take out the stones, we could make a pie. She gave me a big pinny and sat me down with a bowl and a knife, but I'd never been one for fiddly things like that, and after a short while, I was fed up with blinking plums and had two plasters on my fingers.

The water streamed down the windows in long shining strings.

"Weather for ducks," Auntie said, getting up and looking out. "I'll have to take some pails up to the rooms upstairs. There are always leaks when it rains like this. Mimi, you come and help me. Cora, leave those for a minute and wash your hands. You can go and feed the parrot."

She reached behind the tattered curtain under the sink and brought out a brown paper bag full of long black-and-white-striped seeds.

"Just unhook the feed box and pour some of these in," she said. "They're sunflower seeds. The old bird won't peck you."

I took the bag and went down the gloomy passage, past the locked doors, and into the sitting room at the end with its great stone fireplace stacked up on one side with logs. The panelled walls and low beamed ceiling made the room seem very dark, probably more so than usual with the heavy sky outside. I thought how cosy it could be if only Auntie would light the fire so we might be warm.

Near the fireplace was an old red settee, so worn that tufts of hairy brown stuffing hung out of the holes. A broken spring was sticking up right in the middle. I told myself that if ever I had to sit down there, I mustn't forget to check the place first so as not to do myself an injury.

"Hello," came a funny voice like an old door creaking. It was the parrot, sitting on his perch in a huge metal cage behind the settee, the stand resting on sheets of yellowing newspaper.

He eyed me up and down as I took out his feed box and filled it with fresh seeds. Some spilled out onto the threadbare carpet, and I quickly picked up every last one in case Auntie Ida came in and told me off.

"Hello." His voice had something of Auntie's in it.

"Don't you say nothing else?" I said, then thought I might try teaching him to copy some words from me. It would be a good way to pass the hours.

I put my hand through the door of the cage, and taking his time, the parrot climbed down off his perch and walked up and down on my finger, carefully curling and uncurling his claws as he went. He stretched out his wings one by one, as if he were showing me the pretty green and red of his feathers. I moved him close to his feed box and watched how clever he was at taking a seed with his beak and rolling it around with his funny fat tongue, which looked just like a piece of smooth grey rubber. The bits of shell fell to the sand at the bottom of his cage, and he ate the nice soft centre. Really nippy, what he could do with no teeth.

A piano stood beside the window. On the wall above it hung a large mirror in a carved wooden frame pocked with wormholes.

I lifted the parrot back on his perch, saying "Cheerio!" three times. That's what I was going to do every day till he learned it. Then I hooked up his wire door and went across to the piano. I looked up and gazed at myself in the old mirror.

Its misty surface was speckled with black dots. In places, especially in the corners, the glass was so cloudy that it hardly reflected the room back at all. Towards the top there was a hole with dark cracks radiating out from it, as if somebody had thrown something small and heavy at the mirror, not shattering it, but leaving this long crooked spider of a mark. One of the cracks ran almost the full length of the glass. It cut across my face diagonally like a scar.

I peered at my horrid plaits, longing to rip out the elastic and shake loose my scraped-back hair. I wondered if Auntie would believe me if I undid it all and said the rubber bands were so tight that they just snapped of their own accord.

My eyes moved down to the piano. On top was a dusty wooden clock with no hands, and next to it a small sitting lion made of brass, with ugly green stone eyes and a snarling mouth.

I wrote CORA with my finger in the thick dust on the piano lid.

Nan Drumm, Dad's mum, had a piano in her little front room. Some of the notes didn't work, but it didn't matter. Before she went back to Scotland and we didn't see her anymore, she would play it sometimes — old music-hall songs, and carols when we went over for our Christmas dinner. I loved singing and dancing around the room to the music, holding out my skirt and bumping into the furniture. That was before my sister was born.

I'd heard Auntie Ida go upstairs with her, Mimi clanging the buckets. Surely Auntie wouldn't mind if I had a little tinkle on the ivories, as Nan used to say. I would have liked to learn to play the piano like Nan did. She might have shown me how to do it if she had stayed.

I sat down on the stool, one of those that whirled around and went up and down, and I must have whizzed round on it for five minutes at least before I came to a stop, all giddy. I blew at the dust on the lid. The top layer rose up around my name in a thick cloud, making me cough. CORA remained faintly there, even when the dust began to settle. The lid creaked a little as I lifted it to uncover the long row of black and yellow-brown keys.

I wiggled my fingers and put them softly down, thinking I might try and have a go at "Three Blind Mice," which I'd worked out once on Nan's piano.

I found the first three notes, and played them twice and then once more for luck.

My hand moved up the keys a little way for "*See how they run.*" I put the two bits of tune together. Then I tapped out a couple of notes with my left hand to find one that would fit, but it was difficult. None of them sounded right. I played "*Three blind mice, three blind mice,*" over and over—"*See how they run, see how they run,*" four, five, six times—"*Three blind mice, three blind mice . . .*"

Just then, over the noise of my clumsy playing and the steady pattering of the rain, I became aware of another sound, barely on the edge of my hearing. I stopped my fingers.

It grew louder. Inside the room, somewhere behind me, a woman was singing. I lowered my hands silently, trembling, into my lap. The tune was strange, awkward:

"Said my lord to my lady as he mounted his horse:
'Beware of Long Lankin that lives in the moss.'

"Said my lord to my lady as he rode away:
'Beware of Long Lankin that lives in the hay.'"

It wasn't Auntie Ida's voice.

Every nerve prickled on my skin. I could hardly breathe. Out of the corner of my eye I could make out the rain trickling down the diamond panes in silver ribbons.

"'Let the doors be all bolted and the windows all pinned,
And leave not a hole for a mouse to creep in.'"

I felt the blood pumping through the vein in my neck.

"The doors were all bolted and the windows all pinned,
Except one little window where Long Lankin crept in."

"*Hello,*" said the parrot.

The singing stopped.

I gasped, stood up, and whirled round. There was nobody there. The parrot was biting at a seed in his claw. I turned back, and through the black specks scattered on the mirror I saw my white staring face, slashed into two pieces by the crack in the glass.

Auntie Ida and Mimi clattered loudly down the stairs. In my haste to get out of the room, I picked up the wrong end of the paper bag, and the seeds shot out and scattered all over the floor.

I grabbed the seeds in handfuls, tearing the bag in my hurry to get them back inside. In the end, I pushed the rest through a big hole in the carpet, then ran out of the door and back to the kitchen.

❦ ROGER ❧

It was going to be boiling hot. The edges of the puddles down the Chase were cracking as they dried.

Pete and I thought we'd chance going down to Mrs. Eastfield's to see if Cora and Mimi came out. Pete was pretty sure they'd most probably been turned into chickens, but I told him to leave off.

We didn't want to get too close, so if Mrs. Eastfield was with them, we could hide in the triangle of trees or scarper quick before she saw us.

Luckily we only waited about ten minutes, discussing the camp but then thinking it wasn't a good place after all—too near Guerdon Hall really—when we heard Cora's voice. She was shouting at Mimi.

We peeped out first to make sure Mrs. Eastfield wasn't there, then came out from the trees.

Mimi was wobbling on one leg while Cora poured water out of her boot, yelling that she was stupid. Mimi lost her balance and put her wet foot down in a big patch of mud. Cora shouted even louder and slapped her arm. Mimi started crying.

"Someone's in a bad mood," I whispered to Pete.

"Got a booter, then?" he called out.

"Yeah, she flippin' well has!" Cora shouted back. "Auntie got us boots, but Mimi's are too flaming big."

"She didn't do it on purpose," I said.

"Well, I ain't had no sleep, and I'm up to here with her!" said Cora, who frankly did look a bit tired.

She pulled the corner of an envelope out of her skirt pocket. "Look, I didn't post this letter on Tuesday because we went down the church, so don't let me forget to do it today."

"Is it the letter about you going home? I still don't know why you've got to go back when you've only just come."

"I told you—Mum ain't at home and Dad's got to work."

"So who's going to look after you when you get back?"

Cora stared at the ground. "I don't know," she muttered. "I suppose I could make sure Mimi was all right."

"Wouldn't it be easier to stay here until your mum comes home?"

She pushed some water around a puddle with the toe of her boot. "Auntie Ida's too busy to have us," she said.

"Why didn't you go to sleep? Was it the rain?"

"No. Doesn't matter. Stop asking me things."

"Do you want to come down to the church first?"

"Yeah, but best be quick. Auntie'll go mad if she knows I ain't posted the letter."

"Don't like it down there," Mimi sniffed. "Don't like it. That church thing. Auntie said not to go."

"Oh, just shut up, will you? You're a flippin' pest," said Cora, pulling her roughly.

"We thought those words, *Cave bestiam*, might be in Latin," I said.

"I don't know about Latin," Cora said. "How do you know about it?"

I plumped out my chest, then said casually, "Everything at church is in Latin. We all talk Latin, you know, every Sunday, like the Romans—well, most Sundays. Sometimes it's difficult to go because it's three miles to Daneflete, and there aren't many buses, specially on Sunday. You can wait and wait and you might as well have walked it. It's all right in the week because we go up the lane and there's a school bus picks us up at the top, but it's hard for Mum to get us all to church, specially now with Baby Pamela, and then if she does manage it, the old ladies turn round and tut-tut at her if the children make a noise."

"So why doesn't your dad take you, then?" said Cora.

"Because he's a heathen," said Pete.

We'd got to the old gate.

"Trouble is," I told her, "every Monday morning first thing, Sister Aquinas asks who's been to church on Sunday, and if you haven't been, she makes you stand up in front of the whole class for an hour. It's blinking awful, I can tell you, really embarrassing. Nobody else has to do it as much as me."

"Why don't you just say you've been even if you haven't?" asked Cora.

"Flippin' heck!" cried Pete. "Lie to a nun? That's definitely mortal."

"Anyway, there'd always be somebody like that Stephen Mylord," I said. "He's so holy, he never misses church ever, and he'd tell on me to Sister just for another gold star."

"What's all this mortal stuff anyway?" said Cora.

"It's the worst sin there is," said Pete importantly. "If you do one, you'll go to hell."

We looked up at the arch where CAVE BESTIAM was written.

"If only we could find somebody to tell us what it means," said Cora, shading her eyes with her hand.

"Yeah, that's what we were thinking," I said. "The only clever people we know are the Treasures. He's a headmaster."

"Crikey!" said Pete. "I'm not blinking well going round there. It's like Buckinum Paliss."

"I know—we could try Father Mansell. He's nice. He lets Pete and me and Dennis go to the big Christmas party in the big room at the back of the pub even though we don't go to his church—though he might not this Christmas because last year Dennis threw his jelly at the girl who won the musical chairs."

"But Father Mansell lives round the back of the Treasures," said Pete. "You've got to go in their garden first."

Father Mansell was the Church of England priest in Bryers Guerdon. He did services down at this old church, All Hallows, and over at Saint Mary's in North Fairing as well, and he took the Scouts on Monday nights in the Scout Hut. There was Wolf Cubs on Wednesdays, and Mrs. Aylott was the Akela. Grandma Bardock wouldn't let Pete and me join the Wolf Cubs because it was Protestant, but Tooboy let us tag along and help him out when it was Bob-a-Job Week.

Pete held the wide gate open for us. We'd started up the path towards the church when Cora called out, "What's this?"

She was standing beside the remains of a low fancy iron railing enclosing a large overgrown rectangle of ground that stretched all the way to the old chained gate. A gnarled elder tree was growing in the middle, stripped clean of its berries by the birds.

"Don't know — most probably graves," I said, joining her.

"I'm going in. Coming?"

We stepped over the railing.

"You gonna be long?" Pete called, showing Mimi how to stamp through the grass by the path to make the grasshoppers jump out.

Cora and I made our way slowly across the plot, trying to avoid stepping on the flat gravestones, some almost completely hidden by the weeds.

"What a poor old thing," she said, pushing her way past a clump of brambles to reach a straggly rosebush near the far railing, almost at the gate.

Cora knelt and softly touched the single pink bud that drooped on the end of its spindly stem.

"Look at this." Cora seemed lost in thought. "Once this has flowered and gone, there won't be any more. It's the last one."

She began parting the long dry grass beneath the rosebush with her hands. A shallow mat of roots had spread itself over a flat stone slab. I helped her tear the grass away, and with her fingers Cora scraped out the soil from the carved letters of the inscription.

"Oh." She sat back on her heels. "It says—it says *Guerdon.*"

"There's something else," I said, clearing the stone farther down. 'The time' . . . er, 'the time of the' . . . er, 'the time of the singing' . . ."

"Let's go in the church," said Cora, getting up quickly.

Her face had paled. She ran her hand over her forehead and tramped back the way we had come.

"Most probably all Guerdons in this bit, then," I said, following her over the railing.

"We're going in the church," said Cora, pushing Mimi firmly up the path towards the porch.

"Don't like it," said Mimi, and she planted her feet hard and wouldn't move.

"You're a blimmin' nuisance!" said Cora, grabbing her sister's hand and dragging her up the path.

When we got to the porch, Mimi started to cry again.

"You're the flippin' limit!" Cora said. "If you don't blinkin' like it, you can stop out here and wait for us!"

"How long you gonna be?" Mimi asked, wiping her nose on her sleeve. I noticed her glancing at the coffin-shaped grave near the church wall.

"All blinkin' day if we want!" said Cora crossly, and dropped Mimi's hand.

The three of us went through the big wooden door into the church, and I saw Cora look fleetingly back at her sister. Mimi seemed so small, a dark little figure against the light of the graveyard, framed by the shadowy arch of the porch.

"I'll be back in a minute, all right?" said Cora. "Don't move, d'you hear?"

❧ CORA ❧

"It stinks blimmin' awful in here," I said, screwing up my nose.

"Most probably the rain," Roger whispered. "Feels really damp."

"Blimey, I hope we didn't bring this lot in the other

day," I said, pointing to a trail of earth soiling the tiles all the way to the altar.

"Crikey—look at that!"

Five of the huge silver candlesticks were lying on their sides, and the sixth was on the floor. The candles were missing.

"Funny," I said. "There was candles here on Tuesday."

"You sure?" said Roger.

"'Course I'm blinking sure. There was six of them. I counted because I'd never seen great big candles like that before. Where've they gone, then?"

"Perhaps a burglar's been in," said Pete.

"Flipping stupid burglar then," said Roger. "Taking the candles and leaving the candlesticks. Fat chance he'd have of making a living."

We picked up the candlesticks and put them all in a line at the back of the altar where they had been before, three on either side of the cross.

"I'm sure we didn't have muddy shoes when we came in on Tuesday," said Roger.

⚘ ROGER ⚘

On the wall halfway down the church on the left was a huge stone memorial, carved with the names of seven young men of Bryers Guerdon who had been killed in the First World War. I'd never bothered to look at it before, but Cora called me over and we ran our eyes over the names. I recognized all the families. There was a Lieutenant Roland Guerdon, MC; a Campbell; a Holloway; and three Thorstons. I told Cora that Haldane Thorston was an old chap who lived in a cottage down in the Patches. They must have been his sons, three of them lost.

The last name on the stone was Captain James Eastfield, age twenty-two.

❧ IDA EASTFIELD ❧

Ypres, April 1917

Two more weeks, only two more — less by the time you receive this — and we'll dance again under the willows in the garden at North End. If they haven't had the wretched spring mended in the gramophone yet, I'll get Will to play the piano in the drawing room with the windows open.

I'm warning you, I'm going to ask you again, so don't pretend to be surprised. Just so you know, I'm not in the least impressed with all that tosh you came out with last time. You don't have to hang around forever in the ancient ancestral pile. It's Roland who's bagged that job, poor chap, not you. Then, after Gerald Foster caught it at Lesboeufs, I don't suppose

Agnes will be doing anything after this lot is over, and she and Roland are both in line before you, don't forget. There's nothing to hold you there, dearest Ida. I can help you fly free of it. Just let me. You have to let the old place go.

Some little kiddies came round yesterday trying to cadge chocolate. The younger ones will never have known a time without the sound of guns. . . .

His last letter. Roland said he waited for him to die for three hours, then lay next to him in the shell hole for another two until the light faded a little and he managed to drag his body back, still under fire.

Even if he had lived, he would never have danced again under the willows at North End.

⚓ CORA ⚓

An organ, with pipes painted with leaves and flowers, stood in its own small room beside the altar. A little mirror hung over the keys. I caught a movement—my face in the glass—and remembered the woman singing that horrid song in the sitting room at Guerdon Hall, how I had passed the night listening for her voice and watching Mimi's chest peacefully rising and falling, too full of fear to go to sleep myself.

Mimi. Outside. Alone.

"Mimi! We've left her for ages!" I rushed down the aisle. The boys followed, the sound of our pounding feet echoing in the rafters.

I pulled open the heavy wooden door.

Mimi wasn't where we'd left her. For a moment, I thought I saw her, the form of a little child against a gravestone, but I blinked and realized it was the bobbing shadow of a tree. I ran out of the porch. She wasn't anywhere on the path. A lump filled my throat.

"Mimi! Mimi!" we screamed, chasing round the outside of the church. My chest was bursting.

"Roger! What are we gonna do? Where is she? Where is she? Mimi! Mimi!"

"Shh," said Pete, putting his finger on his lips. "Listen!"

It was a wailing noise, coming from a distance.

"I think she's in the lane!" cried Roger, and we shot off down the path and out of the gate.

"Oh, thank God! Look, she's there!" I shouted, spotting the corner of her little white dress fluttering as she turned left into the Chase ahead of us, running as fast as she could in her big boots.

We tore up the lane after her. Even though she fell over once, she sped along so quickly we never caught up with her till we reached Guerdon Hall.

"Auntie Ida! Auntie Ida!" she screamed, rushing over

the bridge and banging with all her might on the great wooden door in the porch. "Auntie Ida!"

From inside the house, Finn started barking furiously. The crying baby stared at us from its place over the arch as Pete, Roger, and I raced over the bridge. Auntie Ida and the dog, bounding with excitement, came out.

"What on earth is going on?" cried Auntie, lifting Mimi up in her arms and pushing her hair off her face. "Get down, Finn! Calm down!"

Auntie rummaged in the pocket of her pinny for a hankie and wiped Mimi's nose. Mimi wouldn't stop crying.

"There was this—this—man!" she gulped. "That— horrible—horrible—man!"

"What are you talking about? What horrible man, Mimi? Where have you been?"

"That—that place where we went. Down there—that church—it's nasty—that—that man's down there!"

"What man? Who?"

"That—that scary man with the black dress! They went in. He—he come and said things!"

Auntie Ida looked up and stared at us. Her eyes hardened into two pieces of jet-black coal. "Cora!" she said in an awful shaking voice. "Have you—have you dared to go down to the church?"

My head went dizzy.

✑ ROGER ✑

In a moment, Mrs. Eastfield had almost thrown Mimi down to the ground and was on us. She grabbed Cora by the arm and dragged her through the door into the house. Cora could hardly keep up with her, squirming as she tried to get away, but Mrs. Eastfield had her fast, her fingernails digging deep into Cora's skin.

Mimi was at their heels, crying, "Cora! Cora! Don't do that, Auntie Ida!"

Pete and me didn't know what to do.

We hung about on the stone flags in the porch for a second, then quickly walked in through the big front door as it began to creak shut.

Following the shouting, we got to the open kitchen door just in time to see Mrs. Eastfield land a great wallop on the side of Cora's face—such a whack that it sent Cora sprawling. As she went down, she banged her leg on the side of the table and then fell hard on her bottom on the stone floor. The money jingled in her pocket. She cried out.

Mrs. Eastfield was breathless with fury, the whites of her eyes wide in her bright-red face.

Cora could hardly get her legs to stand her up again, but Pete and I were too scared to go through the doorway to help her.

ᐤ CORA ᐤ

I tried to get up, but my backside hurt so and my face stung like burning. I tried to push myself up on my hands, but I couldn't get them to work. They didn't seem to belong to me. Mimi was shrieking. I just caught sight of Roger and Pete in the doorway with their mouths hanging open.

I reached up and got hold of the top of the big table with my shaky hands and managed to pull myself up to standing, but my legs were trembling and I couldn't let go.

I didn't want to look at Auntie Ida, but she slammed her two great fists down from the other side of the table and leaned all the way over so her face was right in mine. I could feel her breath and smell tea. Tears were coming down my cheeks in two hot streams.

"I *told* you!" she shouted. "Never—*ever*—to go down to the church! You don't know what you've done—you stupid, *stupid* girl! How *dare* you! How *dare* you! How could you ever—*ever*—leave that child on her own! How *could* you! *You don't know what you've done!*"

Then, through the blur, I saw that her eyes had gone down to my skirt. She snatched something out of my pocket. It was the letter to Dad. She made a horrible noise through her teeth and twisted the envelope so tightly in her hands that it almost ripped.

⚭ ROGER ⚭

Mrs. Eastfield headed for Pete and me. I thought she was going to belt us, too.

"And you!" she yelled. "I'll make sure your mother knows about this! Be sure I will!"

Storming between us, she pushed us aside so hard that Pete's head flew back and banged on the door frame with a clunk. He moaned, staggered slightly, then looked up at me with watery eyes, spilling over into tears.

"I—want—my—mum," Cora sobbed in a small voice.

I just didn't know what to do. The only thing I could think of was to get us all home as fast as possible, but I'd have to confess to Mum about going down to the church. It would be much, much worse if she heard it first from Mrs. Eastfield.

So I had to find Mrs. Eastfield to ask her, but it was the last thing I wanted to do in all the world. She'd gone off down the hall past the big stairs, so I went after her, but every room I tried was locked. The big thick door at the end of the hall was the only one that gave when I pushed. When I peeped in, somebody said, *"Hello."* It was a real live parrot in a cage.

Mrs. Eastfield was sitting hunched up in the corner of an old red settee, kneading a handkerchief in her hands.

She looked up, and her eyes were red and wet. I stared down at the floor.

"Mrs. Eastfield—" I swallowed. "Would it possibly be all right if Cora and Mimi came up to my house for a bit? I absolutely promise we won't go down the church again. I'm really, really sorry. It"—and I took a deep breath—"it was my fault, and Pete's. We'll take them in the woods and over the Patches next time. Honest. We won't do it again."

"Do what you like," she said quietly, wiping her nose on the hankie. "I don't care."

"I'll post that letter. I absolutely promise I'll post it at Mrs. Wickerby's. You can ask her if we bought the stamp. I promise. Honestly. Hope to die. Cross my heart."

She turned and held out the creased letter without even looking at me. "Do what you like," she said again. "It's too late anyway. . . ."

It was a bit of a miserable walk down the Chase, I have to say, with all of them snivelling.

"Dad walloped us the other day, didn't he, Pete, for fighting," I said, doing my best to make Cora feel better.

"That was your fault." Pete sniffed. "You know that green engine's always been mine. Auntie Barbara gave it to me."

"Rubbish!"

"She did!" He stopped dead in the road, his hands curling into fists.

"Oh, for heaven's sake, you can keep the blimmin' thing." I tossed my hand in the air at him, then turned back to Cora. "Sister Laserian at school's the worst for hitting," I said. "She's got this special stick. It's this thick." I held my thumb and first finger at least two inches apart.

"No, Sister Camillus is the worst," said Pete. "She whacks you with her hands. They're hard like leather, like the soles of your shoes, most probably because she does loads of it—whacking."

"Must have hurt her at first, though, when she first started."

"She probably did it for a penance at the beginning," Pete went on. "Then God made her hands hard in a miracle, so she could stop us being so wicked, like if we talk at dinners."

"They're the Sisters of Divine Mercy," I told Cora.

At last she lifted her head.

"There's this teacher at my school—Mr. Diamond," she said. "The boys say if you're naughty and he catches you, he'll hit you with a slipper with nails sticking out of it."

"Blimey! Do you know anybody he's done it to?"

"No—nobody I know."

It was sweltering. Pete pulled out his handkerchief, knotted the corners, and stuck it on his head like Grandpa used to do, except Grandpa's hadn't usually been blown in over and over again then left in his pocket for weeks till the lumps of snot had gone green and hard.

Cora put her head down again. She was walking oddly—I suppose because of her banging her leg against the table and falling on the floor. There was a big red patch on the side of her face and some small half-moon nail marks on her arm. Mimi kept tugging on her skirt and trying to get her to talk to her.

As we got nearly to the top of the hill, we pointed out the old pillbox, a concrete bunker from the war, behind the trees on the right, but Cora didn't seem that bothered. Then, as we passed Glebe Woods on the other side of the road, round the back of the Treasures', I tried to cheer her up by showing her the bit of broken fence where you can get through. As long as you're careful to pull it back behind you, from the road nobody need ever know you were in there.

"There's a ruined castle in the woods," said Pete.

"Oh, yeah," said Cora, as if it was a fib. It wasn't a fib, actually. There were heaps of old stones and half-buried bricks all covered in trees and bushes and moss. It was really fun, climbing over them and exploring. Once, Mr. Crawford, the Treasures' gardener, spotted us from the garden and chased us out, shouting and swearing. We don't go in there that often, because we'd get into big trouble with Mum if we were caught, but if we hear the mower on the front lawn, we know he's round the other side of the house, so we creep through the fence and jump around on the castle until the engine stops, then run away quick.

Just after Glebe Woods, there's a stream that runs under the road and behind the pillbox on the other side. If it's clear, you can drop bits of twig on one side of the road and see if they come out on the other, but more often than not it's choked with grass.

We carried on up the lane and crossed over the main Daneflete road opposite the Thin Man.

To get to Bryers Guerdon, you walk down the Daneflete road a bit, then cross over to go down Ottery Lane, which leads into the village. It's like going through a green tunnel, the top end of the lane, because the trees lean over towards each other and their highest branches meet up in the middle.

There's a deep ditch running along the right-hand side of the road. I pushed Pete in it once when he was little, and felt awful afterwards because Mum had to throw his coat away. He swallowed some of the water, and for days afterwards, I thought he was going to die of the fever.

When you get to the place where the houses start, there are bridges over this ditch. Each house has its own bridge.

The first house on the left is Mr. Granville's shop. He's the butcher, and he's got a big moustache that goes up at the sides in two points. When I asked Mum how it stays up, she said he puts wax on it. A bit farther down on the other side, there's Mrs. Wickerby at the post office, then, over the road from her, there are two grocers together. Mrs. Aylott's is the one we go to—the other one never seems to have much in it. It's called the Dairy. The old lady, Mrs. Rust, sits in there all day with a hair-net on, knitting. Some people must go in, but we never do. Everything on the shelves in the Dairy has a great big space around it. There'll be a loaf of bread and then three feet of empty shelf, then a jar of Golden Shred, then four feet, then a packet of Daz and some Marmite.

Mum sends me down to Mrs. Aylott's with a list, and if I can't carry it all, Mr. Aylott comes round with the stuff in a box when the shop shuts.

I really like Mr. Aylott a lot.

When it was the Garden Fête over on the field in June, Mr. Aylott was Madame Zaza the Fortune-Teller. He wore one of Mrs. Aylott's scarves done up in a turban and some earrings made of brass curtain rings on loops of string. When he came out of his tent for a cup of tea, Dennis and his friend Bernard kept creeping up on him and lifting his skirt. Mr. Aylott would turn suddenly and pretend to take a swipe at them, and they'd go shrieking off. I don't know why they did it over and over again; he still had his trousers on underneath.

I told Cora what Mum had said about Mr. Aylott— that a shell had exploded right next to him in the First World War and he was the only one of his unit left. It left him rather deaf, so you have to shout at him.

"He's got a piece of apple in his head," Pete said.

"What are you going on about?" I said. "What piece of apple?"

"Mum said," said Pete. "From the war, and forty years later it's still in there."

"You idiot!" I said. "A piece of *shrapnel*—not apple. What a dope!"

"What's shrapnel, then?"

"It's a bit of metal stuff out of a bomb, like a bullet," I said.

"Could he go off, then?"

"Go off? Of course he couldn't go off. The blinking bomb's already exploded once. That's why he's got a bit of it in his head. Sometimes you say the most stupid things, Pete. I don't know how you're ever going to get your scholarship. And take that blinking hankie off your head. It's disgusting."

We went into Mrs. Wickerby's to buy a stamp for Cora's letter. Mrs. Wickerby is like one of those little black spiders that eat their husbands, especially when she's sitting in her post-office box, waiting for him to bring her a cup of tea. Mr. Wickerby is very quiet.

She kept us waiting and waiting as she did something important with postal orders, even though she knew we were standing there. Then she caught sight of Cora out of the corner of her eye and leaned right over in her box to look her up and down.

"Yes, can I help you?" she said.

"I need a stamp," said Cora.

"Didn't anyone ever teach you to say *please*? *Please may I have a stamp?*"

"I need a stamp, *please*," Cora said.

We posted the letter in the pillar box outside the shop, then crossed over Ottery Lane.

Our house is up a dirt track called Fieldpath Road, on the left just after the Dairy. The first house is old Gussie Jetherell's. We tend to run past it pretty sharpish because she often comes out shouting rubbish, with her hair sticking out like a big white brush. She always wears the same grubby skirt, the same men's checked slippers with holes in the toes, and the same dirty grey cardigan, all baggy in the front so I don't know where she keeps her bosoms. She's got millions of cats.

The house joined onto old Gussie's is Mrs. Campbell's. She does for the Treasures and cleans the church. I think Mrs. Campbell goes into old Gussie's sometimes to check on her. She must be mad to go in there, it looks so disgusting. Then, after Mrs. Campbell, across the end of Fieldpath Road, there's us, and nobody else.

Our house is wooden with a veranda, and we've got a smashing garden that goes all the way round. Dad grows dahlias out the front, and we're not allowed to touch them. In the winter, he digs them up and puts them in a box in the shed. The back garden's really good because Dad doesn't have time to do it, so it's just left, and there are some climbing trees and lots of wild bits with grass snakes and slow worms, and we can ride our bikes around. The grass isn't all smooth like the Treasures'. Sometimes we get punctures and I have to fix mine quickly before Dad finds out because my bike's new. It's a Raleigh. I got it for passing my scholarship.

Mum was out the back hanging nappies on the line while Pamela slept in the big black pram. Dennis and Terry were having a row by the pond.

"For heaven's sake, let him have the jar, Dennis!" Mum was shouting.

"No, he just gets mud in it!" Dennis shouted back.

"Oh, hello," she said, catching sight of us. "While you're there, Roger, can you look in the shed and see if there's another jar for Terry?"

"Can't Pete go?"

"I asked you. Now, go on! Or I'll get it and you hang up the nappies."

I dragged myself over to the shed to get a jam jar. Of course, by the time I found one and took it over to the pond, Dennis had fished out one of those big newts with the orange belly and spots and was poking it with his finger. He wasn't bothered about his jar anymore and had given it to Terry, so I needn't have bothered. I knew that would happen.

❧ CORA ❧

Mrs. Jotman put down her empty basket, came over to us, bent over, and looked Mimi in the eye.

"And what's your name?" she asked.

"Mimi, and this is Sid."

"Hello, Sid," said Mrs. Jotman, then looked over at me. "And how about you?"

"Cora—Cora Drumm," I said.

"They're staying down at Mrs. Eastfield's," said Pete.

"Are they indeed? It's been a long time since there were any children down there," said Mrs. Jotman.

Suddenly she wrinkled her eyebrows together. "Unless . . . Roger! Come here!"

Roger obviously knew the tone of her voice, and rolled up his eyes.

At least Mrs. Jotman had the decency not to tell Roger off in front of strangers. She caught hold of his elbow and marched him round the side of the house. We could still hear every word she said.

"If I've told you once, I've told you a thousand times . . ." she started.

Pete and me kept our eyes down and scuffed up the earth, while Mimi went off to see what the boys were doing by the pond.

"You've got the woods to play in, the garden. You can even walk into Daneflete to the park, or the pictures!" she was yelling. "Do I have to keep you in? Are you ever going to take notice of anything I say?" Then came a dull thump, but it wasn't much. "You know I don't want you going down to the church. You know that, Roger. I had an idea you'd been down to the marshes. You're covered in gnat bites."

"We were only down at Mrs. Eastfield's, not the church."

"Don't talk rubbish! I know you're lying. Your ears are going red. You are absolutely not ever — ever — to go down there again. Do you hear me? I'm not having this sort of trouble all through the holidays! You're to put your pocket money in Saint Peter's Pence next time you go to church! Understand?!"

They came back round the house again, Roger trailing behind Mrs. Jotman, eyes downcast and rubbing his arm. As he got nearer, he looked up from under his fringe and gave us a grin.

Baby Pamela started making a noise like a little sheep. Mrs. Jotman went over to look at her and told Roger to take me in and make some tea.

In the kitchen, Roger filled up the kettle, put it on the stove, and struck a match to light the gas. Then he emptied the old tea leaves into a bucket under the sink. Pete took some cups and saucers off the draining board and set them out on the table, then we helped ourselves to some broken biscuits from the tin.

"You know what makes me cross?" said Roger as we waited for the kettle to boil. "Everybody shouts at us for going down the church, but nobody ever says why we aren't meant to go."

"Why don't you ask?" I said, rooting around the tin for something with chocolate on.

"Ooh, no," said Roger. "You don't use the word *why* in this house. If we ask Mum *why* anything, she gives us a clout and says, 'Because I say so, that's why.'"

"And if you ask Sister Camillus at school *why*," said Pete, "she says it's a mystery and you'll find out when you die. A fat lot of good it'll do me then."

"Anything they can't explain they say is a mystery. Like me passing my scholarship," said Roger. "Sister Aquinas said it was the biggest mystery in the History of Salvation. Anyway, we never ask *why*, Pete and me, because it just gets you into trouble."

"I suppose they're right, though," I said as the kettle started whistling. "If you can't explain something, then it is a mystery. Anyway, I'll ask your mum about the church if you like. I don't mind."

Suddenly there was a noise like ten trains roaring around the house. I nearly choked on some crumbs.

"Oh, it's all right," said Pete. "It's just Dennis and Terry having a race round the veranda. I expect your sister's joined in as well."

To make matters worse, Mrs. Jotman came in carrying the baby, who was screaming her head off. Not the best time to ask a question.

"I'm just going to feed and change Pamela," said Mrs. Jotman in a loud voice over the racket. "There are some cakes in the tin. Dennis helped me make them."

"I'm not having any," said Roger as she went out. "He'll never have washed his hands."

"Yes, I did, and with soap," said Dennis, running in with Terry and Mimi, and aiming straight for the biscuits. "Blinkin' heck! You've had all the best ones!"

He spat at Pete and poked his tongue out at Roger, and Roger, furious, stood up, took hold of him by the scruff of the neck, and nearly lifted him off his feet. He marched him outside, dropped him on the veranda, then quickly, before Dennis could get up, came back in and shut and bolted the door on him. Terry and Pete laughed and laughed.

Dennis was furious. "I'm gonna break this door down!" he yelled from outside, banging on it so hard that it shook.

"Just try it!" shouted Pete.

All went quiet. He'd gone away, but a minute later, Pete caught sight of him through the kitchen window. He was running back towards the house.

"Flippin' hell!" yelled Pete. "He's only gone and got a hammer out the shed!"

"Blinkin' heck!" shouted Roger. "Out the front! Quick!"

We rushed through the house and out of the front door, but hadn't even got to the steps before we heard him running along the veranda in our direction.

We tore away from Dennis, shrieking and laughing, round and round, our feet thumping over the wooden planks. Dragging my bad leg, I half turned to shout at Roger that next time we passed the door, we should jump down the front steps and into the road and away, but when I turned back, I stopped dead in shock. There in front of me, on the veranda, was Auntie Ida.

As I stood there panting, not knowing what to do, all the rest shot into the back of me one by one, Dennis, the last one in the row, frozen like a statue, holding up the hammer.

Mrs. Jotman came out of the front door with Baby Pamela over her shoulder. "What on earth—? Oh— oh, Mrs. Eastfield—what a surprise," she said, really amazed, like the rest of us. "Goodness. Do—er—do come in. Dennis, go and put the hammer away. He's very fond of woodwork, Mrs. Eastfield."

Dennis walked off quietly.

Auntie Ida went in through the front door without so much as a look at us, and Mrs. Jotman rolled her eyes sideways in the direction of the back garden, so off we went and sat quietly and played Five Stones on the ground, straining our ears as if they were on stalks to hear what was being said in the house.

❦ ROGER ❧

Mimi ran off with Dennis and Terry to play a noisy game of commandos. All we could hear was the kettle whistling and the teacups rattling. With a bit of luck Mrs. Eastfield would eat one of Dennis's cakes and be poisoned. After a while Mum came out, looking serious. She leaned over and gently rubbed Cora's arm.

"Mrs. Eastfield's come to take you back for dinner, love," she said. "Mimi! You'll have to stop the game now! Your Auntie Ida's said you can come back and play with the boys tomorrow!"

Mimi got up off the ground and came running up, absolutely filthy with grass stains all over her nice frock.

"Bit longer? Bit longer?" she asked, wringing her little hands together under her chin.

"Sorry, dear," said Mum. "Come back tomorrow."

Mrs. Eastfield came out of the house, and immediately we shot up. Without looking at her, Cora took Mimi's hand and led her round the side of the house to the front. Mrs. Eastfield followed them.

"See you tomorrow!" I shouted after them. "Oh"— I looked at Mum—"is that all right? Are we allowed to play?"

"Yes, yes, you can," Mum said. "Cora will bring Mimi here first, to play with Dennis and Terry, and you must make me an absolute solemn vow—" She held up her fingers in the Boy Scout salute.

"That we won't go down to the church?"

"There are plenty of other places you can play. Do you promise me?"

I did the Boy Scout salute, too, and pretended to cut my throat and get hanged as well.

"It's really important, Roger. It really worries me that you've been down there with Peter when I'm always telling you not to. Me and your uncle Bill never disobeyed Granny and Grandpa like you've done. We never went there. None of the children did. It's really naughty of you."

"But people go for masses, don't they?"

"They call them services, Roger, in the Church of England. Father Mansell does one a month there, to keep it open, but I don't know if anyone goes down except Mrs. Mansell, of course, and possibly Mr. Hibbert, and probably Mrs. Campbell as well. It's a bit of a trek for the old people up here, to be honest. Everyone else goes to Saint Mary's at North Fairing. Come on, let's go and have some tea."

We all walked up the steps into the kitchen. I opened a tin of Spam, and Pete got the bread and the butter.

✧ CORA ✧

A loud thumping noise woke me, so early it was barely light. I didn't dare make a sound. Something heavy was being dragged along the floor outside our bedroom, then down the passage to the other side of the house. After a while, I heard Auntie's slippered footsteps coming back, then she went downstairs.

The bed was dry for a change. I lay there for a while but could find no comfort in the weight of the heavy blankets pressing down on my sore body. I got out of bed and inspected the huge purple bruise that had spread across the top of my leg.

Walking lopsidedly, I turned into the little passage to the bathroom and was shocked to see a big blank space over the door. A stepladder leaned against the wall. Old Peter had gone.

In that dark place, I had never been able to make him out well, to see if he really was the man Mimi and I had glimpsed standing by the gate. If Auntie had put him somewhere else in the house, maybe I could find him and look at him more closely. What about the man's twisted skin? I was almost certain that Old Peter in the picture didn't have twisted skin.

❧ ROGER ☙

Mum had told Pete and me to get everyone some shredded wheat while she fed Pamela. Pete did the milk but slopped it all over the place, and Terry had almost emptied the whole sugar bowl over his breakfast before I stopped him. Dennis was brewing up for trouble again because there was only one shredded wheat left by the time I got to him. I fished out one of mine and stuck it in his bowl, but he started jumping up and down, yelling that it was soggy.

Then the girls arrived.

"Sorry, there's none left," I said to Cora. "The bread's all gone, and that's the last of the shredded wheat now."

"It's all right. We've had boiled eggs."

"Why can't I have a boiled egg?" cried Dennis.

"Because you've got shredded wheat, you nit!" shouted Pete.

Dennis's face bulged red with temper. He stamped both feet hard on the lino and flailed his arms as he tried to reach Pete, who stuck bits of shredded wheat on the back of his spoon and flicked them at him while dancing around on the floor. Dennis climbed up on the table and trod in Terry's breakfast, spilling milk and sugar every-where. Terry stood up and wailed.

Mum came in with Pamela, who started shrieking at the noise.

"What's going on here?" she yelled. "Who's hit Terry?"

✖ CORA ✖

Before we were able to go out to play, Roger and I went to do some shopping for his mum at Mrs. Aylott's.

"Hello, love," she said to Roger. "Mum all right?"

"Yes, thank you, Mrs. Aylott. Oh, this is my friend Cora."

"Nice to meet you, dear."

"Same to you," I said.

Roger put the list down on the counter, and as Mrs. Aylott went around the shop getting the things, she kept looking over at me out of the corner of her eye. I pulled my sleeve down over my arm but not before she'd spotted the bruises.

Just as another lady came into the shop, Mrs. Aylott asked, "So where are you from, then, dear? London, by the sound of you."

"Yeah. Me and me sister are stopping at Mrs. Eastfield's—just for a bit."

She and the other lady glanced at each other, and Mrs. Aylott made a clicking noise with her tongue.

She added up the bill. "That'll be three and fourpence, Roger," she said, "and take a sweet from the tin—and you, dear."

"Thanks, Mrs. Aylott."

We stood outside the shop. It was getting hot.

"Auntie Ida's took that picture down I told you about—you know, Old Peter—remember? I'm going to find it. I'm going to look at it properly in the light—see if it's the man down the church." Roger didn't look at me as he unwrapped his toffee. "You never believed me, did you? You thought I was fibbing—and Mimi an' all."

He gazed across to Mrs. Wickerby's. "I don't think you're pretending, but"—he popped the toffee in his mouth— "I'm just not sure." Chewing, he stared at the post office. "You see, one day last summer—no, it doesn't matter."

"You can't not tell me now."

"You'll laugh."

"No, I won't. Promise. You know I won't."

"Well, we—Pete and me were playing down there— you know, down the church. We were playing hide-and-seek, and it was my turn to look for Pete and—and, well, I thought he'd come out of his hiding place and spoiled it. I was just going to shout something rude when—when I realized it wasn't him. It was—"

"What was it? Come on, Roger—"

"It was another little boy, much smaller than Pete, standing by himself in the shadows. I looked around to see if his mum or someone was there. Then when I turned back, he'd gone."

We started to walk back up Fieldpath Road.

"Don't say anything to Pete, will you, Cora?" Roger added. "To tell the truth, it gave me the pips. He looked—um—well, scary."

"How on earth can a kid be scary?"

"I'm telling you, this one was. I didn't see his face, but the skin was peeling off his hands, and he had wispy grey hair, like an old man's."

We took the shopping into the kitchen. Mimi was helping Mrs. Jotman feed rose-hip syrup to Baby Pamela with a teaspoon. As we left the house, Pete came tearing down the veranda steps after us.

"Shall we do Patches or woods?" he asked Roger as we strolled back down Fieldpath Road.

"Let's do woods. I ain't never ever been in woods," I said. "What's Patches?"

"It's just where some people live," said Roger. "People from London."

"We've got some camps down there, but they're not as good as the ones in the woods," said Pete.

"Not sure I'm that bothered, then."

"If we did woods, we could show Cora the bomoles," said Pete.

We turned left into Ottery Lane, then took a track off to the right.

"This is the cinder path," said Roger, "where we made our igloo in the snow last year. Tooboy helped, but it was so small we could only get two in at a time. I read somewhere that you're supposed to light a fire inside an igloo so the ice melts and seals up all the cracks, but we didn't have enough room for a fire, so Pete and me took a candle in, but when we lit it, we were so squashed it singed his balaclava."

"And me eyebrows went frizzy," said Pete. "Then this man off the *Lokswood Herald* was going to take a picture with us standing in front of our igloo. He called at our house with his camera and we were all excited and brought him down, but when we got here, someone had kicked it in."

"I think it was most probably Figsy, or Tooboy's friend Malcolm," said Roger. "But Mum and Dad tried to make up for us not being in the paper, so that night when we were in bed, they crept out and made a great big snow-woman in the garden."

"She had big bosoms sticking out," said Pete, showing me what they looked like, "and she was sitting down with her legs straight out and we called her Marilyn Monroe."

"And do you know," said Roger, "there was a little heap of Marilyn Monroe in the garden right up till April."

Ahead of us was a wall of trees. At the edge of the

woods, the cinder path became a narrow track that wound its way around the trunks. I looked up as we walked along to see little sparkles of sunlight gleaming every now and then through the whispering leaves above us.

The bomoles were three miserable bomb craters from the war.

All around us at home in London, there were places that had hardly been cleared up since the bombing, even at the end of our street. Dad said the government didn't have any money to do anything. They'd started building new flats, but it was going to take ages. Some people had lived in prefabs for years. My friends and I played in ruins all the time and found all sorts of stuff in the rubbish—sometimes a few coppers to buy sweets with.

To be frank, these bomoles in the woods weren't up to much—just holes in the ground with wet mushy leaves in the middle. I didn't say anything.

There was a huge rope-swing, though, made by this big boy, Figsy. It was so high you had to climb the giant tree it was hanging from, lean over the fork made by two thick branches and have the swing handed up to you. You sat on the plank of wood with your legs on either side of the rope, then jumped off the tree and swung backwards and forwards. I could wrap my legs right around the plank, then lean back and dangle my head and arms upside down as I went, leaving my stomach behind on the tree.

Roger and Pete showed me some of their camps. The

best one was in a tall tree that had a platform of branches halfway up. Roger and Tooboy, Figsy's brother, had found an old black car door on the cinder path, and they'd dragged it up the tree and wedged it across the branches so you could sit on it, although it did slope down a bit. Pete slid sideways and flattened our bag of jam sandwiches. They ended up squashed thin, but we ate them anyway, sitting on the door, looking out over the tops of the trees and across the yellow cornfield beyond. Roger pointed out the faraway tower of North Fairing church.

When we got back to Roger's, Mimi had fallen in the pond and was wearing a pair of Terry's shorts. Mrs. Jotman told me to say sorry about it to Auntie Ida. She'd washed her frock, and it would be dry for tomorrow.

"You'd better hurry back," she added. "It feels really close, and look at those big dark clouds. You don't want to get caught in a thunderstorm."

Mimi wanted me to carry her all the way down Old Glebe Lane to Auntie Ida's, but I told her if she didn't walk, I'd leave her behind. I couldn't have lifted her if I'd wanted to. Everything ached, and now my shoulders were throbbing, too, from hanging off the rope-swing.

As we got to the top of the hill, the light was changing. The sky on the horizon became an eerie yellow-green, and above us, thick navy-blue clouds like monstrous cauliflowers rolled and gathered. A chilly breeze came whipping up from the marshes.

We heard the first rumble of distant thunder. I noticed Mimi shiver as I held her hand.

"Where's Mum?" she said.

It was the first time Mimi had said anything at all about her.

"I don't know. Nobody's told me nothing."

Even though Mimi's small fingers were locked in mine, I felt so alone, gazing down from the top of the hill over the flat wasteland to the faraway river. It was like standing on the edge of the world.

Suddenly my heart jumped. Something—somebody— was moving up the hill towards us.

Whoever it was, they were between us and Guerdon Hall. We wouldn't be able to get there without passing them. If we turned and ran, I didn't know if we could get back to the main road before they caught up with us. Mimi was so tired, I was so sore—how fast could we run?

"Mimi, we've got to get back to Roger's, fast!" I whispered.

"Why, Cora? Look, it's Auntie Ida down there," she said, pulling away from my hand and beginning to run down the hill. "Auntie Ida's coming."

"Mimi, no—" I began, then stopped.

I must have gone mad for a moment.

It was Auntie Ida. It *was*.

What was the matter with me? What was happening to me in this place?

IDA EASTFIELD

I shouldn't have left it so late before going to meet them, but when the darkness came, it came suddenly. The storm is quite far away still, but with every roll of thunder, it gets closer.

They looked so pathetic, the two of them up there on the hilltop.

Probably a waste of time writing to Harry. It wouldn't surprise me if he didn't even reply, let alone turn up.

I can't believe Cora took Mimi down to the church and then left her on her own. I can't bear to think about it.

But it's been so long now . . . and with the flood . . . I thought the water would have finished him off. I thought so, or maybe just hoped so, until Mimi mentioned the man in the graveyard. Would she make it up, a little girl like that? Maybe it was Reg Hibbert she saw. I just assumed . . . The old fear . . . it will never go away.

I should have taken Old Peter down when Cora first asked. I don't know what is the right thing to do anymore.

He's out of the way now. I've forbidden them to go exploring upstairs. I don't want them snooping around up there. Cora had better not disobey me again.

113

Harry's just going to have to sort out something else. I can't cope with this. They must go home.

That was a huge flash of lightning. The thunder's right behind. The storm must be overhead. I'd better go and fetch the pails. I can't keep this old house going. It's all too much for me.

❧ CORA ☙

I've been trying to keep myself awake for ages now. I'm waiting until Auntie Ida goes to bed. A while ago, I heard her come up and clatter around, unlocking doors, going into different rooms, clanging buckets down on the hard floors.

I haven't heard her since. The storm is blowing stronger, the wind whistling so hard it's rattling the window frames, and the rain beats in furious waves on the old glass.

I might have dozed off and missed Auntie's footsteps. I haven't noticed her candlelight under the door, either. She must have gone to bed by now.

The wind sounds like people crying.

Water is dripping onto the floor somewhere near the cupboard, like the tick of a clock. It's annoying because sometimes it comes when I'm expecting it and at other times it waits on purpose to irritate me.

I'm surprised Mimi's asleep at all, especially when the room flashes bright with lightning and the thunderclaps crash like the whole world is splitting apart. Mum used to make us sit under the kitchen table when there was a storm. I wonder if she can hear this same storm tonight.

If I don't find Old Peter this time, I'll have to try again tomorrow. Auntie might have put him in a locked room. I don't know where she keeps the keys.

She must have gone to bed by now. Why would she stay up all on her own?

I'm very nervous, but I think I'll have to do it now. My heart's beating very fast. I hope it's not going to be too cold.

I tuck Mimi up really close and creep to the door. I know which one of the floorboards creaks, so I step over it and carefully lift the latch. It's stiff. I hold my breath, waiting for the loud click. The wind is gusting strong. I'm hoping it will muffle the sound. I pull the door to but daren't close it right up after me in case the noise wakes Auntie Ida.

A little light comes up the stairs from the hall below. It throws the long shadows of the spindles up onto the wall. Auntie must have left the lamp on for Finn.

There's no sound from her room. She must be fast asleep.

I creep along the passage. It becomes darker with

every step. My shadow goes ahead of me, shifting and changing like a phantom, as if it has a life all its own. I try the latch of a door on my right. It opens quietly, and I make out the odd shapes of furniture covered in sheets. Their black shadows leap up onto the wall behind. On the floorboards, where the door swings open, there is thick undisturbed dust. Nobody has been in for a long time.

I go to the room on the left on the other side of Auntie Ida's. The door is heavy. When I push it into the room, something moves—a thin curtain, hanging from the roof of a huge bed draped with spiders' webs. There are no footprints or marks of dragging in the dust on the floor behind the door. It creaks slowly as I shut it, and the bottom scrapes a little on the wooden boards. I think I can hear some other noise in the house, but then the thunder crashes again.

At the end, before the passage turns a corner to the left, there is a small window looking out over the cobbled yard and the back garden. As I wait, I can hear my breathing over the noise of the rain spattering the black panes. Sweat prickles out over my chilled skin. My pyjamas stick to me, yet I am cold.

Just as I turn to look back to the head of the stairs, I see the lamplight from the hall below flickering, then dying out altogether. I blink for a moment in the darkness.

Then I hear the bell, its lonely distant note tolling

against the wailing of the wind as it speeds across the trees and the reeds, the mud and the water between the church and Guerdon Hall. In my head, I see the church in the gloom of night, the bell rope rising and falling in the empty tower.

By the next flash of lightning, I make out three wooden steps opposite the window, leading up towards the front of the house.

I could easily go back. My bedroom door is still ajar, just at the top of the staircase. It would take only seconds to run to it and bury myself in the warm blankets.

Or I could find Old Peter.

I turn and place my foot on the first step.

A narrow passage goes off to the right. I feel my way along the wall. Moist plaster crumbles under my fingers. The air is filled with the strong smell of damp. I rattle a door to my left, but it will not open. Just after it, the passage turns again.

Suddenly the floor disappears beneath me. I stumble and fall with a dreadful clatter down some steps, banging my elbow on the wall.

For a few seconds, I remain on the floor, rubbing my sore knees, then get up gingerly and move on. The floorboards give slightly under my feet. Treading carefully, I feel for spongy holes or loose splinters of wood and, with my fingers, fumble for doors. This one is locked; this scrapes open only three inches before sticking;

another is nailed shut with a wooden bar. Just before the passage ends, my right hand brushes against the latch of another door. The thumbpiece lowers. It opens.

A cold draught lifts the hairs on my arms. After the thick darkness of the passage, a little light comes through the window from the raging sky outside. The room seems to breathe as cobwebs ripple in the moving air.

Footprints, and beside them a wide line, as if something has been dragged across the dusty floor, lead to an open doorway in the corner, a doorway to another room. From this other, shadowy room comes the sound of water dripping into more water.

I follow the footprints and walk slowly towards the far doorway. When I look into the place beyond, every hair root on my head begins to rise.

A large metal bucket stands on the floor, almost full with the water that falls drop by drop from the beamed ceiling, breaking up the webs into wet strings. At first, in the darkness, I think there is an old chair next to the bucket, a chair covered with a sheet. But then it moves. What I see is not a chair.

It is a woman, bent over, kneeling, with her back to me. It isn't Auntie Ida.

My legs begin to tremble.

The woman holds each side of her head with thin white hands and rocks backwards and forwards on heels hidden by the folds of a long brown skirt crumpled up around her. A thick single plait of fair hair curves down the line of her back.

My heart hammers.

The woman stops rocking and slowly, very slowly, kneels up straight. She takes her hands down from her head, then lifts her right hand and points up to the roof with her finger.

She sits back on her heels, pointing upwards, still facing away from me, not moving.

Suddenly an explosion of thunder and a mighty crackle of lightning shatter the room. I jump, then realize I can see only the bucket. The woman is no longer there. The roar of the pouring rain almost drowns out the steady drip, drip, drip of the water coming down from the roof.

I can't tear my eyes away from the empty space where she was. My breath comes in shudders. I force my legs to move back across the floor to the door I left open. I pull it shut quickly and settle the latch with shaking hands. The thunder roars again. I press myself against the wall and wait there, panting, until the rumble dies away.

Closing my eyes, I take a long, shivering breath, then recall something I saw on the edge of my vision, to the side of the kneeling woman. It was the picture, leaning against the wall under the window, covered with a blanket.

I wait—Is it two minutes? Is it five?—trying to push

119

her image away from the eye in my mind. She was nothing more than a movement of the air, a trick of the storm light, a spectre I conjured up out of bad weather.

If she meant to do me harm, she could have done it already—come up behind me in the dark.

I swallow, pull myself away from the wall, stretch out my hand, and lift the latch again. I can hear my heart thudding in my chest and am barely able to place one foot in front of the other as I move towards the doorway in the corner once more. When I reach it, I hold my breath and slowly peer around the frame.

A lightning bolt cracks, and the room flashes with light. There is nobody there.

As the thunder booms in a long dreadful roll, I move into the room, towards the picture, sit back on my heels in front of it, and, with a swift glance over my shoulder, pull down the blanket.

Old Peter glares at me with wide, wild eyes. His tangled hair hangs around his sharp cheekbones. His right hand grabs at the air, and his left clutches a plain wooden cross as it rests on a block of stone. On this stone are the words CAVE BESTIAM. I know—I am absolutely sure—that he is the man Mimi and I saw by the gate in the churchyard. His skin is smooth and faintly lined, not blistered, but it is the same man.

The rain-streaked windows are drumming in their frames. I think anything is possible now. I saw this man in the painting standing by the gate in the churchyard. I saw an unknown woman kneeling in this empty room. It is as if the world I have known is somewhere else, and I don't know how to be in this one. There is no light but the light of the storm, and the house is alive in the night all around me.

I begin to notice other things in the room—a stone fireplace, beside it a chest of drawers with the handles missing. In the dust on the top is a rusty black box, about a foot square, and next to that a pile of little clothes, neatly folded. I stretch out my hand and pick up a small hand-knitted cardigan. I hold it close to my face and make out the letter *E*, embroidered in blue on the front. The buttons are tiny blue rocking horses. Beside the pile is a grimy basket that may once have been white. Inside are knitted socks and mittens with ribbons, speckled with dirt and crumbs of old plaster.

In the next flare of lightning, I see a beautiful wooden cot painted with marching guardsmen. The folded blankets inside are grey with dust. In that same flash, as I hold the little cardigan in my hands, I become aware of the quiver of a candle flame and hear a voice from the doorway, as hard and as cold as glass:

"What in the name of hell are you doing here?"

SATURDAY 9th AUGUST

❧ ROGER ❧

They didn't come and they didn't come.

Pete was fed up with waiting and had gone over to Mum's friend, Auntie Barbara's, to see her cat Flossy's new kittens. Dennis and Terry were squabbling upstairs.

I hung around the house.

Dad was sitting there with his cup of tea, trying to read the *Express* and have a ciggie. Sometimes he had to go to work on a Saturday morning, but not today, and he was irritated with me.

"Do you have to be under my feet like this?" he said. "Look, it's a lovely day. The storm's cleared the air. Why don't you just go out and play in the woods or something?"

"I'm waiting for Cora and Mimi," I said crossly.

"Crikey. They sound like a pair of glamour girls with names like that," he said with a laugh.

"Shut up, Rex," said Mum, coming in. "They're the girls I told you about, down at Mrs. Eastfield's."

"Oh, right," he said. "Well, why don't you just go over there and call for them?"

"Mum won't let me," I said grumpily.

122

"You know I don't like the boys going down there, Rex," she said, a bit flustered. "Anyway, the thing is, Mrs. Eastfield agreed for Cora to leave the little girl, Mimi, here so the older ones could go off and play on their own. Cora was going to drop her off, but they haven't turned up."

"Well, maybe they just don't fancy it. Maybe she's just gone off you, Roger, me old chum," said Dad, snapping back his paper. My ears burned.

"Make me a cup of tea, will you?" said Mum. "There's a good chap."

I went into the kitchen and put the kettle on the stove.

"I'll have another one, too," called Dad, "but not so much sugar this time. I could stand my spoon up in the last one."

I listened to them talking over the noise of the kettle rattling on the gas ring. I couldn't quite make out everything Mum said because of her quiet way of speaking, but I heard enough. "There's something not right . . ." and "Mrs. Eastfield . . . bruises . . . Roger shouldn't go down on his own. . . ."

Dad's loud voice boomed through the wall. "Why should *I* ruddy go? I work bloody hard all week. I expect a bit of time to myself at the weekend. It's not too much to ask, is it? Why don't you stick Pamela in the pram and go down yourself? I don't even know the bloody kids. That bloody church! You're all living in the bloody Dark Ages round here. As soon as I get old Clark's job, we're moving to Chelmsford, where there's a bit of civilization."

When I went back in with the tray, Mum said, "Look, Roger, your dad's agreed to take you down to Guerdon Hall and you can pick up Cora and Mimi, if everything is all right. They probably just got up late. You may even meet them on the way. Dad won't take the car because there'll be a lot of mud after the storm and he might not be able to get it back up the hill. He can bring Mimi back here to play with Dennis and Terry."

I mumbled, "Thanks, Dad," but knew he didn't really want to do it.

He huffed and puffed all the way down Fieldpath Road, but by the time we got to Ottery Lane, he'd cheered up a bit and even took me into Mrs. Wickerby's and bought some aniseed balls and a *Beezer* for later.

"I've hardly been down here," he said as we went down the hill of Old Glebe Lane, the thick mud clogging our boots. "Your mother's always going on about her and Uncle Bill being told the church was spooky when they were kids. That sort of thing doesn't scare me, you know. I fought Hitler."

"Do you know why they thought it was spooky?" I asked.

"No, I don't ask," he said. "I know people don't like their kids coming down here. Of course, I was born in Great Sawdon, where Granny and Grandpa Jotman live. There was nothing odd in Great Sawdon, unless you count Percy Wheedon, who wore a fez and lived in a shed. I met your mum during the war when she was working in the NAAFI at Colchester—made a great cup of tea, your mum. Let's have a look at this old church, then."

We walked past the end of the Chase and carried on down between the trees. I didn't really like Dad being down here. It was our special place.

"Oh, look at that," he said, going up to the old gate and rattling the chains. "You know what this is, don't you?"

"A gate?"

"Of course it's a gate—it's a lychgate."

"What's that when it's at home, then?"

"A corpse gate," he said. "I wonder why it's all chained up. *Lych* is an old word for a corpse. It's where they'd put the coffin down on its way to be buried. The priest would come and bless it and say some prayers, then he'd let them take it into the churchyard."

I wasn't too surprised at Dad for knowing stuff like that because he was always coming out with all sorts of funny things and knew everything on *Brain of Britain* on the wireless. He read a lot of books, and if he'd been born into a richer family, he'd probably have gone to university.

"Interesting, old lychgates," he continued as we wandered down to the metal gate farther along. "They're like doorways between the holy ground of the churchyard and the unholy ground outside."

"Why's that special, then?" I asked, unlatching it.

"Well, let me tell you," he said. "If you'd died by your own hand—you know, a suicide—or were a murderer, or a lunatic, you'd never have been buried in here, not for anything. You weren't allowed to go to heaven."

"Where would they put you, then?"

"More often than not, they'd bury you at a cross-roads, at night, sometimes facedown."

"Why would they do that?" I asked, popping an aniseed ball in my mouth.

We strolled up the path towards the church.

"To confuse your spirit, if it decided to rise again and cause mischief," said Dad, ruffling my hair. "Little unbaptized babies couldn't be buried in here, either."

"That's really sad. It wasn't their fault."

Dad bent over a grave and picked up one of the wreaths, now brown and soggy, that we'd made with Cora and Mimi. "What's this old thing doing here?" he said, and chucked it in the bushes.

"In Yorkshire, they used to sing a creepy song called 'Lyke-Wake Dirge,'" he went on as we tramped through the grass around the back of the church. "Same word, you see, *lych* and *lyke*. The neighbours would keep a watch, or wake, over the corpse on the night before it was buried, to protect it from being taken over by evil spirits before it could be tucked up safely in consecrated ground. A newly dead body was thought to be very vulnerable, you see, with the spirit being not quite in this world yet not quite in the next, either."

As we walked back along the path and out onto the road, Dad started singing the song. I joined in, stamping in and out of the puddles on our way up the Chase to Guerdon Hall.

"This aye neet, this aye neet, every neet and all,
Fire and fleet and candle leet, may God receive thy soul. . . ."

❧ CORA ❧

I looked in the small mirror on our bedroom wall. My right eye had half closed up and was black and swollen. Down the middle of my bottom lip was a line of dark dried blood. Mimi had cried when she woke up and saw me.

When I went out of our bedroom to go to the bathroom, I saw there was an enamel bowl on the floor, full of white water smelling of Dettol and, next to it, a sponge in an old saucer. Auntie Ida must have left it there. I took the bowl to the bathroom and dabbed as best I could, but it stung. I was so sore and miserable, but my eyes couldn't make any more tears. In the morning, my pillow was soaking, tears mixed with pink watery blood from my mouth.

I went back to my bedroom and just sat on the bed and stared out of the window. It was a lovely sunny day, and the heavy rain had washed all the trees and grass so they looked bright and clean.

Mimi brought me up a boiled egg and soldiers, and then just stood and cried quietly when I said I didn't want it. She climbed on the bed and put her arms round my shoulders and her cheek against mine, but I felt like a stone. After a while, she left and I went over to the mirror, brushed my hair, and tried to put my own plaits in.

I heard banging on the big front door, voices, then Mimi running back up the stairs.

"Cora, Cora, it's Roger! Come and play, come on— oh, *please*, Cora, come *on*," she pleaded, pulling my arm. "Auntie Ida says you can."

I didn't want to go anywhere.

Mimi ran back downstairs. After a while, I heard someone coming up. They knocked on the door. I knew it had to be Auntie Ida. I didn't want to see her.

"Cora, Cora, it's me." It was Roger's voice. "What's the matter? Why won't you come and play? Dad's bought us some aniseed balls from Mrs. Wickerby's. Come and have some."

I opened the door a crack, and when he saw me, he gave a long, low whistle.

"Tell you later," I mumbled.

"Here, have a sweet," he said quietly, holding out the paper bag.

"I don't think I can."

He fiddled around in his back pocket and got out a liquorice pipe, wiped off the fluff, and held it out. "Try this—it's softer," he said. When I smiled, my lip split.

We went downstairs. I heard Auntie Ida going off into the kitchen. Standing just inside the front door with Mimi was a tall man I didn't know. Finn was sniffing around the man's feet, and he patted the dog on the head.

"It's all right—it's Dad," said Roger.

"Crikey! Hello, Cyclops," said Mr. Jotman. "You've been in the wars."

"She tripped down the stairs," muttered Roger.

"Has Mrs. Eastfield seen it?"

"I'm all right—honest, Mr. Jotman."

"It could do with a warm flannel on it," said Mr. Jotman. "Mrs. Jotman will sort you out."

There came the loud clatter of washing-up from the kitchen. We left the house but Auntie didn't come to say good-bye.

Mr. Jotman sang Mimi silly songs all the way along the Chase and up Old Glebe Lane. I hadn't seen her giggle so much in a long while.

We crossed the main road in front of the Thin Man.

"Look, Dad, can you leave us here?" Roger said. "Cora can't keep up. Could you take Mimi down and we'll see you later?"

"Aye aye, Cap'n," said Mr. Jotman, saluting, then, to Mimi, "Are you ready there, shipmate?"

Mimi laughed and saluted back, and they went off together towards Ottery Lane.

Roger and I sat down on the bench under the swinging sign.

I said I had found Old Peter and that *Cave bestiam* was written on the picture. I even told Roger about the little clothes and the cot, but for some reason I couldn't even explain to myself, I didn't mention the woman in the room.

"Dad told me about that old gate," said Roger, and he explained about lychgates, burials, and wakes. Then he added, "We've got to find out what that *Cave bestiam* means. We'll have to try Father Mansell."

ROGER

I've no idea how old Glebe House is, but it's not as old as Mrs. Eastfield's. Mum says the whole house used to be the rectory, but it's so enormous, it's now divided into two. Father Mansell, the rector, and his wife live in one half, the bit round the back, and the grand bit at the front with the great big shiny black door is where Mr. Treasure and his family live.

Mr. Treasure's the headmaster of Lokswood School on the other side of Daneflete. Mum says the boys' parents pay a lot of money for them to go there—that's why the Treasures can live in that big house and have a gardener with a petrol lawn mower you can ride on.

Father Mansell and Mrs. Mansell are really quiet. They have grown-up children who have left home and have families of their own. I wonder what it's like living joined onto the Treasures. I wonder if they can hear them being smart and posh on the other side of the parlour wall.

❧ CORA ❧

Roger took me up to the tall iron gates to Glebe House. We went through a separate, single gate to one side.

The garden was almost as big as Poplar Park near Limehouse Town Hall. The drive curved round towards the house, which was surrounded by dark trees with thick twisted trunks. I didn't know it was possible to live in a house so big, with so many rooms, and not be the Queen. An enormous arched window ran the length of the house from top to bottom. Behind its glass panes, a staircase zigzagged up and down.

"Do they have servants?" I whispered.

"They've got a man who does the garden—Mr. Crawford, remember? Then there's Mrs. Campbell I told you about, who lives near us, who goes in every day to do the housework. Mum says a lady like Mrs. Treasure shouldn't be doing her own ironing and that people who are that clever can't keep their houses clean themselves because they've never learned. She says they do so much reading of books that they never have any time left over to do the washing-up. We'll just creep past their windows and go round the back."

But then we heard an irritating yap-yapping. Around the corner of the house, a girl appeared with a little brown-and-white dog snapping around her fancy black patent-leather shoes. The girl was older than me. She wore a white dress with puffed sleeves and a sash. Her shiny dark hair was caught up on one side with a slide and a wide checked bow.

"Crikey," said Roger through his teeth as she drew nearer. "It's blinkin' Maisie Treasure and that nasty little dog of hers—Pippin or Drippin' or something."

Maisie Treasure was smiling, but it was a pretence. The corners of her mouth turned upwards well enough, but her eyes glittered coldly like two black beetles.

"Hello, Roger!" she said in a voice straight off the Home Service.

She didn't say hello to me even though I was standing right next to Roger, but I could see she was taking me in, all the same.

Roger muttered that we couldn't stop as we were going round the back to see Father Mansell.

"Out of luck—he's in with us, I'm afraid. He and my father get together most Saturdays to discuss the text for Sunday. Father's a lay reader, you know, at North Fairing."

Whatever that is, I thought.

"Annoying about the electricity, isn't it?" she went on.

"What about it?"

"Oh, are you all right in the village? Some power lines blew down in the storm, and we won't be able to put the lights on until Monday, when the men come out to do the repairs. Mrs. Eastfield will be the same."

Unluckily for us, Maisie didn't go in right away but stood there swinging her hands behind her back. I noticed her eyes on my trousers, then she looked up at my scruffy hair and my face. I shrank and looked down at the gravel drive with my one good eye.

"What happened to her?" she asked Roger at last, nodding in my direction.

"This is my friend Cora," said Roger. "She fell down the stairs."

"She's wearing my old clothes," said Maisie.

I felt myself blush scarlet.

A little bell tinkled in the house.

"Must go. Bye!" she said, turning on her smart heels. I listened to their *scrinch scrunch* on the gravel, and just knew they were the sort of shoes that would go *click click click* on the pavement. The dog jumped up and down on its short little legs, looking back at us, growling and barking. I wanted to kick its backside.

Roger stared after her.

"Well, if we can't ask Father Mansell," he said, "it looks as if I'm going to have to go and see one of our priests at Saint Cedd's in Daneflete instead. Mum'll think I've gone mad when I tell her I'm going to church of my own free will tomorrow. She'll think I've had a vision like Saint Paul on the road to Damascus."

ᑑ ROGER ᑐ

Mum said it looked as if it was going to be sunny, so she made me wear my thin blue shirt with the stripes. I shoved the tie in my pocket as soon as I got to the lane.

By the time I reached the main road, the wind had changed and chilly drizzle was blowing up the hill from the marshes. I hung around the bus stop for a while, getting cold, then decided to walk it. Between stops, a bus came along, but the driver wouldn't pull up even though I stuck my hand out.

The rain hit me side on, so I had to hold my hand against my right cheek to stop it going numb; then the feeling in my hand went as well.

As I walked along, I wondered which priest would be saying Mass. I'd be all right if it was old Silverwood, with his round glasses and his fluffy white hair always sticking up like he'd had a fright. But if Geraghty was doing it, he was bound to ask me why I wasn't altar serving anymore; then I'd have to confess it was me who was responsible for the trailing cassock, the hot candle wax, and Brian Buntree having to go to the clinic.

With every step, my heart sank further into my chest.

❧ CORA ☙

Nan used to call this sort of rain Scotch mist. I'd rather be Roger going to Daneflete, even in this weather, than sitting here staring out of the window, remembering the last two nights.

It's dark in the house, but we can't switch on the lights or the wireless. The electricity isn't working. Auntie Ida put a big oil lamp on the kitchen table, with two wicks, telling us to be careful not to jog it or we could burn the place down. I wouldn't mind. At least we could go home. Auntie made Mimi some dolls out of clothes pegs and bits of cloth and wool. I played with them with her for a while, but I'm so tired that I've come upstairs.

I look over at the bed. I should lie down for a nap, get rid of this thick headache, but I hear things when I'm half-asleep and they give me goose pimples. You're supposed to be able to die of fright from a nightmare, but I don't think these things are nightmares. I think they're real.

Last night I heard whispering, very close to me. I peered at Mimi's face, half in shadow on the pillow. She was moving her lips in her sleep, as if she were speaking. I leaned in towards her, and with her breath on my cheek I heard her say, *"Help us . . . help us . . . save us . . ."* but it wasn't her voice, or even one voice alone—it was many voices.

I lay there, my heart thudding, and thought that from somewhere downstairs I could hear a sound like sharp nails scratching slowly on a door. I pulled the eiderdown up around my hunched shoulders.

Then, from another room, far off, somewhere in the house, someone was screaming, crying out, "It's all my fault! It's all my fault!"

I had the same nightmare in London. Horrible noises, sobbing and wailing, came up the fireplace into our bedroom from downstairs. Grown-ups were talking quickly. I wanted to go and crawl into Mum and Dad's big bed and snuggle down in between them, but I knew it would be empty and cold. In the morning, Mum wasn't there. Dad looked washed out. He hadn't shaved. His chin was raspy.

I know it wasn't a nightmare really, but I've always tried to pretend it was.

Last night I heard the same words: "It's all my fault! It's all my fault!"

I lay there through all the hours of the rest of the night, too frightened to shut my eyes again, waiting for the light.

I can't tell Roger. He'd think I was going mad.

❧ ROGER ❧

I imagined knocking on the presbytery door after church and Mrs. O'Hara, the priests' housekeeper, answering.

"What do you want?" she was going to say. "Go away! They're having dinner!"

Mrs. O'Hara was like the nuns. She made you feel like a sinner.

I couldn't face it and turned back to Bryers Guerdon.

I carried on past the end of Ottery Lane and on in the direction of Hilsea, with my wet shirtsleeves clinging to my skin. I glanced at my watch, thinking I'd have to kill time by walking around in the freezing rain for an hour and a half so Mum wouldn't know I'd chickened out of going to church.

Then I caught a whiff of Saint Bruno tobacco. I knew it was Saint Bruno because that's what Grandpa Bardock had smoked.

I looked up and saw a tall figure hunched up against the wall of the Thin Man, coat collar turned up, hat pulled well down, trying to relight his pipe.

As I drew near, the man looked up and I saw myself reflected in Father Mansell's rain-spattered glasses.

"Hello, Father Mansell," I said.

"Oh, hello, er . . ." he said, sucking on the pipe stem.

"Frightful weather."

"Roger," I helped him out. "Roger Jotman."

"Ah, yes."

"You going up to Saint Mary's?"

"Yes. Car wouldn't start. Damp plugs, most likely. Couldn't get a lift from Treasure. They'd already left. Anyway, must get on. Cheerio."

He moved towards the path and began heading for Ottery Lane.

For a moment I hesitated, then ran after him.

"Father Mansell!" I shouted. "What does *Cave bestiam* mean?"

I could see his irritation as he turned.

"What? Look, Roger, I can't be late for Holy Communion."

"*Cave bestiam*. I think it's Latin."

"What? How do you spell it?"

"C-a-v-e b-e—"

"Yes, yes, it's not *cave*, it's pronounced 'cahvay.' It means 'beware.' Is that it? I have to go."

"And the other bit—*bestiam*."

"With *cave* it would be 'of the beast.' Must go, Roger."

I walked all the way to Hilsea, spent ages looking at the twitchy guinea pigs in the murky little pet-shop window, then went back home, thinking of nothing else but what Father Mansell had said.

Cave bestiam—beware of the beast!

❦ CORA ❧

It was pouring again.

The power was still off. The big glass lamp, with the wicks barely showing, shed its feeble light onto the tabletop, while the corners of the kitchen remained colourless, save for the hot glow of the fire under the copper.

Mimi had Sid and the peg dolls lined up under the lamp and was pouring water into cups and saucers for them from an old enamel jug.

Auntie pulled the mangle in from the outhouse and wiped the dust off with the dishcloth.

"When the kettle boils, can you make us some tea, Cora? Oh, and there are some digestives in the pantry."

When the kettle started to get noisy on the big black stove, I emptied the slops out of the teapot, then went to get the biscuits.

I'd never been in the pantry before. It was a dark little room with shelves all the way up to the ceiling, stacked with tins (some of them rusty), bags (mostly torn), and packets of this and that (half of them on their sides and leaking). Searching for the McVitie's, I noticed that a doorway on the end wall had been bricked up. Even though the newer bricks were painted the same dirty white colour as the rest of the room, there was no mistaking the outline. The mortar was rough and poorly finished, as though it had been done in a hurry, and the bricks were a different size.

I reached for the red roll of biscuits and disturbed a few cream-coloured flour moths. As they fluttered up towards the huge rusty meat hooks hanging from the ceiling, I gazed at the wall and wondered what secret place lay behind it.

Auntie Ida and I drank our tea without speaking. Mimi chattered away in dolls' voices, the hot water bubbled in the copper, and the rain beat against the windows. Finn lay under the table and occasionally shifted his feet. I sucked on a digestive with my sore mouth and longed for the wireless.

Suddenly there was a loud banging on the front door. Auntie went white. Finn shot out, barking.

"'S all right. I'll go," I said.

"No, you won't! Ignore it! I'm not expecting anyone!"

"It might be Mr. Aylott with the shopping."

"He comes round the back—and never on a Monday. . . ."

"It might be Roger and Pete, or the postman or something. You might have got a parcel. It might—Auntie Ida, it might be Dad. . . ."

When I said that, she got up and went out of the room towards the front door. The banging started up again.

"Is anybody in there?" a man's voice boomed. "Are you there, Mrs. Eastfield? It's the Electricity Board!"

It was a blessed relief to have the wireless going again.

Ժ ROGER Ҡ

It's awful when Mum does the washing and it's raining. The whole house is damp and steamy and stinks of washing powder. She boils up Dad's handkerchiefs in the big nappy pan, and the smell of the grey soapy water is revolting. I never look in, as I dread to think what I might see floating among the bubbles.

It isn't so bad when the sun's shining. Then the laundry can go on the line outside or on the veranda, but when it's raining, it feels as if the whole world's wet.

Pamela's nappies hang in neat rows from the kitchen airer most days, but on Mondays, if it's wet out, there are clothes everywhere, draped over the small wooden clotheshorse in front of the paraffin stove in the hall, trailing from the big one standing by the fire in the sitting room, and drooping over any chair with a spare back. Everybody walks around slowly with their arms held in so they don't knock the horses over and set fire to Terry's horrible yellow underpants, although that might be a blessing.

The worst thing is, Mum's got me and Pete trapped in the house and she makes us do the worst job of all—the wringer. The wet sheets weigh a flipping ton, and if you don't fold them properly before they go in, they won't go through the rollers. Then you have to wind them all the way back again, and sometimes the handle gets stuck. When Mum does it, the water goes straight back in the tub, but when we do it, it goes all over the blinking floor and our slippers get soaked.

Pete and me were fed up we couldn't go down to Mrs. Eastfield's.

❧ CORA ❧

Auntie Ida got up and went to the window.

"What a cloudburst! It doesn't seem to be easing at all," she said. "I'm going to have to feed the chickens and get the eggs. There's no point in waiting any longer. Cora, watch Mimi doesn't go near the copper while I'm gone. It's getting hot now."

"Everything's steaming up, Auntie. Can't we open the window for a bit?"

"No!" she snapped. "You know you're never to open a window in this house! Never! Do you hear?"

She got her headscarf and coat off the hook on the back of the door and went down the stone passage to the back. I knew she'd be a while putting on her boots.

"Mimi, you all right for a minute?" I whispered, turning up the wireless.

"Yeah," she said, drinking her orange squash out of a teacup. "What you doing that for? It hurts me ears."

"Don't go near the copper, all right, Sis?"

"Where y' goin'?"

"Toilet upstairs, all right? There's rain coming in the other one. Won't be long."

I went quickly out into the hall and rushed up the stairs as fast as I safely could without making too much noise. At the top, instead of going to the bathroom, I turned left and went down the passage. I looked out of the small window at the end. My breath steamed up the small panes of glass. I rubbed one with my finger and saw Auntie Ida, her head bent against the rain, going down the path to the henhouse.

Quickly I went up the three wooden steps, turned right at the top, and went down the stairs I'd stumbled on the other night. A little light reached the passage from a small window almost hidden by netted cobwebs. I could see enough to avoid the chunks of plaster fallen off the walls and the dark rotting holes in the floorboards. Passing the locked rooms on either side, I reached the end of the passage and took a deep breath before raising my hand to the latch and pushing open the last door on the right.

The muffled sound of the Home Service came up through the floor. I heard the pips for the hour and then the man reading the news.

In the gloom, I made out the scuffed trail of footprints leading to the doorway in the corner and felt my heart beating hard as I walked over them once more. Slowly I peeped into the other room before daring to go in.

The cot had been taken to pieces and was leaning up against the wall, the bedding all removed. The baby clothes on the chest of drawers were gone, but Old Peter was still there, just as I'd left him, the blanket that had covered him in an untidy heap on the floor.

I sat down in front of the picture and gazed at the words CAVE BESTIAM, wondering if Roger had found out what they meant.

Then I noticed other words on the painting, written in tiny golden letters on the dark paint in the top corner next to Old Peter's head—words and numbers in curly writing. I would never have seen them in the night, or when he was up on the shadowy wall over the bathroom door where he had hung for so long.

I leaned in close to read the words: PETRUS HILLIARDUS 1584. I couldn't understand them.

I puzzled over them for a while—then I heard something, something I'd heard before. Little by little, the back of my neck began to tingle.

*"'Where's the lord of this house?' said Long Lankin.
'He's away in fair London,' said the false nurse to him."*

It was the same voice I had heard in the sitting room: the woman—singing. I froze as soft footsteps moved across the floor in the other room.

Now the voice came from the doorway.

*"'Where's the heir of this house?' said Long Lankin.
'He's asleep in his cradle,' said the false nurse to him."*

I felt the woman at my back, heard the gentle rustle of her skirt as it touched the floor behind me.

*"'We'll prick him, we'll prick him all over with a pin,
And that'll make my lady to come down to him.'"*

Suddenly the back door slammed downstairs.

"Cora? Where are you? Cora!"

I shot up at once and stood there, trembling. Slowly I turned my head—and saw nothing.

"Who—who are you?' I faltered, my mouth so drained of moisture I was barely able to utter the words.

The name touched my ear like a whisper on the air.

Kittie. I am Kittie.

Auntie Ida's angry voice called up again.

I moved swiftly back to the door to the passage and fumbled with shaking hands to lift the latch.

The passage was empty.

I hurried along the creaking boards, up and down the short flights of steps, and turned towards the head of the staircase.

"Cora! Answer me!"

Rushing along the landing to the toilet, I pulled the chain noisily, waited for a moment to catch my breath, then headed quietly and slowly for the staircase and took my time walking down.

Auntie Ida was in the kitchen. Drops of water flew around her as she shook out her headscarf. While she unbuttoned her coat, she looked across at me with cold, suspicious eyes.

"I told you not to leave Mimi alone!" she snapped.

"I had to go to the toilet. The rain's pouring in the one out the back."

I waited for another angry outburst, but it didn't come. The rain was heavy, the wireless painfully loud. She hadn't heard me running upstairs.

"You should have waited till I got back. You mustn't leave her."

"She was all right. Anyway, Finn was here."

She turned her back and hung up her scarf and coat on the hook.

"Who is Kittie?" I said.

"*What?*"

"Oh, nothing."

I saw her back go stiff as a poker, then her shoulders loosened and she leaned forward, pressing her forehead against the back of the door.

"Don't leave Mimi alone—ever!" she said, still without facing me. Then she went over to the wireless and turned it down.

ROGER

"Roger, I'm running out of washing powder," Mum said after dinner. "Can you nip down to Mrs. Aylott's and get another packet of Fairy Snow for me?"

"Oh, *Mum*, it's *pelting*."

"You can go to Mrs. Wickerby's after, for some sweets," she said. "Take tuppence from the change, and make sure you put the washing powder under your coat or it'll go soggy."

I pulled on my boots and mac.

"Get us a chew, mate," said Pete as I left.

It was rotten out.

I passed the two small houses at the end of Fieldpath Road where Mrs. Campbell and old Gussie live.

Mrs. Campbell's house—number 2 Bull Cottages—was always neat. Mr. Holloway had painted the window frames only the other week. He'd left his blow lamp on the path, and I picked it up and made a noise like flames shooting out. He spotted me and started swearing like a sailor from the top of his ladder. I was so shocked that I dropped the lamp. I didn't hang around to find out if it had broken, but Mr. Holloway never came round to talk to Dad, so it must have been all right.

Number 1 Bull Cottages, where Gussie lives, was a mess, the garden just a heap of weeds. I saw her holding her torn, grey net curtain to one side, watching me as I hurried past. It made me run all the faster.

After Mrs. Aylott's, I went over to Mrs. Wickerby's and got two great big banana chews. I ripped the paper off one of them and shoved it in straight away. It was so huge I could hardly get my mouth around it.

My hair was dripping when I turned back into Fieldpath Road. I was making sure the Fairy Snow was well tucked in under my mac when, to my absolute horror, I saw that Gussie had come out of her front door. I couldn't make up my mind what to do—run past really quickly before she started shouting, or nod politely, then put my head down and scarper back home.

By the time I got there, she was right up at her wonky front gate, getting terribly wet.

She said, "You, boy."

I nearly jumped in the air. I couldn't answer because my teeth were stuck together with banana chew.

"Come and help me."

I tried to push my teeth apart from the back with my tongue. I wanted to explain that I was in a hurry and Mum needed the soap powder, but all that came out was a mumble.

She beckoned to me with her bony white finger. The last thing in the world I wanted to do was go down that weedy path and in through that door. I wondered if I'd come out the same boy who went in, or if I'd come out at all. Dad had always said that if I didn't eat my rhubarb, the witches would get me.

My feet itched to run away, but I looked at Gussie's dried-up, wrinkled old face, the dirty grey cardigan with half the buttons missing, the big checked slippers that were getting wetter and wetter, and was surprised to find myself feeling sorry for her.

So I followed the finger, and went down the path and through the front door.

The hall smelled of rotten meat, rancid fat, and cat wee. There should have been green smoke curling up from the lino. I put my hand over my mouth and held my breath, swallowing my chew in one huge gulp and feeling it stick in a hard lump halfway down to my stomach. What a waste.

Gussie led me in past the stairs. I dripped water over the hall floor. It was quite dark, and I was worried I was going to tread in something nasty. There were filthy saucers of half-eaten cat food everywhere — on the floor and even on the stairs. Lying around the saucers were little hard brown sausages. When I kicked one by mistake and it shot across the floor, I saw it definitely wasn't the kind of sausage you'd want to eat.

Gussie didn't take me far, thank goodness — just through to the grubby little kitchen at the back. Cats shook their tails at me or stood in my way, spitting, the sparse fur in front of their ears riddled with ticks whose metallic-green bodies had grown fat with blood.

"Out there," said Gussie. In the light from the grimy back-door window I could see her bleary eyes rimmed with red. "Pluto's stuck in the coal bunker. I can't get him out. He'll die in there, and I can't get the coal for the fire."

It had never occurred to me that Gussie would be able to talk in sentences like other people did. She was just a weird old woman who came out into the road shouting nonsense. I would run past as quickly as possible, and if I was with Pete, we'd laugh all the way home.

Two of the frosted panes in the back door were cracked. I knew Tooboy had gone into her back garden once for a dare with his brother Figsy, and he'd told us they'd thrown stones at the house. Pete and I'd thought that was really funny at the time.

The rain was coming down in buckets.

The coal bunker had a small hatch at the bottom with coal half falling out of it, and then a big square hole on the top for the coal man to empty his sack into. A wooden lid half covered the hole.

I knew exactly what she wanted—for me to climb into the blinking thing. What could I do?

I put the packet of Fairy Snow down on the kitchen stove, the only spare bit of space I could find. Then I went back out and lifted myself up onto the bunker roof.

It was covered in wet soot and leaves. I pushed back the lid fully and lowered myself through the hole into blackness. Even with the light coming through the opening in the roof, I could hardly see anything except the square of sky above me, dark with rain clouds. I wobbled in my wellingtons, sliding about on the piled-up coal, scraping my back on the roof as I went.

For one odd moment, I thought Gussie was going to put the lid back on with a mad cackle and trap me in there, but then I heard a little mewing sound.

Something jumped on me. Taken off guard, I fell back against the pile of coal and slid down till my bottom hit the concrete floor. Two yellow eyes shone out of the darkness.

As I held on to the cat, it rubbed its face against my cheek. I quickly pushed it up through the hole.

"Pluto, oh, Pluto," I heard Gussie say. "You bad boy."

Getting out was much more difficult than getting in. I couldn't find a foothold on the slippery coal. Eventually I managed to scramble back onto the roof, then jump down to the ground, pulling the wooden lid completely over so that the coal wouldn't get any wetter than it already was and to prevent any more cats finding their way in.

I'd never ever seen Gussie smile before. I can't say it was pleasant to watch, because her teeth were actually just brown stumps, but I did feel the nice warm glow that comes with a good deed.

I picked up the washing powder from the stove. As Pluto jumped out of her arms, Gussie thanked me over and over, but I backed off down the hall, careful where my feet went, desperate to get away from the smell.

Just as I turned to open the front door, the old woman suddenly grabbed my arm, so hard it hurt. *Uh-oh, here it comes*, I thought in a panic—she isn't going to let me go. I turned towards her, and she leaned her face right into mine. Her breath was like old cheese. The smile had gone, and that wild look had come back into her eyes.

"He's here again," she whispered.

"Who—who's here again?"

"I saw the little girl go to your house. You've got to watch her. I saw Ida Guerdon. . . ."

"Ida Guerdon? No, you mean Ida Eastfield—"

"The last of the Guerdons . . ."

"I don't know what you're talking about. I've got to get home."

"He will hunt her down, just like he's done before—"

"I think I need to get back. Mum will wonder where I've got to—"

"Listen to me. I've seen it all before. He knows she's here. He will hunt for her. He will smell her out."

"Who will? I don't know what you mean."

"They won't tell you anything. They all hope he's gone away, but he never goes away. He just waits—waits until the next one comes. I have seen him. I ran away from him. The old priest saved me, many many years ago. Old Father Hillyard saved me, but I remember—I remember it, boy. Watch that little girl. She's not safe down there. . . ."

"Who? Cora? Mimi? Who do you mean?"

"I warned that Will Eastfield. I told him what would happen, but he said I was crazy. He laughed in my face. He wouldn't take any notice of his wife, either. Then they found him in the upper field with the gun in the grass. Don't ever tell me it was an accident. He knew it was his fault. I warned him. Ida Guerdon warned him.

He said I was mad, a crazy old woman, and his wife was a fool. You are listening to me, aren't you, boy?"

"Yes, yes, I'm listening, but I want to go home."

"He'll be looking for her. Then he can rest again . . . until the next one comes. . . ."

"Who? Who are you talking about?"

"*Long Lankin, boy,*" she hissed, holding my collar in her dirty, veined old hands. "*Long Lankin . . .*"

I stumbled up Fieldpath Road, the rain pouring down around me, my head in a daze. I can't even remember what Mum said when I came in through the back door, running black with coal dust from head to foot, clutching to my chest a wet packet of Fairy Snow.

✖ CORA ✖

Roger's mum gave us money to get some ice lollies from Mrs. Wickerby's. We had to go past Gussie's house. The net curtains twitched as we went by.

"How old d'you reckon old Gussie, is, then?" I whispered.

"I don't know," said Roger. "Ninety or a hundred or something. Her house doesn't half stink. I've most probably picked up fleas. Can you get fleas off a bald cat?"

"When d'you suppose she got away from this Long Lankin, then? It must have been when she was a little girl, unless she's going funny and is making it all up."

"You know," said Roger, "if we found out when this priest, this Hillyard chap, was the rector down at the church, then we'd know roughly when it happened — if he *was* the rector here, of course."

"Maybe he was the one before Father Mansell. How do you find out that sort of thing?"

"I don't know," said Roger. "Mum might know, I suppose. She's lived here all her life."

We went into the post office and bent over the big white refrigerator to choose lollies for everyone.

I didn't tell Roger I had heard of Long Lankin already, in that woman's song. I should have done, but I would have had to tell him so many other things as well, and telling him would have made it real. I wouldn't be able to pretend to myself that it might not have happened anymore. I'd had to pretend so many things over the last couple of years—pretending to Mimi, to Dad, to our neighbours in Limehouse, pretending even to myself— that everything was normal and all right, as it seemed to be for everyone else.

Even though Roger told me about the odd little boy he'd seen in the graveyard, I'm not sure he would have believed me if I'd told him about Kittie. *I am Kittie.*

Keep it quiet, and they won't look sideways at you.

"Oh, yes," said Roger, when we were walking back up Fieldpath Road, "I almost forgot. Father Mansell told me what those words mean. We were right. They are in Latin. *'Cave bestiam'* means 'beware of the beast.'"

✿ ROGER ✿

Cora, Pete, and I played in the garden for a while, then thought we'd go up to the woods. Mum said Mimi could stay at home with Terry.

"Only thing is," she said, "I'd better tell you now that

I'm not going to be able to have her tomorrow. I've got to take Pamela to the clinic over in Lokswood. Mrs. Harvey's said Dennis and Terry can go to her house to play with Lynette and Philip, but I really didn't think I could ask her to take a child she doesn't know. Between you and me, she's going to have her work cut out with our two. Her Lynette and Philip are so well behaved, it's unnatural."

I helped Mum put some biscuits in a bread bag to take up to the woods.

"Erm, Mum?" I asked, pushing chocolate bourbons in her direction. "Who was the last rector down at All Hallows before Father Mansell?"

"That's an odd question, Roger," she said, looking at me sideways. "What are you up to now?"

"I don't know, just wondered—just something Gussie said."

"What on earth did Gussie say to you?" she asked, looking at me long and hard. "I thought you just went in to get her cat out of the coal bunker."

"I did—oh, forget it, it doesn't matter," I said, grabbing the bag and heading for the door before I got myself into bother.

"By the way," she said, just as I'd got one foot on the veranda, "when you go out to play tomorrow with Mimi, please stay together and—"

"Don't go down to the church!" I finished off for her.

"We'll get the bikes out. I've mended Pete's puncture. Cora's never been on a bike."

"Don't leave Mimi out. Do something she'd like—in the woods or down the Patches. I'll leave the back door open, and you can make yourself some sandwiches at dinnertime. There's a tin of corned beef in the cupboard."

"All right, all right."

I dashed down the steps and after Cora and Pete, who had already started walking down Ottery Lane.

"Blimey, you took your time for a few biscuits," said Cora when I caught them up.

The path round the woods was really muddy, and a couple of our camps were washed out, specially the one near the wild-pig woman's place. All the sticks had fallen in, so we had to put it back together. When it was finished, we really didn't feel like spending any time in it. Come to think of it, I don't think we ever spent any time in that camp. It only had one entrance, and if the wild-pig woman came out to get us, we'd be trapped.

We could hear some whooping coming from the rope-swing, so headed towards it through the thick trees at the back where people can't see you unless they're looking. If it was Figsy, then we'd run a mile. We told Cora she had to be really quiet as we crept up, but luckily it was only Tooboy and his friend Malcolm.

Mum said Malcolm was rough and we weren't to play with him. He did get up to a few things actually,

159

like letting off bangers in the middle of Ottery Lane before Bonfire Night, so we avoided Malcolm, to be on the safe side, in case he did something to us.

Tooboy was on the swing, and Malcolm was running alongside, shrieking and trying to reach up and pull him off. We came out from behind the trees. When the swing stopped, Tooboy jumped down and walked over. Malcolm came up swaggering, probably because Cora was there.

"Bloody hell!" he said, laughing and pointing at Cora's eye. "Been in a fight? Who gave you that shiner?"

Cora didn't say anything. I knew that meant trouble. Malcolm didn't like it when people ignored him.

"Cat got your tongue, then?" he said, walking around her, obviously narked.

"Leave it, Malc," said Tooboy.

"Fell down the stairs," Cora said in the end.

It was worse than saying nothing. Malcolm started to make fun of her.

"Cor blimey! Fell down the stairs — apples and pears! Proper common little tart, ain't we! Cor blimey!"

He took one of her plaits in his hand and started twisting it around his finger. She stood stock-still, looking straight ahead of her. I could see she was getting upset, because she was blinking a lot.

Suddenly Malcolm took a small flick knife out of his back pocket and clicked it open. Pete and me jumped back about three feet. Cora didn't move an inch. In a second he'd laid the knife across her plait.

"I could cut this right off," he said, his face in hers, really close. Still she didn't move.

"I said, leave it, Malc," said Tooboy. "Look, I've got half a crown out me mum's purse. Let's get the bus and go to the pictures."

Malcolm laughed his head off, let go of the plait with a swing, and put the knife away.

"Come on, mate!" he said, putting his arm over Tooboy's shoulder. As they went off, Tooboy looked behind and gave me a secret thumbs-up behind Malcolm's back.

We just stood there. I felt my legs shaking.

"I don't want to come to the woods again," said Cora.

We went back to my house.

❧ CORA ☙

It was quite late in the morning when Roger and Pete came down to Guerdon Hall. They were on their bikes.

They told Auntie Ida they were taking us back up to Bryers Guerdon, but she obviously didn't trust us, because she came with us all the way to the end of the Chase and watched us nearly to the top of the hill.

We saw her turn back towards Guerdon Hall and waited until she was out of sight. Then Roger and Pete took it in turns to whizz down.

"Do you want me to show you how to ride?" cried Roger as they walked the bikes back up to the top.

"I'd love it!"

The flattest bit of the road, without too many potholes, was at the bottom of the hill. To begin with, Roger held the saddle while I tried to pedal. My legs were still aching and bruised, and after a few tumbles, I had scraped both knees and one elbow as well, but in the end, I was able to get along on my own. Mimi pulled up clumps of grass and threw them at the wheels as I went wobbling by.

"See if you can do the hill," Roger said. At first I squeezed the brakes almost all the way down, but after a couple of attempts, I managed to reach the bottom without them. I took my feet off the pedals and stuck my legs out as I flew, just like Colin Mole, who delivered for the butcher back home. Colin showed off on his bicycle all the time, going round in a circle in the middle of the street and lifting the front wheel in the air when there were girls around to watch him. The bike had a huge wicker basket over the front wheel to carry the meat in, and sometimes Colin didn't get the balance right when he was trying his fancy tricks. Once he went right over and dropped some liver in a pile of dog's business in the gutter. We were in fits, laughing at him.

After an especially good run down, I turned the bike round, all ready to walk it back up again, when I saw someone standing on the brow of the hill, dark against the bright blue sky. There was no mistaking who he was. Mimi had already spotted him.

"Daddy! Daddy!" she yelled, and started running up the road. I threw the bike down and charged after her. Dad had come to take us home!

When we had almost reached him, he smiled that big crinkly grin of his, put down his old kit bag, took the cigarette out of his mouth, and chucked it in the grass. Then he held both arms out wide, and we jumped into them, Mimi giggling like a mad thing. I could smell the lovely familiar smell of his suit. He tickled us, and we wriggled about, laughing. I picked up his kit bag and

163

swung it over my shoulder. Dad lifted Mimi up, and we marched happily down the hill to Auntie Ida's.

☙ ROGER ☙

I knew it had to be their dad straight away. He was much younger and a heck of a lot better looking than our dad. He had a big scar down his cheek, so he looked like some sort of handsome pirate.

Cora had dropped my bike, and the front wheel was still spinning round. I picked it up and checked the handlebars were straight. Pete was looking over at me, and I jerked my head up the hill and we started to push the bikes back up to the top, but I didn't really feel like going down again. The sky had clouded over a bit, so it was best to go home.

Cora, Mimi, and their dad were laughing their heads off when we passed them. Pete said he'd found a penny in his pocket, so we thought we'd call in at Mrs. Wickerby's on the way back and get a couple of gobstoppers.

☙ CORA ☙

As we tramped down the Chase, Dad asked us what it was like at Auntie Ida's, and what on earth had I done to myself to get a black eye and so many bumps. I mumbled something about playing with the boys in the woods and flashed a look at Mimi not to say anything, but she was up on Dad's shoulders trying to twist his hair into two horns and didn't seem to be listening. I told him about Finn and the chickens, and he told us a joke about a three-legged pig.

Dad's hair was usually slicked back off his forehead like James Stewart's, but today his thick fringe flopped around almost into his eyes. He probably couldn't find his Brylcreem. Mum and Dad looked like a pair of film stars. Mum's hair was lovely and soft and wavy, and she never ever had to put curlers in like the other ladies in our street, who wore them all the time under their scarves and only took them out for Christmas and funerals.

"Is she back? Mum?" I whispered excitedly in his ear.

I could see from the way he turned his eyes away that she wasn't.

⚶ IDA EASTFIELD ⚶

I heard them coming long before I saw them. I got his short scrappy letter, but I didn't say anything to the girls because Harry was never reliable and I didn't want them to be disappointed if he didn't turn up. I've lived in this wild place all my life and can predict the direction of the wind more easily than which way Harry is going to blow.

I watch as they come tramping up the Chase, laughing, Mimi up on his shoulders, clapping her hands. He's like Saint George to those two, just like he was for Susan.

Mind you, he's turned up, I'll give him that. Some dodgy deal must have fallen through for him to make his way here in the middle of the week like this.

I stand on the bridge and wave. Finn shoots off towards them, barking as usual, but even the dog is bowled over by him. Finn gives him no trouble at all.

Harry grins and gives me a quick peck on the cheek. "Ooh, I could murder a cup of char, Ida. Nice and strong, two sugars. Ruddy long walk from the station. Don't the ruddy buses run out here?"

"Oh, come on, Harry, it's only a few miles."

❧ CORA ❧

I lay in bed, excited, catching the smell of Dad's cigarette from downstairs, a warm, safe smell. Every Sunday morning, I'd go down to Mrs. Prewitt's and get ten Player's Navy Cut for Dad, five Weights for Mum, and a packet of Spangles for Mimi and me, but the last week at home before we came out here, I just went for the Player's.

166

I was hoping that when Mum did come home again, she wouldn't have got any thinner. She'd changed a lot since their wedding photo was taken. They'd married just after the war. Mum was only eighteen, and Dad wore his demob suit, the blue with red pinstripes that's still hanging in the cupboard. Dad was so young he wasn't long in the war before he was out of it again. Sometimes, when they thought Mimi and I were fast asleep, I could hear Mum and Dad shouting downstairs. Once I heard her yelling that the most Dad had seen of any action was behind the huts at Catterick Camp.

Maybe one day they'd go back to those dances at the British Legion and she would fit into the lovely black dress with the pink roses and ballerinas all over the wide skirt with its layers of white netting underneath. Perhaps this time it wouldn't show up the long bones just below her neck. Sometimes I'd go and look at the dress where it was hanging on the back of their bedroom door and run my fingers over the roses and ballerinas. It made everything else in the room look worn out and grubby. Mum called it her Golden Slippers dress. Dad had won a lot of money on a horse called Golden Slippers, and Mr. Bates had come round and yelled at Dad in the kitchen, and we had cream cakes twice in the same week.

When Mum was in one of her funny moods and went to their bedroom and lay there with the curtains shut for hours and hours, I'd sometimes take Mimi next door to

Auntie Ivy's—that's Mrs. Bedelius next door to us on the other side to the Woolletts—for our tea. Auntie Ivy had six children in a house the same as ours, and once, when they were little, they all had to go to the hospital at the same time because they got a disease with sleeping in the same bed, three up one end and three down the bottom, and one of them died and never came home, and that's why there's only five now, though they're nearly all grown up.

Auntie Ivy's oldest girl, Cissie, was my best friend, even though she was much older than me. She was really funny and made me laugh a lot. Once she told me that the scruffy old geezer at the end of the street called Mr. Pickles had said that if she gave him a penny, he'd show her something worth looking at. Then Cissie laughed and laughed and said that she told Mr. Pickles if he gave her ten bob, she'd go and get her brother Mike, and he could show Mr. Pickles something that was in a jolly sight better condition than anything Mr. Pickles had on offer.

I wasn't quite sure what it was all about, but I laughed anyway because you couldn't help laughing when Cissie did.

There were always young hopefuls knocking on the door for Cissie, but in the end, she fell for a chap from over Hoxton way called Roy Poupart. He was no great looker, but he laughed almost as much as she did. Dad said they were like a pair of hyenas. You could hear them through the wall.

Roy and his mates played in a band called Mervyn

and the Wildfires, and when he and Cissie got married, they set it all up in our street. They put the wires for the guitars and the microphones through Auntie Ivy's window and plugged them into the light fittings. The bloke who was playing bass, Larry, had to stand right next to the wall for the whole afternoon; otherwise his wire wouldn't reach. Every now and then he'd call for me to get him a sausage roll and a bottle of Watneys.

After Roy and Cissie got back from the church, people came from all over the place to join in the dancing and have a drink and a piece of cake, but Mrs. Peake at number 6 told Auntie Ivy that the whole street was going to blow up with all the extra electrics — that's if the noise didn't shred her nerves first. Then Mrs. Woollett came out and said that her mother — that's Mrs. Brace-girdle — was dying, so if they was going to play loud music, it'd better be hymns; then Auntie Ivy said shut up, your bloody mother's been dying for the last three years, and I'm blowed if we're going to have "Abide with Me" all bloody afternoon just on the off chance. Then Mrs. Woollett shouted at Auntie Ivy that she could blimmin' well say what she liked about her mother, but she still had all her own teeth, which was more than Auntie Ivy'd got.

After that Roy got the band to play "Great Balls of Fire," and you could hear Mrs. Bracegirdle shrieking her head off from her bed in the Woolletts' front room, but they just turned up the loudspeakers.

Cissie spent her whole wedding day in fits of laughter, even when Roy spilled his beer down the nice white dress that her dad hadn't finished paying for on the "never never."

Mr. and Mrs. Lan, who ran a Chinese restaurant called the Jade Dragon on the Commercial Road, came with their two little boys, Number One Son and Number Two Son, and a huge bowl of rice mixed up with fried egg, and even a box of chopsticks for us to eat it with, but I couldn't work them out so I had to go indoors for a spoon. Mimi was all by herself in the house, napping in her cot, even with all the noise outside. I shouted for Mum but couldn't find her anywhere.

Dad and Uncle Dick Bedelius got drunk and sang some rude army songs, and Auntie Ivy swore at Uncle Dick in front of all the neighbours, but he couldn't have cared less. Then I think she must have had a bit too much of the Babycham herself because she started another slanging match with Mrs. Peake, saying she was quick to have a go about the music but didn't mind stuffing her gob with the food.

I could hear people singing and laughing and shouting and fighting all night long, and in the morning, the street was a dreadful mess. For ages afterwards, people would talk about what a lovely day it was when Cissie Bedelius got married. It was the best day of my life, or it would have been if it hadn't meant Cissie wasn't going to be there anymore.

After the wedding, Cissie and Roy went to live with his mum and dad in Hoxton. They were going to have the spare bedroom because, luckily for Cissie and Roy, his mum's Hungarian lodger had died.

A few months later, Mum was upstairs in the bedroom asleep and Dad was out. The pans were still dirty in the sink, and I couldn't find anything in the cupboard for Mimi's dinner. There wasn't even a shilling in the blue jug to go and buy some bread, so I popped with Mimi to Auntie Ivy's for something to eat. She squashed us round the table with her family and cooked us all egg and chips. Just as we were finishing, a dreadful wailing noise came through the wall from our house next door. It sounded like *"It's all my fault, it's all my fault,"* over and over again. The Bedeliuses went quiet and looked at each other, then at Mimi and me.

Auntie Ivy shot up, went out the back way, then returned five minutes later and said the old pushchair was in their yard for Uncle Dick to sort out for Cissie now she was expecting, and would I like to take Mimi for a walk in it. I said it would be lovely, so she got a cushion and put it on the seat because some of the stuffing was sticking out.

The pushchair made such a racket, you could hear us coming a mile away. We squeaked over the Commercial Road and I took Mimi to see the big boats and barges coming into the docks from all over everywhere

171

in the world. There was a huge ship unloading bananas. I hadn't had a banana for ages.

One of the dockers winked at me and pinched two off a bunch and gave them to us. They were green and rock hard. I knew the docker's name was Albert because his mate saw him talking to me and said, "Is that your best girl, Albert?"

Albert said if we hung around, we might see a taranchelar, which was a big hairy spider that they sometimes found hiding in the banana bunches, and that a mate of his called Old Jacko got bitten by one on his nose and he'd died of the poison. Albert said spider poison was a special sort called vemon, but I didn't know if it was a joke or not, so we left just in case one jumped out and stuck its teeth in us.

Just as we turned into our street, one of the wheels dropped off the pushchair, so we were really lucky to have got down the docks and back again. By that time, Dad was at Auntie Ivy's, but he looked tired and wouldn't tell me a joke when I asked. He took us round to some friends of his, Auntie Kath and Uncle Norman.

Auntie Kath was pretty and plump, and on hot days wore a blue sunsuit with white polka dots that showed quite a lot of her bosoms. We stayed with them for a few weeks, but I didn't like it. Auntie Kath smacked us sometimes. It wasn't like staying at Nan's, but Nan had gone back to Scotland and couldn't mind us anymore.

Auntie Kath had made Mimi eat dumplings, and she was sick all over her plate. I thought that was why they didn't want to have us again and we had to come all the way out here to Auntie Ida's.

I couldn't sleep, so I threw back the covers and put my feet down on the cool floorboards. Then I opened the door and went out on the landing. The soft light from the lamp in the hall below, and the comforting blue cigarette smoke drew me to the top of the stairs.

I could just hear Dad and Auntie Ida talking quietly in the sitting room. The door was half-open, but their voices were so low there seemed to be something deliberately hushed in the way they were speaking. When I had left the bedroom, I had half thought that I would just go down and see Dad, but now I was curious to hear what he and Auntie Ida were discussing so secretly together.

I already knew every creak on that vast staircase and crept downstairs, avoiding them all. Then I moved as noiselessly as a shadow and settled down on the little old milking stool that stood on its three short legs in the hall beside the sitting-room door. I breathed light shallow breaths so that Dad and Auntie Ida wouldn't hear me.

"Kath and Norman weren't too keen after last time. . . ." Dad was saying.

When Mum came home that time, she couldn't remember some things. She forgot it was Mimi's birthday.

"I'm pretty sure I know why you couldn't ask Kath and Norman, Harry," said Auntie Ida. "Susan used to write to me now and then, you know. She's no fool. She knew what was going on with Kath."

"It was all in Sue's imagination," said Dad quickly. "It must be all part of this—this condition."

"Come off it, Harry. I'm not as ignorant as you think," snapped Auntie Ida. "I've always known what you're like. It's got nothing to do with how Susan is. Anyway, doesn't it occur to you that it's much more likely to be a result of—because of—you know—with Anne?"

"I don't know. I just don't know. She doesn't talk about it, Ida. Ever."

"Maybe that's the problem."

They went quiet for a while. I heard liquid being poured into a glass, then Dad striking a match and the smell of a fresh cigarette.

"What if she's kept in for weeks?" he said at last. "Or . . . what if she never gets better?"

Auntie Ida spoke again. "I don't want them here, Harry."

"There was nowhere else, Ida—you know that," said Dad. "I don't know how long Susan's going to be in this time. It's worse than it's ever been before. I don't know if it's because Mimi is that age, and of course Cora is the older sister like she was—"

"All the more reason they shouldn't be here, Harry.

I've no idea how safe it is. I'm tired of listening and watching. I don't know whether it's all in the past now, or whether there's still something . . . I don't know. . . . "

"I didn't know there was anything wrong with Susan," said Dad. "All the blokes were after her—she was such a corker. We had a real lark at the beginning. You know what it was like just after the war—bloody miserable, freezing bloody weather, nothing to eat, country in flamin' ruins—but we was all right, Sue and me. It was only when she started spinning this daft yarn about Annie, and really believed it, Ida, that I thought, *Uh-oh, what's going on here, then?* I told her to shut up about it—it was just a load of old rubbish and she was to stop going on. I'd had it up to here, Ida. It was enough to try the patience of a bloody saint, I'm telling you."

"No wonder she doesn't talk about it."

There was a moment of silence, then Auntie Ida sighed deeply.

"I can't watch them twenty-four hours a day, Harry. It's beyond me. Thank God Cora's happy to cart Mimi around with her—I'll give her that much at least: she's very patient with her. They've made friends with some local boys. It's fine when they play up in the village—I can almost relax when I know that's where they are— but children can't resist that church. I've tried to stop them going there, but I think they've seen something. I'm not sure. You know what children are like." She paused. "We've come to blows, Harry. I've had to teach Cora a lesson."

"I noticed the bruises," said Dad uncomfortably, shifting in his chair. "I hope you haven't been too hard on her, Ida—what with Susan and everything, she must be feeling bad at the moment. Anyway, for Pete's sake, it's just an old superstition—ruddy crazy, if you ask me."

"I'm not asking you!" Auntie cried. "You don't have a clue what you're talking about, so don't pretend you do! It's dangerous, and that's the end of it! You can't lock them up all day, can you? You can't expect them to stay in the house all the time, and when the weather's hot—"

"Well, this was a bloody stupid place for Agnes to send Susan and Anne then, wasn't it?" Dad cried back at her. "It was hardly safe round here in the war with Hitler just over the water—bloody Battle of Britain up in the bloody air—without all this other ruddy rubbish. What the hell was their ma thinking of, sending them here? They'd have been better off at home in London, even with the Blitz. We got through it all right, me and Ma."

"Well, I'm not sure. Agnes had to work in the factory at Woolwich—you know that. Then—then you know about all her trouble—you know . . . having babies. It was either sending the girls here, to family, or off somewhere hundreds of miles away to strangers. Agnes wouldn't have done that."

"Well, she bloody well should have done, then there'd

never have been this whole bloody mess. I'd have had a bloody easier life, I'll tell you that. Agnes was too ruddy old to be having another baby at her time of life after Anne was lost. It bloody killed her, didn't it, and that good-for-nothing crooked husband of hers, One-Eyed Jack Swift, going off and leaving Susan on her own. It was good of my old ma to take Sue in; otherwise she'd have had nobody."

I was too tired. I didn't know what they were talking about. I knew Agnes was Auntie Ida's sister, Mum's mother, who died having a baby in an air raid, and One-Eyed Jack Swift was her husband. But who was Anne? I'd never heard of her before.

"Well, it's always easy to see things with hindsight," Auntie said. "At least, thank God, you've come to take Cora and Mimi home. It'll be such a weight off my shoulders. Anyway, Cora's too curious, poking and prying around the house. She's really been getting on my nerves. I can't have it, Harry."

There was a long, heavy silence.

"Ida . . ." Dad said quietly. I felt that he wasn't looking at her while he spoke, that he couldn't look at her. "There's nowhere else, Ida. I've got to work. I've got this deal on. I've got to pay the rent. Ma lives in Scotland now. How can I have them? I don't know the first thing about looking after kids, specially girls. They'd be wandering the streets all day. If the Council knew, they'd take them away and put them in a home. What am I supposed to do with them. . . . ? And then there's these people. . . . you know, if they cottoned on there weren't nobody watching my kids . . . I don't know. . . ."

I could feel the wooden floor under my numb feet. It was hard and cold. Suddenly everything in the world was hard and cold.

"Why did you bloody well come, if you weren't going to take them home?" Auntie Ida cried. "What about that neighbour of yours—Susan wrote to me about her once—kind woman, unusual name—beginning with *B*, I think. Why can't she take them in?"

"*B*? Oh, Bedelius—Ivy," said Dad. "To tell the truth, Ivy's not too good herself. Then there's four others still at home, apart from Dick, of course. How can she do it? I ask you, Ida."

"I don't want them here, Harry. Anything could happen!"

"Ida, don't be tough on me," said Dad, sounding wrung out. "I wanted to see them. . . . I wanted them to see their dad. . . ."

I couldn't be bothered to hear any more. I didn't understand any of it, except that Auntie Ida didn't want us and, worst of all, neither did Dad. Mimi and I were nothing but a nuisance.

I crept back upstairs.

✆ IDA EASTFIELD ✇

I almost had to drag Harry by the scruff of his collar and make him go into their room to kiss them good-bye. Even then he only went in because he knew they would be asleep. He hardly touched them he was so frightened of waking them up and making a scene.

✆ CORA ✇

I heard Dad come into our bedroom before he went away. He leaned over and kissed my forehead, so light it was like a breath, but I kept my eyes tight shut.

✆ IDA EASTFIELD ✇

I watched him go down the Chase, his kit bag swinging from side to side. He didn't look back. The sun was up, and the air was already warm for his walk to Daneflete to get the first train to London. If he had waited until the buses started, he would still have been in the house when the girls got up, so he walked.

Everyone turns their back on this place in the end.

Agnes, stupid Agnes, going off with that rogue, Jack Swift, coming down here looking for labouring work, saying he's lost his eye on the Somme, milking it for all it's worth. It turns out it got gouged out in some brawl on the Mile End Road. Of course, he used it to his advantage. All the girls thought he was winking at them.

I lost count of the stillbirths, the miscarriages she had. Susan and Anne. Just Susan and Anne. Just Susan.

Susan screaming—hysterical, running down there in the dark and ripping that little knitted soldier off the gypsy tree in the churchyard where I'd hung him.

I didn't think. It's just what we've always done.

I was making a pot of tea in the kitchen when Cora came down the stairs. I could hear by the sound of her footsteps that she knew he'd gone back without them.

I became so weary that morning—of Mimi's crying and Cora's silence.

❧ ROGER ❧

I don't know—they'd only been here for a little while, but it was funny to think of them back in London. I suppose it would feel like a dream soon, almost as if they'd never come at all. People come and go . . . it happens, Mum said. A few more days and you'll even start to forget what they looked like.

We hung around the house a bit, Pete and me, even though the day was really hot and sunny. We didn't feel like the woods after Malcolm and the flick knife, we didn't think we'd better go down the church, and we didn't fancy the Patches, either. Mum got out the chemistry set Grandma Bardock gave me for my birthday, but I couldn't be bothered with all the instructions, so I shoved it back in the cupboard.

Then she sent Pete and me down to Mrs. Aylott's with a list, but Mrs. Pratt, from Dry Street over near Hobb's Lane, and Mrs. Cleaver, Tooboy and Figsy's mum, were already in there, so we had to wait.

"Yes, Anthony said he saw them in the woods. . . ." Mrs Cleaver was saying in a low voice. I sometimes forgot Tooboy's name was really Anthony. He looked nothing like one.

"A disgrace, if you ask me," said Mrs. Pratt. The three ladies had gathered their heads close together as if they were cooking up something stinky in a cauldron. The bell tinkled when we came in, but they were so busy huddled up talking they didn't even turn round to look at us.

"She shouldn't have been allowed to have children down there," Mrs. Pratt carried on, "after what happened, you know—and two little girls as well, I ask you . . ."

Suddenly Mrs. Aylott caught sight of us and stood up straight.

"Two tins of garden peas was it, Beryl?" she said loudly, rolling her eyes in our direction. Mrs. Pratt and Mrs. Cleaver turned and looked at us and beamed.

"Hello, Roger, Peter," said Mrs. Cleaver. "No, processed if you don't mind, Dulcie. Girls not with you today, boys?"

"Erm, no. They've gone back to London," I said. "Their dad came for them yesterday."

"And not before time," said Mrs. Pratt half under her breath as she turned back to the counter.

◦❧ CORA ❧◦

Auntie Ida sent me to get the milk from down the end of the Chase where the milkman left it every day in a big tin box. Two pints — one pint extra now that Mimi and me were here, and I had to put the money in the box for him to take when he came next. Auntie said she used to have a cow in the barn for the milk, but she never got another one after it died.

It was smashing weather, lovely and sunny. The mud in the Chase was going hard again. I'd been in an irritable mood since Dad left, but walking back up to Guerdon Hall, picking buttercups with my spare hand, and feeling the warm sun on my face, I felt a bit better.

I arranged the buttercups in a jar of water and asked Auntie if we could go up to Roger and Pete's. I think she was glad to see the back of us.

Mimi started skipping as we went down Ottery Lane, in and out of the shadows of the big trees. She seemed to have forgotten all about Dad, even though she'd screamed herself purple the whole day after he left without us.

Roger and his brothers were in the garden, fishing

stuff out of the pond. There was a stinking muddy mess all along the edge, and as we came round the side of the house, they were poking about in it with sticks. Roger was so surprised when he saw us that he nearly stepped back into the water.

"Blimey!" he shouted, a big grin coming over his face. "What the heck are you doing here?"

"Roger! Watch it!" cried Terry. "You've stood right on my best fish!"

"Why aren't you in London?" said Pete, running up. "We thought you'd gone with your dad."

"No," I said, "he's got so much work on right now, but he's coming back to get us really soon. He wanted to make sure we were all right. Came to see us, that's all."

Mrs. Jotman appeared with some orange squash and biscuits and almost dropped the tray.

"Good heavens!" she said. "What a surprise. I'll go and get some more."

"You coming to the cricket tomorrow?" Pete asked as we sat on the grass.

"I dunno," I said. "I ain't never been to cricket."

"Our dad's absolutely the best bowler in the whole team," said Roger.

"Well, Graham Crawford's nearly as good," said Pete. "They're playing Clevedon Mortimer, over on the field. You must come. Roger and me put the scores up.

You can help as well, if you like. Then there's a smashing tea. Mum's already made loads of cakes. Everybody goes, and the weather's going to be brilliant, Dad says."

The distant tinkling sound of "Knick-Knack Paddy-Whack" drifted into the garden. It stopped for a while, then started up again, closer this time.

"Mum! MUM!" shrieked Dennis. *"DAD!* It's the ice-cream man!"

He went running into the house, then shot out again. "Roger! Mum's given me half a crown! Come on!"

We all got up and rushed down Fieldpath Road to where the ice-cream van had stopped outside Mrs. Wickerby's.

"Mum and Dad want wafers," Dennis said, jumping up and down as we waited behind some other children. At last we got our cornets and raced back to the house. Dennis was running so fast that, as he whizzed up the veranda steps with the wafer for his mum in one hand and the change and his cornet in the other, he tripped. His ice cream shot out of its cone and landed with the money in a heap on the wooden floor. A penny rolled round and round, then slipped through a crack between the planks. There was silence, then suddenly Dennis started screaming.

Mrs. Jotman came rushing out, thinking his leg must have come off at the very least.

"Oh, dear," she said, picking him up from where he was thrashing about on the veranda floor. "Here, have my wafer instead."

"Don't—don't like wafers!" he yelled. "Want my cornet!"

We could hear the ice-cream van going off down the lane towards North Fairing. Everyone was eating their cornet really fast so they wouldn't have to share it with Dennis. Mrs. Jotman disappeared into the house and came back with a spoon. She picked up his empty cone and spooned the ice cream from her wafer into it for him.

"'S not the same," he said, sniffing.

"I'll have it, then," she said, and pretended to go for a lick. He snatched it off her and started to eat it, and she went back in the house for a cloth, biting bits off the empty wafers.

❧ ROGER ❧

It was going to be a real scorcher. The sun streamed in around our curtains where they didn't quite fit the window.

I leaned over the side of the bunk. Pete was still asleep. I picked up a sock roll off the top of the cupboard at the end of the bed and chucked it at him.

"Oi! Stop it, will you!"

"It's cricket, Pete!"

He was so excited he shot out of bed like a mad thing, yelling, "Cricket! Wheeeee!" and jumping high in the air, thrusting up his arms in two fists.

After breakfast, Mum made Pete and me help her make ten tons of sandwiches — cucumber, ham, Spam, cheese and pickle, and some really posh ones with tinned salmon. When she had to go off to feed Baby Pamela, we helped ourselves to some fairy cakes and stuffed the paper cases deep down in the bin.

After dinner, Cora and Mimi turned up with a large fruit cake in a tin.

"Auntie Ida made it for the cricket," said Cora, and Mimi gave Mum a box of Roses chocolates in a paper bag.

"Auntie said for the raffle," said Mimi. "I didn't eat none."

"Oh, that's really nice of her," said Mum, putting the bag with the other things.

Dad came in looking very smart in his blazer and whites but irritated because his cap had disappeared.

I remembered Dennis had been in the garden with the cap on his head, practising batting with a big stick. When I went outside to fetch it, he had thrown the stick and the cap away and was chasing a cat through the long grass. Earlier in the morning, Mum had wet Dennis's hair to smooth it down, so when he took the cap off, his hair had dried into a really weird shape like a fried egg.

"Where's Dad's cap?" I yelled after him, but he didn't even look back.

It was lying in the dirt. Rubbing spit in made it even grubbier.

Mum came out. "I'll see to that," she said. "You put the stuff in the pram, and don't squash it all."

We loaded up the pram with tins and bags and plates of sandwiches covered in tinfoil, then off we went, Pete and Dennis reluctantly pushing it between them, Mum carrying Pamela, and Dad swinging his cricket bag.

The way to the field was up a grass track alongside Mrs. Aylott's shop. It was just wide enough for a car, and we had to stand on one side while the Treasures passed us in their shiny black Rover. Mr. Treasure was driving in his straw hat and his big white coat because he was always the umpire. A few other cars came up, but mostly they were bringing the other team, Clevedon Mortimer. I told Cora that she wasn't to cheer or clap for anyone wearing a blue cap with a red badge, but only for the men with the purple caps and gold badges, because they were the Bryers Guerdon and North Fairing team. She said she'd just do what I did.

The ladies set everything up in the Scout Hut. They covered the long trestle tables with starched white tablecloths and laid them out with big plates of sandwiches, cakes, and sausage rolls. We helped put out small plates with a serviette on each one, glasses, and jugs of lemon barley water and orange squash. It looked so tempting, but we didn't dare pinch any of the food because the ladies had eyes everywhere.

I could see one or two of them looking at Cora and Mimi and whispering behind their hands.

While the men were getting into their whites in the changing room, Cora, Pete, and me went outside to make sure the scoreboard was all ready. We checked that all the black metal plates with the numbers on were in the right order. Mr. Bannister from the Elms, farther down Ottery Lane, was going to keep the score on his special pad and make sure we put the right numbers up.

189

"Clevedon Mortimer's won the toss," he told us. "They've decided to bowl first."

We saw Bob Slattery going into the hut, late. I bet Pete sixpence, the next time I ever had one, that Bob Slattery would be out for a duck. His glasses were so thick his eyes looked like big marbles.

"Look," I said to Cora, "over there—it's the Treasures. That's Maisie's pimply brother, Tobias. He never plays cricket for us, thinks he's too posh probably. And that's Father Mansell and Mrs. Mansell, and that's our doctor who lives at North End down the road. He's Doctor Meldrum, and that's his wife, Mrs. Meldrum, and that's their daughter, Caroline, who's a bit older than Maisie Treasure but I think they go to the same school."

They were sitting in the shade around a table spread with an embroidered cloth. It was set with china teacups and saucers and dainty sandwiches, crusts off, on lace doilies. The Treasures, the Meldrums, and the Mansells were all wearing hats, the men in panamas, and the ladies, including Maisie and Caroline, in jaunty little things with a bit of netting. Their wide flowery skirts cascaded down to the grass, completely hiding the small folding chairs they sat on.

Mrs. Campbell came out of the Scout Hut with a tray. I'm surprised she didn't curtsey as she placed a milk jug and sugar bowl with silver tongs on their table. Then she lifted off a huge teapot, covered with a knitted cosy like an enormous Christmas pudding, and nudged it in amongst the little teacups.

Just as she was going back into the hut, the teams came out, so she waited with her tray to let them go by. We all clapped as they came down and took up their positions.

❧ CORA ☙

I hardly had a clue what was going on. Mr. Bannister called out the number of runs, and Pete gave the numbers to Roger, and he changed them on the scoreboard. At one point, a man called Dick Lorimer hit the ball with such a mighty crack it landed over a fence way across the other side of the field, and everybody whooped and shouted, "Six!"

Roger started to change the numbers, but I said what was he doing, because the chap hadn't even bothered running, but Roger said don't be stupid, it was a six, and I said how was I supposed to know what a six was? Then Mr. Bannister said to Pete to go and fetch the ball from Councillor Henderson's garden, and Pete shot off right across the field to climb over the fence and get it. He threw it back to the bowler, who rubbed it on the front of his trousers and made a red mark. I thought it looked a bit rude, actually.

Not long after that, Mr. Granville hit the ball really hard. As it sailed through the air, I started to cheer. A very tall man in a blue cap leaped into the air and caught it. Instead of everybody else cheering like me, they groaned. Roger put a number 1 on the hook where it said WICKETS. Then his dad went in to bat, but I lost track of how many runs he got.

I looked over at Father Mansell and his wife, who sat quietly in the shade, drinking their tea, the same sort of pepper-and-salt hair peeping out from underneath their hats, half brown and half grey.

I wondered if Father Mansell would know when Gussie's Father Hillyard had been rector.

"Roger, Roger," I hissed.

"Not now, Cora, hang on—Yes! Whoopee! A four! Well done, Dad!"

My mind wandered. I saw myself back in the room over the porch in Guerdon Hall, looking at the words I had found on Old Peter's picture—PETRUS HILLIARDUS.

I needed a piece of paper and a pencil. Pete found the stubby end in his pocket and gave it to me.

"Out!" shouted Mr. Bannister. One of the men standing around the field had caught the ball off Mr. Jotman's bat. Pete put his head in his hands, but Roger ran up as Mr. Jotman came off and said, "Never mind, Dad."

Mr. Jotman smiled and ruffled Roger's hair, then

went into the Scout Hut, and Graham Crawford went in to bat.

As Graham walked up to the stumps, I cheekily asked Mr. Bannister if I could possibly have a page off his score pad. He smiled and tore out a clean sheet.

I scribbled out *Petrus Hilliardus — Hillyard.*

"Roger, look! Look at this!"

"Crikey!" Roger laughed. "Look what Bob Slattery's done, Pete."

Bob Slattery had bonked his own nose with the bat. There was so much blood it looked like a hospital job, and they called his wife, Gladys, out of the Scout Hut. She ran up quickly and wiped his white pullover down with her apron. He sat out behind us for a while with his head back. Gladys fetched a spoon and stuck it between his teeth to stop him swallowing. He looked like he'd been attacked by a lion.

They stopped at four o'clock. Bryers Guerdon had scored sixty-eight runs, and Clevedon Mortimer had got six men out, including Dick Lorimer at the end. Roger said that sixty-eight runs wasn't all that brilliant, but it was still anybody's match. I wouldn't have known.

People started to move towards the Scout Hut for tea. I checked up on Mimi, who'd spent most of the first half throwing balls under the trees with Dennis and Terry. I made sure she had a sandwich, a slab of cake, and some cream soda, and was just about to grab some sand-wiches for myself when Mrs. Jotman came up and asked me if I'd like to sell some raffle tickets while people were eating. She tied an old woman's pinny, with pockets in front for the money, around my waist, saying I wasn't to forget to sell tickets to the players, but I had to summon up some courage before I could approach them in the middle of their sausage rolls. One or two of them made fun of the way I spoke. I pretended I didn't mind.

I thought Father Mansell was never going to come into the hut, but then I saw him edging his way through the crowd to the gents. I waited for him by the door, then, when he emerged, waved my book of tickets under his nose.

"Would you like to buy some, Father Mansell?" I said. "A penny a strip."

He smiled, dug around in his pocket for some change, and came up with sixpence. "A London girl, I hear," he said as I made heavy weather of tearing off the strips of tickets so I would have more time.

"Yeah, I'm stopping at Mrs. Eastfield's," I said. "Do you know her?"

"Oh, yes, I know Mrs. Eastfield," he replied. "Do you like that old house?"

"Well, not really," I said. "Oh, I shouldn't have said that, after she's taken us in an' all, but the thing is, I like my home in Limehouse better—not so big."

He laughed.

"I've seen your house," I added. "It's big like Auntie's."

"Oh, yes, yes, but like you, Mrs. Mansell and I would much prefer something smaller. It's too large for us. When my predecessor—sorry, the rector before me, Reverend Scaplehorn—was living there, it was converted into two. The Treasures live in the front half. Mr. Treasure is the headmaster of Lokswood School. He's the umpire today."

"Yes, I've seen him."

"He has a charming daughter, Maisie—very bright, you know. She's a little older than you, but if you like, I could introduce you. It would be pleasant for you to make a friend here during your stay. She's at the match today."

"I've met her already."

"Excellent, excellent. Well, I won't keep you, my dear. Nice to talk to you."

One of the Clevedon Mortimer team pushed past us to get to the toilet. The rector was pinned against the wall for a moment.

"Er, is that a ruined castle in your garden—in the woods, a bit farther down the hill?" I asked quickly.

"Castle? Ruined castle? Ah, I know what you're thinking of. Yes, you must be able to see it from the lane—just a pile of blackened stones now. It's the old rectory, my dear. I can see the remains from my bedroom window. I have a lovely view over the marshes. In the winter especially, when the trees are bare, I can see the spire of All Hallows and the chimneys of Guerdon Hall as well. They're very fine chimneys, aren't they?"

"What happened to that old rectory?"

"Well, it burned down—end of the sixteenth century, I believe, a dreadful fire by all accounts. I think the Guerdons began to build it, and the church, when they first came to the land at Bryers just after the Norman Conquest. I think Guerdon Hall was originally built in stone, and it's been sinking into the marshes ever since. The existing manor was rebuilt and altered over the centuries by successive Guerdon knights. There are probably extensive cellars, dating back to the original building, although frightfully grim and damp, I should think. You should ask your aunt about it. I'm not much of a historian, I'm afraid. Reverend Scaplehorn was, though. He knew a lot about it all—far too much if you ask me."

He laughed, and then stopped himself suddenly. Then he said, "It must be odd to be always surrounded by the ebb and flow of the tides."

"Auntie never stops looking out the windows to see if they're in or out. It's like a habit." I was desperate to keep Father Mansell talking. "Erm, I ain't seen nobody go down the church."

"Oh, yes, very quiet. People prefer to go to Saint

Mary's, up at North Fairing. It's a shame because All Hallows is a much prettier church. You know, I haven't done one baptism or wedding down at All Hallows since I've been here, although we do have funerals."

"Why don't people like it, do you think?"

"Oh, I don't know. It's a long way from the village, of course, and there are some stories, but I don't pay much attention to them. I'm an old sceptic myself. Still, I'll be retiring soon."

"So why did this Mr. Scaplehorn go, then? Did he retire an' all?"

"Goodness, look at the time! You're going to have to get those tickets folded. They'll be calling the raffle soon."

"Erm, how can you find out who were the rectors at Bryers Guerdon from way back?"

"Goodness me, child, you *are* curious."

"Just can't stop meself asking things," I said.

"Well, of course, there are always the parish records, but most of the really old documents were destroyed in the fire. Look, let me help you fold up those tickets. Time's moving on. We can put them in here."

Father Mansell took off his panama and put it by his feet. We tore up the strips, folded each ticket, and dropped them into the hat.

"Come to think of it," he said suddenly, "I'd almost forgotten. You can look inside the church. There's a list of all the rectors of the parish almost from the earliest incumbents right up to Reverend Scaple—"

"Cora!" yelled Pete, dodging through the crowd. "Where on earth have you been? Oh, hello, Father Mansell. Cora, they're waiting to do the raffle. Where are your tickets?"

"Oh, lummy!" I said. "They're here in Father Mansell's hat."

Father Mansell smiled. "Don't you worry," he said. "I'll take them. I'll say I kept you talking—which indeed I did."

I folded up the last ticket and threw it in. Father Mansell said good-bye, and very nice to make my acquaintance, and took his hat over to the tombola and emptied it into the drum.

A large woman called Mrs. Teale whirled the tombola around by the handle, opened up the front, and asked Father Mansell to choose a ticket, as he was standing there. Everybody laughed and clapped their hands when he won himself a bottle of Sanatogen Tonic Wine. The ladies thought it was hilarious and refused to take it back.

The best thing was that Pete won a prize—shame it was a tea towel and not the box of Roses chocolates from Auntie Ida. He came up to me with the tea towel draped over his head and said, "I can be the Red Shadow in this."

❦ ROGER ❧

Flaming girls don't have any flippin' idea about cricket. Clevedon Mortimer's innings was really exciting. Their first man was caught out after only two runs, but Cora was annoying. She would keep trying to get my attention.

You could see time was moving on because the shadows on the grass were getting longer, but everything was going brilliantly for us because Pete and I were changing the numbers on the wickets hook over and over again.

We got them all out for only fifty runs. It wasn't even seven o'clock yet. When it was over, the men came off the pitch, the Clevedon Mortimer team being sporting and shaking each other by the hand and slapping the Bryers Guerdon team on the back. Pete and I whooped at them as they came by. Dad and Graham Crawford put their caps on our heads, then we sorted out the scoreboard with Mr. Bannister and he gave us some Murray Mints out of his pocket.

Back in the Scout Hut, the ladies had done most of the clearing up during Clevedon Mortimer's innings. Cora still kept pestering me as we helped pile up Mum's empty plates, then stacked the chairs back against the walls.

"All right, you can tell me when we've finished," I said, "but we can't chat now or they'll tell us off for not helping. Honest, I'll listen when it's all done."

But there never was time that evening. Suddenly everything in the Scout Hut went quiet, apart from the rattling of cutlery and the distant murmur of chatting out in the kitchen. Mrs. Eastfield had walked in, holding Mimi by the hand. She looked around and saw Cora.

"Come along," she said. "It's getting late. Go and thank Mrs. Jotman for having you."

As soon as they left, everyone started talking again, but I don't think it was only the match they were muttering about.

✖ CORA ✖

Mimi's wet the bed again. Auntie Ida gets the copper going for the hot water, and I sort out the clothes from the sheets and blankets. Then Auntie goes down the stone passage to let Finn out for his run and to get the big tin bath.

Mimi is in a silly mood, still excited from the cricket match. I rummage behind the curtain under the sink and find a bag of peanuts. I pull it out, and nibbled empty shells, crumbs, and mouse droppings fall through the shredded brown paper onto the floor.

"The parrot can have some of these for a special treat," I tell Mimi, putting the few remaining whole nuts into a teacup. "Hold them through the bars of his cage one at a time. See if you can get him to say 'Hello.' And you're not to go mucking about on the piano or a giant'll come along and tread on you, and I'll know because I'll hear you doing it. I'll make you some squash when you come back."

Auntie pushes the tin bath through the door. I let her know where Mimi has gone. She switches on the wireless, rolls up her sleeves, and gets stuck in with the washboard and some green soap. I help her wring out the big sheet. We have some tea and a biscuit, and while

I'm washing up the teacups, we hear the pips for the hour. The news comes on.

"Is that the time?" I say. "I bet Mimi's eaten them peanuts herself."

Suddenly, with a great splash, Auntie Ida drops the heavy wet towel she is scrubbing into the bath. Soap suds wash over the floor.

"It must have been half an hour!" she cries, getting up and frantically wiping her hands on her apron.

"She's most probably in the toilet," I say.

"For half an hour? *Mimi!*" Auntie shouts as she rushes down the hall to the front door and checks to see it is still locked. "*Mimi!* Oh, God, did I lock the back door when I let Finn out? Check the back, Cora! Oh, God, is the tide out?"

I run back into the kitchen and down the stone passage. The back door is locked and the key hanging up on the big hook.

When I get back into the hall, Auntie is rushing in and out of rooms, banging on locked doors. "*Mimi! Mimi!* Answer me! *MIMI!*"

I dash up the stairs, the sound of my pounding feet echoing along the landing. I lift the latch on our bedroom door and push it open. Mimi isn't there.

"You in the toilet, Mimi?" I shout. I stop and listen, then run to the bathroom and check the toilet. The doors stand open. The rooms are empty.

202

"Auntie! Can I go along the passage up here?" I call down, leaning over the rail. "Am I allowed?"

Auntie comes racing up the stairs. Her face is white. "Yes! No—no! I'll go! *MIMI!* Where are you?!"

I hear her footsteps on the wooden floorboards, going in and out of the rooms along the landing, opening and slamming doors. When she comes back, her hands are trembling and her wide eyes move everywhere. She rubs her forehead and says, "Oh, God, oh, God . . ." over and over.

"I bet she's hiding. She does it sometimes—thinks it's a lark," I say, trying to be calm, but my voice is shaking like Auntie's hands. "She's most probably behind the settee in the sitting room, giggling at us getting all in a lather. I'll go back and look. I tell you, I'll give her a ruddy good spanking when I get hold of her."

I run quickly down the stairs, turn right at the bottom beside the dark panelled wall, and go towards the sitting room.

There is a soft knocking sound, quite close to me. I stand still. It stops. Then comes a scuffling. The knocking begins again, a few little taps. After a few seconds, all is quiet again.

The stairs creak as Auntie Ida comes down.

"*Mimi! MIMI!*" I shout. "Stop playing this ruddy stupid game! Are you making that noise? Say something! It ain't funny!"

I move into the sitting room. Auntie follows me. I lean over the settee to look behind it. The parrot says, *"Hello."* I glance up, and there is Mimi, standing in the doorway.

Auntie sinks into a chair and covers her face with her hands. I storm up to Mimi and shake her and shake her by the shoulders.

"What are you bloody playing at?" I scream. She starts to cry. Tears fly out as I shake her. I find I'm crying as well.

Then I put my arms around her and squeeze her really tight.

"It ain't funny," I say. "It ain't funny hiding like that. Where've you been? We looked all over the blimmin' place."

There's dirt on her dress and bits of spiders' webs in her hair. "What's all this?" I say as I pick them off. "Where've you been, Mimi?"

She looks over at Auntie Ida, then at me. "Can I have my squash now?" she says.

Auntie Ida goes out into the hall.

"You're not to play hide-and-seek here!" I say to Mimi. "You're not to go off on your own!"

"I weren't on my own," she says. "I went in this little house."

"Are you fibbing me, Mimi?"

"I ain't fibbing. I weren't on my own."

I see Sid sticking out of her hand.

"You mean you had Sid?"

"Nah, but she knows Sid. She see'd him before."

"What on earth you talking about? Who's seen him before?"

"I ain't saying," says Mimi. "I ain't saying nothing."

"Mimi, if you don't tell me, I'll give you the worst arm burn in the world." I take her arm in my two hands and start to twist the skin.

"I ain't saying," she says, baring her little teeth in pain. More tears drop out of her eyes. I can't carry on. I let her go.

"I ain't saying," she sobs, rubbing her arm. "I promised, hope to die."

"Don't say that!"

We go out of the room and back into the hall. Auntie's standing at the bottom of the staircase with her back to us, her arm clutching the big post. After a minute, she lifts her apron up and wipes her face with it, then, still without turning round, goes into the kitchen.

"Can I have my squash now?" Mimi says.

"Shut up, Mimi," I say as we follow Auntie. "You've been a bad, bad girl. You ain't having no squash, not for ages."

Finn is barking at the back door. Auntie goes off to let him in.

"Another cup of tea?" I ask when she returns.

"No," she says. "Why don't you take Mimi up to

Bryers Guerdon and see if the Jotman boys can come out to play. I'll walk you up the hill."

"We'll be all right," I say. "You don't have to do that."

"Yes, it would be better," she says, taking her scarf off the hook, "and we haven't picked up the milk yet."

Mimi runs on ahead, throwing sticks for Finn. Auntie Ida and I say nothing. Now and then I catch her looking over to where the church is, behind the trees.

By Glebe Woods, Auntie stops for a moment and looks back down the hill with her hand shading her eyes. Then she leaves us to go and pick up the milk from the box and get back to the washing.

Mimi and I walk up to the main road. I'm cross with her for keeping this secret from me.

"Where did you go?" I ask for the umpteenth time.

She looks away from me across the wheat field.

⊰ ROGER ⊱

I went with Pete to the top of the lane and put him on the bus to Daneflete. He was going to Pip Bracken's birthday party. Pip lives on Corsey Island, and his mum was meeting all his friends outside the Longship in Daneflete, then taking them back to their house. Pete said they were going to pick winkles off the mud right outside Pip's house and pull them out of their shells with a needle and eat them. Wasn't my idea of a party.

Just as the bus pulled away, I spotted Cora and Mimi coming along by the Thin Man. Cora said Mimi had been a flipping idiot, hiding somewhere, and she wasn't to have any treats at my house like biscuits or ice cream.

When we got there, I wished we hadn't gone round the back because Mum saw us and gave us this big basket of washing to hang up on the line. Still, at least we could talk while we were doing it.

"You know," said Cora, "Father Mansell said the rector before was called Mr. Scaplehorn. He said there was this rectory before Glebe House, but it burned down in this great huge fire hundreds of years ago, and that's the ruins in the woods. It never was a castle, you know — it never was."

Cora took a pair of my pants out of the basket and was getting two pegs ready to hang them up. What was worse, they were the pants that were all thin round the back. I snatched them off her and stuffed them in my pocket.

"Pete's," I muttered.

❧ CORA ☙

When we'd finished pegging up, I showed Roger the piece of paper from Mr. Bannister's score pad.

"Look," I said. *"Petrus Hilliardus—Hillyard*. This is what I wanted to show you yesterday at the cricket. Look, the name's nearly the same. I think that painting is a picture of this Father Hillyard what Gussie was going on about, but the picture's really really old. He must've been dead for ages."

"Unless it's the person's name who painted the picture—the artist. They always put their names on."

"Well, it's still old."

"That first word, *Petrus*," he said. "It's Latin for Peter. It's in my missal—*Tu es Petrus*—it means 'Thou art Peter.'"

Mrs. Jotman came out. "Roger, I'm going over to Auntie Barbara's. She's poorly, so I've done some of her laundry. Pamela's just gone down for her nap, so she won't be any bother. If I'm not back, can you do cheese on toast for everyone for dinner? Don't forget to bring anything in that's dry, and *fold* it—don't just shove it in the basket. If Pamela wakes up, you'd better come and get me, but she should be all right for a couple of hours. And keep an eye on Dennis. Pete couldn't find his penknife this morning, and I expect Dennis's got it. He swears blind he hasn't, but I know he's fibbing. I don't want him ripping up the curtains."

"All right. See you."

"The best bit, though," I said, when Mrs. Jotman had gone round the side of the house, "is that Father

208

Mansell said there was this list of all the rectors there's been at All Hallows, and it's somewhere in the church."

"But like I said, we don't even know if this bloke Hillyard was a rector, do we?" said Roger.

"Well, we won't know nothing if we don't look."

"All right, but we'll have to wait till Mum comes back."

⚜ ROGER ⚜

Cora and I had a quick look round to make sure nobody was about, then squeezed ourselves through the bit of broken fence. The old ruins aren't far from the lane. There's so many trees growing around, you wouldn't know the ruins were there if you didn't really look—not that there's much to see: some bits of wall, all green and mossy, and small heaps of half-buried stuff with weeds all over. Most of it is just smooth mounds, but if you scrape away the earth and moss with a stick, some of the bricks are quite near the top.

"Once you know there's been a fire, then you can see," said Cora, poking about among the stones. "Some of these bricks are black."

We went a bit farther into the woods, wondering how far the ruins went.

"Must have been an enormous great place," Cora said.

We went back into the lane, then put our heads down and ran all the way to the church.

"What are we looking for, actually?" I panted, pushing open the door.

"No idea. Pete interrupted Father Mansell just as he was saying."

We went inside.

"Don't it feel horrible in here today," Cora whispered.

"Just what I was thinking," I said. "Somebody's cleared up since we last came in. There are new candles in the candlesticks. Was there a service yesterday morning?"

"Haven't a clue," Cora said. "Mrs. Campbell must've been in and done it."

⟡ CORA ⟡

We look everywhere for the list of rectors—on the memorials on the walls, in hymnbooks, out in the porch, on the grave slabs set into the floor.

"What about behind that curtain then?" says Roger.

We stand in front of the altar and gaze at the heavy embroidered curtain that hangs behind it, the full width of the stained-glass window. Running along the whole length of the bottom of the wall from one side of the church to the other is a wooden step.

"If I stand on this, I might be able to see round the back of the curtain," I say. I climb up, but the step is too narrow for my feet. I begin to lose my balance. I grab the fabric. The metal rings slip to one side with a coarse jangling. I land on the floor, having dragged the curtain along the pole as I went.

"Crikey!" Roger whispers.

"What is it?"

"Pull it all the way back," he says, "then come and stand here."

I gather up the curtain to one side, then go and join Roger.

I draw in my breath.

On the wall, scratched deep into the stone in huge jagged letters, is written:

LIBERA ME DE MORTE AETERNA LIBERA ME DE ORE LEONIS
LIBERA ME LIBERA ME LIBERA ME PH 1584

And underneath is more scrawled writing, gouged out with a screwdriver or a chisel by someone in such a frenzy that the plaster has broken off in flakes around the letters:

DELIVER ME FROM ETERNAL DEATH DELIVER ME FROM
THE MOUTH OF THE LION DELIVER ME DELIVER ME
DELIVER ME JS 1948

We walk quickly back down the aisle, yank open the church door, and rush out into the sunshine.

I balance myself on a gravestone.

For a long time, we can't speak.

"We'll have to go back in," Roger says. "We'll have to cover it up again."

"I don't know if I can."

"I'll—I'll go if you like."

"No, it's all right. I'll come."

We drag ourselves back to the porch and go into the church once more. The air inside seems thick. Together we pull the curtain over the writing and turn our backs on it.

"We'll have to try in here," I say as we walk towards the arch of the tower. "I don't ever want to come back in this church again as long as I live, and this is the only place left we haven't looked in."

❧ ROGER ❧

Cora's skin was damp and shiny. She stared up at the ceiling of the tower almost as if she were seeing straight through it. She rubbed her hand on her forehead.

"Can we be quick?" she said irritably. "I can't stand it in here."

On the right-hand wall was a locked wooden door that I thought must lead up to the bells, and on the left hung the other thick curtain. I took hold of the edge. "Shall we look?"

Cora sighed, then nodded.

Behind the curtain was an old wooden door, small, grey with age, riddled with wormholes and rotten at the bottom. I rattled the bolt and drew it open. The long plate on the door slipped away from the wood and into my hand.

"Oi!" cried Cora. "What are you playing at?"

"Most of the screws are missing," I said, carefully trying to line up the remaining rusty screws and pushing the bolt back in place.

"Leave the blimmin' thing alone. Look, this is it."

Above the door was a long slab of marble carved with a list of names in two columns under the heading RECTORS OF THIS PARISH.

At the top of the list were just names: *Guillaume de Pycard, Guillaume de Machaut, Jean de Fontcheval*. The first with a date was *William de Sutton 1231–1237* and the last, *Jasper Scaplehorn 1932–1948*.

"Jasper Scaplehorn—JS. Could he have written that stuff on the wall?"

"Could have done, I suppose. *JS 1948*—the year he left."

Cora reached up and ran her finger down the names,

and there it was, towards the bottom of the first column: *Piers Hillyard 1540–1584*. After Piers Hillyard there was no rector named until *Walter Gomeringe 1643–1652*.

We replaced the curtain.

"Let's get out," said Cora. "I don't feel well."

I pulled open the door and screwed up my eyes against the bright sunlight that blazed from the churchyard on the other side of the dark arch of the porch. For a second, through my half-closed eyes, I thought I saw something move.

❧ CORA ❧

Just as Roger and I step onto the path, the sky is disturbed with squawks of alarm and the rushing of wings. Hundreds of birds take off from the surrounding trees. As the cries fade and the birds wheel and turn and gradually disappear over the line of the hill, an odd stillness falls upon the graveyard. We seem to have brought the tight, close air of the church outside with us, air that feels charged with discomfort.

We start to walk towards the lane. A light wind begins to drift through the grass among the gravestones. All is quiet, but for a low buzzing in my ears like the noise of flies. Maybe it is the sound of my own blood.

Something makes me look towards the old gate.

My feet freeze to the path. Roger doesn't move. He has seen him, too, the man standing by the gate, the man wearing a long black robe. Wisps of grey hair frame the man's blistered face. The top of his head is bald. His thin beard blows to one side.

He gazes at us, at Roger and me, without blinking.

In a moment, he vanishes. As I gasp with relief, he appears again, behind a headstone a little nearer to us. He disappears again, then reappears still closer, each time closer, closer still, disappearing and then appearing once more.

My mouth goes dry.

The man is only ten feet away. His skin looks raw.

Then, out of him, though his lips barely move, comes a voice, a thin faraway voice that seems to reach out to us from across some great sea of time, from another shore a million miles away.

Leave this place, he says from this distant country, this other world. *He walks again. Leave this place. Take the child away. He is hunting. He will find her.*

Then, among the tombstones, out of the air, small figures appear. They are the size of little children, but their colourless faces are old and rotten, like the faces of the dead, their eyes nothing more than black holes, their hair grizzled and sparse.

They open their pale, cracked lips and begin to cry out with high, wailing voices, *Save us, save us. . . .*

As I stare, open-mouthed, mute with horror, I see that some are not as far decayed as the others. One of these little ones, a girl with her fair wavy hair still remaining, steps forward from the group and reaches out to me. I stand rigid. She looks like Mimi. . . . She fixes me with her dark hollow eyes. *Save me, save me.* . . .

The old man calls out to the children, *You are lost. Go back. Go back.*

They begin to moan, their voices rising and falling in desolate waves.

After what seems a long, long time, I begin to see the grass, the wildflowers, and the gravestones through the children's bodies. They are fading into nothing, but the moaning goes on and on, long after they have gone. The small girl is the last to disappear, her arms still stretched out in front of her, towards me.

Take the child away, the man says again as his body becomes air. *He walks again. He knows she is here.* . . .

I don't know how many minutes pass by. The breeze dies down. Shadows move across the grass as the birds return and the trees fill with song once more. I am not sure I am in the world I know or not.

"I've heard those children before," I whisper, still staring at the place where they were standing.

"What? When?" rasps Roger.

"I've heard them in Guerdon Hall, in the night. I

thought I was dreaming. He's the man in the picture, Piers Hillyard. He's come to warn us."

"*Cave bestiam*." Roger shudders. "Beware of the beast."

⤜ ROGER ⤛

I lie here listening to the kitchen clock chiming away the hours of the night. My eyes feel hard, like two lead bullets. I see the man's face in the flower pattern on my bedroom curtains. I turn to the wall. I feel his fingers on my back. I shiver.

I can't say anything to Pete. How could I tell him what we've seen?

⤜ CORA ⤛

I don't want to go to sleep. I don't know what I might dream of. I make myself stay awake, listening to the mice scratching under the floorboards.

Mimi dozes. She's kicked off the top blanket. It is such a hot night. My hair is wet and sticky. Mimi turns towards me, and her mouth falls open. I push her bottom lip up and move her head so her mouth stays shut, then take a deep breath and get out of bed.

My feet are cool on the wooden floor. I go to the window and pull the curtains aside. A great yellow moon hangs in a clear sky full of stars, so bright the garden is alive with shadows, rippling behind the dirty panes. The bar of the horizon glows turquoise.

I lift the rusty metal catch and try to open the window, but it will not budge. I push hard on the wood with my palms and feel a slight movement, then pound with my fists a couple of times. I listen for a while to see if I have woken Auntie Ida. Hearing no sound from beyond the door, I punch at the frame with all my strength. At last it rattles. Small splinters of wood break off, old paint flakes and dust come away, and gradually the window scrapes across the stone ledge and creaks outwards but will not open completely. The frame stops against the sharp broken ends of rusty nails.

I lean as far as I can into the gap and breathe in the warm air as I gaze down at the wilderness of a garden, the dark curve of the empty creek surrounding it, and the wasteland of marshes beyond.

A soft breeze bends the grass blades and rustles the leaves on the overgrown shrubs below. A smell drifts up to me, rotten and sweet at the same time, the smell of dead animals, of an opened grave. I smelled it today in the church tower.

I catch a movement in the trees near the henhouse. If a fox is coming for the chickens, I'll make a noise, clap my hands, throw something — I hold my breath and wait for it to clear the bushes.

It is not a fox.

Moving slowly, creeping along the ground, it approaches a bright patch of moonlight by the wire fence. It is shaped like a long tall man, yet it crawls like an animal.

It draws closer to the light, closer, one hand stretched out and then the other.

My breath rushes out.

Heart thumping, I drag the window shut.

Swiftly it turns its head and looks up. Through the diamond panes, I see a bony face like a skull. It looks at me from the dark orbits of its eyes and opens its jaws wide, showing me long, pointed yellow teeth that flicker behind the old shifting glass like the flames of candles.

Somewhere in the house, Finn stirs and growls.

∝ ROGER ∞

Pete was upstairs playing with his soldiers and said to call him when we were going out.

Mum had gone to feed and change Baby Pamela. Cora and I sat in the kitchen, hardly speaking. She looked messy, with her hair hanging down and dark rings under her eyes.

I stared at a crust of bread on the lino.

"Are you sure?" I said.

"'Course I'm blinkin' sure."

"Could've been a nightmare. You know, after what we saw an' all."

"I've had enough flippin' nightmares since I've been here to know the difference. I ain't stupid."

"Moonlight plays funny tricks—"

"Shut up, will you! I saw the flippin' thing! Just like we saw that man at the church!"

Mum came in. We both stared at the bit of bread.

"You two had a row?" she asked, then added breezily, "Couldn't you find any ribbon, Cora? Do you want me to do your plaits for you? I don't mind if you don't want me to, but Mrs. Eastfield isn't used to having kids

220

around. She's not in a routine. I'll do it for you, if you like. I never get to do a girl's hair in this house. Baby Pamela hasn't got any yet."

"Oh, ta," said Cora, making herself smile. "Thanks. Auntie does it sometimes, but it's really tight. Feels like she's pulling me roots out."

Mum took down her basket of odds and ends from the dresser. "What colour ribbon, Cora? This red's nice, isn't it?" she said.

"Yeah, very nice, lovely," said Cora, and Mum reached over for her big black bristle brush and started to tidy up Cora's hair.

"Mrs. Jotman, you know you said Mrs. Eastfield isn't used to having kids around?" asked Cora. "Well, what happened to her little boy?"

Mum's mouth fell open, and so did mine. She stopped the brush halfway down Cora's head.

"Well, what a question," she said, then started brushing again, but quicker.

"She did have one, didn't she?"

Mum ran her fingers through her own hair. She always did that when she was flustered.

"Well, yes, to be completely truthful, she did have one as it happens," said Mum, making a back parting. "Erm, I think he was called Edward. You mustn't be too hard on your auntie, Cora. She's had a tough time."

"What happened to him?"

"Look, why don't you ask her? I really don't think it's my place. You've got lovely thick hair, dear. You're really lucky. Does it come from your mum or your dad?"

"What happened to her baby? I can hardly ask *her*, can I?"

"Well, Cora, if you don't think she'd want you to know, it isn't fair to ask me, is it? It's just gossip, anyway."

"What's gossip? If it's gossip and everybody round here knows, why shouldn't I know and all? It's my family, ain't it. If anything ain't fair, it's me not knowing what's gone on with me own flesh and blood."

Mum sighed. Cora's eyes went wet round the edges, and she sniffed. I honestly couldn't tell if she was really starting to cry or just pretending, but Mum's a sucker for tears, soft as butter, and Cora knew it.

"Oh, Cora, please don't upset yourself. Oh, dear, you've put me in such an awkward position. Look, don't tell anybody I said anything, especially your aunt. . . . To be honest, Cora, nobody really knows for sure. Nobody knows what happened to the little chap — that's the problem. When I was a girl, I just picked things up here and there from bits of grown-ups' conversations. All I know is, he died . . . disappeared . . . somewhere down there. . . .'

"Did her husband die as well?" I asked. Mum shot me such a look, I swallowed.

"Well, yes, he did, obviously — otherwise he'd be around, wouldn't he," she said uncomfortably.

"How did he die?" I asked, boldly for me.

"You're going too far now, Roger. Why have you suddenly started asking all these questions? It's Mrs. Eastfield's private business. It's nothing to do with us."

"Did he kill himself?" Cora asked.

"Cora! What a question!" Mum cried. "Nobody—nobody knows what happened. He was found in the upper field, just below Glebe Woods, not long after the little boy went missing. He'd been out shooting rabbits or something. It was most likely an accident. These things happen. A gun can go off the wrong way."

Mum went quiet. Then, to my amazement, she continued.

"Mrs. Eastfield started to give it all up after that. Her family, the Guerdons, farmed all the land round here. It went as far as Daneflete and the river, then over to Hilsea, and nearly to Fairing the other way—a lot of it marshland, of course, not much use to man nor beast. The Guerdons were a titled family many years ago, but sometimes titles go sideways or get lost, and the Guerdons ended up wealthy gentleman farmers. There's no lack of money, never has been.

"When I was a child, I remember seeing Mrs. Eastfield quite often driving a tractor along the main road. During the war she had some help from land girls and labourers, but none of them stayed for long. It was all too much for her. Gradually she sold off some

223

land to other farmers, and what she didn't sell, she rents out."

"Well, if she's got money, why doesn't she sort the blinkin' house out, then?" said Cora. "It's falling to bits."

"Oh, Cora," said Mum, twisting Cora's hair around her fingers. "Sometimes, when an awful lot of rotten things happen to a person, they—they sort of lose heart, I suppose. It must be hard. After hundreds of years, with that old house never going out of the family in all that time, she's—well, she's the last of the Guerdons, the only one left to have been born with that name."

That's what old Gussie had said—*the last of the Guerdons.*

"She probably just couldn't be bothered," Mum went on, "and anyway, why should she? It isn't worth wasting money on, is it? After she's gone, who's going to want to live down there, in that lonely place, near that funny old church . . . all those weird stories. Nobody in their right mind would choose to live down there. It'll be pulled down or left to fall down all on its own."

"Why don't she move away, then?" asked Cora.

"Where would she go?"

Cora wouldn't stop. "Why don't people round here want their kids to go down the church, then, Mrs. Jotman? What's the matter with it? What are them weird stories you said? And why doesn't anyone like Auntie Ida? Why do they all whisper behind her back? Why do they go quiet when she walks in anywhere?"

"That's an end to it, Cora! Quite frankly, they're not the sort of things children should be asking. That's enough now!"

"Why don't grown-ups tell kids nothing?" Cora cried. "Like we're stupid."

Mum sighed. "It was the same when I was little."

She tied up the end of the first plait, then busied herself brushing and then sorting the rest of Cora's hair into three strands.

"Look," she went on. "People around here are funny about the church, always have been. It's probably a lot of old superstitious nonsense, but, well, some strange and, to be honest, awful things have happened down there that just haven't ever been understood. As for your Auntie Ida, people are funny with folks who've been touched by tragedy. I suppose they think it's catching or something, so best to keep your distance. People can be very self-righteous, especially in small villages like this. You have to know how your neighbours stand, what they think. You have to know where you are with them. It makes you feel safe. Folk can be uncomfortable with someone who is different, or odd or unpredictable. And, of course, it gives them something to talk about. All right?"

"But it's cruel not to talk to Auntie Ida," said Cora. "It's bad enough if your whole family's gone and died, without people gossiping about you—"

"Well, it's other things as well, Cora," said Mum. "It's

not just Mrs. Eastfield's husband and son. I mean, more recently, during the war— Look, I'm really unhappy telling you this. It isn't my place—"

"So you keep saying."

"There's no need to be rude, Cora. It's awkward."

"Sorry—sorry, Mrs. Jotman."

"There are people who would be horrified that I'm saying all this, especially your aunt. If you breathe a word—"

"Promise, cross me heart."

"Well, during the war . . ." said Mum, and I leaned right in. "Not so close, Roger, I can't breathe. During the war, two sisters were evacuated to Mrs. Eastfield's from London—relatives, I think, a bit like you and Mimi, I suppose—one older and the other much younger, just a toddler really. Well, the little girl disappeared just like little Edward Eastfield."

"What happened to her, then?"

"Well—um—she could so easily have wandered off. The marshes can be treacherous. The reeds can grow as high as a house, and there's hidden pools and thick mud. You've really got to know where you're going as you get closer to the river. Then the creeks come right round the house, and they're tidal. It's not a place for a child. . . ."

"Didn't they look for her? Didn't the police send out search parties?" I asked.

"Yes, they gave as much time as they could spare, but

it was wartime, of course. They had many more demands on their resources than they could manage as it was. The Local Defence Volunteers got involved — or I think they were called the Home Guard by then. I know, because your Grandpa Bardock went down on the marshes with his unit to look for the little girl, Roger, but they gave it up in the end. I don't think they actually thought they would find her. I remember hearing Grandma and Grandpa whispering about it when they thought I couldn't hear. He hoped it would be different this time. Then I heard her ask him, under her breath, whether they'd gone through the door — some door some-where — to look for the child, but he whispered back that it was bolted. I could hear he was — um — scared, which unsettled me, because your grandpa wasn't easily upset. Then he said maybe there would be a miracle and she would turn up. But there wasn't. She never did.

"I — I hate to tell you this, to be honest, but the police took Mrs. Eastfield away for questioning at one point. There was no evidence of foul play, as they say, and in the end they let her go."

"Crikey!" I said, amazed to think of Mrs. Eastfield being arrested like a murderer.

"What happened to the older sister?" Cora asked.

"Eventually someone came and took her back to London on her own," said Mum, "and I even remember overhearing some gossip a year or so later that the girl's mother had just died, on top of everything else."

"So do people not like Auntie Ida because they think she kills children or something?"

"No, nobody thinks that, Cora, honestly," said Mum. "There are lots of reasons. She doesn't need them, for a start. She isn't interested in being part of Bryers Guerdon. She doesn't give anything, and she doesn't take anything, unless she absolutely has to. They probably think she's a bit uppity as well, speaking with that accent. Anyway, that probably wouldn't matter if she got herself involved in the community, like Mr. and Mrs. Treasure, for example, but she doesn't. She chooses to live apart, all alone in that lonely old house, and anyway, the Guerdons have always been thought a really strange lot, from way back."

Mum tied off the second plait tightly with the red ribbon.

"There have always been stories about Guerdon Hall," she continued. "And it's odd that the church is all on its own down there with the village up here. We were always told as children that the marshes bred the plague, and that sometime long ago, the people moved up here to healthier ground. Fear of catching the Black Death was enough to keep us away when we were little, apart from all the other tales." Mum laughed. "Father Mansell doesn't bother with All Hallows much. Almost all his services are held at Saint Mary's, in North Fairing. Even Mr. Hibbert, the sexton, gives All Hallows a wide berth if he can help it. When we were children—I've never forgotten—he scared me and your uncle Bill half to death with a ghost story he'd made up about something he'd seen down there in the churchyard. Really gave me the pips, I can tell you. Irresponsible, silly man.

"Anyway, the simple fact is, folks up here in Bryers Guerdon like to think that if you ignore unpleasant things for long enough, they'll just go away. They'd rather not be reminded of those unwholesome events concerning Mrs. Eastfield, so when she turns up here in the village, they don't like it. She makes them recall things they'd rather forget."

"I suppose Mrs. Aylott and her friends thought Mrs. Eastfield wasn't a fit person to have Cora and Mimi staying with her, then," I said. "No wonder they were gossiping in the shop."

"Oh, yes, of course," Mum said. "Were they? Oh, dear."

"Mrs. Jotman," said Cora, "you said 'superstitious nonsense'? What's all that, then?"

"Oh, Cora, I thought we'd finished," she said. "Look, when you're . . . er . . . warned about certain things from being very little, when you grow up with daft stories, it's very difficult to be sensible about them when you've got children of your own. It's always, well, *just in case there's something in it* . . . you know what I mean. . . ."

"What daft stories?"

"Oh, Cora"—Mum threw her hands in the air—"can't you leave anything alone? It's just silly when I think about it."

"About what?"

"Oh," Mum sighed, turning her back and heading for the door, "oh, they used to tell us . . . Look, I'll show you something. Won't be a minute."

Cora and I met each other's gaze as Mum left the kitchen with her basket. She returned with her big red scrapbook. I'd never really looked through it, put off by some of the soppy things she'd stuck in it, like tickets for the pictures when she and Dad were courting.

She shuffled through the huge grey pages. "Ah, here we are," she said, spreading the book out on the table. It was a page of newspaper cuttings, stuck in with old brown Sellotape. They were dirty yellow with age but had come out of the paper we still had delivered every Wednesday, the *Lokswood Herald*.

Mum laughed a little while she turned the scrapbook round on the table so we could see.

"Most of the reporters around then," she said, "were either really young juniors, straight out of school, not old enough for active service yet, or old chaps. Really silly things got put in the paper, but with the war on, local stories didn't last long. Obviously, when that little girl went missing and Mrs. Eastfield was taken to the police station, there was a certain amount of interest, and they sent a reporter and a photographer down to have a bit of a snoop around, but they found out very little because people here tend to clam up when outsiders come poking their noses in.

"I suppose the chaps felt they ought to print something, though, having come all the way down here. They must have picked something up from somebody, some remark. Look at this. Daft, isn't it?"

It was an inside page of the newspaper. A half-inch-high headline read: A MONSTER ON THE MARSHES?

"The—the grown-ups used to frighten us with it," Mum said quietly.

I turned to Cora. I wasn't quite expecting what I saw.

Her face had gone pale. She wasn't reading the article, but was staring at a small, grainy photograph in the corner at the bottom of the page. The photo had originally been of two girls, standing arm in arm, one much taller than the other, but the paper had only printed half of it, the smaller girl. Underneath the picture were printed the words: *Anne Swift, the Missing Child*.

Mum noticed Cora was upset. She quickly closed the scrapbook before I could get a proper look at the photo, and took it out of the room. When I went to search for the book later, I couldn't find it.

Cora didn't say a thing. She got up and went out into the garden.

❧ CORA ❧

I watched Auntie Ida adjust her brown hat in the hall mirror.

"Edith Shardlow and I were at boarding school together," she said. "We see each other once a year or so, just to keep in touch."

She picked up an old comb off the small table and ran it through the ends of her hair, then wiped a smudge from her cheek. Who would have thought that Auntie Ida had a friend? I realized how little I knew about her, except that under that chestnut hat, her head was full of secrets.

"Though Edith's had a better life," she added quietly.

Auntie Ida would know quite well who the child in the newspaper was, the same little girl who had reached out to me in the graveyard: *The Missing Child. Anne Swift.*

"We're meeting at Wren's Coffee House in Lokswood at eleven thirty."

Anne Swift. Two sisters. Mum was Susan Swift before she married Dad. Susan and Anne. Dad and Auntie Ida had talked about them in the sitting room that night last week. But surely it wasn't Mum, that older girl whose arm was still in the photograph in the newspaper, hooked through her little sister's. If she'd had a sister, I would have known—surely someone would have said.

It couldn't have been Mum, the girl who'd had to go back to London on her own, whose mother had died not long after—Agnes Swift, Auntie Ida's sister. Dad always said her husband, One-Eyed Jack, thought he'd get rich marrying her because the Guerdons had loads of money, but he didn't reckon on Agnes's father disowning her for marrying him. Agnes Swift—the black sheep. Old Guerdon never gave them so much as a penny.

"I'm going to treat Mimi to a banana split," Auntie said. "They are very good in Wren's, smothered in chocolate sauce. Then, as it's early closing, we might take her to the seaside on the open-top bus, if the weather stays fine."

Auntie never even asked me if I wanted to go, too. I wondered whether she didn't want me to come because she'd be ashamed of me in front of this friend from her smart boarding-school days, of the way I spoke or where I came from, or because Edith Shardlow might ask me about my eye, from which the purple bruising had faded to a spreading yellow stain. Maybe Auntie hadn't asked me because she didn't want to run the risk of my saying yes.

It was possible she didn't want to take Mimi, either, and was just suffering her because she didn't trust me to keep an eye on her properly.

I'd never had a banana split smothered in chocolate sauce or been to the seaside.

Auntie had smartened herself up for the occasion. When Mimi, in the little white dress with the pink and green smocking, came into the hall from the kitchen and Auntie bent down to do up her shoe buckles, I caught the whiff of mothballs.

"I'll take Mimi up to the bathroom," said Auntie. "Father Mansell is giving us a lift to the station in Dane-flete. If there's a knock at the door, make sure it's him before you answer."

I watched Mimi's little figure, her hand locked in Auntie Ida's, lifting her knees high to climb the treads, Auntie moving slowly, patiently, alongside her.

Had Auntie taken little Anne upstairs just like this? Had Mum watched the two of them, just as I was doing now?

The knocker thudded dully on the door. I opened it to Father Mansell, who smiled, touched his hat to me like a gentleman, and said the chauffeur was ready and waiting to take Mrs. Eastfield and the little girl to the station in Daneflete.

"You've got a load of dust on your hat," I told him as he came through the door.

"Oh, so I have," he said, taking it off and giving it a good brush. Then he ran his fingers nervously round and round the brim while he stood there, not quite sure what else to say to me. I was pretty sure he'd forgotten he'd met me before until I asked if he had drunk up all the Sanatogen he'd won in the raffle.

"Ah, yes, the tickets, the raffle tickets . . ." he said, his eyes taking in the cobwebs, the thick dust, the shredded curtains at the window on the stairs. "By the way, did you know there was a bowl of tomatoes in the porch, and a dead rabbit?"

"I'll tell Auntie," I said. "Erm — at the cricket, you was telling me about Mr. Scaplehorn, the rector before you," I reminded him.

"Ah, yes, so I did. He came to this house a great deal, I believe. He and Mrs. Eastfield were great friends, you know." He looked up the stairs to see if there was any sign of Auntie Ida and Mimi.

"You was saying he knew a lot about this place, and the church an' all."

"Er — yes, he — um — carried out a great deal of research into the history of this area, travelled to county record offices and up to town and all sorts of other places in his spare time — bicycled everywhere, so I'm told."

He took his handkerchief out of his pocket and mopped his forehead. I got the feeling he really didn't want to talk about Reverend Scaplehorn, or about anything really, with me.

"What did he do with all the stuff he found out, then?"

"Goodness, I've never known such a child for

235

questions. Well—er—when Mrs. Mansell and I first moved into Glebe House," the rector continued uncomfortably, "most of his papers were left behind. In one of the drawers in his desk, I found notebooks, letters, and copies he'd made of historical documents connected with Guerdon Hall, the rectory, and the church. I barely glanced at them, to be honest. I'm more of a mathematician than a historian. I'm not a great one for dwelling on the past."

He folded the handkerchief and replaced it in his pocket, then took a sideways glance at his watch while he rocked backwards and forwards, creaking in his shoes.

"I suppose you chucked it all out, then, seeing as you wasn't interested."

"No, no," he continued, taking another sneaky look up the staircase. "You can't throw things like that away. No, I popped it all in an old tin box and gave it to Mrs. Eastfield. I thought she would be the only one who might remotely want it, as most of the material concerned her family. You should ask her if she still has it. It would be a jolly thing to do on a rainy day, have a look at what's inside, as you seem to be so fascinated. It may be lying around somewhere. You'll know it because I painted *JS*, for Jasper Scaplehorn, on the lid. The box is black. Of course, it might all be frightfully boring. When Mrs. Eastfield comes down, I'll ask her about it."

"No, don't worry," I said. "If a rainy day comes, I'll

look for it." I went up three stairs and shouted, "Father Mansell's here! He's been here ages! There's a rabbit and some tomatoes in the porch!"

I heard Mimi's little feet running along the floorboards. Auntie Ida's footfalls followed.

"Leave the rabbit inside the door," she said. "Mr. Crawford will have brought it down. I'll stew it tomorrow."

Auntie shut Finn up in the house. He made such a fuss she had trouble pushing the door closed on him before she locked it.

We walked down the Chase. Father Mansell had left the Wolseley at Glebe House.

"You needn't have bothered to come down," Auntie Ida was saying. I was trying to remember where I'd seen a black box like the one the rector had described.

"Oh, I fancied the stroll," said Father Mansell. "Looks as though it's going to be a beautiful day for your outing. They say we're in for a heat wave."

"Hoo, they say all sorts of things," said Auntie Ida. "Now, are you sure you're all right to pick us up from the six forty? We can always catch the bus."

It was in the room with the painting of Old Peter, on the chest of drawers, next to the basket of baby clothes.

"No bother at all, Mrs. Eastfield. Glad to be of service, and I've a couple of jobs to do in Daneflete today anyway. I've got to check some printing they're doing for me at Cottle's, next to the Longship. Might even pop in for a little tipple. Then I'm going to call in on Edgar Selwyn at Prospect Hall. I haven't seen him for a while."

They chattered on, and then, just as we turned left to go up the hill, who should come running down it at top speed but Roger and Pete, so fast that they couldn't stop. They whizzed past us, yelling their heads off.

"I'll stop here till they come up again," I said. "See you, Mimi. Have a nice time. Cheerio, Father Mansell."

Father Mansell touched his hat, and Mimi wiggled Sid at me and I waved to him. Auntie Ida pointed in the direction of the church, shook her finger, then turned back towards the hill.

Roger and Pete were bent over with their hands on their knees, catching their breath and laughing.

"You nearly went over there, mate," said Pete.

I sat down on the grass verge and waited for them to stop panting.

"Cor, got a real stitch," said Roger, rubbing his side. "I won, though."

"Yeah, but I'll win you tomorrow," Pete said, tumbling down on the grass on his back.

"Where they all going, then?" Roger asked me.

"Auntie Ida's meeting this friend in Lokswood. Father Mansell's giving them a lift to Daneflete station. We'd better start walking up, or Auntie Ida'll be worried we're going down the church."

We dusted ourselves down and started to climb the hill. Sure enough, although they were a long way in front, Auntie Ida turned round, shaded her eyes with her hand, and looked down at us. When she was certain we were coming up behind, she turned again and continued walking with Mimi and Father Mansell.

"Look, I don't want to go down the church," I said. "I want to go back to the house. Can we just listen out for Father Mansell's car to go off first?"

"What on earth do you want to go back there for?" said Pete.

"I want to try and get in and look for something," I said. "A box. I can't look for anything with Auntie around."

"How're you going to find a box in that great big old place? Could be anywhere. What's in it, then?" said Pete.

"Just history stuff. It's a tin box. I think I might know where it is already, so we won't be long."

We carried on walking up the hill. As we passed Glebe Woods, we heard car doors slamming, an engine starting up, then the Wolseley scrunching over the gravel. As it poked its nose out of the drive to Glebe House, I saw Auntie Ida lean forward in the passenger seat, looking to see if we were still coming up the hill. I gave her a wave, then the car turned to the left and they drove off up the lane.

"Come on!" I shouted. We turned on our heels and

239

ran all the way back down the hill, so fast that we couldn't stop our legs taking us down into the Chase all on their own.

As we got up to the house, Finn started barking. We went into the porch at the front, and I tried rattling the huge door. I heard the dog's claws padding towards us over the floorboards, and he gruffed and whined at us from the other side.

"Let's try the windows," I said to Roger, pulling him away from the spot on the path where he was staring up at the carving of the crying baby.

"Look, they've all been nailed up, every one of them," he said as we moved from one window to the next towards the back of the house, framing our faces with our hands and peering through the glass into the rooms as we went. Long rusty iron nails had been hammered into the ledges hard up against the frames so that the windows couldn't be opened.

"Someone must've been really scared of burglars," said Pete.

"Must be boiling hot in there," said Roger as we got to the back garden. "Won't any of them open at all? Poor old dog must be baking."

"Auntie's left him some water. He'll be all right," I said. "Remember I told you I opened my window the other night? It was a heck of a job. The nails was so rusty, they broke. Look, that's my bedroom."

I pointed upwards to the damaged window frame. Among the dandelions on the path we found splinters of wood, so rotten they crumbled in our fingers.

"Look here!" said Roger. "Look at this! What's happened here?"

We were standing in the cobbled yard between the two wings of the house; a mass of ivy had spread itself over the eaves and up onto the roof. Somehow, whole branches, their torn ends still white and fresh, had been ripped off and lay on the path on a carpet of scattered leaves.

"Somebody's climbed up it," said Roger.

"Right up to the roof," Pete added, pointing. "Look, those tiles have slipped."

"Was it your auntie?" asked Roger.

"What would she flippin' well have gone up on the roof for? To get a suntan?"

We moved on around the house, thumping on the nailed-up windows, with Finn barking at us occasionally from inside, until we reached the far side of the garden where Auntie had forbidden Mimi and me to go because of the well. Under the trees were drifts of stinging nettles and knotted brambles as vicious as barbed wire. The blackberries were sweet after the few days of sunshine.

On the outside of the end wall of the house was an enormous stone chimney, rising up from below ground level. The house was badly sunken in on this side, for along the bottom of the wall, on either side of the chimney, were the very tops of windows, criss-crossed with iron bars. The glass was cracked and dirty and almost obscured by weeds, grass, and old rotting leaves.

To one side of this massive chimney was another, smaller chimney of bricks, obviously added much later. I pressed my face to the nearest window and saw that this more recent chimney rose up behind the big black stove in Auntie Ida's kitchen.

"Look," said Roger. "Someone's been digging."

A few feet from the wall, heaps of fresh damp earth were piled up around three sides of a dark hole.

"Careful," he said, approaching gingerly. "Might be the well." He knelt down on the flattened grass, spread out his hands on either side, and leaned over. "Chuck a stone in, Pete!"

It landed almost immediately, with a soft thud.

"Don't sound like a well to me," I said, kneeling down beside Roger and peering over the grassy edges of the hole. "It ain't deep enough, unless they've stuck a lid on. Here, lower me down."

"Don't be stupid. If there is a lid, it's most probably rotten, and then you'll fall through and drown."

"Hang on to me arms."

"You're bonkers. Here, Pete. Come and help."

242

They held my hands, and I wriggled backwards. My feet touched a firm surface that gave a little as I moved. I straightened up, only in up to my knees.

"Be ready to grab me," I said, "and give us a stick."

Pete found a short piece of dead branch. I scratched with it around my feet. Most of the soil had been removed. I found I was standing on wooden planks that sank in slightly when I changed position. I moved with care. The stick scraped over metal, two muddy rings linked by an old iron chain.

Suddenly a piece of plank sheered off. My foot dropped into a jagged hole. I felt a jab of pain, lurched, and grabbed the boys' arms. They pulled me out. My ankle was bleeding.

"It's trapdoors, with rings you pull them up with," I said, blotting the blood with my filthy sock. "They've got them just the same in the street round the back of the Half Moon at home. The men from the brewery roll the barrels down off the cart and into the cellar."

"I still think it's the well," said Roger. "That's what your auntie said. And they've put these door things on to stop people falling in."

"Yeah, maybe," I said, "but we'd better move away. Come on, Pete. The wood's gone rotten. Be careful."

Pete stared over the edge. "Who's dug it all out, then?" he said. "Was it Mrs. Eastfield? What does she want a blimmin' great hole in her garden for?"

The house was nailed and barred so completely we could find no way in. I was really irritated.

"Do you want to look at the old pillbox from the war?" Roger suggested as we walked up the hill towards Bryers Guerdon. "Dad said soldiers sat in there eating sandwiches, playing cards, and looking out for Hitler."

The stream, overhung with trees on the hilltop side, ran under the road and marked the boundary between two fields, one on the flat land at the top of the hill that led all the way to the main road, and the other on the slope.

"It goes along the back of the pillbox"—Roger pointed out its course with his finger—"and through all the fields from Bryers Guerdon to South Fairing and Daneflete. Then it gets much wider and ends up in the estuary."

The barred gate into the field was farther down the hill, so instead of walking back, we squeezed through a gap in the hedge. The sloes and hawthorns scratched our arms and legs half to death.

The tall yellow wheat, almost ripe for harvesting, was spread out before us, moving gently in curving waves under the blue, cloudless sky. Among the stalks, clusters of poppies held their scarlet flower cups up to the hot sun.

"This way," Roger cried, plunging into the wheat.

"Ain't the farmer going to blow his top if he sees us squashing his field?"

"No, it's only old Ferguson. He's a great big bloke with a face like a big purple balloon. He'd never catch us. He can't run for toffee."

Pete and I trailed upwards through the field behind Roger, stamping down the wheat as we went. I tore up some poppies and held them in a loose bunch.

The pillbox was a plain concrete bunker standing in front of the stream and the hedgerow behind it. It had been abandoned for so many years that the wildflowers and nettles grew tall and lush for yards around it, and the briars, bristling with rose hips, rose as high as the windows, open slits that faced the marshes and the river and the sea beyond.

A thick extra wall stood about two feet away from the doorway. Roger said it was to shield the soldiers from bomb blasts and to provide a bit of extra shelter from the wind and rain, but it looked like the entrance to a gents' toilet to me.

Inside, it smelled like a gents' toilet as well. I held my breath.

"I bet that Mr. Ferguson's wee'd in here," I said, gulping in air.

"And more than once," said Roger.

It was impossible to see anything in the darkness at first, but little by little I made out the shapes of old smashed bottles, sweet papers, newspapers, and other rubbish trodden into the damp earth floor.

"Pete and me were going to make a camp here once," said Roger, "but we didn't want to sit down—"

"Or eat anything," added Pete, "in case we got a disease."

"Imagine if you was a soldier and had to stay in here all night long, waiting for the invasion," I said. "It must have made you want to be sick."

"Yeah, but they wouldn't have wee'd in it then," said Roger. "They'd have gone outside."

Pete began to hop from one foot to the other. "Why did you have to start talking about widdling?" he said. "I'm nipping out for a minute."

I'm not sure how long it was before Roger and I fell silent, beginning to feel that there was something outside, something that wasn't Pete.

When did we start to hear the low, swishing, crunching noise of something coming nearer and nearer still, pushing its way through the wheat? When did we first notice the smell, like something old, damp, and rotten, stronger even than the smell inside the pillbox? Why did we look at each other with great wide-open eyes, not daring to blink, not daring even to whisper?

Why did my skin tingle and my breath become a shallow tremor?

We slid our eyes towards the doorway.

A huge black shadow was moving slowly across the concrete slabs of the outside wall, in the shape of a long, crawling man. As it neared the entrance, the shadow loomed up, so massive that it shut out every inch of sunlight on the wall.

A hand, with thin, almost transparent, blotched flesh, crooked, bony fingers, and curved black fingernails like iron claws, reached out and curled around the edge of the doorway.

It waited for a moment, then made a rattling, rasping sound as if it were drawing in breath, or *smelling*.

There was no way out. My legs began to tremble. The flowers fell from my hand. My head swam. I felt myself swaying.

Suddenly I realized Roger was holding me up. My knees had given way. I had sunk down halfway to the floor.

"It's gone! It's gone!" croaked Roger.

"Pete! Where's Pete?" I panted. We roused ourselves and rushed out through the doorway.

Pete was crashing through the bushes on the other side of the ditch, then he jumped over it and landed on the bank.

"We going home now?" he chirped.

"Yeah," said Roger weakly. "Yeah, mate."

"Blimey, what's the matter with you two? Look like you've seen a ghost."

As Pete leaped through the wheat on his way to the gap in the hedge, Roger and I stood and stared at the flattened trails through the field. One track, ours, curved towards the lane. In the other track something large and heavy was moving, on all fours, towards the edge of the graveyard beyond the hedgerow at the bottom. Where the wheat had been crushed, the channel ran blood-red with the scattered petals of broken poppies.

ROGER

We put together some matchbox boats for Dennis and Terry, like the ones Dad had made in the flood, a little twig pushed through a square of paper for a sail stuck on with a small ball of Plasticine. The Plasticine has to be placed just right or the boat will keel over.

We pushed them round the pond with garden canes and had quite a nice little fleet going, until Dennis picked an argument with Terry, went crazy, chucked handfuls of stones in the water, and sank half of the boats. When Terry wailed, Dennis hit him with his cane and made a huge red mark. Mum came running out of the house and walloped him.

Dinner was toad-in-the-hole and mash, but I hadn't much of an appetite. Mum felt my forehead and asked if I was coming down with something. After dinner we turned on the hose. Dennis and Terry loved it, whooping up and down the garden in their pants, shrieking, while Cora and I chased after them, spraying their legs with jets of cold water, but with no heart for laughing.

Cora became more and more quiet as the afternoon wore on.

"I'd better get back," she said as we hid behind the shed to avoid the washing-up. "Auntie Ida and Mimi'll be home by now."

I walked with her up Ottery Lane. The shadows of the trees were long on the road.

"I'm going to try and find that tin box," she said. "It's got a load of Mr. Scaplehorn's things in it. I bet there's stuff in there we should know."

"You're going to have to be careful, though," I said, "or you'll end up with another black eye."

Cora looked down at the ground. "I should have said before," she said. "Maybe I'm going mad, but last time I went in that room, I heard this woman, singing. . . ."

"Was it your auntie Ida?"

"No, she'd gone outside in the rain, to the chickens."

"Maybe somebody else is living in the house. Have you asked her?"

"Roger, there ain't nobody else living in that flaming house, I'm telling you!"

"They could be hiding."

249

"Why would anybody be flippin' well hiding? Use your blinking common sense."

"Are you saying it's a ghost, then?"

"How the flaming hell would I know? I—I asked her who she was."

"Flippin' heck! Did she say anything?"

"*'Kittie.'* She said, *'I am Kittie.'*"

"We've—we've seen some queer things, Cora."

"Forget it. I'm most probably just going bonkers. That flippin' house'd drive anybody up the wall."

"Shall I call for you tomorrow?"

"No, don't worry. I'll bring Mimi up. Cheerio."

Cora crossed over the main road by herself.

❧ CORA ❧

I knew it wasn't Roger, or Pete, or me it was hunting. It wanted smaller children than we were. That's why it left us alone in the pillbox. It took little ones like Anne and—and Mimi, like the small souls in the graveyard.

I reached the brow of the hill. As I stood and listened to the trickling of the stream running underneath the lane, an evening blackbird warbled its loud, clear song from the hedgerow. I took a few paces forward and shivered. Crossing over the hidden water, I felt I was moving from somewhere that was safe and comforting to another place altogether, a place that was uncertain and dangerous.

I gazed across the marshes. Among the soft grey reed beds, the warm light was glimmering golden on the water in the pools. Perhaps there are places people should never live in, never even go to, no matter how beautiful they seem to be.

Auntie Ida and Mimi weren't back yet. I knew it even before I reached Guerdon Hall. As I drew near, I could hear Finn howling. I imagined his claws had been clattering aimlessly over the floorboards all day long.

I was too scared to go round to the back of the house on my own. I didn't even want to go over the bridge.

Instead, I picked my way through the old farm machinery to the big barn with its door half hanging off. The walls were dark brown wooden boards, the roof tiled like the house. A rusty old gent's bike lay half-hidden in the dirty straw, its tyres flat as pancakes. It looked as if the barn hadn't been cleaned out since cows were there. I pulled some of the straw over to the doorway and made myself a cushion, then sat down to watch for anything coming along the Chase.

Tears began to spill out of my eyes. I didn't want to be here with that great dog howling like nobody was going to let it out ever again, and no one near me, just all that sky, and the trees rustling and the dried mud in the road. I wanted to be far away from that big old sinking house and the skeleton cottages opposite, with their weeds and broken windows like empty blind eyes. What were all these things that were happening here, and that had happened before—horrible things that I couldn't understand?

I wanted to be back in Limehouse—Dad with his feet stuck up on the mantelpiece reading the *Eagle* and Mum in the kitchen making scrambled egg on toast.

❧ IDA EASTFIELD ❧

I should have known Hugh Mansell would let us down. Even the best of clergymen have their weaknesses, just like the rest of us. Father Mansell's is his fondness for whisky. A couple of glasses of Buchanan's with Edgar Selwyn in Daneflete and the last thing on his mind would have been the six-forty train.

I only hope he and the Wolseley got home in one piece. I waited for him too long, then carried Mimi over two miles before a bus came.

Where is Cora? If she's at the Jotmans', how will I get her home? Surely she won't be down here on her own.

I trudge down the darkening Chase. Mimi is heavy in my arms. In her sleep, she still clings to Sid and the coloured windmill on a stick from the seaside. Her pretty smocked dress is smeared with chocolate sauce.

In the house, Finn is howling like a wolf. As a single star begins to twinkle low in the sky beside the rising moon, a small dark figure moves towards me from the barn.

✿ CORA ✿

After slipping off Mimi's grubby dress and tucking her up in bed, I went down and made Auntie Ida a cup of tea. She was flaked out in the kitchen, rubbing her feet through her stockings. We ate some cold sausages left over from the evening before, then cleared up the bloody mess by the front door where Finn had helped himself to the rabbit and scattered and squashed the tomatoes.

I only vaguely remember dragging myself back upstairs for the night, too exhausted to think about searching for the box.

THURSDAY 21st AUGUST

❦ CORA ❧

I expected to sleep long into the morning, and for Auntie to be so weary that she would let me be, but I was woken by a bark, followed by the sound of the back door opening then shutting. In the quiet of the early morning I heard the big iron key turning in the back-door lock, its loud distinctive click echoing down the stone passage leading to the kitchen. Finn barked again.

Gripped by both bewilderment and fear, I jumped out of bed and dashed to the window. I pulled aside the curtains a little and peeped out. Hearing footsteps and looking down, I saw, in the half-light of dawn, Auntie Ida, wearing her coat and scarf, walking along the path under my window. She continued round the corner of the house and out of sight. Where was she going? It was far too early to get the milk. Why would she leave the two of us alone?

I was too alert to return to bed, so decided that now Auntie had gone out, I would look for Jasper Scaplehorn's box. I'd heard Auntie locking us in. Finn was downstairs. If anything happened, I would hear him bark.

I picked up Mimi's windmill from where it had dropped on the floor and put it next to her on the pillow, then I opened the door and set off along the landing. I passed Auntie's empty bedroom, then paused where the passage turns to the left, just before the three steps, and looked out of the window to check she wasn't coming back. In the garden, pale sunlight was spreading itself across the grass until each moist blade glittered in its own coat of dew. There was no sign of her.

I ran up the three steps, along the passage, down the other side, and through the musty corridor, then stopped outside the door at the end and lifted the latch.

The room and the far room beyond were dark as night, the windows obscured by some heaving, humming mass, shutting out the light of the coming day.

I moved forward across the floorboards, leaned in towards the window, then reeled back in shock.

It was thickly covered with huge flies, crawling over the diamond panes, their fat black-and-white bodies packed tightly together. Flesh flies—flies that don't bother to lay eggs, just maggots. Nan told me about them once.

As I gazed in horror, little patches of light began to appear on the glass. Flies were lifting off and heading for the open door behind me, buzzing close to my head, brushing against my body, landing for a moment, then taking off.

Where would they go to in a house where the windows were always shut tight, the doors always locked? They might fly around the house for ever and ever. Round and round. Up and down the stairs. In and out of the rooms. Big dirty flies. Going into the kitchen cupboards. Filling up the pantry. Crawling on the food.

Shivering with disgust, I crossed to the chest of drawers and looked at the box I had noticed before. It was a black tin, about a foot square, scratched and spotted with rust. On the lid were two neatly painted gold letters: *JS*. I breathed deeply, stroked the lid, then picked up the box, surprised at how heavy it was. I glanced behind at Piers Hillyard, staring at me from his frame. A fly crawled across his face.

On the slab at the bottom of the stone fireplace, I noticed something shrivelled. I couldn't tell what it might once have been—maybe part of a bird or animal that had fallen down the chimney from the roof and had lain there in the hearth, a feast for the maggots. I took up the heavy iron poker that was leaning against the wall and prodded it. It was like a piece of dried-up, grey-coloured skin.

Back in my bedroom, I dragged the wooden chair over to the window so I could look out for Auntie Ida.

"What you doing, Cora? Is it breakfast?"

"'S all right, Mimi. Ain't time yet. Go back to sleep."

256

I sat down with the box on my knees, then broke two fingernails before I got it open. The underside of the lid gleamed like new, with a sunburst pattern in bright yellow and green surrounding the words: HORNER'S CREAM TOFFEE — THE TOFFEE OF SUPERLATIVE TASTE.

The box was full of old papers, all different shapes and sizes, white and crisp, old and yellow, brown and flaky round the edges, torn, folded, and creased. There were pages ripped out of jotters, some printed, some out of old newspapers, and others written by hand. At the bottom of the box was a burgundy leather-bound notebook, about four inches by three. I put the papers on the floor beside me and lifted out the book. Flicking through the handwritten pages, I noticed the writing was untidy, rushed, sometimes upright, then occasionally sloping to the right, with words heavily scratched out or corrected, and all over the place, little sprays of ink as if the writer had been careless of the deep pressure of the nib on the page.

Each of the entries had been signed *JS*—Jasper Scaplehorn.

I put it back in the box and took up an envelope from the top of the pile on the floor. It was made of beautiful thick cream paper, embossed with the words DIOCESE OF LOKSWOOD.

It had been opened cleanly with a paper knife. I read the letter inside.

The Bishop's House
Lokswood

30th September 1940

Dear Jasper,

With reference to your recent letter, the Bishop is very happy to make any documents you require available to you. I am usually to be found in the library on Monday and Tuesday afternoons between 2 o'clock and 4 o'clock. Just call in and I will be happy to help you to track down the relevant material. Come at 1 o'clock and we'll have lunch.

Tuesday is Mrs. Berry's day off, so if you come then, I'll take you to the Blue Anchor. Their mushroom soup is delicious.

I look forward very much to seeing you again. It has been too long.

Kindest regards,

Henry Massinger
Archivist to the Diocese of Lokswood

I replaced the letter in its envelope and took up the leather notebook again. On the very first page was scrawled:

The Norman knight, Guillaume de Guerdon, landed with the Conqueror and fought alongside the Duke at Hastings. William rewarded his faithful knight with the land at Bryers and the gift is recorded in Domesday. The land, bordered by Daneflete and Faring to the east and Hilsey marshes to the west, is rich and fertile.

The Guerdons built their house down on the marshlands, originally fortified and almost completely surrounded by a natural creek, to more easily defend it against the Saxon dispossessed. They also built the church, All Hallows, and became lords over the cattle herders and shepherds who dwelt there.

War, pestilence, and famine passed through Bryers Guerdon on their way along the world as they've always done and the tides came and went, rose and ebbed, day upon day upon week and month and year upon year.

The church is peculiarly isolated. At the present day the village of Bryers Guerdon lies away to the north, and the ancient quiet of the immediate surroundings remains undisturbed. The church was erected on a site in a central position between the dwellings of the peasants on the marshes and the house of the lord of the manor, which was Guerdon Hall.

One of the earliest military effigies in England lies in the sanctuary beside the altar. It is of Sir John Guerdon, d. 1348, probably of the Black Death.

In the age of the first Elizabeth, Sir Edmund Carey

Guerdon was the lord of the manor. He married Ygurne,
youngest daughter of the old family of Pleshett, and it was
in their time that Cain Lankin lived rough on the marshes.

I closed the book and put it back in the box, then
reached down for more letters.

Hunsham Vicarage
Hunsham Parva
Lokswood

13th February 1941

My dear Jasper,

The Bishop has asked me to write to you, as your old friend,
and in confidence, as he feels I may be able to make more
headway with you than he has been able to do hitherto. I
am aware that things are a little strained between the two
of you at present, but I am writing in good faith, to let
you know that he is extremely anxious about your well-
being, particularly in the light of the illness from which
you suffered some years ago.

He felt that the solitude and relative ease of the living
at Bryers Guerdon would be to your benefit, but now feels
he may have been misguided in suggesting it to you. In
his report following your recent consultation at Coldwell

Hospital, Dr. Rowstone has recommended that a transfer to a busier parish, with a curate to assist you and keep you company, may be in your best interests. The Bishop will inform you of a suitable vacancy should one arise.

The Bishop feels it is imperative that you dissociate yourself from the bizarre rumours that appear to be circulating in Bryers Guerdon concerning the disappearance of little Anne Swift last summer. You mention in your most recent letter that you feel that some kind of supernatural agent was also involved in the death of Edward Eastfield in August 1925. I can only reiterate what the Bishop has already written to you in the course of your lengthy correspondence: that the police investigated both disappearances most thoroughly, with all the resources and manpower at their disposal, and came to the conclusion that there was no evidence whatsoever of any activity of this kind.

It was agreed that the marshland to the rear of Guerdon Hall is treacherous, and that, unfortunately, once the small body of a young child was sucked down under the mud or the water, it would be extremely difficult to locate it, especially in a desolate area such as this, covering many square miles and extending all the way to the estuary. You have been told this on several occasions, and yet you insist on troubling the Bishop with your deluded theories (his words, Jasper, not mine).

My old friend, for the last time, he will absolutely not

261

condone any further investigation into the area around All Hallows church. He maintains that you, as an ordained minister of the Church, should lead by example, and that it is your paramount duty to allay suspicions of this dubious nature among your parishioners. Superstitious beliefs persist in some rural areas, and you must be seen to discourage them. We are, after all, living in the twentieth century and not in the Dark Ages, although I have to say, in this time of war, I truly wonder how far we have come.

If you continue to give credence to these wild and preposterous ideas, the Bishop feels that you will seriously interfere with the natural process of grieving most necessary to the well-being of the Swift family, and indeed of Mrs. Ida Eastfield, who we understand is suffering tremendously under the strain of these events. It must be a huge burden to her, to bear the weight of guilt that two children in her immediate care have been lost in this way in separate incidents many years apart, compounded by the added misery of the death of her husband, William Eastfield. The investigations into his demise proved inconclusive, but it is generally believed that he took his own life while suffering a mental breakdown following the disappearance of his son.

Mrs. Eastfield needs your unremitting support and spiritual guidance at this time. We understand that in the circumstances she naturally fell under suspicion, resulting in her having to undergo the most extensive and humiliating investigations by the police, most mortifying for anyone, let alone a lady of her social standing.

You bear heavy responsibilities for many people in your parish in these difficult years. We understand that Mrs. Avis Goodwin, of Ottery Lane, lost her husband during the evacuation of Dunkirk, leaving her with three small children. The parents and sister of another parishioner, Mrs. Josephine Bennett, have been killed in a bombing raid which destroyed her old family home in Shadwell, and now she will be expected to bring up the two nephews who have been staying with her since the beginning of the war, as well as her own four children.

These people need your care and attention, Jasper. The sexton, Reginald Hibbert, informed us of these needy families so that we might assist them with monies from the Bishop's Fund. If he had not done so, we would not have been made aware of their difficulties. You absolutely must not neglect the duties imposed upon you by your calling.

I beg you to consider carefully all that I have written, Jasper. The Bishop will not enter into any further correspondence with you at present, but will pass on to me any letters from you unopened, so I will be dealing with you directly for the foreseeable future. He told me to make sure I informed you of this so that you know that any further *petitioning would be futile. Naturally, he will continue to support you in regard to the usual parochial matters. I know you do not wish to be transferred to another living, and I will do my utmost to prevent it, but I have little confidence in succeeding if you persist in continuing along the path you have chosen.*

On a personal note, you know my door is always open to you, Jasper. I still have some of that fine Napoleon brandy we brought back from France in '32.

Most sincerely and humbly, your friend,

Martin Godfrey Gilbert

Suddenly I heard footsteps on the path below. Out of the corner of my eye, I noticed a movement outside and peered through the window. Auntie Ida was coming along the side of the house. She quickly looked round and up, and I pulled my head back, hoping she hadn't seen me. I heard the big key turning in the lock and the sound of Finn's paws on the stone flags as he went to meet her.

Auntie wouldn't expect me to be awake yet. I was sure it was safe to read more and opened another letter. It had been written over four years after the one before.

Hunsham Vicarage
Hunsham Parva
Lokswood

25th June 1945

My dear Jasper,

A new beginning for all of us, I sincerely hope. I trust all is much better with you and that eventually you will recover fully. I was most distressed that you did not appear to recognize me all the time you were in Coldwell Hospital, so it was with a lighter heart that I left you after my visit to Bryers Guerdon on Tuesday last. Your spirits seem to be somewhat restored, and I am assured by Dr. Meldrum that eventually most of your memories will return to you. Sometimes treatments that seem the most harsh and brutal do us the greatest good.

Mrs. Eastfield informed me that your temporary replacement, young John Fox-Leigh, kept All Hallows locked up during your absence and conducted all the services at Saint Mary's, North Fairing. I understand his wife was uncomfortable with All Hallows and didn't like to be in the building, but we all know how women can be when they are anticipating a happy event. I well remember Audrey when Bernard was on the way—she suffered from nightmares, too.

As soon as you feel able, I urge you to reopen the church or the fabric of the building will deteriorate beyond help. I understand it suffers dreadfully from damp and is prone to smells. It could do with a regular dose of fresh air. Perhaps a Victory Thanksgiving service would be appropriate and encourage a joyful association with this church. I am aware that your parishioners favour North Fairing, even though All Hallows is strictly their parish church. It would be a great tragedy if it fell into disuse and disrepair. It is a beautiful old building.

I must let you know, Jasper, that I have gone to great trouble on your behalf to persuade the Bishop to let you stay on as rector of Bryers Guerdon. I know you do not wish to leave the place, so I urge you to keep your peace with him. Please do not make things more difficult for yourself than they are already. Fortunately, Bryers Guerdon is not an arduous living, and I feel sure you will gradually be restored to your former strength, and will be able to manage your duties perfectly well.

One last thing: the Bishop wishes to go ahead with the plans to divide Glebe House into two separate dwellings. As you are aware, for a long time now he has felt it to be much too large for modern needs. Representatives from the Ecclesiastical Commissioners will be getting in touch with you in the near future to arrange a meeting to discuss the proposals.

Look after yourself, Jasper. Let me know if there is anything I can do for you.

Your most sincere friend,

Martin Godfrey Gilbert

Almost feverish with curiosity, and hardly knowing what to look at next, I went back to the notebook.

Glebe House

7th April 1947

I must write, for I fear I am losing my remaining reason and what is left of my memory. I know what they are saying about me in Bishop's House. Martin tells me, may God bless him, but it is difficult for him, I know, for he must remain the Bishop's man. When I am alone, and it is late into the night, I sometimes wonder if they are right, because it seems like madness, but I have seen the children in the churchyard. They are trapped in a place that Hillyard called the half-world. I have seen him, too, keeping his eternal vigil, in recompense for what he did, always watching with his poor burned face.

Haldane Thorston has entrusted to my view the

documents rescued from Old Glebe House by his forebear,
who risked everything to save them from the conflagration.
Piers Hillyard, it seems, attempted to destroy the beast with
flame and expired in the attempt (if only I could say God
rest his soul), but he could not have succeeded, for it cannot
be vanquished with the elements of this world. It hung in
the air, was buried in the earth, was burned with fire, and,
as far as I can understand, avoids the water. I believe it is
sustained by the energy in the lifeblood of the very young.

"And the Lord said unto Cain: And now art thou
cursed from the earth. . . . And Cain said unto the Lord:
Behold, thou hast driven me out from the face of the earth;
and from thy face shall I be hid; and I shall be a fugitive and
a vagabond in the earth. . . ."

I must find out more. . . . God help us all.

JS

Then, on the next page:

23 November 25 Eliz. Indictment of Aphra Rushes of
Shersted, Boxton, Bryers Guerdon and others, spinster,
*being a common enchantress and witch (*communis
incantatrix et magica*), as well of men as of beasts and*
other things, and exercising art of witchcraft, sorcery, and
enchantment, not having God before her eyes but led by
diabolical instigation, of her malice aforethought, contrary

to the Act of 5 Eliz., cunningly bewitched and enchanted John, son of Edmund Carey Guerdon, knight, at Guerdon Hall, Bryers Guerdon, aged 1 year, whereof he died 1 August 25 Eliz.; and that the said Aphra bewitched Ygurne, wife of the same Edmund Carey Guerdon, knt., at Guerdon Hall, Bryers Guerdon, on 1 August and thereby killed her, and that the said Aphra Rushes by her charms and enchantments and of her malice aforethought slew and murdered the said John Guerdon and Ygurne Guerdon.

A witch.

Denied.

Fails to confess.

Judgement that she be returned to prison and be pilloried four times for 6 hours and each time to confess her offence.

Indictments of felony taken anno 25 and certified to the next Assizes.

I turned over.

16 December 25 Eliz. Inquisition held in the Mote Hall at Lokswood taken before Robert Lord Myldmaye, Thomas Petrie, John Fawkes, Henry Cottingly, knts., William Chunce, Thomas Vernon, Edmund Purton, and Henry Coker, esqs., and others. The jurors say that the said Aphra Rushes of Shersted and Bryers Guerdon, spinster, there bewitched and killed the said John Guerdon, son of Edmund

Carey Guerdon, knt., and Ygurne Guerdon, wife of the same.

Judgement according to the form of the Statute Incendetur ad Cindres (to be burned to ashes).

My hands had gone clammy and left marks on the fine paper.

Thereupon the Judge proceeded and pronounced the sentence of death against her, as worthily she had deserved. After she had received her judgement, she was conveyed from the bar back again to prison, where she had not stayed above two hours but the officers prepared themselves to conduct her to the place of execution, which is Bryers Guerdon. To which place they led her, and being come thither, on the day appointed, one master Fortyce, a learned divine, being desired by the justices, did exhort this wicked woman to repentance, and persuade her that she should show unto the people the truth of her wickedness, and to call upon God for mercy with a penitent heart, and to ask pardon at His hands for the same. But she would not so, and went to die deserving of the punishment of the law.

Suddenly I heard a noise — Auntie Ida's footsteps on the stairs.

As quickly as I could, I gathered up the papers from

the floor, tiptoed across to the bed, jumped in with the box, the notebook, and everything, and covered myself right up to my chin with the eiderdown. I held my breath and squeezed my eyes tight shut. The box was hard and cold against me, and a corner of the leather book dug into my neck.

Mimi turned over.

Auntie Ida stopped outside the door, listening. I was holding my breath so long I thought I'd die.

I hadn't shut the curtains. Would she see the strip of light under the door and know I was awake?

The latch clicked. I swallowed. The papers rustled slightly. I didn't dare, dare move.

The latch went back down again. There was quiet for a minute, then I heard Auntie's feet moving away down the passage towards her own room. Her door opened with a creak, then banged shut. I came out from under the covers, and my breath rushed out.

I put the loose paper and letters back in the box and rested it on the eiderdown between Mimi and me, then sat up and propped the soft feather pillow behind my head.

I opened the notebook once more. The warm sunlight streamed across the bed. I pulled the eiderdown up around me. Mimi's little toes touched my legs, but as I read, I began to feel a creeping chill in my bones.

❦ ROGER ❧

Cora was banging on the back door. I was only up because Dad woke me before he went to work saying Mum wasn't feeling too good, so could I take her a cup of tea in bed.

"Blimey, you're early," I said, peering round the door, trying to hide the cowboy pyjamas I'd got from Grandma.

"I've got to show you something! It's really important!" Cora was breathless. She pushed her way in, dragging Mimi, looking bleary-eyed, behind her.

"Don't slam it! Mum's still in bed. Pamela's had a fever and been sick all night. Mum's whacked. I don't think Terry's all that well, either. Keep Mimi in here for a minute."

I took Mum her tea, though I don't think she noticed, then I went into my bedroom to find myself some clothes. Pete was still asleep.

My old shirt from yesterday was still on the floor, so I stuck it on again. Just as I shut the door, I heard a horrible retching noise coming from Terry and Dennis's room. I waited for a few seconds, hoping Mum would come, but when she didn't, I knew I'd have to go in.

Terry came lurching towards me and whooshed sick

all over my shirt and trousers. Smartly I took a step backwards and the rest sprayed over the lino.

"Blinkin' hell, Terry!" I yelled.

"I was trying to get to the toilet," he said, wiping his mouth on the back of his hand. "I feel horrible, Roger. Ooh, there's more coming. . . ."

And it did.

❧ CORA ❧

We didn't know how to start off the washing machine, so filled up the bath with hot water and tipped in the whole packet of powder. Then we dumped the clothes in and swished them around with a wooden spoon from the kitchen.

Baby Pamela started crying, so Roger got her from his mum's room. I could see Mrs. Jotman through the crack of the door, flaked out on the bed. Pamela smelled awful. Roger said I should change her nappy, but luckily Mrs. Jotman, her eyes bloodshot and her hair sticking out, came and took the baby.

We tried mopping Terry's bedroom floor with a bottle of Dettol and made him stay in the bathroom in case he was sick again.

Dennis and Mimi went to play in the garden. Pete

was still fast asleep. Mrs. Jotman wandered around rocking Pamela in her arms, trying to make up her mind whether or not to bother the doctor.

❧ ROGER ❧

We couldn't find much in the cupboard, so made ourselves some sugar sandwiches, then sat side by side in the crook of the big oak tree.

Cora took a small leather notebook and some old squashed letters out of her pocket.

"They've all come out of that box I told you about," she said. "I found it. Auntie went out first thing, really early, and I sneaked in and got it."

"Where's the box now?"

"I hid it under the bed. I couldn't bring all the stuff that's in it, but this is the most important. I had to wear these trousers because they were the only things I had with a pocket big enough. Look at this."

She opened the notebook and forced it under my nose.

"It's rotten handwriting," I said, reading.

She would not so, and went to die deserving of the punishment of the law.

"What's all this about, then?" I said, when I'd finished

274

all the letters and pages Cora wanted me to read for the time being. "It's horrible."

"And that Anne Swift in the letter is the girl in the photo from the paper in your mum's scrapbook. And — and she's the same little girl in the graveyard, the one with her arms out. On my mum's side, they're all Swifts, you know. Mum's name was Swift before she married my dad. Her mum was Auntie Ida's sister, Agnes Guerdon, and her dad was One-Eyed Jack Swift. Dad and Auntie Ida said something about Anne when he came. I overheard them. It's all something to do with my family."

I looked over the letters again.

"You see this — Coldwell Hospital," I pointed out, "where it says Mr. Scaplehorn went — it's an asylum, where people go when — when they've gone mad. It's out in the country on the other side of Lokswood. In the Easter holidays when Mum was having Terry, Dad had to go over there to do some surveying. He took Pete and Dennis and me with him to keep us out from under Mum's feet.

"We went through some huge gates in this great high wall with bits of broken glass stuck in the top. He left us in the car while he went in to do whatever he had to do. There were lots of little windows with bars across, and the walls went up and up. I saw a face look out, and they had a white nightie thing on, even though I think it was a man, and I was really scared till Dad got back."

"Maybe Mr. Scaplehorn was going crazy then. . . . Look at this," said Cora, thumbing through the leather notebook again and showing me a page.

Applications were made to the Bishops of Lokswood in 1753, 1812, and then in 1878, and again in 1902 to carry out the Rite of Exorcism at Guerdon Hall, Bryers Guerdon, each time by request of the Guerdon family. "What's this word here?" She jabbed her finger at the word *Exorcism.* "Look, it says the names of the priests who did it— *'Francis Payne, Inigo Ryecart, Percival Wormald'*—"

"Hang on a minute," I said, getting up. "I'll go and get my dictionary."

The house still smelled revolting and was full of steam from the big pan bubbling away on the gas, full of boiling nappies. Mum was opening the windows. She said Terry had been sick again, so I might have to go down to Mrs. Aylott's to get more Dettol. Pete was tying up his shoes, ready to pop down to fetch Dr. Meldrum from North End.

I found my dictionary under a cushion on the settee in the sitting room. It was open on the *B*s. Pete must have been looking up *bloomers* or *bosoms* again.

I took the book outside and we found the word *exorcism*. Apparently it was a ritual carried out in a haunted place by a priest with a special licence from the bishop to make ghosts or evil spirits go away.

"But those exorcisms couldn't have worked, could

they," I said, "or they wouldn't have had to keep asking to do them all over again."

"Then here, look," said Cora. "The Guerdon family asked for some sort of ceremony — maybe the same thing, maybe an exorcism, but it doesn't say — in the churchyard, and that was in 1910!"

"Crikey!" I said. "Mrs. Eastfield must have known about it. It would have been a big thing. She must have been about our age."

"Well, we know that whatever they did, it didn't make any difference because we've seen things in the church-yard ourselves. And look at this. . . ." Cora searched quickly through the notebook. "It's the most biggest thing of all —"

Just then, a plump lady in a dark-blue uniform came round the side of the house. She spotted us in the tree.

"Hello there, Roger!" she cried. "Dr. Meldrum is tied up, so I've come instead. Ha, ha — when I say 'tied up,' I mean he's busy, not that a robber's got him. Ha, ha. There's a lot of this about, this sickness. Is your mum inside?"

I jumped down. "Oh, yes. She'll be really glad to see you, Nurse."

She went up the veranda steps and knocked on the frame of the back door, which was standing wide open. "Hello!" she called. "It's Nurse Smallbone, Mrs. Jotman!" before disappearing inside.

"Funny name for a big lady," Cora said.

"She brought all of us into the world," I told her. "It's a shame, though—when Dennis was on the way, Nurse Smallbone was rushing up Fieldpath Road in her old Ford Prefect to get to Mum when our dog, Bonzo, shot out in the road right into her car—*smack bang*—dead as a doornail. He was a great dog, old Bonzo. I can't tell you how many times I wish we still had him instead of Dennis."

Mum came to the door and called to us, rubbing her forehead with her hand. "Can you go down to Mrs. Aylott's and get some more Dettol and washing powder? Here's the money."

We were on our way back, and at the bottom of Fieldpath Road, when I pulled Cora's arm and stopped her.

"Here," I said, "can't you let me see what you were going to show me before Nurse Smallbone came round? We might not get another chance."

I noticed out of the corner of my eye some torn, grey net curtains twitching, and realized we were standing right by old Gussie's broken front gate.

"Not right now," Cora whispered. "Not here. Later."

At home, Nurse Smallbone was trying to get Baby Pamela to take a bit of boiled water and sugar from a bottle. She said if she didn't settle down in a couple of hours, she'd get her over to the cottage hospital in Daneflete.

Terry kept whining and hanging onto Mum's skirt, miserable because nobody was taking much notice of him. Mum was getting irritated. If Nurse Smallbone hadn't been there, I think Mum would have whacked him.

Cora and me got the dry washing down and pegged up the nappies. Dennis and Mimi ran off when we asked them to come and help with the folding. We took the big basket in, and Mum and the nurse were having a cup of tea, but Mum was only sipping at it. Even though Pamela was asleep at last and Nurse Smallbone thought she might be over the worst, Mum looked a bit weepy and didn't seem to care that there was water all over the floor.

"Couldn't your mother come and help?" Nurse Smallbone was saying.

"Oh, you know her," Mum said quietly. "She can't cope with too much. It's her nerves. You wait and see— when we're all feeling better, she'll have the boys over for dinner, so she can tell her friends at the WI how much she did for me. It's all right—honestly."

"I'll go and speak to her."

"No, no. And she's not been too good since Father died. I'm used to it. I'd rather not have the hassle."

I managed to squeeze two more cups out of the teapot for Cora and me. We went back into the garden with them and found a nice quiet spot in the shade.

"Look," said Cora. "Mr. Scaplehorn copied this into his book from some old scorched papers that this bloke,

Haldane Thorston, had in his house. He says it took them days to work out what it all said—and where these dots are, the paper had burned through so there's some bits missing."

"Remember when we were in the church, I told you Haldane Thorston's this old chap who lives over the Patches?" I said. "His three sons had their names on that memorial from the First World War. He comes up this end sometimes to Mrs. Aylott's or Mrs. Wickerby's. Pete and me see him now and then when we go and check on our camps down there."

"Well, somebody in Haldane Thorston's family, way, way back, was this servant who worked in the old rectory," said Cora, "and it looks like he took some papers out, saved them like, before the whole place went up in flames. Jasper Scaplehorn thought that that thing—you know, that beast thing—must have been in the house, and Piers Hillyard tried to kill it by fire but ended up burning the whole rectory down and himself as well. I think this stuff must have been in those papers."

I drank down my tea, took the pages from Cora, and began to read.

PIERS HILLYARD

I tremble in my deepest heart when I think what I have done. I write this in my chamber, and it is late into the night. I fear my candle will soon burn out, and who knows now what lurks in the darkness beyond these walls? I write this in mortal dread of the thing I have unwittingly . . . [illegible section, scorched] . . . I must write, for I know that somehow my life is forfeit. I must pay the price of my folly. I know my mind is leaving me, and while I still have some wits left me, by the grace of God, I must write. I must write. . . .

I know Cain Lankin had threatened the Guerdons with mischief and had confronted Sir Edmund on two occasions, so that when Sir Edmund was summoned to attend the Privy Council by Our Most Gracious Majesty Queene Elizabeth, and would therefore be absent from home for some time, he did exhort his household to beware him.

But there was no proof that Lankin was in Guerdon Hall on that lamentable night when Lady Ygurne and her child were killed, may God grant their poor souls rest and mercy. Surely I could not refuse to inter his body in consecrated ground on rumour and hearsay alone.

The witch, Aphra Rushes, never said he had been there, even when they lowered her into the pitch barrel, even when she was dragged forth, lifted up, and chained to the stake. Even when they held the torch to the wood, she never spoke. Miles Fortyce, having come hither with the condemned woman from the Assizes at Lokswood, did endeavour to persuade her to repent her wickedness, but she said nothing. She did not utter a single cry, even when the flames began to take the wood. There are those who said she smiled, and that they saw the black shadow of Lucifer embrace her in the fire, but I saw nothing, only the dark cloud of smoke from the burning pitch. Even the stake itself began to take the fire. I turned my head away and covered my face. The smoke came over me, and the stench of broiling flesh overwhelmed me. Only then, in her death agony, did Aphra Rushes let forth a scream that pierced the hearts of all who stood there, and a hush came upon the crowd. In that hoarse cry were words that rent the choking air. Aphra Rushes cursed all those that bore the name of Guerdon, in every age that was to come.

Then she fell silent and was consumed. I felt hot ashes in my nostrils.

Of all the divers ways in which man may quit his wretched life, the flame is like to be the worst of all. I am mortally afeared of . . .

I found his body in the wasteland. It might have been nothing more than a heap of wet rags blowing in the wind by the side of the creek. There was blood on those tattered clothes and around his mouth and in his hair, but I did not come too near, for I could see he had been a leper.

I sent away the parish women who prepare our deceased brethren for burial, so they would be spared the touching of him. The sexton's men came with the rough wooden box they had quickly put together, longer by far than the coffin of any man I had known. In fear and haste, they hammered down the lid upon his unwashed corpse. We did not know whose blood it was upon him. Which one of us was man enough to search his body? Who would risk such a death—and such a life?

But the people would not let me rest until I had the box opened and had Lankin hung in the gibbet. I paid the sexton and the gravediggers two sovereigns to hang him up, for they would not do it for less. Such was the length of his body that only with great trouble did they fit it inside, and for three days he swung there, out in the lane on the brow of the hill, for all to see, though none would draw near the place.

An unnatural tempest blew over the land, and my man, Moses, came to tell me that corpse-lights had been seen among the graves in the churchyard.

A great shaft of lightning, like a thunderbolt from Jove himself, struck the steeple of the church, the very place in which Aphra Rushes had been confined, and as we worked to quench the flames, I felt in my heart that it was a sign unto us from the very throne of God. We had convicted an innocent man, a man who had died alone and in desolation, without any proof, and therefore he must be accorded Christian burial.

As the people had accused him, so now they turned their ire upon me.

When, at further great expense to my purse, the sexton removed him from the cage on the third day, the rot that had consumed Lankin's diseased body in life seemed to have made no further progress upon him after death. He was unchanged since I had discovered him on the marshes. I could not look upon that hideous corpse for longer than it took to sign the cross over him before they hammered down the lid once more.

Still the people plagued me to bury him out of sanctuary, where four roads meet, pinned to the earth, but I could not believe that Aphra Rushes could have suffered so, under torture and by the flame, and not laid blame against another. Still I refused to judge Cain Lankin a guilty man.

Alone but for the poor simpleton, Shem, who daily gathered grass for my horse, to assist me, as I had no more sovereigns to give to the sexton or his men, I dragged the wretched box that held Lankin's body, under the shadow of darkness, across the threshold of the lychgate. It lay upon the earth, on the midway unto hallowed ground, and holding my lantern aloft to read the text, I began to recite the prayer of commission.

At that moment a terrible sense of foreboding came upon me, and I felt almost that my very soul was being wrenched from my body and was gazing upon me from some other place, outside the confines of the lychgate, beyond the world itself. I could hear noises and lamentations in mine own head, screeching and wailing, causing me grievous pain. In this feverish stupor, I glimpsed Shem with his hands grasping his temples, moaning in affliction like to mine.

I sent up a desperate entreaty unto the Lord, and

sensing some answer from heaven, prevailed upon Shem to aid me in drawing the rude coffin through the gate into the churchyard. I was obliged to seize the good soul's hands and place them steady on the box, and together we heaved it unto sacred ground.

The tumult ceased. I gave thanks unto my maker, but with my eyelids yet sealed in prayer, I felt a pull upon my arm. Shem, his face wild and distracted, pointed to the wooden box with a trembling hand. I swear upon my oath that it had shifted at the least half a foot to the side from the spot where we had placed it. As we watched, it rocked back and forth, without human aid. I felt cold blood course through my body and was overcome with a dread such as I had never before felt.

Shem would have departed the place forthwith, but I was afeared to be left with the corpse alone and in darkness, save for my lantern, and persuaded the poor lad to assist me in moving the box farther into the churchyard.

I would have made a resting place for the box on the far side, to the north, but we were both consumed so with misgiving and fear that we could not make the passage thereunto. I brought to mind the cavity that Cain Lankin himself had laboured to dig close by the church wall, which no man had filled, in the vain hope he had entertained of drawing forth the woman Aphra Rushes.

For long hours, in utter weariness, with black dust and ashes from the charred timbers of the stricken steeple

285

darkening our moistened skin, we laboured to dig farther into the earth in this place. Lankin's coffin lay upon the path, and as we toiled, we saw it move thrice more. Shem was agitated and consumed with terror, but carried out my bidding as his priest.

At last we had made an opening sufficient deep to take the rude casket. With great difficulty, we interred the frightful remains and covered over all with earth.

Shem fled from the church in a great disturbance. After that night, I never beheld the poor wretch again. To this very day, I know not whither he went.

I am a man of God, but I do not understand many of those things of which our world is made. I believe now that even while he had lived, Cain Lankin was already half in death, in some manner a part of the very fabric of that wilderness which he had made his dwelling place.

I am a man of God, but I am weak, and now my foolishness and my failure have caused a curse so terrible to fall upon these people of the marshes that I, and I alone, must find the means to save them. It is a curse no less terrible than that which Aphra Rushes brought down upon the heads of the Guerdons. I know in my soul that my life is forfeit. I have condemned myself to that hell I sought to spare Cain Lankin.

It did not end with the unnatural deaths of Lady Ygurne and her baby son. Merciful God, it has only just begun. Two more young ones . . . The people are moving *away from the marshlands with their cattle to make new lives on the high lands beyond the . . .*

I fear for my own household. A washer girl, Kittie Wicken, has come up to this house from Guerdon Hall and has been safely delivered of a son, thanks be to God. Kittie would not remain in the Hall in her travail, but struggled up the hill alone and at the eleventh hour. She is a strange young woman, somewhat afflicted in the mind, I believe, or consumed by dark secrets that disturb her peace. She will not leave her infant alone by day nor by night and sings constantly to the babe, always the same vile tortured melody, scarcely fit for the ears of a child. I do not linger to attend to the words, for Kittie's voice has the power to pierce the soul. It fills my head and will cause me to lose whatever reason still remains to me. Before much longer, we shall all be mad here.

Kittie must go back to the Hall, for she is bound in duty to the Guerdons, though she pleads to remain here. I hear her fearful sobbing and wailing in the night.

One of her secrets she has confided to my keeping, which grieves me most sorely and is a burden to me. Kittie has confessed that Sir Edmund Guerdon is the father of her child. She informs me also that other maidservants in Guerdon Hall are fearful of his appetites.

I can keep Kittie here no longer, though we may all be beyond help now.

Here, and in Daneflete, Hilsey, and Faring, I can find

*no carpenter who will repair the damage to the steeple.
Maybe beyond Lokswood . . .*

*They cried out against me, but I allowed the body of a
murderer to pass through the lychgate to burial in consecrated ground. In that moment, Cain Lankin passed into
the half-world between the heavens and the earth.*

Who can undo the terrible deed I have done?

I felt tired, numb.

"I don't know what to say," I told Cora. "There's so
much. . . ."

After a few moments she spoke quietly. "That's my
Kittie—Kittie Wicken. She is still singing that song, but
not in the old rectory, in—in Guerdon Hall."

❧ CORA ❧

We stood at the top of the hill. I held Mimi's hand. It felt
sweaty.

"What we waiting for?" she said, pulling at my arm.

The sides of my head began to press in. I felt a dull
ache in my shoulders and knees.

*For three days he swung there, out in the lane on the brow
of the hill, for all to see. . . .*

The gibbet must have hung here.

"Come on, Sis," I murmured. "I don't like it here. Let's run."

"Can't run. Feel sick," she said, swallowing.

"I hope you ain't got what Baby Pamela's got."

I tried to hurry her, but she pulled back.

"Mimi, I want to get off this hill. You've got to run. Hold my hand tight."

"I can't," she whined. "My tummy feels bad."

"You've got to — you've just got to," I said, pulling her roughly. I dragged her faster and faster, until her little feet slapped up and down on the road behind me.

"Don't do that," she sobbed. "Don't like you. Sid! Sid's dropped!"

She dug in her heels. I had to stop. In the second that it took for her to pick Sid up, I looked back and noticed a tall, dark figure moving swiftly down the hill behind us.

Swaying, dizzy, I swept Mimi up in my arms and started to run, staggering under her weight. She was too heavy for me.

"Please come, Auntie Ida," I breathed. "Please come."

Mimi wailed, her head bobbing from side to side. I tottered into the Chase, tripping in and out of the ruts.

A man was shouting. "Cora! Cora! What's the matter? Stop!"

Still running, I turned my head back. Father Mansell was puffing along the track. I stopped, exhausted. Mimi fell out of my arms. My stomach churned. I swayed,

289

turned away, and was sick in the grass by the side of the road.

"Dear girl," said the rector, trying to catch his breath. "Dear, dear, dear. Is that everything? Dear, dear, let's get you home."

I stumbled down the Chase.

"I came down," Father Mansell was saying, still breathlessly, "to apologize to your aunt Ida for not picking her up in Daneflete yesterday. It was a terrible thing to do, and I've had the deuce of a headache today, so I'm paying for it."

I just wanted to lie down, right there, and sleep on the cool, hard earth.

"Not far now," Father Mansell droned on, his hand under my elbow. "As I was visiting Mrs. Pembroke in Bryers Guerdon this evening, your aunt asked if I could pick you up from the Jotmans' and walk you home, but by the time I got there, you'd already left."

I lurched towards the verge, then was aware of standing in the hall, with Auntie Ida, in a misty haze, holding me gently by the shoulders and peering into my eyes. I turned away, and the wooden floorboards came rushing up towards my face.

❧ ROGER ☙

The bread in the bread bin was going mouldy.

Mrs. Lester, next door to the Wickerbys, brought round a couple of cans of tomato soup for me to heat up in a pan if anyone was well enough for dinner. Then she bundled Pamela up and said I was to take her for a walk. I went up Back Lane because there's only one broken-down old house there and nobody would see me pushing the pram.

I thought Cora must have been ill or she would have come.

❧ CORA ❧

The day becomes the night, but I don't know when it happens. My throat and my tongue taste bitter. My stomach aches. Mimi isn't here. I spread myself out over the big bed. Sometimes I am so hot, I push the eiderdown and blankets away with my feet. At other times, I shiver with cold and reach for them, wrapping myself up uselessly in a tight cocoon, unable to still my chattering teeth.

Auntie Ida tries to make me take a cool drink. As soon as it reaches my stomach, it rushes out again into the bucket by the bed. I hear the swishing of the mop on the floor, again and again.

Somebody sponges my arms and legs with cold water and wipes my face and my hair with a warm flannel. Sometimes I think it is Auntie Ida and sometimes the lady in the uniform at Roger's house. Other faces appear—an old burned man, a witch with flaming hair screaming, *Libera me! Libera me!*

The children come.

Cora, save us. . . . Save us, Cora. . . .

Kittie bends over me, singing:

"'The nurse how she slumbers, the nurse how she sleeps.
My little son John how he cries and he weeps.'"

I can smell her warm breath and feel her plaited hair fall across my cheek.

Two people are talking quietly in the room, their soft voices coming and going. My eyes are closed, but I am only half-asleep. I feel a little stick being tucked gently into my armpit. Someone holds on to my wrist lightly.

"I've always wondered what this old house was like, Mrs. Eastfield," a man whispers. "What with living at North End, you know. I'm sorry. Please forgive me. It's not my place."

"Oh, it's all right, Doctor," murmurs Auntie Ida. "It's all so long ago now."

"What were they like, the Eastfields? We only met the daughter, Rosalie, when we bought the house. A charming woman, extremely elegant."

"Ah, Rosalie was beautiful. But then they all were. It was one of those golden families, Doctor, one of those families that always seemed to be bathed in sunlight."

"Old Colonel Eastfield was dead, of course, by the time we came," he said, "but Mrs. Eastfield and Rosalie moved to Sussex. I believe there were relatives there. Strange she never married, a woman like that."

"Many women were left all alone after the Great War, Dr. Meldrum."

They fall silent. The man lifts my arm briskly and removes the stick.

"I'm truly sorry, Mrs. Eastfield," he mutters. "I should never have brought it up."

Someone tucks the covers in close around me. It seems a long time before Auntie Ida speaks again.

"Well, what difference does it make now? So long ago, it feels I lived another life, yet these days I seem to be thinking of the past more than I have done for a long, long time." She sighs. "It was the wrong thing to do, Doctor—marry Will, I mean. I only married him because he looked like his brother."

The man coughs awkwardly.

"Always looking at him and wishing he was someone else, sometimes even pretending he was that other person."

"I—I think I'd better be off now, Mrs. Eastfield," the man mumbles.

I don't think Auntie Ida is really talking to him anymore. I don't think she is bothered whether he is listening or not. She is in her own place.

"My brother, Roland, and . . . and . . . they met at Marlborough. Strange, how they lived so close to each other but only really met when they were away from home. But then we were always isolated from other children. Nobody wanted to come and play here—their parents wouldn't let them, anyway. And we were never

allowed to associate with the children of the labourers in the farm cottages, you understand. We just had
each other for company until we went away to school.

"Of course, the tragedy for the Eastfields was that
they ever became involved with the Guerdons. Little by
little, we drained them of their lustre. . . ."

The man is uncomfortable. "Yes, well—" he begins.

"It's a dangerous thing to do, to fall in love with a
Guerdon. I should know—my mother did the same
thing," Auntie continues, in her own world. "He knew
he was going to have his work cut out persuading the
Colonel. The old chap would never have allowed it, and
we were so young. He didn't even approve of his friend-
ship with Roland, so we kept it secret. Then, after the
war, the world was changed—"

"The girls are both on the mend now," the man says
quickly. "As I said, this germ has gone through a lot of
people in the village, but it doesn't last long. I haven't
lost anyone yet. By Monday this one will probably be
eating like a horse. It might take the younger girl a little
longer, but you're doing all the right things. Call me
back immediately if things don't improve."

A bag clicks shut.

"If I might be so bold," he says, "I do think you
should seriously think about getting connected to the
telephone. You're very isolated here. It's a good job the
rector rang to tell me I should come down and take a

295

look at the girls. But what if he hadn't known? What if it had been something more dangerous? You don't even have anybody to run a message for you."

He rests his warm hand on my forehead. I feel peaceful.

The curtains darken. I slumber, I wake, I doze, and my visitors drift in and out of my dreams. I have no way of knowing how real they are.

Suddenly bright sunshine fills the room.

"Cora, try some of this, dear," says a soothing voice. A hand cradles my head, and I sip sweet water, and a little more. Then it rests me gently back on my pillow.

Auntie says, "I don't think you need this pail anymore."

Half in and half out of waking, I see her lift the bucket from the floor. There is a thud, and Auntie cries out in pain. She goes down on her knees, lifts up the edge of the eiderdown, and looks under the bed. I hear her suck in her breath through clenched teeth, scuffle around, then get up quickly, clanging the bucket against something metal. She leaves the room with quick hard footsteps and slams the door behind her.

❧ IDA EASTFIELD ☙

How dare she! How dare she prowl around my house! Jasper's box—how the hell did she find out about it? Has she shown anything to the Jotman boy? Prying into things, snooping and prying!

I've written another letter to Harry, but I can't even go and post it with the two of them sick. I'm going to have to light the copper and do the washing. I can't leave that stinking stuff soaking until tomorrow.

There are flies everywhere. If only I could fling all the windows open and let the fresh air blow through the house, but even if I could do it—they've been nailed up so long—I wouldn't dare. Not now.

I'm so angry with Cora—raking up the past like this. How dare she—making me go through all this—all over again.

Oh, God, it's the photograph they put in the newspaper. Oh, Agnes . . . Annie was such a sweet child.

I'm so weary.

❧ ROGER ❧

Mrs. Campbell's turned up with some shopping and a great big steak-and-kidney pie for dinner. The pastry's an inch thick. She said I had to wrap it up in tinfoil and put it in the oven on number five for half an hour. I've never put the flippin' oven on. Do you just stick a match in? What if I blow the house up?

Everything's messy. Dennis has left his cars all over the place. Mrs. Campbell said I should tidy up and do the dishes, but I can't find the cloth, and why should I pick up Dennis's rubbish, anyway? I thought I'd do the lino in the kitchen, but when I got the mop out, it had some dried sick on it, so I just stuck it back in the bucket in the corner. Mum'll sort it all out later.

❧ IDA EASTFIELD ❧

I shall have to take Cora and Mimi back to London myself, as soon as Mimi is up on her feet again, but will Harry be there? Cora says there is a public house called the Half Moon where the landlord will pass on a message to her father. I should have been connected to the telephone when I had the chance. Hugh Mansell would let me use his or, failing that, Geoffrey Treasure.

Just a few more years, that's all it would have taken. Once I have gone, this house will sink back into the marshes where it belongs, from where it should never have risen up in the first place, and one day they will shut up the church forever. Nobody will come down to this wilderness again. He will not cross the water, and it will all be over—all be over.

Everything was all right until they came.

❧ ROGER ☙

I couldn't believe it when Cora turned up at the back door. She looked washed out.

"I couldn't stay there a minute longer," she said. "Auntie gave me this other letter to post to me dad. I did it on the way up. Oh, and she took Mr. Scaplehorn's tin box."

I poured us out some of Mrs. Campbell's Lucozade.

"Blimey!" I said. "Was she cross with you?"

"Dunno," said Cora. "She ain't said a blimmin' thing about it. She's just going round looking miserable as sin.

Mimi ain't right yet, neither. It's like a wet weekend in June down there."

"That's it, then, is it?" I said. "What are we going to do now?"

"Well, I was thinking on the way up. This Haldane Thorston bloke—do you reckon he'd tell us anything about it? What's he like?"

"I don't know really. He's not like the other people down the Patches. He speaks with this posh voice. You wouldn't think he'd talk like that just to look at him, you know. He's got a big beard and old clothes and boots on, and he's always doing his garden. I asked Mum about him once, and she said that she'd heard Mr. Thorston had had an uncle who'd made a lot of money in India and that this uncle paid for him to go away to boarding school, then to university. But Mr. Thorston didn't do anything with all the stuff he'd learned. He just came back to Bryers Guerdon and married some girl and had loads of kids. Remember, three of them died in the First World War?"

"Yeah, rotten," said Cora. "Anyway, why don't we go and see him? There'd be no harm, would there? He can only tell us to push off."

"Yeah, could do. You haven't been down the Patches yet, have you?"

Pete came whizzing in, almost back to his old self again, not that he'd been really ill like everybody else—

most probably stuck two fingers down his throat to make himself sick and get the attention.

"You going down the Patches, then?" said Pete. "Can I come?"

"Yeah, all right, mate."

We found Mum on the settee in the sitting room, with her eyes closed and Pamela fidgety on her lap.

"Can we go out?" I asked her. Mum half opened her eyes and said Auntie Barbara was going to come later and get Dennis and Terry to go over there, so it was all right—she'd manage.

✎ CORA ✎

We went towards North Fairing. The houses petered out and the road narrowed until the footpath gave way to muddy banks on either side, forcing us to walk on the pitted tarmac. Above our heads, the treetops met in a high rustling arch.

A little way into this green tunnel, the right bank sloped downwards into a wall, the brickwork dotted with small purple flowers and the lacy fingers of tiny ferns. After twenty feet or so, we stopped in front of a pair of tall wrought-iron gates, standing open, a lovely garden spreading out beyond them. Three weeping willows cast their huge round shadows onto a lush green lawn that swept down to an elegant cream-coloured house, its walls almost hidden by cascades of pink roses.

"Close your mouth," Roger said, "or you'll swallow a fly. That's North End, where Dr. Meldrum lives. You know, he was at the cricket with Mrs. Meldrum and Caroline."

"Oh, yeah," I said. "Dr. Meldrum came to Guerdon Hall when I was out of sorts. I heard him and Auntie Ida talking in the room when they thought I was asleep. Did you know this is where the Eastfields lived, before Dr. Meldrum moved here—you know, Auntie's husband's family?"

"Well, I'll be—blimey—I never knew."

"Yeah, this was their house—'one of those families that always seemed to be bathed in sunlight,' Auntie said. 'A golden family'—how lovely. Fancy being a golden family, a golden family in a beautiful cream-coloured house. The father was a colonel in the army."

"That Captain James Eastfield, whose name's on the memorial in the church," said Roger, "the one who was killed in the Great War . . . this must've been his home then. . . ."

We moved forward and found ourselves standing in the cold, dark shadow of the wall.

"Roger," I said, "Auntie Ida said to the doctor she shouldn't have married Will Eastfield. She said she only married him because he looked like his brother.

That Captain James Eastfield—I suppose that was the brother she was talking about. It was secret. Nobody knew anything was going on between them."

❧ IDA GUERDON—MAY 1917 ❧

Rosalie and I are going up to town together. I am walking to North End, and then Hedley is taking us to Daneflete station in the trap. Rosalie is all set to buy a new hat at Rachel Byng's in South Molton Street; then we will go on to the theatre before spending the night with Mother in Onslow Gardens.

It is all so delicious. I find I must keep biting my tongue to stop myself mentioning his name. Yesterday I couldn't conceal a ridiculous grin when she talked about him coming home on leave—only another week—one more week—seven more days—one hundred and sixty-eight hours (give or take twelve hours or so for delays).

I am pretty certain Will knows. He gives me rather an odd look sometimes. I believe he may have seen us in the garden. He signed up the day after his birthday apparently—keen as mustard. Decided not to go up to Oxford until after the war. Starts training next month. It would be grand if they could be in the same unit together, and with Roland, too. That would be splendid luck. But of course, they may not put new recruits in with the chaps who have been out since Mons. I don't know what they do.

I walk down the lane. There are bluebells among the trees near the cinder path. I bend to pick a small bunch for Rosalie and hear the creak of a bicycle as it comes towards me. The creak repeats again and again. I look up and see the boy from the Daneflete telegraph office. At least I see the top of his cap. His head is down, and he rides fast.

I drop the bluebells. They fall among the others, and everything swims together in a kind of haze. It really is far too hot for a coat. I should have left it at home — Agnes did say twice.

What an unpleasant job for a young lad like that to have to do.

Of course, there are several other houses on the way to North Fairing, not just North End. The Bendalls at Whitebeams have a son, Nicholas, in the army, and there are the Thorstons, of course. They lost George and young Hal within a day of each other on the Somme. Roland was their officer. He said he had to down half a bottle of whisky before he could bring himself to write the letter of condolence. Frank Thorston, the youngest, is still out there. Then there's Walter Paget from Lamp Cottage. He's in the navy. Who else? Ah, yes, Albert Hatton — no, he is in hospital and will be returning home soon.

I will be calm. One hundred and sixty-eight hours (roughly).

304

I walk on down the lane. The boy on the bicycle passes me and touches his cap but doesn't look up. The creak repeats and repeats and fills my head, then fades, then there comes a moment when I think I hear it but possibly don't. My legs feel a little hollow. I am dizzy, but it's quite warm. I really should not have worn my coat.

My bag is heavy. Mother insisted I bring her the two books she left behind last time she was here. I lift my chin. The gateposts of North End are just a short way off. I deliberately keep my head up. I don't want to look down and see the marks of bicycle wheels in the gravel. My heart is beginning to race rather too quickly.

I really, truly do not wish the Thorstons to suffer yet another loss, or the Bendalls, or Mrs. Paget; I truly truly do not, but . . .

He must know that I will say yes this time.

I stand at the gatepost, just about hidden from the house by the willows. I lean against it. The solid brickwork holds me up. I find I am biting my fingernail.

The parlour maid, Betty, stands between the pillars at the open front door with a small envelope in her hand. She waits for a long time, rubs her forehead with trembling fingers, then turns and calls into the house. A girl comes to the door, her glossy fair hair caught in a loose knot above the lace collar of her green silk dress—Rosalie. The maid points down the path and shows her the envelope. The girl's hand flies up to her mouth. They stand there for quite a while before they go in.

Ten minutes, fifteen minutes go by.

One by one, the curtains are drawn shut and the light in the house goes out.

✖ CORA ✖

We went back to the lane, where we found Pete balancing a beetle on a twig.

"If you keep going for half a mile or so, you get to North Fairing," said Roger, "but there's not much there, just the church and a couple of farms. The best thing, though, is Mr. Hancock's bull. It's in the field next to the lane, and it's blinking huge. Sometimes it's standing there hiding behind the hedge and it snorts when you go past and you get such a fright it makes you jump. I wouldn't go in that field for a million pounds — well, I suppose I might for a million, but not for a hundred." He chewed his lip thoughtfully. "Well, maybe I might for a hundred, but not for ten."

"Can I see it?"

"Yeah, I'll take you later, or tomorrow."

"Maybe tomorrow. My legs are still a bit wobbly. How far is it to the Patches?"

"We're here."

A grassy track curved off the lane to the left, just wide enough for a car, although it probably wouldn't do the car much good.

There wasn't a scrap of wind. We made our way along a well-beaten path, grateful for the shade cast by the tall bushes and overhanging trees. In clearings behind the high hedges were small wooden houses, many of them painted—green, blue, pink—some with verandas like the Jotmans'.

Each house was surrounded by a garden brimming with fruit, flowers, and vegetables—fat green pea pods ready to burst, tender runner beans hanging among masses of small red flowers twisting their way up wigwams of sticks, bunches of plump scarlet tomatoes shining on their bamboo canes alongside monstrous marrows, feathery carrot tops, bolting lettuces, and juicy red raspberries—while around and about, ignored by the birds, small squares of tinfoil and old polished cans hung limply from strings.

We stood and breathed in the sweetness. Pete wanted to nip in and pinch something, but Roger and I were scared someone might see. Instead we made do with the blackberries that grew along the path, black-ripe and soft.

Everywhere, flowers overflowed their beds, jostling with each other for the light, scrambling through trees or spilling over the tops of the hedges above us.

"Ooh, smell this," said Pete, pulling down a branch tangled with yellow flowers and squashing it into his face. "Honeysuckle . . . yum, yum."

An apple tree, bending under the weight of ripening fruit, was leaning out over the track.

"The apples in our garden are still tiny," said Roger. "These are really early."

We scrabbled about in the grass looking for windfalls and managed to gather a couple of handfuls. Most were small, hard, and sour, but a few were just about soft enough to eat. Roger said the really unripe apples were collected up and fed to pigs. We cut the maggots out with Roger's penknife. You have to be careful with maggots. Once, when I was at Nan's, she got one in her apple and spat so hard her false teeth shot out and landed in the fireplace.

In one of the gardens, two brown cows, tied up on long ropes to a tree, stood and stared at us, chewing nonstop, their mouths going round and round and round. I noticed their huge eyes were ringed with thick eyelashes, just like Cissie Bedelius's when she spat into her little box with the mirror in and rubbed the wet black cake with a tiny brush and put it on to make her eyes look bigger.

"What sort of people live down here, then?" I asked.

"People came out from the East End of London between the wars and built these places for themselves," said Roger. "We don't see much of them in Bryers Guerdon. I suppose they've got everything they need here, really."

"It's like they escaped, then."

"I suppose so."

Dad told me that the chances are we'd have to move to one of the new flats eventually, when the Council had finished knocking down all the old houses like ours in Limehouse. I asked him where Mum would hang out the washing and where the dustbin would go, and whether we could still be in between Auntie Ivy and the Woolletts, but he didn't know. Then, just after Easter, on my way home from school, I passed a huge iron demolition ball swinging on the end of a crane, and it was only a few streets away.

Now I decided that if the big ball came to our street, I'd tell Dad about the Patches—maybe we could escape like these people had done. Dad could build us a wooden house—I'd help him, and I wouldn't have to worry about the men who made him have to go to the hospital and have stitches in his face, and maybe Mum wouldn't go away so much. It would be nice to live in the Patches, and have a garden full of raspberries for nothing.

A large tabby cat twisted itself around our legs to be petted, then turned its tail and wandered off towards a green railway carriage under a tree. The brightly polished brass fittings gleamed in the sunshine. Lace curtains hung at the windows, and a crooked chimney, with a small steel hat like a Chinese coolie's, poked out of the roof. Tethered to a post in the garden was an old white nanny goat.

"Is this where Mr. Thorston lives?" I asked, excited, but Roger pointed to an ancient thatched cottage on the other side of the track.

"He isn't the same as these other people," he said. "He lives there."

Mr. Thorston's cottage was like the picture on the lid of the huge box of chocolates that lay for months in Mrs. Prewitt's shop window. It was much too dear for anybody around us to buy, even if they spent their Christmas Club all at once. One day the box was gone. I expect Mrs. Prewitt ended up eating the lot herself.

The place looked as old as Guerdon Hall. Tall purple and pink flowers reached the windows, and the huge straw roof hung down almost to the top of the frames. The thatch was a dirty grey colour and was covered with chicken wire. A bird with a tail like a V swooped out from under the roof.

Pete pushed the gate, and it creaked open. We followed as he marched up the path between the tumbling plants to the low front door and banged loudly with the iron knocker. Nobody answered.

"I'll pop round the back," he chirped. Before we could stop him, he ran down the side of the house.

Seconds later, we heard his feet thudding back. He turned the corner, hopping from one leg to another, holding his head and yelling, "Oi! Oi! Flippin' heck!"

The front door opened, and an old face looked out, half of it hidden under a white bush of a beard.

"What the blazes is going on here?" the man called in a voice like the prime minister's on the wireless, well spoken, deep.

"I don't know," said Roger. "Pete ran round the side."

The man stepped out, and was so tall he seemed to unfold himself upwards.

"Idiot boy!" he scolded Pete, who was red and cross and crying. "You ran straight through my bees' flight path."

"How the heck was I supposed to know?"

"For heaven's sake, come here," Mr. Thorston snapped. "Get your hands down a minute. How am I supposed to help if you won't let me see?"

The old man peered at Pete's face. Then he pinched it a few times here and there, checking his fingers after each pinch.

"You're a nincompoop," he muttered. "You've killed some perfectly good bees! These black specks, they're their poor little backsides!"

"I don't care about their blinkin' little backsides!" cried Pete. "Me face is on fire!"

"Come in, then." The old chap bent and led us

through his low front door. I decided I might have been better off in London after all, where we were unlikely to be troubled by bees. The only wildlife around us came out after the pubs shut on a Saturday night.

The front door opened straight into the sitting room. A few framed photographs, brown and faded, of young men in uniform stood on windowsills that must have been all of a foot and a half thick. I lowered my eyes, not wanting to look in their faces.

The brick fireplace was almost as wide as the end wall, and on either side was a deep flowery armchair, comfortable with cushions. In the chair on the right, I was surprised to see a thin, frail-looking old lady, fast asleep with her head bent over her chest, gently snoring. A ginger cat lay curled up on her lap, napping with her.

Against the side wall behind her chair was a large wooden chest, so old it was almost black. Carved on the front was a row of arches, and inside each arch was a little wooden person in old-fashioned clothes, looking out with tiny hole eyes.

The floor sloped even more crazily than at Guerdon Hall. I was surprised the furniture had stayed where it was and hadn't slid down the boards and ended up in a heap at one end.

"Sit down there," Mr. Thorston told Pete, pointing to a small cane-bottomed chair. Mr. Thorston's head barely cleared the dark heavy beams, and he had to bend quite low to get through the door into the next room.

Pete sat down, writhing and moaning.

"Shut your cakehole," Roger whispered loudly, "or you'll wake up Mrs. Thorston over there." Then, behind his hand to me, "I never knew there was a Mrs. Thorston still in the land of the living."

Through a crack in the door, I could see a round wooden table and chairs, and a dresser brimming with cups, plates, and jugs. Mr. Thorston was in yet another room beyond. We heard splashing water, mixing, stirring. He returned carrying a tin cup. Dipping his finger in, he dabbed a thin paste onto the pink bumps that had swollen up on Pete's face.

"Just a bit of bicarb," said Mr. Thorston. "Here, hold the cup yourself. Every time you feel stinging, slosh some mixture on."

"Rub them over with an onion," someone said. To our great surprise, we realized it was Mrs. Thorston. No sooner had she uttered the words than she dropped her head again.

"No fear," said Pete, rudely snatching the cup. "This stuff'll do, thanks."

Mr. Thorston turned to Roger and me. "What are you doing here, anyway?" he said. "And what's the hurry? For heaven's sake, give an old codger a chance to get to his own front door."

"Sorry, Mr. Thorston," said Roger. "Pete, say sorry."

"Sorry, Mr. Thorston," said Pete, as though he really thought Mr. Thorston should be saying sorry to *him*.

"Sorry, Mr. Thorston," I joined in. "We only wanted to ask you a couple of things."

"Sorry, Mr. Thorston. Very sorry, Mr. Thorston," said Mrs. Thorston from her chair in a childlike, quavering voice, without raising her head. She was so odd she made me want to giggle, but I knew I mustn't. Not Pete, though. He just couldn't stop himself having a bit of a smirk at poor Mrs. Thorston's expense. Roger kicked his ankle, and some of the bicarb spilled out of the cup onto Pete's knee.

"You all right, Gracie?" said Mr. Thorston.

"I'm all right, Hal. You all right?" returned his wife, her head on her chest, her eyes closed.

"Now I know you are two of Rosie Jotman's boys, but who might *you* be—from the East End, if I'm not much mistaken?"

"I'm Cora Drumm, Mr. Thorston," I said, "and Mrs. Eastfield is my great-auntie Ida. Her sister Agnes, my gran, went and died in the war. Me and me little sister Mimi—that's Elizabeth—we're stopping with Auntie Ida for the time being 'cause our mum ain't at home at the moment."

"And how old is Elizabeth?" he asked, looking at me intently, his eyes narrowing.

"Oh, please say Mimi, Mr. Thorston. Mum and Dad called her Elizabeth after the queen, but she don't look nothing like an Elizabeth. She's four, but she's very small for four."

He sat for a moment, staring at a spot on the floor, then he got up and went back through the door into the other room without saying a word. Roger and I pulled questioning faces at each other. Pete slapped more fingerfuls of bicarb onto his face until it was covered with thick white blobs.

"You look a right stupid bonce," Roger hissed at him. Pete flicked his fingers in Roger's direction, but the mixture landed on the floor. I stretched out my foot and rubbed it in.

Mr. Thorston came back carrying a plate glistening with yellow waxy lumps. He passed across the window, bending to show us the plate more closely, and a ray of sunlight caught the pieces of wax as they dripped strings of molten gold into a thick syrupy pool.

"Would you like some?"

"Cor, thanks, Mr. Thorston," cried Roger. "Look, Pete, honeycomb!"

"Come and sit round the table in the other room," said Mr. Thorston, "then it won't matter if you get messy."

Pete looked as if he wasn't sure he should eat something that had come from his enemies the bees, but in the end the plateful of shining honeycomb was too much to resist.

We sucked and slurped, swallowing the sweet running honey and spitting out the largest pieces of wax into our sticky hands.

Mr. Thorston smiled as we gorged ourselves, and he told us he had three hives and a machine out in the shed that spun the combs to extract the honey. Then he disappeared out of the back door for a few minutes and returned with an enormous veiled hat, big thick gloves that stopped the bees stinging his hands, and a metal smoker that made them sleepy so he could get into the hives.

"Even with all this stuff on," he said, "I still get stung sometimes, but it doesn't bother me."

A voice reached us from the next room: "What do you want to show them all that stuff for? They don't want to see that stuff."

"It's all right," Mr. Thorston called out. "I'm putting it away in a minute. You all right, Gracie?"

"I'm all right, Hal. You all right?"

Mr. Thorston soaked an old towel in water in the sink, and we cleaned ourselves up. Pete asked to put on the big hat and looked a proper charlie in it.

"Now, then," said Mr. Thorston as we helped him wipe down the table, "why have you come all the way down here to see me?"

✎ ROGER ✎

As we sat round the table once more, Mr. Thorston looked expectantly at Cora, then at me. I wish we'd thought of some excuse not to bring Pete. I didn't want to say too much in front of him, but how could I tell Mr. Thorston that? As he studied my face for the third time, I sort of rolled my eyes in Pete's direction. Then I noticed the whisper of a smile around Mr. Thorston's mouth.

"Now, Peter," he said, getting up. "I need a big strong boy to do a really important job for me. If I let you out the back—nowhere near the hives, mind—you'll see some peas and runner beans that need picking, and some lovely red tomatoes. Come with me."

Mr. Thorston took Pete into the kitchen and gave him a large basket. Pete came to the door with his blotchy face to show it to us and stuck out his tongue as if it was a really special task he'd been picked for and we hadn't.

"Save the tomatoes till last," said Mr. Thorston, "or you'll squash them with the beans. Take this little box, and you can put some raspberries in there, but watch your fingers. There might even be some late strawberries. You'll have to poke about under the leaves. See what you can find to take home with you."

Pete ran off, all excited.

Mr. Thorston came back carrying some glasses and a jug on a tin tray. "That'll keep him busy for a while," he said. "Now, who fancies some lemonade? Grace! Would you like some lemonade?"

She said nothing.

The lemonade was smashing, not fizzy like the stuff in Mrs. Aylott's. It wasn't even transparent, but pale yellow and not too sweet. Even after we'd had a drink, Cora and me still sat there like a pair of prize idiots, not daring to open our mouths.

Mr. Thorston looked thoughtful. He leaned towards us. "You said you wanted to ask me something," he said quietly.

"Yes, we—" Cora stuttered.

"It's all right." Mr. Thorston sighed. "If you and your little sister are staying at Guerdon Hall, Cora, I expect you've—er—noticed some—some odd things. Am I right?"

Cora waited a moment, then blurted, "When we ask people questions, they don't want to tell us nothing, but—but we've already worked it out. We know about Long Lankin, Mr. Thorston. I've—I've seen him. I'm—I'm really worried about Mimi. I want us to go back to London."

"Well," said Mr. Thorston, drawing in his breath and sitting back in his chair. "Does—does your aunt Ida know?"

"No. At least—she doesn't know how much we've found out and—and she couldn't know the things we've seen. I couldn't tell her, neither."

He studied our faces for a moment before he spoke. "Of course you must understand the adults are only trying to protect you. Obviously they don't want any harm to come to you, and don't want you to be frightened. It's as simple as that. It's also a case of ignore it and it'll go away, but don't take any unnecessary risks. Don't let the children go down there, just in case.

"It's been especially hard for your auntie Ida, Cora, living in that old, old family house. She has been touched by tragedy so often—her own child, her brother—"

"You mean the one killed in the First World War—on the stone on the wall in the church?" I said.

A shadow seemed to pass over Mr. Thorston's face. He looked at his hands. The veins were raised and swollen under the thin skin, and deep grooves ran down his thick yellow nails. His head drooped slightly, and I noticed his shiny scalp was peppered with brown spots. "Oh, no, no, I wasn't thinking of Roland—but yes, she lost him, too, of course. Much earlier than that—she must have been about five, I would think, maybe older—her little brother, Thomas Guerdon, disappeared."

Our mouths dropped open.

"Crikey!" I said. "Would that have been in about 1902? Would that've been anything to do with them having one of those things—you know, exorcism—done?"

"Goodness, where did you find that out?" said Mr. Thorston. Then he went on before I could answer him.

"Cora, to be blunt, I am awfully surprised she agreed to look after you and— and especially your little sister."

"She hates us being there," said Cora, "but I don't think she had much of a say in it. Me mum, well . . . then me dad—well, there wasn't nowhere else really. Dad just dumped us on her. She's the only family we got—proper family, I mean. Me nan went back to Glasgow. We used to stop with Auntie Kath, but she won't have us no more."

Mr. Thorston went quiet for a moment, stroking the white wires of his beard and staring at the window behind us.

Then he said, "How much do you know?"

Cora and I looked at each other. She shrugged her shoulders. I shrugged mine. Then we began. And once we started talking, it all flooded out in a rush. We blurted out everything we could remember—about Cora seeing somebody by the lychgate, about Mrs. Eastfield being so angry, the gypsy tree, and how Cora had seen something crawling in the garden. We mentioned the children in the graveyard, expecting Mr. Thorston to laugh, but he sat there quietly pulling at his frayed cuffs while he gazed at us. We told him we were pretty sure we'd seen Piers Hillyard, and how we first found the words *Cave bestiam*, and how Father Mansell told me what they meant, and all about the letters we'd read out of Mr. Scaplehorn's box, and the leather notebook, until Mrs. Eastfield took the box away, which was how we'd known about the exorcisms. Then we had to stop to catch our breath.

"We might have left a few things out," I said.

"Hmm . . ." Mr. Thorston poured some lemonade for himself, drank it down, deep in thought, then spat out a lemon pip into the empty glass. "Now, can you remember what you saw in that box?"

"Right," said Cora. "There were these letters from some bloke at the bishop's, and then something he wrote himself saying you'd given him some stuff to copy. That's how we knew to come here."

"Well," said Mr. Thorston, leaning back, "you managed to read quite a lot one way and another."

There was a bump from the other room. The cat had jumped off Mrs. Thorston's lap. It walked in through the doorway and on into the kitchen.

"You all right, Gracie?"

"I'm all right, Hal. You all right?"

"You can understand, I suppose, having read what you have, why Piers Hillyard lost his wits. He believed that he was responsible for unleashing this—this monster into his community. He was consumed by guilt that he had given Lankin a Christian burial, even though he did it for the best possible reasons—"

"Because he didn't want a poor innocent man to be buried at a crossroads and not be able to go to heaven," I said, remembering what Dad had said when we stood by the lychgate.

"That's right. Hillyard obviously felt that something strange, something unnatural, had been awakened when he brought the coffin through the lychgate, the boundary between hallowed and unhallowed ground. Then, later, when things happened, when babies and little children began to disappear, he carved *Cave bestiam*— *Beware of the beast*—in a wild frenzy, everywhere—on doorframes, furniture, panelling, using any knife or tool he had to hand, and he scratched it all over the walls of the church as well."

"Er . . . and that stuff behind the altar?" I started. *"Lib—libera—"*

"Ah, yes," said Mr. Thorston. *"Libera me de morte aeterna, libera me de ore leonis.* They are words taken from the text of the Latin Mass for the Dead."

"And underneath they were in English," said Cora. "'Deliver me from eternal death, deliver me from the mouth of the lion.'"

"A cry from one man's desperate soul, taken up hundreds of years later by another."

"And what about the thing over the front door at Guerdon Hall—the thing with the baby's head on?" asked Cora. "Did he do that an' all?"

"It was saved from the fire," said Mr. Thorston. "We know that much. You can see the scorch marks—and you're sure you saw Hillyard? How do you know it was him?"

"There's this picture at Guerdon Hall—"

"Ah, yes—the portrait—Old Peter. It's still there, then."

"Auntie took it down off the wall and hid it, but I found it. His name's on it in these teeny-weeny gold letters. And he's definitely the bloke in the churchyard, honest he is."

"I believe you, Cora. Others have seen him, too. Of course," Mr. Thorston went on, "you must understand that All Hallows, in the old days when Hillyard was rector, was rather different. The walls of the church were covered in brilliant paintings—scenes from the Bible and suchlike. The paintings survived the Reformation, possibly pro-tected by the Guerdon family, but after the dreadful events concerning Lankin and the fire in 1584, All Hallows was locked up and abandoned for many many years."

"Oh," cried Cora. "That was the number on the paint-ing, next to Piers Hillyard's name—it said 1584."

"The year it was painted—the year he died," said Mr. Thorston. "Then, in the 1640s, during the Civil War, another rectory was built—Glebe House, farther up the hill beyond the stream, and the church reopened.

"The new rector, Walter Gomeringe, was a strong supporter of Parliament, and he swept in like a new broom. It was a period of terrible unrest, a bleak time for England. People were frightened, superstitious. Neighbour turned against neighbour. The iconoclasts arrived, whitewashed the painted walls of All Hallows, and smashed the statues, but they never completely destroyed Hillyard's warnings, hidden deep in the stones.

"You mustn't forget," he went on, "that churches were often built on ancient sites, sacred long before known history and known time. Who knows what strange forces the people of prehistory detected in the place where All Hallows stands? I'm pretty certain that if you were to go down deep enough, below the medieval, then the Anglo-Saxon bones, deeper and deeper still, you would come upon layer upon layer of ancient remains, going back how far . . . how far . . . I couldn't say.

"The Guerdons only did what hundreds of other people have done, before and after them: built a church on a site that was already connected, in some way now lost to us, to the unseen, but sensed, world of the spirit. They may well have demolished an ancient house of worship to do it. As for the lychgate, maybe there has always been some kind of portal there—who knows?"

We sat lost in thought.

Cora broke the silence. "Mr. Thorston," she said, "the bathroom at Auntie Ida's—"

"Yes, I know it. I'm pretty sure that would once have been the Guerdons' own chapel. You see, they were recusants."

"What?"

"Well, through those difficult years, people were

324

expected to change their way of worship, their faith, with each new monarch—it all started when Henry the Eighth split from the Church of Rome when he wanted to divorce Catherine of Aragon and marry Anne Boleyn. Edward the Sixth remained staunchly true to his father, but his sister, Bloody Mary Tudor, restored the Catholic faith. When she died, Elizabeth came to the throne; she became head of the Church of England. It was very difficult for people. Of course, many blew with the wind, but some refused to, and they are known as recusants. They risked serious consequences, as you can imagine, but some English families managed to steer their way through the storms by means of power and influence and fortune, continuing to worship in their own way, smuggling priests into their own homes and hiding them if things got hot. If the Guerdons harboured priests at Guerdon Hall, there might well be a priest's hole there."

"A what?" Cora and I said almost together.

"In 1585, in the reign of Elizabeth, an act of Parliament made it a treasonable offence to house a Catholic priest, so people devised ingenious means to conceal them if the place was searched—secret spaces, hidden rooms, and suchlike."

We sat quietly, trying to take in Mr. Thorston's words. Suddenly Mrs. Thorston spoke from the other room.

"I can hear you. I know what you're talking about in there."

For a moment Mr. Thorston seemed worn out. He rubbed his forehead with his hand. "You all right in there, Gracie?"

"I'm all right, Hal. You all right? What about the witch?"

Mr. Thorston looked towards the open doorway, sighed, then got up from the table and went to fill the jug.

❧ CORA ❧

"We — we know a bit about her, the witch," I called after him. "She was Aphra Rushes. She was burned. Mr. Hillyard was there."

"Have some seedcake." Mr. Thorston returned with the fresh lemonade and a large round tin. "My own recipe."

He put the tin on the table and lifted the lid. The smell was wonderful.

"I ain't never heard of a man baking before," I said.

"Would you like a piece of the seedcake, Gracie?" Mr. Thorston called.

There was no reply.

"The thing is," he said while he cut three slices and placed them carefully on side plates from the dresser, "most people think witches were burned at the stake. In

326

Scotland it was relatively common, but in England, for the most part they were hanged. Sometimes iron rivets were driven into the knees and elbows after execution to prevent the witch rising from the grave. People were very frightened of the dead."

"Pin him to the ground," I said, "that's what the villagers wanted to do to Cain Lankin, Hillyard said—bury him at a crossroads and pin him to the ground."

"To stop him rising up and causing mischief," said Roger. He swallowed down some cake before he spoke again. "Why was this Aphra Rushes burned then?"

"Well, in this country, only a very small number died by the flame. It was an extremely expensive method of execution, for a start. Wood was precious, and it took time and expertise to construct the bonfire. Witches who died in that way must have been mortally feared. Fire was considered to cleanse and purify, you see. Often, even after the body was burned, anything that was left of it was carefully collected up and burned again, so that any spells lingering in the corpse could not remain behind to pollute and taint the living."

"So why were the people more frightened of Aphra Rushes than of other witches?" Roger asked.

"Well, most poor souls hanged for witchcraft were accused by a terrified or vindictive neighbour whose cow or child had died or was sick with some unknown disease. It was a dangerous time for people who were different, or who happened to say the wrong thing in earshot of the wrong person, but what happened at Guerdon Hall was not like that."

"She really did do something bad, then."

"Aphra Rushes was convicted of a pair of brutal, wicked murders. The victims were the wife of Sir Edmund Guerdon, Lady Ygurne, and the son and heir, their baby, John. It was particularly horrific because Aphra Rushes was the baby's wet nurse."

"Eh?"

"Well, either because Lady Ygurne couldn't feed her own baby or because it was considered unseemly for such a high-born lady to do so, Aphra Rushes was the baby's wet nurse. She was employed to feed him, having just lost an infant of her own.

"There was one crime on the statute for which a witch could be executed by burning, a crime called petty treason. The woman could be accused of petty treason if she was thought to have used her powers against her master or her husband."

"And her master was Sir Edmund," said Roger.

"Yes," said Mr. Thorston, "and what's more, as lord of the manor, he had the authority to decide her punishment. It is believed that Sir Edmund and Lord Myldmaye, the judge at Aphra Rushes's trial, were great friends. To condemn a woman to die in this way, you would have to be determined to make her suffer."

Mr. Thorston looked tired. He rested his elbows on the table and rubbed his eyes. "I sometimes think," he added quietly, "that if I had lived then, I might have been condemned as a witch."

"You? But you're a man!" cried Roger.

"No difference. Men, women, children, even animals—they all ended up on a rope."

"Animals!"

❧ ROGER ❧

Suddenly the back door burst open and, banging and clattering, Pete staggered in with the basket crammed full of vegetables and fruit. For a second, I thought someone had shot him, but it was raspberry juice smeared all down his shirt. A huge marrow rolled off the top of the basket and landed on the floor with a thud. I could have picked it up and flattened him with it for coming in just then, just at the wrong time, just when we were getting somewhere.

"How the hell are we going to get that lot back?" I said, irritated at his silly face, mottled with dried bicarb paste and bright red juice. I felt like sticking two carrots up his nose.

"Don't worry," said Mr. Thorston. If he was annoyed

with Pete, he was good at hiding it. "We'll divide it up amongst you. I've some nice strong bags."

"Ta very much," said Pete. "Smashing peas!"

"Don't think anything of it," said Mr. Thorston. "We can't possibly eat all that fruit and veg ourselves. I make jam and chutney, but it's never as good as Gracie's used to be. You all right there, Gracie?"

"I'm all right, Hal."

He rummaged around in the bottom of the dresser and brought out just one bag made of old canvas, like the postman's.

"Oh, dear, this is all I can find," he said, getting up off his knees. "I don't suppose you can come back tomorrow? It'll give me time to get some more bags from the shed." He winked sideways at me and Cora.

❧ CORA ❧

I wake and sit straight up. My face is filmy with sweat. I am all alone. Auntie has taken Mimi into her own bed with her. I can hear a ripping noise, scratching, tearing, the sound of something slipping and sliding.

ಲ ROGER ੍

How on earth am I going to put Pete off coming back to Mr. Thorston's with us? My head aches with trying to think of something that isn't cruel or dangerous. Short of nailing his feet to the veranda, I'm stuck.

I slop into the bathroom to find an Aspro.

Mum saves the day, without even realizing it. "Grandma's having you all over for dinner," she says wearily, "so I can put my feet up." I can't wipe the grin off my face. "Why are you so cheerful about it?" she adds. "The only reason you ever go there at all is for the Smarties."

True. Going to Grandma's is really trying. Behaving oneself for hours on end can be a terrible strain on the nerves. The one good thing about going there today, though, is that Pete loves Grandma's thousand-piece jigsaws. The picture is always of something to do with the royal family. They've done the crown jewels, the coronation, and even the corgis. Personally, I haven't the patience, but once Pete and Grandma get stuck in, you pretty much have to look after yourself, getting your own Ribena and thumbing through Grandma's knitting patterns looking for pretty girls in cardigans. With a bit of luck, there's every chance I might be able to slip away back to the Patches without him.

I wouldn't have to keep an eye on Dennis and Terry, either, because Grandma keeps two donkeys, Flora and Heather, at the end of her garden. Dennis and Terry can spend hours down there, jumping out of the bushes and poking them with sticks.

"By the way, Grandma says it's fine for Cora and Mimi to come to dinner, too. She's doing stew. But I don't think we'll be seeing Mimi. She's really poorly.'

Even better.

Grandma lives in a big house called York Lodge, which is in Hobb's Lane. Pete and I call it the Dead End because it's all old people down there.

✎ CORA ✎

Roger's grandma had permed hair and wore a string of pearls and shiny brown shoes with little tassels on the front.

She wasn't very nice to me.

When she answered the door, I said hello and told her that I was staying at Mrs. Eastfield's, with my sister, and that she was my great-aunt. I also made sure before we started that I thanked her for having me over for dinner in case I forgot afterwards. She looked at me in a queer way and said something quietly to Roger that I couldn't quite hear, and he never told me what it was, even when I asked.

While we were having the stew, she kept glancing at me across the table and making a clicking noise with her teeth. I felt I must be doing something wrong with the potatoes. It ruined my appetite, but I dared not leave the dinner. In the end, I forced it down without chewing.

Afterwards I tried to help clear away by piling up the china, but she said, "Leave those, please!"

I wouldn't mind, but Dennis mucked about with his glass of water, spilling some onto his plate, yet his grandma didn't scold him, and Terry, turning his nose up at the stew, only ate bread and jam, but she still let him have jelly.

When the table had been cleared, she brought out a brand-new jigsaw. The picture was of a military band. Pete ripped off the cellophane, then the lid, tipped all the pieces out onto the table, and started making a little heap of edges.

"Grandma, is it all right if Cora and me go out to play for a couple of hours?" said Roger. "Er — are we having tea here as well?"

"No, not tea. I told your mother you would be back at about half past four, so you can come and pick your brothers up at a quarter past. Do you have your Christmas watch on, Roger? I don't suppose you have a watch, Cora."

"Don't worry, Grandma, I've got it here," said Roger. "Thanks for dinner."

"Thanks for dinner," I mumbled, looking down at the carpet.

"Cheerio!" Roger shouted back as we shot out of the door and down the driveway to Hobb's Lane.

"Whoopee! Wasn't it lucky we went to Grandma's today?"

I didn't say anything.

✺ ROGER ✺

Mrs. Thorston was sitting in the same chair as before, her head down, the big ginger cat on her lap. Mr. Thorston led us into the other room. On top of the table were two pieces of paper. The first looked very old and fragile, the curly script so difficult to read it might as well have been Chinese. The second sheet was freshly torn out of an exercise book, the handwriting sloping evenly to the right with perfect capital letters. If Mr. Thorston had written it in Sister Aquinas's class, she would have given him a gold star and put it up on the wall. He spread his hands over the pieces of paper very gently and asked us to sit down.

"Way back in my family, on my mother's side, there

was a man called Thomas Sumner," Mr. Thorston began. "He was a servant in the old rectory when Piers Hillyard was the rector. When the fire broke out, it seems that Hillyard and Sumner were together in the same room. Hillyard ordered Sumner to escape and take some documents with him—documents that Hillyard thought extremely important. Although Sumner seems to have been reluctant to leave without his master, Hillyard forced him to take the papers and he managed to get out of the house, but not without great injury to himself.

"Those papers have remained in that chest in the next room ever since, and from what you say, you have already read the transcriptions that Jasper Scaplehorn made, including that shocking account of the burning of Aphra Rushes written by Hillyard himself.

"Jasper researched many other documents in the Public Record Office in London, in the county and diocesan archives, and in all kinds of other places. The history of Long Lankin, you see, became his obsession—and his undoing.

"It would probably take all afternoon for you two to work out what this paper says. Old handwriting and spelling like this can take some getting used to. Jasper's transcription must still be in the old tin box with Mrs. Eastfield, so I spent this morning making this copy of my own for you."

17 August 26 Eliz. Examination made by Neville Harper, surgeon, upon Thomas Sumner, aged 23 years, servant to the late Reverend Piers Hillyard of Glebe House, Bryers Guerdon, may God have mercy upon his soul. The above named Thomas Sumner, languishing vehemently, being close to death of burns and injuries suffered in dyvers parts of his body at Glebe House on 15 August, most gravely wishes to make it known that at about eleven of the clock in the night time, upon the Solemnity of the Assumption of our Most Blessed Ladye, a great spirit in the likeness of one Cain Lankin, late of Bryers Guerdon, came unto Glebe House with intent to do mischief unto Margery Skynner, infant daughter of Miles Skynner, servant.

The said examinate saith that he did witness the Reverend Piers Hillyard exhort the spirit to depart in the name of our Most Soveryn Lord Jesus Christ, but that the said spirit would not so, whereupon the above named Piers Hillyard did take up a lighted candle and did throw the candle with great force upon the spirit. The spirit was not consumed, but roared and danced and caused the fire to take upon dyvers furniture and hangings in the chamber.

The above named Piers Hillyard commanded the said Thomas Sumner to depart forthwith and remove dyvers papers, but Thomas Sumner would not so unless Piers Hillyard did come forth also and save his person that he might prolong his life. Thomas Sumner affirmeth that he being badly burned and Piers Hillyard gravely burned

336

also, he agreed to depart with him together, but before they quitted the chamber, Piers Hillyard fell down upon the floor and died, and the spirit of the said Cain Lankin took the life of the above named Piers Hillyard unto himself, whereupon Thomas Sumner removed himself in haste from Glebe House with sundry articles as Piers Hillyard had commanded him so to do.

By the grace of God no servants, maidservants, grooms-men, or their children perished, nor any animal, save Piers Hillyard, and the said Thomas Sumner who is like to die this day of his injuries. May God have mercy on their souls.

Hereunto I put my hand, this day 17 August 26 Eliza-beth (AD 1584),

Neville Harper, surgeon
Crawden, Daneflete

We sat staring down at the paper, even when we'd finished reading it. All I could hear now was the slow *tick tick tick* of a clock somewhere in the cottage. It was like the ticking of the whole world, on and on and on, through all the years that have ever been.

"So he pricked him, he pricked him all over with a pin,
And the nurse held the basin for the blood to flow in."

I nearly jumped out of my skin.

337

"Flippin' hell!" cried Cora, shooting to her feet.

It was Mrs. Thorston, singing in a voice like a little girl's. We rushed into the other room. She was still in the chair but staring straight ahead with her mouth wide open, her eyes a strange milky blue.

"Gracie! Gracie! That's enough!" said Mr. Thorston, kneeling down in front of her and taking hold of her shoulders. The cat jumped down, spitting.

"My lady came down then, all fearful of harm.
Long Lankin stood ready, she fell in his arm."

"She's scaring the living daylights out of me!" Cora shouted. "Make her be quiet!"

"Stop it, Gracie, do you hear?" said Mr. Thorston.

Mrs. Thorston's head slumped down.

"I shouldn't have mentioned Long Lankin," said Mr. Thorston. "You all right, Gracie?"

"I'm all right, Hal."

Cora was white. "That's Kittie's song," she said, "Kittie Wicken's. I've seen her, Mr. Thorston. How is Mrs. Thorston singing it? What's going on?"

"Sit down, Cora, sit down," he urged gently, guiding her into the cane-bottomed chair.

"Everyone in Bryers Guerdon knows that song — all the old people anyway. Kittie was a laundress at Guerdon Hall when — when the murders happened."

"I know. She had a baby—a boy," Cora said. "It was born at the rectory, then Kittie had to go back to Guerdon Hall, but she didn't want to. She was frightened. What happened to the baby?"

"There's no record," said Mr. Thorston. He studied his rough old hands. "At least, not of the baby, but we know what happened to Kittie. She—she was found dead in the creek."

"The creek at Guerdon Hall?" said Cora.

"Jasper—Jasper Scaplehorn thought she might have been trying to save her baby from Long Lankin."

"Was the tide in or out?"

"When they found her, the tide was in—she was floating—but it didn't mean there was water in the creek when she died. She might have been trying to cross the mud after Lankin and somehow he killed her. Or poor Kittie could have taken her own life, drowned herself."

"Why would she do that?"

"Piers Hillyard says she was bearing the burden of some terrible secret she wouldn't even confide to him. Whatever it was, she was a very, very frightened girl."

❧ CORA ❧

Somebody knocked firmly on the door.

"It's only me, Mr. Thorston! Can I come in?"

I recognized Nurse Smallbone's voice.

"I'll go," said Roger, heading for the door.

"And how's Mrs. Thorston today?" Nurse Smallbone called over, entering like a breeze. "Oh, hello, you two, fancy meeting you here. Nice to see you on your feet again, dear. How's Mum, Roger?"

"Still a bit tired."

"Only to be expected. I'll pop in and see her on my way home. Good afternoon, Grace. Lovely day, isn't it? I've got your new tablets here. I'm going to have to give Grace the once-over, Mr. Thorston. Do you mind — the children —?"

"Yes, yes, of course. Come along, you two, best be going."

"Oh, all right," said Roger. "Bye-bye, Nurse Smallbone. Bye, Mrs. Thorston."

"Bye," I said.

Just then, Mrs. Thorston sat bolt upright. She turned her head and looked straight at me with her cloudy eyes. "He ate my brother," she said.

"Really, Grace, what nonsense you do talk," muttered Nurse Smallbone, opening her black bag. "Have you been making her that tea with plants again, Mr. Thorston? I've told you before, it won't do her a bit of good."

"He didn't have any toys," said Mrs. Thorston, holding my gaze. "I took the little rag he carried about and tied it on the gypsy tree."

340

"Come on, Cora, come on," said Mr. Thorston. "I—I'll walk you both down the lane for a bit. Don't forget the rest of the vegetables, Roger. I'll be back soon, Nurse."

In a daze, I picked up one of the bulging shopping bags that were resting on the floor by the front door, and left the cottage, relieved to feel the sunshine on my face.

"Mr. Thorston," I asked, "what did she mean—'He ate my brother'?"

❧ ROGER ❧

"Could we sit down for a moment?" said Mr. Thorston as we passed a wooden bench. We stretched out our legs and watched a cat washing itself as it lay in a sunny patch of grass beside the path.

"You know," Mr. Thorston went on, "Mrs. Thorston— if you could have seen her when she was young, you wouldn't have laughed then."

"We didn't laugh, Mr. Thorston," I said. "It was—"

"It doesn't matter. Don't worry." He gazed at the hedge opposite. "You know, I could have made a fortune for myself out in India. Oh, the colours of the place— blood red, ochre, burnished gold, the fragrance of spices, the baked earth, painted birds, the jewels, the palaces, the beautiful women . . . My uncle Leonard lived like a maharajah, and I could have done the same. He laid out an embroidered carpet before my feet but—but I couldn't bring myself to walk upon it."

"Crikey, why not?"

"Because Grace could not have walked beside me."

"Oh, come on, Mr. Thorston, lots of English ladies went out to India," I said. "Though I've always thought they must've been really hot in those great long dresses."

"And ladies had tight corsets on in them days, all laced up," said Cora. "Must've been stifling."

"Ah, well, that's it," said Mr. Thorston. "Grace Jetherell would never have been considered a lady."

"Jetherell? Grace Jetherell?" I cried. "Like—like old Gussie Jetherell?"

"Her sister," said Mr. Thorston. "They were a large brood, the Jetherell children. When they were all very young, their father worked—when he could stand up, that is—as a labourer on the farm at Guerdon Hall. They lived in one of the cottages opposite the house. God knows where they all slept. Davy Jetherell drank away every last penny he made at the Thin Man. In the end, there was a nasty accident at harvesttime and he was killed. I doubt he would have lived much longer anyway, considering the probable state of his liver.

"I first caught sight of Grace when I was just a boy. She was the most exquisite creature you ever saw—like a water sprite, with her hair blowing loose in twisted golden ropes.

342

When I went away to school, and then to Oxford, I wrote her poems I knew she wouldn't be able to read. Whenever I got back to Bryers Guerdon, I went straight down to the marshes to find her and recite my silly poems, waving my arms about in huge romantic gestures. Of course, she thought I was a prize idiot, which indeed I was.

"She and her brothers and sisters ran wild when their father wasn't around. The oldest boy, Charlie, was a nasty piece of work—got into a lot of trouble, hated me. Nellie, their mother, began to suffer early on from the same trouble that's ailing Grace now. The youngest boy, Bobsy, disappeared."

"What happened?" asked Cora. "Did—was it Long Lankin?"

"I can't tell you," said Mr. Thorston. "Grace would never speak of it. That's the first time she ever said . . . what she said just now."

"Only one of them disappeared? Living so close an' all?" Cora said.

"Well, Davy Jetherell was never a God-fearing man," said Mr. Thorston. "He had no time for religion, and the children knew he'd beat them if they went anywhere near the church. Grace used to tell me how her father terrified the children witless with his stories of Long Lankin. I'm pretty certain the Jetherells knew exactly where they could and couldn't go. You probably know that Lankin seems to avoid crossing water, and of course the whole area around the church and Guerdon Hall is a network of streams and channels, some freshwater, others salt and tidal. Many of the freshwater brooks flow underground from springs on the hillside. They run round and into each other so that some places are actually safe from him—the Chase, for example."

"Yeah, the safe bit starts where the farm cottages are," said Cora. "There's a stream that disappears under the track there."

"When the inspectors went down there to try to get them to go to the school in North Fairing," Mr. Thorston went on, "the children would flee onto the marshes by the path behind the big barn, because they had worked out that Lankin would never go that way, but they didn't dare go near All Hallows.

"When Davy Jetherell died, your great-grandfather, Henry Guerdon, Cora, evicted the family. He wanted the cottage for another labourer, but Guerdon's wife let the Jetherells live in the first of the two Bull Cottages in Fieldpath Road without her husband ever knowing. The two Bull Cottages are still part of the Guerdon estate. Mrs. Campbell pays rent to your auntie Ida, Cora, for number 2, but as far as I know Gussie's never paid any rent for number 1. I don't know what she lives on, to be honest. She never married. I think Mrs. Eastfield may give her some small allowance and sees that she's all right. It's none of my business."

"It'd all go on cat food, anyway," I said.

"So I hear," said Mr. Thorston, getting up from the bench. "Well, Gussie and Grace are the only Jetherells left now. I'm afraid, though, you're a few years too late with your questions. Grace could have told you some of the old stories about Long Lankin, but, well . . . not now . . . not anymore. . . ."

Cora had gone quiet.

"Look," Mr. Thorston said, "I'd better be getting back, or that Nurse Smallbone will be wondering where I've got to. Will you two be all right with those bags?"

"Yeah, fine," I said. "Thanks, Mr. Thorston. Cheerio."

He started to walk away, then stopped and turned back. "Cora," he said.

She seemed to wake up from some private thought. "Yes, Mr. Thorston?"

"You really need to speak to your aunt about this. She knows many things she shouldn't keep from you. It's your family, Cora. You must ask her."

"She won't tell me nothing, Mr. Thorston."

❧ CORA ☙

"Flip!" said Roger, noticing the time on his watch. "It's nearly four o'clock. We'd better get back to Grandma's and pick up the boys. She hates it when you're late."

"I ain't coming," I said.

"What? She'll go mad."

"Don't be daft. She won't go mad with *me*, will she? She don't like me. She thinks I'm common. You go on. I'll help you with this other bag of greens as far as her house, then Pete can carry it."

"Aw, come with me," said Roger. "She might give you some Smarties."

"It wouldn't make a scrap of difference. I wouldn't care if she gave me ten tubes of Smarties in a gold box with brass knobs on, I ain't coming."

Roger gave up. I went with him halfway up Hobb's Lane, then we said cheerio. I handed him my bag and he carried them both up to York Lodge.

I knew where I was going, and it wasn't back to Guerdon Hall—not yet, anyway.

I crossed over Ottery Lane at Mrs. Wickerby's and turned right up Fieldpath Road, but I wasn't going as far as Roger's.

The garden of number 1 Bull Cottages was ten feet high in stinging nettles. As I went up the path, I saw the nets moving. The door opened before I got to it, and Old Gussie grinned at me, her mouth all brown gums and stumps of teeth. Through her thin, uncombed hair, I could see her scalp was thick with scabby crusts.

Flies crawled across the bowls of half-eaten cat food on the stairs.

Gussie shut the front door behind me and then beckoned with a dirty finger. I followed her into the front room, which was piled up with junk, most of it tins of cat food, half of the cans long opened and abandoned on the floor. Gussie had the remains of a meal all down the front of her cardigan. It looked like Kitekat.

She pointed to a filthy armchair beside the fireplace, so worn and covered in stains and loose threads it was difficult to tell what colour it might once have been. I perched on the very edge of the seat, unwilling to breathe in any deeper than I had to.

Gussie picked up the skinny cat that lay asleep in the armchair opposite mine. It had barely any fur, its tail like a long pink pencil.

"Off you go," she said, putting it on the floor. It picked its way through the empty cans and slunk out of the door while Gussie sat down.

There was no messing about with Gussie. She didn't waste any time on the weather.

"I've seen you go up and down the road," she said in a voice like a loud hard whisper, as if she had a problem with her throat, and whistling on her s's through her rotten teeth. "I've watched you. You've got a little sister and you're staying at Ida Eastfield's. You've come because of what I said to the Jotman boy the other day."

"I suppose so," I said, "though it ain't just that. You see, I've just been over Mr. and Mrs. Thorston's—"

"Ha!" she said, so suddenly it made me jump. "*Mrs.* Thorston. She's no more *Mrs.* Thorston than I am!"

She chewed on her gums for a minute. I didn't dare say a word.

"Grace would never have gone to church for no one. She'd never have got herself tied down by no bit of paper. We were all scared of churches, all of us. Dad told us churches were bad places. He'd strap us if we went down."

I pushed a cat away with my foot.

"I used to watch them — Grace and Hal Thorston — down on the marshes," Gussie went on. "I used to hide in the reeds. They're higher than a man, you know, those reeds, and sharp, too, if you're not careful. I'm a great watcher, I am. Hal was a tall, handsome devil, all right. He spouted poems at her, and she'd laugh. She didn't know what they meant. Sometimes she'd grab the paper and drop it. When the two of them went off, I looked for the pages. If they'd landed in the water, I fished them out with a stick. The ink ran, but it was no matter because I couldn't read the words. I just liked to look at his writing, and touch it."

Suddenly Gussie got up and leaned right over to me. "It was very pretty writing. Would you like to see?"

I nodded.

Gussie reached up to the mantelpiece for a small brown teapot with a broken spout. Inside was a dirty grey ball of old papers, wrapped around in layers like an onion. She stretched forward and put the ball in my hands.

"What am I supposed to do with this, then?" I asked.

She leaned towards me, took the ball in her grimy fingers, and unwrapped the first piece of paper. I held it, stiff and curved like a cup, impossible to smooth flat. Looking closely, I made out some lines of faded writing, in script that matched Mr. Thorston's. I read it with difficulty. Sixty years before, maybe more, he had written it for Grace Jetherell.

Your dwelling place is the airy world between the sky
  and the water,
You . . . footprint, you are the marsh-king's daughter,
And . . . moistened vapour of your breath,
You leave a . . . which . . . I follow, though . . .

"I can't read it," I said. "It's all smudged."

"Try another one, then," said Gussie.

I removed the next layer of paper. It was much easier to read:

She fashions from a skein of mossy weeds
A wreath, then weaves from drops of water hanging
  on the reeds
Long dripping strands of silver beads.

She twists these glistening threads of liquid jewels
Into her crown, then from her rushy throne, she rules
The kingdom of the green glass pools.

I couldn't undo the next piece of paper. The rest of the ball was a hard lump, and when I tried to peel the top layer away, the corner tore off and crumbled.

"I've kept them all these years," Gussie said, grinning with her rotten teeth. Then, before I knew what was happening, she snatched the ball out of my hands, wrapped the two poems around it again, and pushed it back into the teapot on the mantelpiece.

"But I know what you want." She turned to me again. "You want to know about Long Lankin."

"Well, I suppose—"

"'Course you do. Hang on, though. I'm parched."

Gussie shuffled out of the room in her grubby slippers and returned with a dirty tin mug. I could smell strong alcohol. She sat down, took a swig, then, as it went down, screwed up her eyes, shook her head, stuck out her horrible tongue, and went *"Haaaa!"*

"Are you going to tell me about him, then?" I didn't want to have to stay in the filthy chair any longer than I needed to, and the cats were coming in. "Do you remember the story?"

"Oh, yes, yes, yes," she said. "My old dad told us over and over, so we'd never ever forget it. Remember

350

it? Ha! You never forget about Lankin and his poor old mother. Leastways, she wasn't old but just looked it, like everybody down there on the marshes in them days. She was always sick, and all her babies died before they was even born. When this ugly child come along, and stayed alive, she thought it was a changeling left by the fairies and they'd stole her own baby away. She gave him a cursed name because she didn't own him and she didn't want him—she called him Cain."

"Who was his father?"

"Not even his mother knew that."

Gussie took another gulp from the tin mug.

"When he grew up, Cain Lankin was an outcast, taller than any other man, thin as bones, and ugly as sin. Folk shunned him and began calling him Long Lankin. He did some bad things—a bit of thieving to get food, killed animals in the night. They said he ate them raw and got a taste for blood. He never wandered far from the water, but wouldn't cross it, even then. He thought it took his strength away. Then he fell in with this young woman—Aphra Rushes, a vagrant. No one knew where she'd come from. In them days people liked to know their own. Why should anyone leave where they was born and choose to wander about like a stranger, unless they was driven away by their own folk?"

Old Gussie took another sip from her cup—"*Haaaa!*"—before continuing.

"Aphra Rushes had just gave birth to a dead baby. Still full up with milk, she was taken on as wet nurse to the Guerdons' baby son, John. In them far-off days, a woman of her kind was only fit to be a nursemaid or a midwife, then the lowest calling on God's earth."

Gussie wiped her mouth. "In this life, bad finds bad," she said.

She leaned forward again and fixed her bloodshot eyes on mine.

"One night, when Sir Edmund Guerdon was away in London, his wife and son were killed in the old kitchen down at Guerdon Hall. Her ladyship tried to escape and left her lifeblood all up the stone stairs before she died. They found the woman, Aphra Rushes, with the baby's body still in her bloody hands, and there was strange things on the table—burning candles, a silver bowl, a silver knife stole from the master.

"Rushes was taken for murder and witchcraft. Whispers started that the outcast Cain Lankin needed to drink the blood of an infant, caught in a silver bowl, to cure his terrible affliction, for he was a leper."

"But why did she kill the baby's mother?" I asked.

"Maybe she was jealous because her own baby was dead and she had to feed this other one," Gussie said, "or she hated Sir Edmund Guerdon and wanted to make him suffer. The master went after women, you know. Maybe he tried to get her to go with him and she didn't like it, or maybe he ignored her and she didn't like that either, or maybe she was just plain wicked."

A black cat jumped onto the arm of my chair, sat down, and began to scratch itself furiously behind the ear. I gently pushed at its legs with my hand, and it jumped off.

"The thing is, Long Lankin wasn't in the old kitchen when the servants found Aphra Rushes with the dead baby, but they were sure he'd been there. If she'd done the baby in, who'd done in her ladyship lying halfway up the steps? The men swore that they'd seen these bloody footprints leading away across the kitchen floor, footprints that just stopped and went into nothing. The story spread around that Long Lankin could be somewhere then nowhere in the time it took to blink your eye, that he could slip through narrow gaps and spaces, could pass through keyholes and under doors."

Gussie leaned towards me again, and I breathed in the smell of whisky.

"Nothing could be proved against him," she said, "and Aphra Rushes never let on, even to save her own skin."

She sat back.

"Aphra Rushes was packed off to Lokswood Gaol," she continued. "They jabbed pins an inch into her flesh all over her body to find the Devil's Mark, and she was stuck in the pillory and they did all sorts of other nasty things to her, but she never told on Lankin.

"Then, before they could get her in the big court, this horrible sickness spread through the gaol, something like the plague. Lots of prisoners died, as they would, all squashed close together in the filth like they were in them days. Of course nobody wanted Aphra Rushes to die like that. They wanted her to be punished properly for everyone to see it, so they had to take her out and put her somewhere else, where she couldn't get out. And do you know where they brought her? Back to Bryers Guerdon. They locked her up in the bell tower in the steeple at All Hallows church. She stayed in there for weeks, sick with all the torture they'd done to her. It was said you could hear her crying out across the marshes, half-starved and going crazy.

"They couldn't find nobody brave enough to guard her, especially at night, not for a fortune, so they chained her up with only a bit of slack and put strong locks on the doors. Only the priest, Piers Hillyard, out of his good Christian heart, brought her bread and water."

Gussie took another drink from the tin mug.

"Sometimes," she continued, "on stormy nights, when we was children down in the cottage, we could hear the sound of the passing bell coming from the church, though no human hand was ringing it. My ma said it was the wind wailing and whining its way through the tower and snatching at the rope, but my dad would say, 'Hush, it is not the wind that shakes the

354

rope; it is Aphra Rushes tolling the bell, calling for Long Lankin. . . .'"

Then Gussie looked at me hard. "Sometimes," she whispered, "I think I can hear it still, even up here."

She drank again.

"The story goes that Cain Lankin would come each night from his hiding place on the marshes and creep around the church, looking for a way to set Aphra Rushes free, but he couldn't. They said he'd scrape away at the earth in the graveyard with his fingernails like claws, so that he could tunnel his way under the walls of the church. But before he could finish digging with his hands into the dwelling place of the dead, Aphra Rushes was taken out and sent to Lokswood for her trial and condemned to death. Then she was brought back to Bryers Guerdon and burned.

"Piers Hillyard found Lankin's body down on the marshes, but even with his death, this was a tale that wouldn't have no ending . . . not now, not ever . . . no ending. . . ."

Gussie stared down at the floor, then, without moving her head, slid her eyelids up and fixed me with her gaze.

"My old dad said that the priest buried Lankin at night, in the very hole he'd dug out with his own hands. As the years went by, some old sexton put another tomb over where Lankin's grave had been, but that wasn't the end of it, was it? . . . Oh, no, it wasn't. . . ."

I said, "Tell me what happened to your brother."

Her mouth twisted. She closed her eyes and rubbed her cheek hard with her hand. "Oh dear, oh dear, oh dear . . ." she muttered.

"I'm sorry—"

She rubbed the thin skin even harder so it creased into deep folds under her fingers, then she sat and chewed her gums for a long while.

"Oh dear, oh dear . . ." she said at last. "There were a lot of us children. Charlie was the oldest, and he was a bad boy—ended bad, too. Charlie had this pair of boots. He must have thieved them from somewhere because we didn't have proper shoes. They were everything to him, these boots. He was always polishing them to a shine with his spit. One evening Dad was up at the Thin Man like usual and Ma was sick, like usual, too. Charlie thrashed my little brother, Bobsy, like he always did for sport, but Bobsy'd had enough. When Charlie went out, Bobsy got hold of those boots where they were standing in the hearth and threw them right into the fire. When Charlie come in and saw them all black and scorched in the flames, he went crazy like a madman. He took down a rope, then got hold of Bobsy and dragged him out the cottage and down the Chase and out in the lane towards the church. Me and Grace ran after, screaming, but Charlie wouldn't stop.

"He lugged Bobsy across the graveyard and over to

356

the gypsy tree by the water. We thought he was going to hang him. Me and Grace, we pulled Charlie's arms and hit him, but he was too strong. Grace was older than me, but we were both little. But Charlie wasn't going to hang Bobsy. That wasn't his plan at all. He pushed Bobsy up against the trunk and tied him up really tight to it with the rope. Then he got hold of our hands, Grace's and mine, and dragged us away. Bobsy screamed after us. Even Charlie wasn't strong enough to hold on to the both of us girls for that long. Halfway back up the Chase, I managed to get free and wriggle away. As I ran back, I heard Charlie laughing.

"I ran and ran fast as I could, and by the time I got back to Bobsy, he was yelling and crying and there were things in the churchyard moving, like children. I was so scared. I tried and tried to undo the rope. The skin came off my fingers I tried so hard, but Charlie'd made big tight knots. I half fell in the water behind the tree. My feet were soaked. I cried and cried.

"Then this voice came, this strange voice. I looked up, and there was an old man standing there in front of me. 'You cannot save him,' he said. 'Save yourself; run away. Long Lankin is coming.' 'What?' I said. 'Who are you? Help me—help me untie the rope! Please help me!' 'I am Piers Hillyard. I cannot save your brother now,' he said. 'You must run away or he will take both of you. Listen to me. It is too late to save your brother. He is coming.

He is coming. Run away!' Then he turned and looked over his shoulder, and behind him, round the corner of the church, this dreadful thing was crawling towards us through the graves. Bobsy screamed. I tugged once more at the rope, then, then . . ."

Gussie rubbed her cheek again.

"I ran away."

❧ ROGER ☙

Dennis and Terry whizzed up the lane towards Fieldpath Road. Pete and I followed, carrying the heavy bags, changing hands from time to time.

I looked up and spotted Cora, sitting on the bench by the pillar box outside Mrs. Wickerby's. The first thing I thought was that Grandma hadn't given me a tube of Smarties for Cora, so should I hide mine in my pocket and eat them later, or should I share them with her, and would she be one of those people who always took the orange ones so I wouldn't get so many for myself? I was pondering all this when she got up and started walking in our direction.

She looked dreadful—grim, pale face, drooping shoulders.

"What on earth's the matter?" I called.

"Nothing," she mumbled, shooting a glance at Pete.

"Just thinking about school next week. I don't know what's happening, what I'm supposed to do, and I ain't got no pencil case."

She didn't look me in the eye, so I knew she was fibbing.

"Here, have some Smarties."

She held out her hand.

Back at home, the two of us sat in the garden with some squash while Mum got liver and bacon on the go.

"I didn't want to say nothing in front of Pete," she muttered. "I—I went to Old Gussie's."

"Crikey! What did you want to go in there for?"

CORA

I pushed a bit of liver around the plate with my fork.

"Don't you like liver and bacon?" asked Mrs. Jotman.

I didn't want to upset her. "Well, it was a big stew at Roger's gran's."

"You won't be wanting that bit of bacon, then," said Roger, leaning across the table to stab it with his fork.

Mrs. Jotman flicked the back of his hand. "Leave it alone. Cora's been ill. She might want it later."

Terry was eating bread and jam as usual.

"Have some of these lovely vegetables from down

the Patches," said Mrs. Jotman, pushing the bowl of runner beans towards him.

"Terry says if he eats anything green, he'll get that dangerous disease Grandpa died of, a *new-mown ear*," said Pete.

I was aware of Mrs. Jotman glancing at me every now and then. "Rex," she said to Mr. Jotman, "Cora's really tired. You know she's had that germ as well. When we've finished, is there any chance you could take her down to Mrs. Eastfield's in the car?"

Mr. Jotman sighed loudly. It was obvious he didn't want to. I should have told him not to bother, but the truth was I couldn't face the walk on my own. I stared down at the cold gravy on my plate, feeling terribly tired, wondering how I could get Mimi back to London.

"We've had all this out before, Rosie, you know that," he grumbled. "Even in this weather, you'll never get a car down that Chase."

"You could drive to the bottom of the hill and walk her the rest of the way. It wouldn't take long. Just look at her."

"Well, it looks as though I've got no choice, doesn't it?" said Mr. Jotman. "Did you say there were raspberries?"

"Well, there were, but the bowl's mysteriously empty. I'll open a tin of peaches."

After the meal Mr. Jotman got up and took his keys off the dresser.

"Can I come?" Roger cried, jumping up.

❧ ROGER ❧

The car bounced along Old Glebe Lane, while the cow parsley on either side blurred into balls of white fluff. Cora sat next to me, shoulders turned away, staring out of the window. Dad obviously couldn't bear the silence.

"I'm thinking of renting a television from Yateman's," he said. "It's only two bob a week."

"Hooray! We can see *The Lone Ranger*!" I whooped, grinning from one ear to the other. Then I caught the look on Cora's face, a mixture of misery and fury.

We pulled up at the end of the Chase.

"Do you want to walk Cora up to the house?" said Dad, taking out his cigarettes. "I'll just sit and wait here for you."

Cora and I walked away from the car. She wouldn't look at me.

"What's the matter?" I asked. Then, thinking to cheer her up, I added, "You'll feel better soon, you know. Mum always says worse things happen at sea and every cloud has a silver lining." It was a mistake. I was too breezy, too excited about the television.

Cora's anger was like a huge blast of wind in my face.

"How the hell can you blinkin' well go on like that?" she bawled. I took a step backwards, my mouth dropping open like a cod's.

"Are you a flippin' idiot or something?" she carried on. "Didn't you take a blind bit of notice of anything Mr. Thorston or Gussie said? After everything we've seen an' all? Don't you think I'm scared stiff about me sister? How can you just switch yourself on and off like that, like—like a flippin' lightbulb! I can't believe I'm walking along with you! All you're bothered about is whether I'm going to give you me blinkin' bacon! You don't care about nothing except a ruddy telly and how much you'll get for ruddy dinner!"

Then she burst into tears. I didn't know what to do. I touched her arm.

"I'm really sorry, Cora," I said. She shrugged off my hand and wiped her eyes with the cuff of her sleeve.

I looked at the ground, not knowing what to say to stop her crying. After a few moments, her shoulders dropped. She bit her bottom lip to hold back the tears, then looked up, her face blotched and puffy.

"I—I think the same thing's going to happen to me and Mimi," she said. "The same thing what happened to my mum and her sister."

"Oh, come on, don't be daft. Lightning doesn't strike twice in the same place. . . ."

"Down here it does, Roger. Down here, bloody lightning bloody well strikes over and over again."

❧ CORA ☙

A heavy door slammed downstairs; a key turned in a lock. I woke up with my heart thumping. Auntie Ida must have gone out again. I reached over for Mimi and felt only a cold pillow.

I opened my eyes. The entire room burned crimson. I shook myself and blinked. The sunlight was shining so brilliantly through the old brick-coloured curtains that everything was drenched in a livid red—the walls, the floor, the bedspread—everything.

I jumped out of bed and pulled open the curtains so forcefully that a couple of the brass rings flew off and landed somewhere on the wooden floorboards. My eyes were sore; my head felt heavy.

I had slept fitfully. Every now and then, slipping, slithering sounds had broken into my sleep, and the odd crash like the shattering of flowerpots on the gravel.

Recalling the noises, my stomach twisted and my chest tightened. I wiped my moist forehead with the palm of my hand. How could Auntie Ida have left us on our own again—left Mimi?

I pattered down the landing on my bare feet and pushed open Auntie's bedroom door.

I stood on the threshold for a few moments, barely breathing, as if I were about to enter a sacred place.

Only partly lit by the thin sheets of sunlight that pierced the spaces between the thick curtains, I saw Mimi's little outline under the blankets of a vast wooden bed with, at its head and foot, heavily carved panels of fruits and curling leaves.

In the half-darkness, Mimi looked tiny, pale, and fragile as bone china. One hand, with Sid loosely cradled in it, rested on the bedspread, embroidered with so many scattered flowers it looked as if she were lying in a meadow. I brushed her fingers gently with the back of my own, leaned over, and kissed her soft hair.

"I'll get you home, Mimi," I whispered. "Honest. Soon as Auntie gets back, I'll tell her we're going, even if I've got to carry you all the way to London myself. I'll look after you, keep you safe."

She stirred a little and closed her hand around Sid.

I sat with Mimi until I heard Finn's bark of greeting. Auntie must have returned.

As I made my way back along the landing, I heard another noise from below, from the direction of the kitchen. I leaned over the rail and listened, then crept down a few stairs. Taking each tread one by one, I moved farther down still, until I reached the bottom and stood in the hall, uncertain what I should do.

It was dreadful sobbing, terrible to hear, the sound of a shattered heart.

I tiptoed along the hall and peeped through the crack between the open kitchen door and its frame.

Auntie Ida was sitting at the big table, holding her head in her hands, clutching a sodden handkerchief, her whole body racked and shuddering. Finn sat looking up at her, whining, putting a paw on her knee then bringing it down and shifting on his back legs.

I still didn't know what to do and had just decided to creep away and not let on that I'd heard anything when Finn got up, padded over to me, and whimpered. I tried to shoo him away quietly, but he gave a soft bark and I knew I had to come out from behind the door.

Auntie Ida looked over with bloodshot eyes, swollen and streaming. Her mouth trembled; her hair hung down in wet strings. She turned away, but the tears and the noise kept coming.

I moved towards the table. In front of Auntie lay an old book, the open pages wet with teardrops. I looked down. It was *The Pilgrim's Progress*. We'd read some of it at school.

But now, in this Valley of Humiliation, *poor* Christian *was hard put to it; for he had gone but a little way, before he espied a foul* Fiend *coming over the field to meet him; his name is* Apollyon. *Then did* Christian *begin to be afraid, and to cast in his mind whether to go back or to stand his ground: But he considered again that he had no Armor for his back, and therefore thought that to turn the back to him might give him the greater advantage with ease to pierce him with his Darts. Therefore he resolved to venture and stand his ground; For, thought he, had I no more in mine eye than the saving of my life,* "'*twould be the best way to stand.*

"Can—can I help, Auntie Ida? Is it something I've done?"

"No—no," she sobbed at last, groping for the words. "It—it isn't you, Cora."

"Shall I make a cup of tea?" I went to the big stone sink and filled up the kettle.

"There are lots—lots of things I should have told you," she said in the end, mopping her eyes.

"I probably know most of them." I lit the stove and put the kettle on to boil. "I know about Long Lankin, Auntie."

She stared at the open book for quite a while. I stood against her shoulder and looked, too.

So he went on, and Apollyon *met him. Now the Monster was hideous to behold; he was cloathed with scales like a Fish (and they are his pride); he had wings like a Dragon, feet like a Bear, and out of his belly came Fire and Smoke;*

366

and his mouth was as the mouth of a Lion. When he was come up to Christian, *he beheld him with a disdainful countenance, and thus began to question with him.*

APOLLYON. Whence come you? And whither are you bound? . . .

"Cora—" said Auntie at last, tears beginning to spill from her eyes again. "Cora, I saw my little—my little boy this morning—Edward—I saw him. . . ."

"What?"

"Down—down at the church. I—I've begun to go there again, and—and sometimes the children come, and other times they don't come," she sobbed. "I go because I hope I'll see him, but if I do, it's terrible, because he's neither dead nor alive. He still knows me. He—he calls out to me, Cora, he calls—'Mummy!'—but I can't—I can't reach him." A horrible rattle left her throat. Her shoulders shook, and the pitiful crying began again.

"But even—even if I knew how to set him free," she was weeping, the words running into each other, "but even if I knew how, even if I was able to do it, then I would never see him again. He would be lost to me forever. And—and the worst thing is—he fills me with fear—my own little boy—he frightens me—there's only a bit of the real him left—but I can't stop wanting to see him—even though he's become—I don't know what he's become—"

I warmed the teapot and spooned in some fresh tea leaves.

"I thought—I thought it had all finished when the great flood came. How could it have gone on? How could Lankin have survived, being afraid of the water? Then— then, when Mimi said she saw the man in the grave- yard, I went—I went down to see if I—if I could still see my son . . . and it took me a long time. . . . If he hadn't come to me first . . . I—I don't know which is my brother Tom, because the longer the children are with him, the more like him—the more like him they become. But my son—his eyes . . . his little eyes . . . Yet he still knows me, he knows me, Cora . . . even now that I'm getting old."

I took down two cups and saucers from the dresser, found a jug of yesterday's milk in the pantry, and poured out the tea. We sat down opposite each other at the table and stirred in a lot of sugar. Auntie Ida dabbed her eyes and blew her nose with the same soaking handkerchief.

"I'll have to get another," she said.

"I'll go." I left the kitchen to fetch one from the pile of clean laundry in the outhouse. When I returned, more tears were running down Auntie's cheeks. She looked old and worn out, shredded into pieces.

"I've—I've seen the children, Auntie Ida," I said. "I think I've seen Mum's little sister, Anne."

"Yes, I've seen her, and all the others, all the others. . . . I used to go and see my brother Tom all the time when

I was a little girl—it was as if he had never gone—as if he were just in a different place—and it made me feel better because, Cora, when he was taken—when he disappeared—"

She covered her eyes with the fresh handkerchief and groaned, and the groan was so laden with misgiving and regret that I found helpless tears pricking my own eyes at the sound.

"When he disappeared—Roland—my big brother, Roland, and my sister, Agnes—Roland, and Agnes—and me—" she said, taking the handkerchief from her face and pulling it around in her hands. "Cora, we were—we were hiding from him—we were teasing him. We could hear him running around the house looking for us. We were hiding—hiding in the priest's hole. Roland said some woman had shown him where it was, but we thought he was pretending about the woman and had just come across it himself. Sometimes—sometimes Roland would disappear for a long time. He would go into the dark places in the house, places where Agnes and Tom and me would never go. We went inside the hole, but we thought it was funny to hide from Tom. We were . . . laughing at him, laughing at him crying and calling for us.

"Our parents were up in town. We had hardly any house servants here. They were frightened of what they saw and heard and couldn't bear the doors and windows always having to be kept locked. None of them ever stayed for long, and Mother could never get anyone from the village to work for us.

"Our old nurse, Joan, was fast asleep as usual. It was so hot that day, and she was almost completely deaf. She never noticed anything that went on. But there was a new maid-of-all-work from Hilsea only started a couple of days before—she must have opened the back door to let in some air—she probably thought the whole business of locking the doors was nonsense, as most strangers do—we were used to a stifling house—we just thought that was how houses were.

"We were hidden away in the priest's hole, squashed together, laughing, when Tom screamed—it was terrible—we tried to get out but we couldn't work the hidden doors—they're so old. There are two doors, one after the other, and we couldn't get the first one open again. We were trapped for what seemed like hours, banging and banging on the panelling and shouting, exhausted, before Roland managed to release it, but we were too late—too late."

Auntie sat there, wringing and unwringing the soaking handkerchief.

"Then, some time later, I let it slip to my mother that I used to go and see Tom in the churchyard and that maybe she'd like to go down and talk to him and it might make her feel better. Her fury was unimaginable, like nothing I'd ever seen. She had the most appalling temper.

"My father felt—he felt guilty—for Tom. He felt he should have taken his family away from this house, but . . . somehow he couldn't do it. I think I understand that now.

"Then, when—when Roland was killed in April 1918, Father spent most of the rest of his life, which wasn't long, staying at his London club, and then Agnes ran away with Jack Swift. Eventually Mother died as well, in the house in Onslow Gardens. Everyone—everyone left."

It was ages before Auntie could speak again; then, when she did, I could hardly hear her. I don't think she could bear to say it.

"It's all my fault—all of it—my neglect. I left Susan and Anne in the house alone. If I'd told Susan *why* she had to keep the door locked, instead of losing my temper with her, she wouldn't have opened it, and Anne would have been all right. We had a land girl, Vera, staying here just before it happened. I lost my temper with her as well. She was so fond of Annie. She would have watched her, if I had just explained, but I didn't expect anyone to believe me. . . . If I had just told her to keep Annie safe when the tide went out, to guard her when the mud went dry. . . ."

Auntie Ida wiped her face and got up out of the chair. She swayed a little, waited a few seconds, then went over to the dresser and opened the right-hand drawer. It was stuffed full of old bills and letters. Auntie shuffled through them. Creased brown envelopes, pieces of paper, and yellowing postcards spilled out of the drawer and drifted down to the floor. She found the letter she was searching for and didn't bother to pick up the scattered things or even close the drawer.

❧ IDA EASTFIELD ☙

The address is written in a child's hand. A painstaking effort to be neat.

My fingers shake as I remove the folded page from its envelope. I remember thinking, when it arrived all those years ago, that the small splash marks all over the cheap lined paper were careless smudges. They irritated me at the time. Now I run my eyes down the letter and I see that they are teardrops.

With an anguished heart, I hand the letter to Cora.

Limehouse
London E14

14th August 1940

Dear Auntie Ida,

I am so sorry. I do not know how to tell you how sorry I am. I have never been so sorry in all of my life. Everyone is so angry with me. Mum won't talk to anyone, specially not to me. She cries all the time and I make her cups of tea but she leaves them to go cold. Dad goes down the pub and won't come home, or when he does, he's had too much beer and shouts at me and wallops me, and says Annie was his favourite and he's going to leave us.

But Auntie Ida, I want to tell you what happened so you'll know. Then you can write a letter to Mum and Dad and say it wasn't all my fault, not all of it, so they won't be so horrible to me and Dad won't go away.

I miss Annie so terribly. She used to follow me all over the house and in the street, and sometimes I'd shout at her to go away, but I didn't mean it like it sounded, and now she really has gone away and there's this empty space behind me and I keep thinking if I turn round she'll be there saying "Soo, Soo, Soo," and I can't stop crying, thinking about her and missing her and wishing she was here. All I've got of her is Sid. He sleeps next to me in bed and he smells of her.

I tried to be so good for you because you were kind taking us in with the bombing. I didn't take Annie down that church like you said not to—it was that girl, Vera, that one you gave the sack to afterwards. I heard you shouting at her for it. She shouted back that the house was horrible and she wouldn't have stayed anyway. See? I heard it all.

Then, that day I was just trying to work out "Carolina Moon" on the piano, Annie was having her nap upstairs, *and you'd gone out to the barn to milk Tilly. It was so hot, Auntie, I was sweltering, and this was the bad thing I did: I opened the back door to let some air in, even though you told me to keep it bolted till you knocked, but you never said why it always had to be locked. You never said anything. I could see the barn from the window, so I knew I'd have time to nip up and close the door before you got back, but I'm so sorry I opened the door.*

I was messing about on the piano when I heard something coming down the hall. I was worried you had finished in the barn without me seeing you and you'd be really cross with me for opening the door when you specially told me not to, specially because the tide was out, you said, but I didn't know why you said that.

There was this really nasty smell, like old earth and dead things, sort of mouldy, and a slithering noise, like something crawling along the floorboards. The smell got stronger and the sound got louder till it was right by the door.

My mouth went watery like metal and my hands went all sticky.

I couldn't turn round to look. I was so scared I was frozen to the stool. I could feel my blood throbbing and my neck was so stiff tight, it hurt.

The parrot said, "Hello" in his little goblin's voice.

I forced my head up and looked in the mirror over the piano. I saw something so, so terrible in the room behind

me, looking at me. I've never seen anything like that in all
my life before. My breath rushed out and I did the next bad
thing. I picked up that brass lion from the top of the piano
and threw it at the horrible thing in the mirror with all my
might and cracked the glass. I'm so sorry I did that to your
mirror, Auntie Ida, but I didn't know what to do.

What was that horrible thing, Auntie Ida? Did you
know it was coming so I had to keep the door bolted? Why
didn't you tell me about it? I'd have kept the door locked if
you'd said. I'd have been terrified the monster would come
in. Did you think I wouldn't believe you?

It went out of the room. The door slammed shut. I heard
feet slapping on the boards, heading for the stairs, then it
started to climb. My tongue was like a hard lump in my
mouth. I wanted to shout but no words would come out. I
was stuck on the piano stool, sweating, so scared I couldn't
move.

I heard it on the landing, and doors opening and shut-
ting. There was scuffling, a dragging sound, banging, hor-
rible noises.

Then I got my feet to work. I rushed to the door, and
that's when I started shouting, "Annie! Auntie Ida!"

Fast as I could I ran up the stairs. Our bedroom door
was wide open. The bed was empty. Sid was on the floor.
Annie was gone.

Please, please, Auntie Ida, do you know where she is?
Please tell those old soldiers to keep looking for her. I want

to hear her say "Soo, Soo, Soo," and buy her one of those
little red lollipops she likes.

Please make it better for me with Mum and Dad. Please.
Please write them a letter saying it wasn't my fault.

Your loving niece,

Susan

Cora sinks into herself. "Poor Mum," she sobs. "Poor Mum . . . did you send a letter?"

"No . . ." I say, numb with remorse, "I didn't send any letter."

❧ CORA ☙

Auntie hid her face in her hands and moaned.

I mopped my own tears, my running nose, on my cuff. Nobody ever told Mum she wasn't to blame, and every day since Annie was lost, she has suffered for it.

"It was all my fault," said Auntie, "and I still don't learn, Cora—I didn't tell you, either. I hoped and prayed that Lankin was finished."

"How can he be finished, Auntie Ida?" I sobbed. "What is he?"

"He has ruined life after life," she said, bringing her hands down from her swollen, red face and staring at the far wall. "Not just the lives of the little children he stole away, but many, many others."

"Then what can we do?"

"The only one who has ever come close to an answer was Jasper—Jasper Scaplehorn. You read some of his research—I don't know how much."

"I—I don't know how much there was."

"I went to see him at Glebe House not long after Annie disappeared. I was desperate, consumed with misery. I hoped that Jasper, with all his knowledge, could help me, that together we could do something, but—but the poor, dear soul had burdens of his own."

⌘ IDA EASTFIELD ✎

It was one of those still, warm summer evenings. Jasper and I sat together in the drawing room at Glebe House.

On the floor, in front of the two tall windows, rectangles of light stretched themselves out over the fat, faded pink roses on the worn carpet. Between the windows, the French doors stood wide open, framing the lawn as it sloped down the hill to the woods. Beyond the treetops, the land swept away across the

377

wide, flat marshlands to the shimmering estuary in the far distance. There was no way of knowing, on that hazy horizon, where the earth finished and the sky began, or what was water and what was not. Over this vast expanse of grey, thin rosy pink fingers were feeling their way from the west, where the sun was beginning to go down.

It was a rare hour of respite from the constant drumming of British or enemy planes, wheeling like great black birds in and out of the clouds.

Jasper sat as always, legs out and ankles crossed, in that old, scratched leather wing chair of his, with the bowl of his wineglass cupped in his long fingers. Beside him on a small leather-topped table was a jumble of papers; some had spilled off the pile and fallen onto the carpet.

Jasper was tall, with a striking nose, hooked like a Roman emperor's, and thick wavy hair. In the First World War, Jasper was a young chaplain, hardly older than some of the lads he'd had to pray over. I think he went out to Flanders with dark brown hair and came back with grey.

If you'd happened to peep in through the window that evening and had chanced upon us sitting there with the long shadows spreading over the grass just outside and the warm sunshine sparkling on our glasses, you might have thought we made quite a contented, comfortable couple. But after a little while, if you'd stayed there long enough, and looked closely enough, you might have noticed how tense we were. I remember the loud slow ticking of the slate clock on the mantelpiece, and how I anxiously turned towards it as, on every quarter-hour, it chimed with a soft rolling peal of bells.

"Jasper . . ."

Jasper drew in his legs, then nearly spilled his wine as he put the glass down on the floor beside his chair.

"Let me warm up the soup I've brought," I said. "It's carrot—really good."

He pulled his jacket straight, gave me a quick, nervous smile, and shook his head.

"When did you last eat?" I asked gently.

He didn't answer.

"Or sleep?"

"Sometimes, in the afternoons, I find I have drifted off in this chair. It's enough."

A warm draught lifted the fringes on the flowered curtains that draped a full ten feet from their iron rail. I left my chair and moved to the open French windows. He joined me with his glass and the bottle of wine.

The shouting and whistling coming from the upper field meant that Peter Bardock had his men out on manoeuvres. They would wind up soon and finish their evening in the Thin Man.

It grew steadily darker. The deep, blue vault of the sky arched above us, and the moon hung there in a sprinkling of stars, but to the southwest all the heavens were aflame. Jagged bars of scarlet partly hid the low golden ball of the setting sun. As we stood looking out at the garden, our faces were flushed with its light.

"Is he sleeping—out there—Lankin?" I wondered.

"Maybe it's a kind of sleep," said Jasper, "but it's an existence we can't even imagine, a hovering between worlds. I think if a baby or a very young child comes close to his dwelling place, then he somehow connects with this strong life force. He begins to hunt for the child."

Jasper filled his glass again.

The dusk deepened, until a band of turquoise across the horizon was all that was left of the day. A few bats swooped and darted in their scattered flight over the garden. Jasper lit a couple of lamps, but the glow around them was pale and cold, intensifying with greenish shadows the pallor of his face.

It was getting late. The breeze that had been so comfortable before was now chilly. I reached for the cardigan I'd slung over the back of my chair, and Jasper, taking the hint, partly closed the doors, then went back to his armchair.

"But is he properly alive?" I asked.

"He is alive, but not in the way that you or I are. He

straddles the plane between the living and the dead. Lankin can't be wholly spirit. He needs some kind of sustenance to preserve his immortality in the physical world. Of course, the bodies of very young children are full of the energy of growth. In theory, I suppose their flesh could sustain a creature such as Lankin for many years in this half-world he inhabits. We can be pretty sure that he had already drunk the blood of the infant John Guerdon as part of a ritual spell to cure his leprosy."

Jasper drained his glass and poured into it the remnants of the bottle. The hand that held the glass was beginning to tremble a little.

"Why don't I get you some soup—?"

"No, no. I don't want it," said Jasper. "Let me go on." He sipped the last of his wine. "I—I believe Lankin is a creature of the boundary between land and water, partly in the social world and partly in the untamed wilderness of bog and marshland, confined by the water that flows around the margins of his territory.

"Even as a living man, we know he dwelt on the edge of society, an outcast, a bastard, avoiding the habitation of normal men. Maybe the process of becoming this thing that he is started even before he died."

I turned my empty wineglass around in my hand.

"As far as we know," Jasper continued, "Cain Lankin was found on the marshes by Piers Hillyard, not long after Aphra Rushes was burned at the stake.

"The rector and the sexton's men were so frightened of catching leprosy from the corpse that no thorough investigation was made, and I doubt whether they had the resources to determine the cause of death, anyway. We must assume that the body had all the appearance of death, but remember, it did not start to decompose when it was hung in the gibbet."

"So possibly, at that point, for some reason, Lankin was on the verge of being taken up—fully—into this half-world?" I ventured.

Jasper shifted in his chair. "Well, yes, possibly," he said. "During his life, he was partially assimilated, but then some cataclysmic event, some travesty of the accepted spiritual and social norm, might well have caused him to pass into it completely.

"Lankin's transition may have come about as a result of many things. He must have been in a highly charged emotional state. He failed to rescue Aphra Rushes from the bell tower and probably saw her burned to death, even if from a distance—"

"Jasper," I said, "Piers Hillyard himself was most specific. He seems to have been convinced that by allowing this body, the body of a murderer, to pass through the lychgate into consecrated ground, he was responsible for establishing Lankin's permanent existence in this half-world. He had an unnerving physical experience, and a feeling of utter dread, if his account is to be believed, when he and this lad, Shem, dragged Lankin's coffin into the churchyard. And it was only after that that Lankin began to move the box from inside. Could that be the cataclysmic event you mention?"

"Well, gates are definitely significant," said Jasper, "even in ordinary, everyday places. But down here, where there are uncertain, shifting boundaries between one element and another, doorways and gates would be even more important—portals between the worlds, perhaps."

"The villagers must have sensed there was something sinister about the lychgate. It has been abandoned and chained up ever since. They made another entrance to the churchyard farther down," I said.

"Well, then, perhaps they would have done better to leave it open." He stared into space.

"What do you mean?"

"As I said before, maybe Lankin was becoming this— this creature even during his lifetime. Possibly there was some kind of folk memory of something similar happening in the past that stirred up the villagers' fear. They were desperate for Hillyard to let him rot in the gibbet, but he insisted on removing him on the third day. Maybe—maybe if he had been left in the cage after that third day and had not passed through the gate, his body would have started to decompose naturally. Or if he had been buried at the crossroads and riveted down, we would not be here together in this room today—but Hillyard's compassionate heart prevailed. If what it took for the transformation to be complete was for Cain Lankin to pass through the ancient, elemental portal where the lychgate stands, I can only think . . . that maybe if he passed back through it . . . the other way . . ."

"But he would never do that, knowing it might be the end of him, would he?"

"You're right, Ida. How on earth could it be done?"

The night had closed us in. Behind the windows, the living darkness crept around the house, and the weak light from the two lamps in the room was all that kept it at bay. An owl hooted from somewhere in the woods.

"I'm so weary, Ida," said Jasper.

"You need to sleep."

"Don't tell me what I need to do!" he snapped suddenly. "What do you know? I see him everywhere!"

"He doesn't come up here. He will not cross the stream—"

"I said I see him everywhere, Ida. Even when I shut my eyes, he is on the inside of my eyelids, inside my head. . . ."

The clock chimed the half hour. It gave me a moment to collect myself.

"What are you doing about the church services?" I said. "Apparently everyone was waiting for you at Saint

384

Mary's on Sunday. Where were you? It's happening more and more. . . ."

Jasper leaned his elbows on his gaunt knees, lowered his head, and pushed his long fingertips into his hair, rocking gently backwards and forwards. I saw tears trickling down his face.

A part of me ached for him, but I had so hoped for comfort myself. Who would ache for me? Jasper had not slept in a long time, but neither had I. My nights were haunted by bleak despair over Annie and plagued by a fury at Susan that I could not bear to shake off. With Susan at the heart of my rage, I didn't have to confront my own guilt.

After a while, Jasper sniffed, wiped his cheeks, and sat up straight.

"Sometimes I feel like two people," he said, "one looking in a mirror at the other, and I'm not even sure which of those two men I am."

I also saw two people, two little girls—one Annie on that last morning, with me tucking her in for her nap, a cup of warm milk and honey on the cupboard by the bed—the other a child in the graveyard in years to come—hollow-eyed, dry-skinned, wasted, ragged, old . . .

"Jasper," I said, hoping to catch this fleeting moment of calm in him. "Why is my brother Tom less and less my brother? Why is my son Edward not quite my son? Although I can't keep away from the churchyard because I long to see them, I am also afraid of them. As the years have gone by, they've become more—more like Lankin himself. Of course, they are no longer of this world, but they are also . . . not of heaven."

Jasper stared at the carpet and pondered this for a while, but the moment was disturbed by the dull throbbing of aircraft engines.

He got up, walked to the half-closed doors, and looked up at the night. "Wellington bombers," he said, "heading for the sea."

"To Germany?"

"Maybe."

He watched as the silhouettes of the heavy planes passed over the house.

"If Lankin drank their blood, as you suggest," he said at last, his back still towards me, "then I think he has taken part of their life force into himself. He has fed off them, and now they are compelled to dwell with him in this strange place, which is neither of the earth nor of paradise. The longer they inhabit the world of the monster, the more monstrous they themselves become. They are bound to Lankin, therefore they cannot be saved unless Lankin's own life is forfeit."

He turned towards me, the bones of his face unnaturally highlighted, the hollows of his cheeks dark and shrunken. Again, slow tears fell from his eyes, but he did nothing to check their flow, raised not so much as a finger to his face.

"Why are you weeping, Jasper?"

"I seem—I seem to cry for nothing most days, Ida," he said. "But now I cannot bear the thought of what may have to be done, and I know I am the one who must do it."

"What are you talking about?"

He moved to his chair and cast his watery eyes over the papers on the table beside it. He rifled through them, dropping page after page onto the floor, then grasped a sheet with tremulous fingers.

"This is the statement of Neville Harper, the surgeon who attended poor Thomas Sumner as he was dying of his burns after the fire at the old rectory. Remember I showed it to you before? It was in Haldane Thorston's chest. Lankin came into the house to steal a child, Margery Skynner, and Piers Hillyard threw a candle at him?"

"Yes, I recall it."

"Well, I don't think I read it before today with any kind of particular insight, but listen—what does this mean? 'But before they quitted the chamber, Piers Hillyard fell down upon the floor and died.'" Then Jasper spoke very slowly: "'And the spirit of the said Cain Lankin took the life of the above named Piers Hillyard unto himself. . . .' What on earth does it mean, Ida? Have you ever asked yourself why Piers Hillyard is in the churchyard, and how he actually died?"

"Well, we've always known how he died," I said. "In the fire, of course. I have always believed that it was his choice to remain on earth to warn others, in recompense for the fateful decision he made to bury Cain Lankin's body in consecrated ground. He tried to warn in life by carving out *Cave bestiam* everywhere, and . . . he warns in death. He appears, especially to children. . . ."

"Well," said Jasper, "in this statement it also says, 'Thomas Sumner affirmeth that he being badly burned and Piers Hillyard gravely burned also, he agreed to depart with him together.' Obviously Hillyard was in a bad way, but he was not *in extremis* at that moment. I would think that he and Sumner possibly suffered a similar degree of injury, but Sumner didn't actually succumb until two days later. Hillyard seems to have fallen down and died suddenly, unexpectedly, just as they were about to leave the room. Lankin, on the other hand, was in the thick of things, *not consumed*, but rather *roared and danced*. Somehow, when he believed he was on the point of death, he was able to preserve himself by *taking the life of the one who was causing him to lose his own*."

We sat in a kind of daze.

"So, just as the children are condemned to remain with Lankin because he has consumed their blood," Jasper continued, "so Hillyard is trapped in the half-world, too, because the monster absorbed his life."

I struggled to make sense of it. "Are you saying," I

388

said, "that if you try to take Lankin's life, you forfeit yours?"

Jasper sat down slowly, his body shrinking into the depths of the chair.

"Maybe Kittie Wicken tried to kill Lankin as well," I said, "when he came for her baby."

"She died in the creek," added Jasper. "Could it be that she attempted to destroy him with water?"

"As Hillyard tried with fire," I said. "Like Hillyard, she comes when there are children in the house. I have never seen Kittie clearly, just a fleeting glance, a shadow in the wrong place, but as a child, I did hear her singing, sometimes quite close to me. My brother Roland must certainly have seen her. He always said that a woman had shown him where the priest's hole was, somewhere to hide if Lankin came in. Kittie must still have been employed at Guerdon Hall when they were constructing it. She knew the secret. But Roland used it against his brother. Instead of saving Tom, it—it—"

"Hush, hush, Ida," sighed Jasper.

He rested his elbows on the arms of the chair, bowed his head, and closed his palms together as if in prayer.

"I keep thinking of Christian," he said, "prepared to stand his ground in the Valley of Humiliation against the monster Apollyon. Apollyon was wounded by a blow from Christian's sword, but he still spread his dragon's wings and flew away. How can we be certain that, in that moment of sacrifice, when someone is prepared to confront Long Lankin, no matter what it might cost them, Lankin still won't confound death, as he has confounded it for centuries?"

"So you fear that the sacrifice will be in vain?"

"I do, Ida."

"But Hillyard and maybe Kittie Wicken were not aware of the consequences of what they did. Maybe — maybe if someone was willing . . ."

"How can we know, Ida? . . ."

And he began to weep again.

❧ CORA ☙

"Not long into the following year, Jasper was in Coldwell Hospital," said Auntie Ida, staring into space.

"Auntie Ida, is — is Mum in a hospital like that — like Coldwell?"

"Oh, Cora . . ."

I shut my eyes. Auntie reached across the table to take my hand. I snatched it away. It could all have been so different. Auntie should have written a letter to my mum's mum and dad.

It's all my fault — all my fault. Nobody had ever told Mum it wasn't.

"He — Jasper — was discharged just as the war

ended," Auntie Ida went on quickly, "but—but a couple of years later, he was taken back in again. That's when Hugh Mansell came."

"I'm really scared, Auntie Ida," I said, looking down at the tabletop. "I want to take Mimi home."

"You must go home, Cora." Auntie leaned her forehead on her outstretched fingers. "I feel Lankin is getting closer and closer. Three times now I have seen him near the house. He is waiting for one little moment of weakness, one small second when we let down our guard. We're all trapped, Cora, you and me too, not just the children down in the graveyard . . . my little lost Edward . . . we're all trapped. . . ."

Auntie raised her head.

"Maybe—maybe I could find somebody in the village to look after the two of you for the time being, until I can get you back to London. And then, somehow I could try to undo what Hillyard did. . . ."

"Auntie, please don't say such a dreadful thing. It can't be done."

"Maybe that's what I have to do . . . but who would help me?" She sank down again. "Nobody would want to help me."

Auntie's tears began to flow again.

I found myself putting my hands on her drooping shoulders and giving them a little squeeze. Then I leaned over and put my cheek against hers.

Auntie reached up and touched my hand. I didn't shake it off this time.

"I'll see if Hugh Mansell's in," she said, "so I can leave a telephone message for your father at the pub. I'll need to run a flannel over my face first."

❧ ROGER ❧

I was tying up my shoelaces when Pete came in.

"Where we going, then?" he said, slopping the milk over his shredded wheat so it overflowed onto some spilled sugar.

"Thought I'd go down Mrs. Eastfield's. Don't put the box on top of that milk. It'll stick to the table."

"Mum'll wipe it up," he said. "Wait for me. I've got to find some socks."

"Hurry up then. I'll get the bikes out."

It was going to be a really blazing day. On the main road, the tarmac was slightly soft, and the air above it already shimmering.

We stood at the top of the hill on Old Glebe Lane, levelling up to race each other down to the bottom.

"Can you feel that buzzing feeling?" I asked Pete.

"Don't be daft. What buzzing feeling?"

"Like—I dunno, like when you're standing under an electric pylon—you know, like the big one near the woods."

"Nah. You ready?" Pete took off.

"Oi! Hang on! We're meant to go together!" I shouted after him.

The ground was so hard we whizzed round at the bottom and into the Chase without stopping. The mud was baked into big lumps. Sometimes we had to stand up on the pedals to get along, but mostly it was a case of getting off the bikes altogether and pushing.

We waited for a while on the bridge outside Mrs. Eastfield's.

"D'you reckon there are frogs?" said Pete.

"I don't expect there'll be any here. I think the water's salty."

"Don't you get frogs in the sea, then?"

The tide was just about out. Only a trickle of water remained in the middle of the creek.

The electricity wire drooped from its pole near the bridge. All seemed strangely still, despite the busy humming of the insects in the wildflowers and the quiet babbling of the stream as it disappeared under the road. Not a single bird was singing from the trees around Guerdon Hall.

We dropped our bikes on the path and walked up

to the house. I banged on the front door, and the dog started barking.

"Who is it?" came a voice from the other side of the door. "Quiet, Finn. I can't hear."

"It's us."

We heard the sound of a key turning in the lock. The door opened a tiny crack, and I saw Cora's eye.

I'd already decided that if she was still going to be in a mood, Pete and me should just leave it and go down the woods instead, but she called out over her shoulder to Mrs. Eastfield, waited for a reply, then opened the door wide.

"Auntie Ida's gone to get washed," said Cora. "Best come in the kitchen."

❧ CORA ☙

Auntie Ida came down, scrubbed up but a little flushed and puffy.

"Mimi's still asleep but stirring," she said. "In ten minutes or so, go up and check her. If she's too hot, wring out a flannel in some cold water and wipe her forehead with it. I'm going up to Father Mansell's to make this telephone call, and you absolutely must promise me you won't leave the house, absolutely promise."

We stood listening, our eyes round with serious attention.

"I should be less than half an hour. I've checked the windows. The front-door key is still in the lock."

"What a blimmin' palaver," whispered Pete as Auntie put on her scarf.

She locked the back door behind her, taking the key. For some time, Finn jumped up on his back legs and scrabbled at the door, whining.

"It's blinking sweltering in here," said Pete, getting himself some water to drink from the tap. "Why's she locked us in? What if there's a fire and we're stuck and get burned to death?"

"We can get out the front," I said. "Anyway, you get used to it."

"I'm flippin' sweating," he said.

"We can go up to your house when she gets back."

"Blinkin' well hope she won't be long," he grumbled. "It's like a great big oven in this place. How do you stand it with the windows all shut? What's there to do in here?"

"There's a parrot," said Roger.

I got the bag of seeds out from under the sink and took Pete to show him how to take out the feed box.

Auntie Ida said the parrot had been in that same cage for years and years, that if you opened the door and told him he could fly away, he wouldn't want to, wouldn't even know how.

"He's lost loads of feathers," said Pete, fascinated. "You can see his skin."

When the parrot said, *"Hello,"* Pete laughed his head off and kept saying, "Hello" till the old bird said it again. I left him and went back into the kitchen, where Roger and I started washing up the dishes from breakfast. Roger was blinking hopeless at it, just slooshing the things around in the water instead of wiping them properly with the dishcloth. I tried to tell him as much as I could about what Auntie Ida had said.

❧ IDA EASTFIELD ❧

Harry must come. It's urgent now. How could I send Cora with the message I'm going to leave? He is her father, after all. It's bad enough her mother being the way she is. He must come. There's still time today — if not, then tomorrow. He must come quickly.

Everything's locked up. I checked every window. I've got the back-door key here in my pocket. I hope to God Hugh is in. Maureen Mansell must be there, or I can try the Treasures. Somebody will be around. How will I find the telephone number of the Half Moon? Hugh will help me. Why am I so uneasy? I must hurry. It's so hot. I'll have to take my scarf off.

They've got Finn. I won't be long.

I must take off my coat. The air is laden. Another storm must be on the way.

❧ CORA ❧

Finn starts pawing at me. Maybe Auntie Ida hasn't fed him, what with everything going on this morning. I open up a can of Chappie and fork it into his dish. He wolfs it down.

He's still unsettled, gruffling and whining. I can't give him any more food. Auntie would be cross.

When Roger and I go out into the hall, Finn sits at the bottom of the stairs and looks up, fitful, his eyes wide open, his whole body bristling and alert.

Roger and I leave him and go into the sitting room, where Pete is trying to make the parrot say "Bye-bye."

Roger sits down on the settee on one side of the spring, and I sit on the other, the loose stuffing itchy on the back of my legs. It's stifling. We lean back, close our eyes, and blow out hot air.

Pete is starting to get annoying with his "Bye-bye, bye-bye."

"Leave off, mate," says Roger. "He's too flippin' old. He's never going to say 'Bye-bye.'"

Finn comes in and sits restlessly on the floor by our feet. He puts his paw up on my knee.

It just occurs to me to go up and check Mimi when a sudden, massive thud from upstairs rattles the parrot's cage.

"Blimey! I hope Mimi ain't fallen out of bed," I say, quickly standing.

Finn gets up. He growls from deep in his throat, then, drawing back the sides of his mouth, bares his curved teeth in a snarl.

"Shut up, Finn!" I say. "Why're you doing that? Shut up!"

Down the length of his back, the hair begins to rise. Half crouching, he moves towards the door. Puzzled, I slowly follow him. Roger gets up. Pete stops saying "Bye-bye" and looks over.

"What's the matter with him?" he says.

A nasty smell fills the hall. I hear light, faltering footsteps on the staircase. Finn growls a long, menacing growl.

A small figure in white brushed cotton pyjamas, dotted with yellow ducks, is descending the stairs. A little white hand with Sid dangling from it moves downwards, loosely touching the thick wooden rail. Mimi herself is as quiet as a whisper, but from farther up the stairs comes the sound of creaking and the noise of slow, rasping breathing.

With one huge bound, Finn leaps along the hall to

the bottom of the staircase. He crouches at the bottom, threatening and snapping, his eyes fixed on something higher up the stairs, something beyond Mimi.

"Cora, Cora . . ." Mimi cries in a small, weak voice.

Finn barks wildly, his eyes bulging, saliva spilling out of his mouth.

I rush to the stairs and look up. My jaw drops open. Behind Mimi, Cain Lankin is crawling down like an animal. The tip of his tongue, wet with thick grey spit, is sticking out from between his sharp yellow teeth like a black pointed stone.

Mimi is in a dream.

I push past Finn, leap up four stairs, and fling my arms round her. Long fingernails, hard as iron, snatch at me. I stagger backwards with Mimi. I fall onto the wooden floorboards, gather her up, and dash back to Roger and Pete. They stand there, open-mouthed. Finn leaps forward a few steps, barking and growling, barring Lankin's way.

Mimi sways as I stand her on the hall floor by the sitting-room door. My mind is racing, back to Haldane Thorston, Auntie Ida, to Mimi's disappearance on washing day.

"Mimi! Mimi! Listen! Where's the little house you went in with that lady? How did you get in?" I shout at her, holding her shoulders. "Mimi!"

She's half closing her eyes.

"Mimi! Where's the little house? How d'you get in the little house?"

She lifts up her hand and waves towards the panelling. "There," she whispers. "You push it—there."

She's floppy. I hold her up.

"Roger! Pete!" I shout. "Push the wood! Push it!"

They don't know where to push. They prod the wood from top to bottom where it joins the door frame. Roger clenches his teeth and pushes his shoulder against it.

Finn yelps. A rattling sound comes from his throat, like gargling.

"Not there," Mimi says, so quietly I have to put my ear to her lips. "This side. Here."

"This side!" I yell. "This side!"

✄ ROGER ✄

We dash to the next section of panelling.

Mimi points limply towards a particular square of wood. In desperation I thump it with my fist. Nothing happens. I push my damp hair out of my eyes.

The scuffling continues on the staircase. There's a loud thud. Finn is gasping for breath.

"Are you sure, Mimi? This one?"

She nods faintly.

I press the wooden square firmly with both hands and feel a movement. From behind the wall, near the floor, comes the sound of stone grating on stone, then a slow scraping noise. The whole panel of five carved squares gives way under my hands and swivels around on itself vertically, bringing threads of cobwebs with it. Behind, there is a dark hole.

"Quick! Quick!" I yell. Cora pushes Mimi in and follows. Pete squeezes in next, and I squash myself into the only bit of space left. It is so tight we struggle to push the panel back into place.

"Breathe in!" Cora mumbles. I bend my arms and knees and push at the edge of the panel, straining with all my might. It begins to move and is inches from shutting when a grey hand, the slimy, stinking flesh stretched taut over the bones, grabs the edge. I feel a sear of pain as a fingernail, sharp as a razor, takes skin off my cheek. Pete strains to reach the door and begins pushing it, little by little, until the grisly fingers are trapped. We push together, and at last, bit by bit, they withdraw. The panel closes, and we are entombed in thick black darkness.

There is no sound from outside, but we know Lankin is still there. We can smell him.

"I can't breathe," whispers Pete right against my face so his lips touch me. "What are we going to do? We're using up the air. We'll die in a minute."

Mimi is whimpering. I can't work out whether the hand pressed into my back is hers or Pete's or Cora's. I try to stretch my neck, but my head scrapes against the underside of a stair tread. I'm so completely wedged in, I can only take shallow breaths from the top of my lungs. The metal mechanism on the back of the panel presses against my ear. I am desperate not to release the spring and reopen the door.

"What are we going to do, Cora?" I hiss through my teeth. "How long is Mrs. Eastfield going to be?"

"If she comes back now," Cora breathes, "I don't know what'll happen. I—I can't hear Finn."

Pete starts crying. I feel his body shuddering, his cheek wet against mine.

❧ CORA ☙

Then the slow scratching begins. Now I understand how the long grooved marks came to be on the front door of Guerdon Hall, on the back door, on the door of the church.

"Will—will he get in?" Pete sobs.

We are packed together so tightly I can feel the hammering of Pete's heart as well as my own.

"We're—we're going to squash to death in here," he cries faintly.

Then I remember something Auntie Ida told me just this morning.

"Auntie—Auntie Ida," I stammer. "She said there were two doors, one after the other. This hole was built to hide a priest. If—if they found this hole here but there was nobody in it, they'd think the hiding place was empty and go away, but—but if this hole had a secret door itself that went into another hidden room—a hidden room they didn't even think about—"

"But we're so squashed and it's black as night," Roger says. "How could we find another door? There's no room to move—"

The scratching stops. Lankin thumps the panelling. It rattles.

"What if he pushes in the right place?" croaks Pete.

"Don't—don't worry, mate," says Roger. "With us lot here, there's no room for it to swing round."

"Mimi knows," I whisper.

"Knows what?"

"Mimi—Mimi, listen to me. Did the lady show you another door? Was there another door in the little house? Mimi, can you hear me?"

She makes no sound. I try to touch her, terrified she has suffocated.

I find her hair, her face. "Mimi! Answer me! Mimi! Wake up!"

"She kicked the wall," Mimi says in a small, quavering

voice, "at the bottom . . . where the stairs go down . . . she kicked it. . . ."

"Whose foot's near where the stairs go down?" whispers Roger.

"I don't know. I've gone all numb," whines Pete.

"I think you must be nearest, Cora," says Roger. "Can you move your foot?"

"How the flippin' hell can I move me foot—there ain't no space."

Lankin begins to pummel the wall with both hands. We shake with it.

I stretch out my foot and somehow manage to run it a short way along the bottom of the side wall. I press my shoe tight against it, then, wriggling myself down, try to move it farther along, but am wedged in by Pete. I feel for Mimi's skinny legs. There is a tiny space of wall in between them. I might just reach it if I stretch my foot a little more.

"Keep still, Mimi. Don't move an inch!"

I kick at the bottom of the wall between Mimi's feet. The blow is so feeble that I expect nothing and sigh with frustration. All I can do is try once more. The second kick is a little harder.

To my amazement, there is a grating sound, and half the wall slips sideways behind the other half. My foot falls into nothing. Cold, damp air rushes in from somewhere under the ground.

ᴄᴋ ROGER ᴣᴐ

"Crikey! You've done it!"

"Hang on. I'll see what it is."

Cora wriggles down and pushes forward through the hole with her feet, making extra space for the rest of us. We breathe more easily.

"There's a bit of a landing, then wooden steps going down—quite steep, I think. This must be how the priests escaped." Cora snakes her body through the hole. "Mimi, come here. Come down to me. We're going to get out this way. Come here. I'll carry you."

Mimi's too poorly to complain or cry. I twist myself round and manage to bend and help her through the hole into Cora's arms.

Lankin is hammering furiously on the wood, making a kind of strangled roaring sound in his throat. There is room now for the door to swing open if he hits the right panel.

"Go on, Pete, hurry up," I urge him. "Get through the hole. Quick, quick! I'll follow you."

Pete is all over the place. He can't get his bearings, bumps his head, and cries out.

"Rub it hard. Rub it really hard! You'll be all right, mate. Just get in there. Go on."

I push him through, then fold myself double, turn,

405

and go through backwards so that I can shut the hole behind me. It's tight. I crouch on the little landing, feeling a draught rising from the steep empty space under my heels.

Despite Lankin's heavy beating from the hall, I can hear Cora and Pete descending carefully, one step at a time, down under the ground.

I have to work out how to shut the door, but I can't see anything.

I catch hold of the edge of the panel and try to slide it back to the left, but it only gives an inch or so. Feeling for a jammed spring, I run my fingers around the sides, but all I find are thick tangles of dusty webs. Grunting with effort, I try once more to wrench the square of wood across the opening.

A wave of panic sweeps over me. I thump on the wood with my fist.

"You all right?" comes Cora's echoing voice.

"Yeah, all right," I pant. "Just trying to close the door. It's a bit stiff."

I feel in the dark, over my head, to the left and right, for some kind of mechanism. In desperation, I thrust my hand back through the hole and grope around the inner wall.

Somebody grabs my hand. I shriek with fright and fall back so quickly onto the landing that half my backside hangs out over the steep staircase. I lose my balance.

My arms flail about, trying to find a grip. Just as I'm about to go sprawling backwards, someone snatches my right arm, then my left.

"Roger, you all right?" Pete calls up. "What is it?"

The hands pull me back towards the door, holding me until I'm steady and kneeling on the landing. I stay there, shaking, gasping for breath. The hands are small, like a woman's. They let me go. I am rigid with fear; my heart thuds in my chest.

Lankin's blows become muffled as the second door is slowly drawn shut, but not by me.

"Nothing!" I shout back hoarsely. "Just coming."

✥ CORA ✥

Mimi's fingers are knotted so tightly in my hair that my eyes water.

I feel my way in the dark with the toes of my shoes. The stairs twist sharply to the right, then left again, so steep I have to lean backwards and take them one at a time. The dense mats of hanging webs brush our faces. Mimi shifts her weight and throws me off balance. I wait, hoist her into a different position, my hair roots straining, and make sure I'm steady before going any farther.

The sound of tiny pattering feet reaches my ears,

and I realize I can see the vague movements of scurrying mice. I am no longer blind in the dark. Somewhere there is a source of light. In the murky gloom, I make out the lines of the steps, which are becoming damp and slightly slippery. Then I see the grey edge of a panel, on a slant, blocking my way. Holding Mimi tight with one arm, I push it and it falls to one side, crashing to the ground and crumbling into pieces.

In some large empty vault to my right, drops of water echo as they fall to the floor with a hollow plopping sound. I catch a gleam of brightness among the confusing, colourless shapes.

"I'm down!" I call, my foot crunching on a pile of small bones.

Directly ahead, beyond a low archway, some broken barrels lie half-sunken in mud, the curved pieces of wood sticking up like the rib bones of a great decaying fish.

To the left the passage goes off into blackness under the house. Mimi is flopping on my shoulder, a dead weight. With heavy arms, I carry her across the dank ground towards the echoing chamber.

Pete clings to my cardigan as we peer through the open doorway.

The room is alive. In the washed-out half-light, mice scatter into the dirty corners, and long-legged spiders retreat into cloudy webs that hang in sheets like old, torn banners from the ceiling. Beetles creep along the dust-laden shelves, drop into the big black iron pans, and plop into holes, while two glossy rats slide out of an untidy stack of logs piled against the back wall and disappear into the shadows. Something slithers off the huge, cracked wooden table and flops with a light thud onto a floor littered with broken pottery, shards of glass, small bones, and other, unidentifiable rubbish, once lifted by floodwater, moved, shifted, muddied, and left adrift to settle where it would.

A shaft of light glances downwards from an alcove to the side of the curved arch of the wide fireplace. Iron chains and hooks dangle in rusty loops from the chimney. Below the chains is a long metal frame, veiled with rippling cobwebs, which supports a heavy bar, pronged at one end.

Small grimy windows are set high up, hard against the angle of the ceiling, the same windows we saw almost buried at the bottom of the wall when we went searching around the house for a way in. Daylight barely penetrates the thick, green-stained glass.

We are directly under Auntie Ida's kitchen. Auntie Ida and Mimi and I sit at the table in the room just above, drink our tea, eat our dinner, wash our clothes, and listen to *Woman's Hour* on the wireless—only a floor away from this cellar.

Pete tucks himself close behind me as we step through the open doorway and over the threshold. On my left I make out in the dusky light a stone staircase spiralling upwards.

Roger follows us into the room.

"This—this is the old kitchen," I stammer.

He swallows. "Crikey—where—where it all happened."

"What? What are you talking about?" says Pete. Roger and I cannot answer him. "What about these stairs?" he continues. "I'll go up and see if there's a way out."

"Careful, mate!" says Roger as, gingerly, Pete begins to climb from one step to the next, kicking down small lumps of crumbly mortar and pieces of old brick and wood as he goes. A couple of times we hear him stumble, muttering to himself.

Then, as if waking, Mimi raises herself in my arms, untwines her fingers from my hair, and gazes over my shoulder into the empty space beyond the wooden stairs.

"She's here," she whispers in my ear.

"What? What are talking about?"

"Behind you."

Roger and I turn our heads and look back. My blood runs like ice.

Standing in the dim passage beyond, framed by the dark rectangle of the doorway, is a young woman, her face half in shadow. She begins to sing.

"Here's blood in the kitchen. Here's blood in the hall.
Here's blood on the stairs where my lady did fall."

Roger is trembling so violently, I can feel it against my arm.

The girl starts to speak softly, hoarsely, in a kind of breathless babble.

". . . the silver basin on the table . . . one for you, Cain Lankin, says the false nurse, and one for me . . . the thin dagger — a flash in the firelight — crimson splashes in the basin — an infant screaming in the night —

"Who is behind the door? Pull her out! Pull her out! Ha! Little Kittie Wicken, is it! Ha! Little Kittie Wicken, that bad girl, is it! She won't tell or I'll call up Old Nick, the Prince of the Power of the Air, I will, and he'll rip that biddy biddy baby out, he will, and serve it up for you, Cain Lankin, my dear. . . . He will drag little Kittie down to the lake of fire and brimstone because she's a wicked sinner, with that biddy baby in her belly that should not be there. . . . I know who put that biddy biddy baby in your belly. I know, I do.

"Stop your snivelling. Stop your grizzling. She can be of use to us, Cain Lankin, my dear. She can fetch the moon-white mistress from her sleep, and if little Kittie Wicken snitches, out that biddy baby comes and we'll stick him with this bloody pin.

"I can do it, Kittie Wicken. I can do it while I live. I can do it if I die. I will search you out. I can play with living and with

dying, I can. Be sure of that, Kittie Wicken. I have charmed the spirits, I have.

"Look at little Johnny, Kittie, poor little boy. . . . The infant is crying for his mother. Fetch her down for us, fetch down the mother, Kittie Wicken. Poor little Johnny . . .

"If you whisper to a living soul, I will make a charm and bring you to the feet of the Demon."

Kittie steps forward. A little light outlines half her head in a golden curve. One eye remains in darkness; the other glistens with a feverish glow.

"I should have fetched the men, but—but I stole away aloft. My lady slept in her chamber, her hair golden on the silken pillow, her cheek flushed like a summer rose. 'My lady'—I touched the small white hand on the counterpane—'the baby cries for you; he will not lie still.'

"'How durst I go down in the dead of the night
Where there's no fire a-kindled and no candle alight?'

"The baby shrieks from below. My lady throws aside her coverlet, searches for her robe.

"'You have three silver mantles as bright as the sun.
Come down, my fair lady, all by light of one.'

"A footstep on the stair . . . the babe for you, Cain Lankin, and ah—the mother for me—here she comes—her lord

gone—that'll learn him when he comes back—that'll learn
his high lordship—good little Kittie Wicken brings her down.
Sew your lips, Kittie, or I'll find you out. One for you, Cain
Lankin, and one for me—and away before the light. . . ."

"Is that you, Cora?" Pete shouts down. "What are
you saying?"

"There goes my lady—crawling up the stone steps—the
mantle ripped—a trail of blood . . . too late . . . too late . . . I should
have fetched the men. . . . I should have fetched the men. . . .

"'O master, O master, don't lay blame on me.
'Twas the false nurse and Lankin that killed your lady.'

"'. . . scarlet blood drying in dark pools on the floor . . .'"
"It's bricked up up here!" Pete calls down. "We can't
get out!"

"'Long Lankin was hung on a gibbet so high
And the false nurse was burned in a fire close by.'

". . . he came for my little baby . . . snatched him from me
and took him across the creek . . . my little Robin . . . my angel
from heaven, my little lost boy . . . I brought my lady down
to them. . . . I was afeared of the cunning woman, of the long
man. . . . I should have fetched the men. . . ."

The woman slips away backwards and is swallowed
up by the black tunnel. Mimi moves her fingers up and

413

down in a tender wave before laying her head back on my shoulder.

Pete blunders down the last couple of steps and looks frantically around the kitchen.

"Didn't you hear me? It's bricked up up there!"

"The pantry," I say in a daze. "The staircase leads to the pantry."

"Eh?" hisses Roger.

"The end wall of the pantry upstairs was bricked up, a long time ago."

"What's the matter with you?" says Pete, looking around wildly. "I'm going to climb up that chimney."

He moves forward, picking his way quickly through the debris on the floor. He reaches the fireplace, climbs over the metal frame in the hearth, and looks up the chimney, his nose and forehead lit from far above.

Even in the gloom, I can see Roger's face is drained of colour. "Cora—upstairs—a minute ago," he says under his breath, "the sliding door was stuck. I couldn't close it. I lost my balance and somebody—some woman—grabbed me and stopped me falling down the steps. Then she shut the door for me. I think—I think it must have been her."

Mimi's lips are soft on my neck. "It was Kittie."

Suddenly we hear a muffled crash from upstairs.

"Blimey! Lankin! He must've got through the first door!"

414

"We've got to get out!" My arms are aching. I put Mimi down. She is unsteady on her feet and holds her arms up to me. "Hang on, Mimi. Give us a minute."

I guide her across the floor to the fireplace.

"Any luck, Pete?" asks Roger as we gaze up the huge chimney to the small circle of light way above our heads. The walls slope inwards to a narrow opening at the top. Even if one of us could climb it, we would never get Mimi up as well.

The banging starts again. Mimi clings to my skirt.

"He's trying to get through the second door," cries Roger.

I run my eyes along the curve of the fireplace, to the stack of ancient logs under their grey filmy shroud, to the strong bar of light that shines down from inside the overhanging alcove above them. In the beam, swirling dust sparkles like glitter.

"Where's this light coming from, then?"

Two chains ending in large hooks hang down inside the recess. Roger catches hold of the thicker one.

"I'll pull myself up on this and have a look."

He tugs on the chain hard. There's a mighty crack. Roger lets go. We stumble back into the room as stones, small pieces of brick, and wood shower around us. The chain falls into the fireplace in a tangled heap, sending up a dense cloud of dust.

Wiping his eyes, coughing, Roger waits a few seconds

for it to settle a little, then goes back to the alcove and leans over the log pile.

"It goes right back, a sort of shaft. That's sunlight shining down. Pete, come and help me move some of this wood."

⁓ ROGER ⁓

Pete and I grab as many logs as we can and toss them behind us onto the floor. The wood crumbles into powdery pieces, irritating our throats, making us choke. Beetles, fat spiders, and wood lice slither in and out of the flaking bark. Our grubby hands are fringed with cobwebs.

We clear a space. I climb over the remains of the stack and bend to get through the short tunnel beyond. The ground is covered with soil. After a few paces, I can stand upright and see white-blue sky through a small jagged hole over my head. Pete is behind me. A quick scramble and he is up on my shoulders while I hold on to his legs.

"I might be able to climb up," he calls down. "It isn't high, and some of the bricks are missing, so I can stick my feet in the gaps."

"Careful, then, mate."

One hand, then the other goes up into the shaft. One foot, then the other comes off my shoulders.

I look up and get an eyeful of dirt. With his legs wide apart, Pete has wedged himself across the shaft. He is holding on to the wall with one hand, and with the other he is reaching up and pulling at something. Scraps of wood, bits of earth, and dust rain down on my head.

"It's a sort of trapdoor," he shouts. "I think it's where Cora's foot went through—you know, that hole in the garden. You got a long stick? I might be able to push it up."

I think quickly. "Get that spit thing!" I yell to Cora.

"What spit thing?"

"That long pole thing in the fireplace. Hurry up!"

I hear her mumbling. "The flippin' thing's rusted."

"Hurry up!"

The prongs on the end of the pole, wrapped in cobwebs, are coming towards me through the tunnel. On the other end of the pole is a short metal handle. I stretch it upwards and Pete takes it from me in his raw, dirty hands.

He hits the bottom of the trapdoor with it, over and over again.

"Me arms are aching!" he calls.

"Don't stop, mate!"

"I'm getting blimmin' great blisters!"

At the next blow, there is a crack, and a huge chunk of wood misses my shoulder by a whisker. The shaft floods with hot light.

"You all right?" My open mouth fills with loose soil and leaves. "Blimmin' hell!" I blink and spit out stones.

417

Pete hits the trapdoor with a last mighty thump, and a whole plank becomes dislodged and wedges itself against his body and the side of the shaft.

"I'll have to drop the pole, then I can get hold of this wood." The pole slides past my face, and the handle hits me hard on the nose. I feel warm blood streaming into my mouth and down my chin.

"Watch out!" cries Pete. "Here comes the door!"

Half-blinded and spitting out blood, I'm not ready for it. The piece of wood falls. On its way to the ground, it slams into my elbow with a jarring blast of pain. I see popping lights, feel sick, stagger.

"Oi! Roger! Flippin' heck! Stop wobbling about! Don't drop me!"

I feel Pete's calves on my shoulders. He scrambles down. "Crikey, what happened to you?" he says, brushing the dirt off his shirt.

I wipe my nose with the back of my hand. "Got to get Mimi out. Quick."

The banging from upstairs has become frenzied. Any minute now and the second door must cave in.

"Cora! Get Mimi over here! We've got to go now! Pete, you get out first, then I'll lift Mimi up, and then you can pull her arms while I push."

Pete climbs back onto my shoulders, stretches up, and begins to climb, finding hand- and footholds in the crumbling brickwork. The last I see of him are the soles of his shoes wriggling up and out of the hole and into the brilliant sunshine. He calls down that he is in the garden.

Cora pushes Mimi, who is crying, through the tunnel.

"Quick, lift her up on my shoulders!"

"You ready, mate?" I shout to Pete. "Grab Mimi as she comes out!"

"Won't go. Won't," sobs Mimi, twisting her hands into Cora's skirt.

"You flippin' will!" Cora grits her teeth and snatches Sid from Mimi's hand. "You can have him back when you're a good girl."

Grizzling, Mimi lets Cora lift her up.

Pete is leaning over the edge of the hole, balanced on the other side of the trapdoor. I can see it moving. I don't know how long it will bear his weight. He reaches down, but though I stretch up on my toes, I can't get Mimi near enough.

"I can't reach!" he shouts.

"You'll have to go piggyback," I say to her. She whines.

"If you let me carry you up, Cora will give Sid back."

❧ CORA ❧

Still complaining, Mimi lets Roger lower her down onto his back.

"Hold really tight," he says to her. "Don't let go."

I give her Sid. He dangles from her hands under Roger's bloody chin. She wraps her legs tightly around his middle. He takes a deep breath and starts to climb up the shaft.

I hear a pushing, scraping noise from the top of the wooden staircase beyond the kitchen.

"Mimi, get your blinking hands off my eyes," I hear Roger say as he looks for handholds in the shaft. "I can't see a blimmin' thing."

Suddenly his foot slips. I catch it in both hands and gasp as skin slides off my palms. I groan and lose my balance.

At that moment, Roger finds a foothold and hoists himself upwards out of my reach.

Shading my eyes with my hands, I can make out his shape moving up the shaft. I see Mimi being lifted out, Roger manoeuvring himself onto the remains of the trapdoor, which is now leaning inwards from its frame at an awkward angle, one iron ring a black circle against the sky.

⤜ ROGER ⤛

My feet slide sideways as the trapdoor begins to give way. Bending my knees, I quickly swing up my hands to clutch at the long grass on the edge of the hole. My left hand grabs a clump; my right hand seizes another but loses its grip. My arm flails and crashes into the broken, ragged frame. Long rusty nails pierce the flesh of my wrist and rip the skin into deep bloody lines. I cry out. I think I will faint. Swallowing, grunting, I fling up my streaming hand, grasp a sheaf of grass, and pull myself up as the remains of the trapdoor crack, sheer off, and plummet down the shaft towards Cora.

✎ CORA ✎

I am showered with earth and splinters of wood. There is a ripping sound, a cracking. Choking, I jump backwards into the tunnel, banging my head on the rim of the arch. Part of the trapdoor falls, crashing into the ground, bringing with it rocks, stones, and soil. The rest, I can tell by the instant darkness, has lodged itself in the shaft, blocking my escape.

Behind me, I hear the sound of feet stumbling blindly, awkwardly, down the wooden stairs from the priest's hole. Something heavy, metal, is being dragged along behind, scraping on the edges of the treads.

My blood pounds as if it will burst out of my skin.

I rush to the kitchen doorway, slipping on the floor, bumping against the table. The footsteps are just above the last bend, almost at the bottom of the stairs. In front of me is the long passage under the house.

It is all I can do—go down the black tunnel and hide in the dark.

I stretch out my hands in front of me but can't even see my fingers. I stop, standing frozen on the soft, damp ground, listening. I have no sight, no touch, but I can hear sharp as needles.

The footsteps stop behind me. They crunch on the bones at the bottom of the stairs and then go through the doorway into the kitchen, followed by the sound of some weighty metallic tool.

If I make a dash now, I could get to the steps and rush upstairs, but just as I begin to turn, the footsteps come padding back across the kitchen floor, back to the staircase.

I run down the dark, dark tunnel, my feet slapping on patches of moisture.

The footsteps follow, slipping like mine. The heavy object trails behind.

Faster. Faster still.

My forehead cracks on stone. I see stabs of light, sparks. My head buzzes. I crumple.

I hear panting. The metal thing drops. Arms grip me tight, enfolding.

I smell soap.

"Cora! Cora! Is it you? Oh, thank God. Where's Mimi?"

It's Auntie Ida.

"Where's Mimi? Didn't you hear me?" she says. "I called and called — the second door was stuck. Where are they? Where's Mimi?"

My head throbs. My knees are buckling. I feel giddy.

"They've gone through this trapdoor, into the garden. They've escaped."

"Through the trapdoor? The log shaft? Oh, my God! Oh, my God!" Auntie cries, turning, hurrying back, pulling me with her to the wooden steps, stumbling in the darkness.

I trip over the long handle of the axe she is dragging behind her. It is the huge one that was hanging on hooks by the back door.

My head is spinning. Auntie Ida yanks me, slipping, stumbling, up the wooden steps. We squeeze ourselves back through the gap in the panelling. She pulls me down the hall. With horror, I see Finn, still and silent, slumped at a strange angle across the bottom of the staircase.

ROGER

Gasping, I lift my face and see Lankin snatch Mimi away from Pete. Pete shrieks, falls to his knees, and covers his face with his hands.

I pick myself up and stumble down the garden after Lankin.

Mimi's little body dangles limply under his arm. He knows where he is going, darting over the dry mud at the bottom of the empty creek, then leaping over the barbed-wire fence on the other side and into some huge brambles.

For a second, he stops and looks back at me. Grey saliva dribbles down his chin.

The creek is too wide, the mud too soft. I can't get across.

He drops onto all fours, stretching himself out like some huge insect, and moving so quickly, with Mimi's floppy head just skimming the ground, that in a moment he is gone.

I bolt back past Pete to the front of the house, pick up my bike from the ground, and hurry on, pushing it over the bridge and hopping onto the saddle in the Chase. The hard lumps of baked mud make it impossible to go fast. I drop the bike and run. My side and throat hurt, but I speed on, round the end of the Chase and down towards the church.

I stop at the lychgate, shoulders heaving, catching my breath, hearing that buzzing noise in my ears like a million flies swarming. The sun burns my cheeks.

❧ CORA ❧

We dash through the back door, standing wide open, and into the garden. Auntie won't let go of my dirty, sweaty hand. My breath is sharp in my throat. She rushes me along the path and around the side of the house.

Pete is alone, cowering next to the outside wall of the huge chimney. Tears pour out of his eyes and down his filthy cheeks in two pale streaks.

"Peter, Peter, where are they?" shouts Auntie Ida, kneeling in front of him, dropping the axe, and shaking him by the arms.

His bottom lip trembles. He wipes his eyes with his fists.

"Come on, you two!" cries Auntie, picking up the axe and starting to run to the front of the house.

"What was that shaft?" I call after her.

"They used to use it for getting stuff down into the kitchen — in the old days," she shouts breathlessly over her shoulder. "It's — it's probably the way Lankin got out after the killings. He must have started to dig it out again."

"But how did he know that's where we'd come out?"

"There's no other way — he knew that. Hurry, Cora!"

We turn the corner and race along the weed-covered gravel. "Oh, please don't let it be too late!"

We thunder over the wooden bridge. The creek is dry. The tide is out.

Pete follows us, pulling up the front of his shirt to wipe his face.

Auntie Ida staggers with the huge axe in her hands. "I never—I never thought he'd come through the roof!" she pants. "Oh—my chest—you carry on—my chest—"

"Let me take that!"

"No—no—" She leans on the axe and takes in great gulping breaths. "All right—I'm all right now—let's go. . . ."

We run on. Glancing towards the marshes, towards the church, Auntie doesn't see Roger's bike lying in her path until it's too late.

She goes sprawling. The axe flies out of her hands.

She clutches at her chest. Her face reddens. Pete and I help her to her feet. Her chin is cut and her knees grazed through her ripped stockings.

"I'm all right. I'm all right. We must go on! I'm all right!"

Pete reaches for the axe. "I'll take this, Mrs. Eastfield. I'll carry it for you."

"Give it to me!" she snaps. "I said, *give it to me!*"

She snatches the axe out of his hands, turns it upside down, and sticks the head under her armpit like a crutch.

"Come on—come on—we must hurry! I'm all right. Hurry!"

We are at the end of the Chase. Auntie Ida is hobbling, her face a strange greyish white.

"Peter," she says, gritting her teeth, "do you know where Father Mansell lives?"

In a daze, he nods.

"Go and get him! Quickly!"

Pete turns and starts running up the hill.

Auntie Ida and I press on to the church. As we enter the churchyard, her breathing is heavy, her face pinched.

She stops, panting, for a moment, drawing in her strength. I squeeze her arm, and as I do so, my eye is caught by a smudge of pink just above the ground on this side of the lychgate. The small tight rosebud I'd seen hanging over the grave slab just after we came to Auntie Ida's has bloomed and is dying.

We see Roger standing by the old coffin-shaped tomb with the stone lid half off, where Pete put the wreath we'd made.

Auntie and I draw closer. Roger bends down and picks something up from the ground. It's Sid.

"I think he's taken her in here," he says, pointing to the tomb.

"I'll go first," says Auntie Ida.

She gives me the axe, lifts her injured leg in her hands, and, grunting, hoists it over the side of the stone box. Then, taking some deep breaths and holding on to the sides of the tomb, she lifts the good leg over. With her backside resting on the edge, she braces herself for a minute, then lowers herself in, crying out in pain as she lands.

"Give me the axe!" she calls up, her voice sounding muffled from under the ground.

I lift it with both hands and drop it in after Auntie Ida, then climb up onto the stone lid and swing my legs over the edge. The lid shifts a little as I look down the inner walls of the tomb into the dark earth. The hole is edged with the fine threads of white roots.

"Just jump, Cora," I hear Auntie say. "It isn't deep. Bend your knees when you come down. I'm here."

With my eyes shut tight, I launch myself into the hole. Auntie steadies me as I land. I open my eyes and, for a moment, can't see in front of me. My mouth tastes of soil.

"Follow me," whispers Auntie, stooping to crawl through the tunnel, dragging the axe behind her.

Steadying myself, I crouch down like Auntie, reaching out on both sides, feeling hard earth, stones, and ancient bones. My hand runs over something round and smooth. I turn my head. It is a half-buried, dirt-brown skull. Two eye sockets, stopped up with earth, gaze back at me. A fat worm moves like a tongue in and out of the old yellow teeth. The lower jaw is missing.

Roger flops down behind me. "How did he do this tunnel?" he breathes.

"Lankin tried to rescue Aphra Rushes from the church by digging his way in with his bare hands," whispers Auntie Ida. "Then Piers Hillyard buried him in his rough coffin in the very same place. Lankin had begun to dig his own grave without knowing it and then, later, must have clawed his way out of it."

The tunnel is narrow and short. In only a few paces, we have reached the foundations of the church.

Some of the stones have been hacked out for an entrance. A makeshift door, a piece of rotting wood, is propped up in front of the hole. Auntie removes it and leans it against the tunnel wall, then peers into the darkness.

"The smell . . ." she says, wrinkling her nose in disgust.

She crouches down and, with great care, puts one leg, then the other, over the rim of the hole and passes into the dark space on the other side. Then she reaches back for the axe.

Roger and I follow.

❧ IDA EASTFIELD ❧

We are in the crypt beneath the church. It reeks of the sweet odour of rotting flesh and burning wax.

I peer round a stone pillar, wipe soil out of my eyes, blink, and am dazzled.

The walls are flickering with light. A myriad of candle flames splutter and spit from niches and ledges, coffin lids and tombs, sending up wandering strings of smoke to curl under the vault of the ceiling.

My moist hands clasp and unclasp the handle of the axe as my blurred vision clears. Then I let out a long, low gasp.

In front of us is a vast pile of bones in a high jagged heap—skulls and leg bones and vertebrae, knee bones and jaws, whole and broken, crushed, splintered, sharp, the larger ones gathered from the tombs of the under-croft, the ancient tombs of the Guerdons, my family, now standing broken and empty. The only Guerdons Lankin has spared lie safe in the plot near the old gate in the graveyard above us.

But most of the bones in this massive pile are very small, delicate even. All are discoloured—dark brown, yellow, ivory, dirty grey.

The floor is littered with fragments, scraps of cloth, little pieces of shoes.

On the far wall, the huge black shadow of the pile quivers in the candlelight.

Sitting cross-legged on top of this grisly mound is Long Lankin, sitting on this ghastly throne made of the bones of the poor damned children condemned to wander in the half-world so long as he himself has life. One by one, they were called to play in his garden of souls.

Blood of my blood, flesh of my flesh, bone of my bone — somewhere there, in that wretched charnel heap, are shreds of my own self — my ancestors, my brother, and . . . and my son.

Lankin looks down at us, holding Mimi out towards us, mocking us. Her small thin body is limp and drooping. He lifts her floppy arm and shakes her little hand at us.

He can wait. He has her in his grasp. Even if we were able to climb the shifting bone pile, how could we stop a creature who has defied death for generation upon generation? He gloats at us, drawing back his thin, wasted lips and showing us his pointed yellow teeth.

He is smiling.

❧ CORA ☙

We stand completely rigid, staring in horror. I take a glance at Auntie. She looks defeated, bleak with pain. I feel utterly helpless.

Suddenly Roger hisses out of the side of his mouth, "Help me, Cora. Pull out the bones. Make the heap fall down."

"What? Don't be stupid. What about Mimi?"

431

"Leave her to me," whispers Auntie Ida with a hint of excitement in her voice. "You help Roger."

"But your leg—"

"It's all we can do, but we must do it now. Move!"

"Right. Give me the axe!"

I grab it from Auntie as we run towards the pile. It's so heavy, the head hits the ground with a clunk. Long Lankin looks down at us and tips his chin to the side and stops grinning.

Roger starts at the bottom of the heap, furiously tearing out leg bones, ribs.

I lift the axe as high as I can, then strike at the tangled mass, thrusting the metal head deep inside, turning it around with all my strength, and yanking it towards me. A couple of little skulls drop to the floor.

❧ ROGER ❧

I claw at the pile with both hands, pulling out a shredded sock, bones, a dirty blue rag, bones, and more bones.

Cora is struggling. I snatch the axe from her and bring it down once, twice, into the heap, and once again. Mrs. Eastfield drags out a piece of a ragged blanket, and with it comes a large bundle of bones knotted together. They dislodge and shoot across the floor. The heap is creaking. It's beginning to move. Where the axe head falls, bones spill out and roll away. A space opens up in front, stretching back into the middle of the pile, overhung with the platform of bones on which Long Lankin sits.

He leans over, snarling. Dangling Mimi under one arm, he starts to crawl down towards us. The shifting sound becomes louder, more urgent. As his weight presses down on the front of the heap, the tangled bones under his feet begin to slip.

❧ IDA EASTFIELD ❧

Lankin and Mimi are sliding down the pile. There's a mighty rushing sound. Bones clatter onto the floor all around us. There's no stopping them. Lankin loses his balance. He's tumbling down amongst the unravelling bones. Mimi is slithering down with him. She wakes. I hear her cry.

He's falling towards us. Mimi is entangled in his legs. Everything is rushing. The bones are spilling over our feet. Roger is shouting. We are all caught up in the bones. Lighted candles are toppling on their sides. Thin lines of smoke rise to the roof.

Mimi will be crushed. Lankin's great stinking body is in the way. His legs are sprawling, his arms flailing.

Where is Mimi? I can't get to her. The long bones are twisting around one another. The ribs are sharp. My leg hurts. There is barely room to stand.

❧ CORA ☙

Beneath the pile of bones, a hem of Mimi's pyjamas appears.

Roger snatches her ankle.

Lankin's long feet lurch towards my face. I can see through the shredded skin to the flesh underneath. He is covered in sores. He stinks. The bones are sliding on top of him. He is howling.

The crypt is filling with dust. The candles are going out. I step on the axe handle and drag it up in my hands.

Mimi clings to Roger. Her arms are about his neck.

We stumble out of the mess. We dash behind the pillar in the corner to the hole in the wall, but the huge crash of the bone pile has dislodged the earth in the tunnel roof. It caves in and falls so quickly that soil flies into the crypt in a thick, filthy cloud. We cough out the dirt and, choking, try to rub it from our eyes.

I look in every direction, trying to see through the clouds of earth and dust.

Through my stinging eyes, I spot a dark oblong like a small door in the back wall. I throw myself at it. It moves a little but doesn't open. I feel for a latch, but I can't find anything. I can't see.

"It's all right, Mimi. It's all right," I say over her wailing. "We'll get you out. We just have to open the door."

Auntie Ida grabs the axe back from me. I hear a noise, look behind, and through half-blind eyes see a large shadowy shape beginning to rise up from the scattered bones on the floor.

"He's coming, Auntie Ida—hurry, hurry!"

"Move back! Move back!" she yells.

❧ ROGER ❧

Mrs. Eastfield swings the axe and—*wham!*—splinters the door. The axe head is stuck in the wood. She drags it out—*wham! wham!*

Lankin is standing, tottering, shaking his head—*wham!*—Mrs. Eastfield's made a hole, the edges jagged and sharp. Panting, she tugs at the broken pieces and throws them down, then hits the door with the axe again. The hole is bigger.

Cora yanks Mimi out of my arms and pushes her through the broken door. Mrs. Eastfield leans towards me, gets hold of my shirt with her filthy, sweaty hands, and pulls me up to the doorway. I climb through, tearing my sleeve and cutting my arm on a splintered edge of wood. There is a dark stone staircase curving upwards. I climb after Cora and Mimi. Mrs. Eastfield hobbles up behind, groaning and gasping for breath, dragging the axe. It clangs up the steps—*bang! bang! bang!*—one at a time.

✣ CORA ✣

There's a small door up there, worm-eaten and rotten at the bottom. I shift Mimi onto my hip, crouch forward, and, with all my might, push at the door over and over. It shudders against my fists. Roger squeezes past me and starts kicking at the decaying wood. Auntie Ida passes up the axe. There is no room to swing it. He bangs relentlessly at the bottom of the door with the top of the shaft. It cracks and splinters, but there is no room for me even to push Mimi underneath.

"Move back!" cries Roger. "The bolt on the other side's rusty. Don't you remember? It's the little door behind the curtain in the tower. Most of the screws have gone. Move back!"

He thumps the door halfway up with the back of the axe head. Suddenly, at one thud, the door moves out a few inches. Behind it, something metal clatters to the floor.

"The bolt's come away!" says Roger. He pushes the

door a few inches. The long, heavy curtain hangs behind it. He forces his way through the gap, gathers up the folds of fabric, and holds the curtain to one side to let us out. The light stings my eyes.

On the wall above the door is the marble slab naming the rectors of Bryers Guerdon.

"Quick! Quick!" says Auntie Ida, pushing us forward as she turns. Then, with a huge effort, she shuts the door behind the curtain. I hear the slapping of Lankin's feet as he comes up the staircase behind us, and I scrape my elbow on the font in my hurry to reach the church door. Roger yanks it open. We rush out into the churchyard and, breathless, start to run down the path. I hold Mimi's head tightly against my shoulder, my hand over her eyes.

I hear her muffled voice: "You're hurting me."

"Come on, Auntie Ida!" I call. "Hurry up! We've got to get to the top of the hill!"

She falters beside the porch, leaning on the axe, breathing hard, kneading her chest with her free hand.

"Come *on*! We'll help you!" Roger shouts.

"You go. Run! Go on!" she urges.

We hear the heavy church door creaking open.

"Auntie Ida. He's coming!"

"Get away! Get away!" she grunts, pushing the air with her hand.

"You're hurting me!" Mimi whines again.

Lankin's repulsive form appears round the corner of

437

the wall. I make a sound like a groan. His head turns towards me, but it is Mimi he sees. At the same moment, she wrenches my hand from her eyes and, for a second, gazes at his face. Then, taking me by surprise, she begins to writhe in my arms, pummelling my chest with her fists and kicking out with the soles of her feet.

"Let me go! Let me go!" she yells.

"Roger! Help me!" He is almost at the metal gate. He turns towards me. I grapple with Mimi, but she seems to have summoned up some furious energy. She beats me so hard on my rib cage, I am thrown off balance. Before Roger can reach us, she forces me backwards with one mighty shove, wriggles out of my arms, and begins to run through the graveyard, in and out of the tangles of weeds and grass, dodging the crosses and tombstones, past the tower, and up the shadowy side of the church. Roger and I give chase. I look back. Lankin is crawling swiftly behind us on all fours, twisting his long body this way and that around the graves. I can't see Auntie Ida, but what I do see, gathering against the wall of the church, are the little ghostly children, their dark, hollow eyes following us as we run.

Mimi zigzags through the churchyard. Sobbing, she passes the last ragged crop of gravestones and jumps over the tufts of grass as she draws closer to the pool on the far boundary. Above the water soars the bare, white, double hook of the gypsy tree.

❦ ROGER ❧

Mimi slows down, her bare feet sodden in the spongy ground this side of the tree. Trying to head her off, Cora and I find ourselves floundering in marshy water. I look behind. Lankin is no longer behind us. He is on another course altogether, avoiding the bog, taking a wide circular route onto the dry, higher ground at the back. I've lost sight of Mrs. Eastfield.

"Oh, God, where's Auntie Ida?" Cora shades her eyes with her hand and scans the graveyard. "She must have fallen!"

Mimi is grizzling and whining, crossly drumming her soaking feet in the moss. She starts to head for the tree.

"Mimi! Stay where you are!" Cora yells at her. "He won't get you in the water! Roger, she's not listening."

We try to wade but are sucked in. I reach out for a clump of reeds, but my feet remain where they are and I splash into the bog. My head goes under the water. My mouth fills with threads of weed. Cora reaches out to help me. I lift my face and, wiping it with filthy wet hands, struggle to my feet.

"Get Mimi!" I shout, spitting to clear my mouth. "He must be behind the tree. She can't see him!"

Desperately, Cora tries to lift her right foot. "I'm stuck!" She begins to panic. "Mimi! Stay where it's wet!"

"It's no use; she won't take any notice."

Whimpering, Mimi leaves the marshy ground and begins to climb the shallow bank a couple of feet from the tree. A grey-fleshed hand creeps inch by inch around the edge of the trunk.

Mimi stamps her feet, then pulls up a handful of grass and starts to wipe her toes with it.

"Mimi! Mimi! Come back to the water!"

She looks across at us, her little eyebrows knitted, her face flushed.

Lankin's body emerges.

❧ CORA ☙

Mimi turns her head, sees Lankin, moans, and in one swift movement rushes along the edge of the grassy bank, then climbs up onto the fan of massive roots rising out of the pool. She presses her back to the tree trunk, arms spread out against it, her chest fluttering. Lankin disappears behind the tree. Mimi's eyes, wide with terror, swivel from one side to the other.

We must get Mimi to the shallow water. Seconds pass while I struggle to move my feet. Then I look up and see Lankin again.

"Roger! Up there!"

Slowly, branch by branch, Long Lankin is climbing up towards the great bald hook of the tree. As he stretches upwards, his skin glistens and the sunlight catches the raised lines of the veins and sinews on his elongated arms and legs. When he reaches the upper part of the dry white trunk, where it forks into two, he wraps his legs around the crook and sits down, the top of his head shining under the blazing sun.

Then he bends forward, jerks his head, and, leaning out, studies Mimi, who is still darting her eyes right and left, stiff with fear. He bares his teeth.

"Mimi! Mimi! Run away!"

Long Lankin looks across to us, grins, and, headfirst, begins to lower his body slowly and deliberately down the trunk. He stretches out first one arm, then the other. Only when the fingers of his right hand touch her hair does Mimi look up and see him.

She groans and squeezes her eyes shut tight.

To the right, someone is stumbling through the grass.

"Oh, Auntie—" I gasp. "Auntie Ida!"

She reaches the tree. Lankin twists his head, bares his teeth at her, and snarls. Then, locking his legs around each side of a forked branch, he lashes out with his left hand, trying to hook her clothes with his nails.

Auntie Ida moves backwards one step, out of his reach. She grips the axe, white-knuckled, fists tightly

441

clenched, her face set, grim and determined. She lifts her shoulders, swings the axe around her back, and, with a loud grunt, smashes it with a tremendous blow into Lankin's body. There is a spurt of liquid, a terrible shriek.

Auntie struggles to release the axe from the tree trunk. For a moment, it remains embedded, then drops to the ground with a thud. With it comes a long grey arm.

A monstrous shudder runs through Lankin's body. With legs twitching, he slumps out of the tree, slithers past the axe and past Mimi's trembling figure, then flops into the water in a froth of bubbles. Auntie totters for a moment, then leans round the trunk.

"O-open your eyes, Mimi," she pants. "He's—he's gone. Grab my hand."

Auntie Ida leads Mimi onto the grass beside her. Mimi throws her arms around Auntie Ida's neck and buries her head under her chin. With Mimi still clinging there, Auntie falls to her knees, gasping for breath.

Roger struggles towards me, his feet squelching. He grips both my hands and tries to drag me through the bog towards the tree.

"I can't move," I moan.

"Can you get your shoes off?"

I think, *How am I going to undo the buckles?* then remember they are the red slip-on shoes from Maisie Treasure, without any straps.

With a loud sucking, slurping sound, I wrench my right foot out, then my left. In turn my feet sink into the soft peaty mud. Roger pulls me hard, and I move forwards.

We trudge through the shallow, mossy water towards the bank, where I fling off my wringing socks before rushing to Auntie Ida and Mimi, kneeling, hugging them, my voice choking.

"Oh, Auntie Ida, it's all over."

With a huge effort, Auntie lifts her head and clutches my arm. "No, no. Take Mimi!"

She looks away from me towards the pool. Below the swirling surface, the water is heaving.

"Take Mimi! Quickly!" she says.

I unwind Mimi from Auntie's neck and take her in my arms. Auntie staggers to her feet, then falls again.

"Come on, Mrs. Eastfield, I'll help you," says Roger, picking up the axe.

Auntie pushes him away and says through gritted teeth as she sinks down into the grass, "Get Mimi out of here."

Take her away. Take the child away.

It is the voice of Piers Hillyard. We turn from Auntie. He is standing a few feet from us. Roger, dragging the axe behind him, and I, with Mimi wrapped around me, move in a wide circle around the bog, then back away towards the church and the silent, staring children.

❧ IDA EASTFIELD ☙

I lie on the edge of the pool in a gentle nest of reeds, my hair trailing in the water. I watch the movement under the surface, the ripples, the bubbles. I know he will rise from this water as he rose from the waters of the flood. He is weakened, but not finished.

Piers Hillyard bends over me, his lips close to my ear.

It is not enough, Ida, he says. *He is drawing the life from your body, his strength gathering as yours grows weaker. If you do not rise now, it will be too late. It will all begin again. You know what has to be done. It is the gate. It is the lychgate. Now is the time.*

I am weary. Let me be. Let me rest here.

Let us all rest, Ida. Open your eyes; raise your head. Look at the children.

Leave me. Let me sleep.

Look at Edward.

Edward. At the sound of my child's name, I feel my eyelids flutter open. Through the fringes of my lashes, I see him, standing in front of the others, his poor wasted face turned towards mine.

Another small boy moves forward to Edward's side, then a little girl. I know it is my brother, Tom. It is Annie.

The gate, Ida. He is feeble. Now is the time.

Something breaks the surface of the pool. The water is rising towards me. I lift my head. Small waves lap against the bank, gurgling into my nose and mouth. I struggle to raise my chin.

I see Long Lankin floundering through the choking waterweed as he struggles to reach the side. With his one arm, he propels himself, splashing clumsily towards me, then lunges with his hand to clutch at the reeds. Drawing himself up with one mighty effort, he heaves himself above me, then plunges downwards. The water sweeps over my head. When it recedes, I smell Lankin's fetid breath. He steadies himself against the bank by twisting my floating hair around his hard black tongue.

Ida, the gate.

As Lankin's teeth draw closer to my scalp, my head turns to one side, and all I see in the line of my vision is the sad face of my son. Lankin grips my hair tighter, but gazing at Edward, I feel a strange tension enter my body, as if I were being stretched by a steel thread that becomes a hard, solid rod.

Grunting with effort, gritting my teeth, I roll my hands into fists, bend my elbows, and push myself upwards from the mud. My scalp is burning. I dig my knees into the ground and, groaning, inch my way backwards from the water's edge, dragging Lankin with me.

Pausing for a moment for breath, I summon up the strength to crawl again, pulling away from him, away

445

from the pool. I feel my hair roots stretching—straining, then ripping away from my scalp. I cry out. Lankin collapses into the reeds, gasping, and spits my hair out of his mouth.

I stagger up and lean against the tree, panting.

Piers Hillyard is standing among the gravestones. The children have not moved from their place near the church wall. Cora, Mimi, and Roger are in front of the lychgate, staring, their mouths gaping open.

Hillyard breaks the silence.

Ida, the gate, he says. *Draw him back.*

❧ ROGER ☙

Mrs. Eastfield totters towards us. Behind her, Lankin is on his knees by the water's edge. He rubs his dripping forehead with his hand. Liquid is dribbling out of the shreds of his left shoulder and running down his side.

Mrs. Eastfield stops, swaying. "Roger!" she cries in a trembling voice. "Smash the chains! Do you hear me? Break open the gates! Use the axe—quickly!"

"I—I don't think I can do it anymore. . . ."

"Quickly! Quickly!"

I turn and anxiously size up the chains and ropes binding the two old gates together. I swallow, take a breath, then bolt forward towards them with the heavy axe firm in my sore, weary hands.

I swing the axe high and feel the sockets of my arms straining against the weight. Mustering all my strength, I smash the head down against the rusty chains. As it crashes into the thick metal links, a jarring shock passes through my body. For a second, I am so weak, my arms shake.

I bring the axe up again and strike once more, then again. With the last blow, the chains and old frayed ropes split apart. I drop the axe and try to push the gates open, but they barely move. My arms hurt. I kick at the earth and weeds packed around the bottom.

"Roger! Roger!" Cora screams. I snatch a look over my shoulder. Mrs. Eastfield is almost at the lychgate, but behind her, his face twisted with both agony and hatred, the crippled Long Lankin crawls through the graveyard.

"Don't stop, Roger!" Mrs. Eastfield cries.

"Here, climb over the gates!" I call to Cora. "Quick! Quick!"

With Mimi clinging tightly to her, Cora puts one leg over the right-hand gate. I take Mimi's weight for a moment, and Cora scrambles over.

I swallow, wipe each hand on my trousers, then lift the axe once more. I strike at the gates over and over again. They begin to split. My shoulders ache. The palms of my hands are ripped.

447

A huge piece of the right gate shatters. I drop the axe, kick against the jagged pieces with my heel, and throw the loose bits aside. My hands are slippery. There is blood on the axe handle. I pull and push at the wood with my torn hands until the smashed gates move apart.

At last the way stands open.

I rush under the arch and stand on the roadside, where Cora and Mimi are locked together. On the other side of the arch, Mrs. Eastfield is at the gate.

❧ CORA ❧

Auntie Ida turns slowly and faces Long Lankin. He rises up on his feet, stands at his full height, and fixes her with his spiteful eyes. Behind him the children stand watching.

I wrap my arms tightly around Mimi, folding her to me, and stare at the beast caught in a beam of sunlight, framed by the pillars and dark roof of the lychgate. I see the words: CAVE BESTIAM.

Lankin's eyes move from Auntie Ida and fall on Mimi. The grey saliva trickles out of his mouth and down his chin.

"What shall we do?" I breathe.

"Pass Mimi to me," Roger whispers. "I can run faster than you."

I hear a hissing noise. It is Auntie Ida.

"Put Mimi down!" she is saying through her teeth. "Put her down and move away!"

"What?!"

"Put her down on your side of the gate."

"No! I'm going to run—"

"Put her down—facing you! Hurry up!"

"I—I can't do it, Auntie."

Piers Hillyard appears to the left of the gate. He nods his head at me.

I let Roger take Mimi out of my arms. He moves forwards, stands her a couple of feet away from the broken gates, turns her to face the road, then steps back. She remains there, bewildered, wringing her hands.

"Stay there, Mimi," he says quietly to her, moving back a little more.

She looks tiny, her fair hair like a golden halo around her dirty face, her pyjamas filthy and torn.

A hot stillness hangs over the churchyard.

Long Lankin gazes at Mimi's back. He snarls and begins to move towards the gate. Auntie shifts her feet but remains where she is, standing between Lankin and Mimi.

Suddenly Mimi screws up her face and looks across from Roger to me, her eyes wide with terror. She takes a faltering step towards us.

Roger shoves his blood-smeared hand in his pocket,

449

drags out Sid, and holds him up. "Mimi," he says, "if you don't stay where you are, I'll—I'll stamp on Sid till he's dead."

Mimi moans. Her eyes fill up.

Slowly Lankin places one foot in front of the other until he is face-to-face with Auntie Ida. Then she moves a step backwards, and another.

Lankin advances towards her, his eyes over her shoulder, taking in Mimi, the tip of his tongue running across his lips.

Auntie takes another step backwards, this time between the broken gates, under the shadow of the roof. Then she takes a small sidestep so there is nothing between Lankin and Mimi.

Lankin is about to move forward once more: one last step and he will be across the threshold of the lychgate.

All at once, he seems to see where he is standing. A savage, furious light comes into his eyes. He raises his chin, opens his gaping mouth, and rolling his head from side to side, utters a long, hellish roar.

Mimi cries out, darts towards me, scrambles into my arms, and hides her face against my cheek.

In an instant, Auntie Ida throws herself forward. Flinging her arms around Lankin's waist, she locks her wrists behind his back. Howling with rage, he tears at her with the iron fingernails of his right hand. Her body pressed tightly against his mottled, festering skin, she drags herself backwards. He tries to reach her head with his teeth and pushes against her forehead with his remaining hand.

"I'll help you!" cries Roger, moving forward.

"*Get back!*" Auntie moans, sweat glistening on her forehead. "*Get back!*"

Then, with a deep, pitiful groan, summoning the last remnants of her strength, Auntie Ida hauls Long Lankin's broken body back through the lychgate.

☙ ROGER ❧

Under the arch, Long Lankin drops to his knees, places his hand on the ground in front of him, and leaning on it for support, raises his chest and shoulders and turns to look at Mimi in Cora's arms. Two spiteful pinpoints of light gleam in his eyes. I feel a cold tingling on the back of my neck.

Then something drops out of his mouth, something curved and yellow.

A tooth.

Curiously, he tilts his head and looks at it on the ground. Another tooth falls; then, after a moment, another and another. They drop from his shrunken gums one by one and settle among the broken pieces of the gate, the rusty chains, the weeds.

All at once, a tremendous shudder runs through his body. He raises his head upwards to the sky and screams a long, last dreadful scream that echoes again and again around the walls of the church.

Then Long Lankin crashes, his body jolting and twitching, full length across the ground. As his skull hits the earth, the neck twists and cracks and is still.

In the dark sockets of his eyes, the lights dim, then go out.

❧ CORA ❧

For a few long seconds, we stand in silence, numbed and exhausted, gazing at Long Lankin's motionless form.

At first I barely notice it, but gradually, as it increases, I see that a fine powder of grey dust is flowing from Lankin's mouth, nose, and ears. In wonder, we watch as it draws together and moves slowly down his body in one long smoky stream over the shrivelling skin and the crumpling limbs.

Then Piers Hillyard is there, on his knees. He lowers his head, draws in a smooth deep breath, and begins to blow the dust away. It rises into the air as a swirling mist, little by little gathering up into itself every particle of Lankin's hideous body until it forms a snakelike, trailing vapour, which, after a while, leaves not a single trace of him on the ground where he fell.

The ribbon of cloud moves towards the church, towards the huddle of ghostly children standing against the wall. It encircles them, sweeping over their heads and around their bodies. Where the grey dust touches and then enfolds them, the shredded skin falls away, the deep dark eye hollows vanish, and the grizzled hair disappears. They appear as they were when they were first snatched away—dressed in the little handmade clothes of lost, faraway times.

The children are changed, yet gaze at one another in bewilderment, barely recognizing their companions. They study their own hands, then each other's, touch their hair, their skin, their eyelids, blinking in the sunshine, as if they have no memory of how they once looked.

For most of them, their brief lives were lived many years ago, yet they have remained here, in this place, while all the people who ever cared for them are long buried.

The children turn and look at us across the gravestones, then gradually fade away into nothing.

The mist curls upwards, spreads lazily for a moment, and is gone.

Piers Hillyard stands quietly, closes his eyes, and sighs deeply. A light breeze begins to lift his hair. The sleeves of his black robe flutter. The hem starts to flap and twist. Leaves and dry grass rise into the air. Small twigs whirl and fly.

All at once, a great gust like a wall of wind blasts its way through the churchyard. Our own hair whips up behind us.

Suddenly, from the far boundary, there comes an immense tearing sound. We feel the ground begin to tremble under our feet.

"What is it?" I cry, pressing Mimi close into my shoulder.

"Look over there!" Roger calls against the gale.

I turn. The wind is hard on my back. I steady myself and gaze out through half-closed eyes.

The gypsy tree is tilting towards the water. One by one, the wind rips the thick gnarled roots out of the earth. Creaking and groaning, the great tree leans farther and farther forward, the massive trunk juddering. Inch by inch, the huge bald hook lowers itself until it is hovering over the pool. The few remaining roots, so stretched they can bear the strain no longer, begin to snap in rapid succession.

With a deafening roar, the mighty, ugly tree thunders down, crashing into the water in a monstrous pile of rustling leaves and cracking, splintering branches. The old toys, the rags, and the remnants of little shoes are drowned forever.

The wind gradually loses strength until it is nothing more than a gentle motion of the air. It spins the leaves for a while until they drop to the surface of the churning, bubbling pool, where they settle, bobbing over the muddy ripples.

I search the graveyard for Piers Hillyard, but he has gone.

The tower wall glows golden in the sunshine.

"Roger! Roger! Cora! Father Mansell's coming! Father Mansell's coming!"

In a daze, I realize it is Pete shouting. Father Mansell and Mr. Crawford are a little way behind him in the lane.

Mimi raises her head. "Where is Auntie Ida?"

I shield my eyes with my spare hand and see her, slumped across the grave in the plot beside the gate, her feet straddling the broken iron railing. Mimi climbs down from my arms, goes to her, and gently shakes her shoulder.

"Wake up, Auntie, wake up."

One of Auntie Ida's hands lies loosely across her chest; the other rests on the slab. The last remaining rose on the old worn-out bush above her drops its pink petals one by one over her fingers. I kneel beside her, gently brush the petals aside, and read the inscription:

THE TIME OF THE SINGING OF BIRDS HAS COME

ACKNOWLEDGMENTS

Warmest thanks to Annie Eaton, Sophie Nelson, Sarah Dudman, Natalie Doherty, and the whole team at Random House. Thanks also to my husband and children, in particular Eleanor for her helpful comments over hot chocolate and cinnamon buns, and to Rosemary Leclercq.